WII

MW00415231

# ★ PRAISE ★

## For the #1 Bestselling Blake Carver Series

"Immensely entertaining and startlingly plausible."
– *Ragazine*

"Hard to put down. "
— *Paul Harris, author of The Candidate*

"Astonishing. "
— *Jerry Gabriel, prizewinning author of Drowned Boy*

"Believable and sophisticated. "
— *Publisher's Weekly*

"An espionage thriller for our times. "
—*Amazon.com Breakthrough Novel Award Review*

"Chilling. Will keep you up at night long after you've turned the final page."
— *Keir Graff, author of The Price of Liberty*

Rogue Empire

Published worldwide by Massive Publishing.
ISBN: 9781535319553
Library of Congress Control Number: 2013909551
Copyright © 2016 by William Tyree

For my parents.

# PART I

# BREAKING: U.S. Drone Destroys Chinese Embassy in Libya

*—25 feared dead*
*—Pentagon investigating "a tragic accident"*
*—Beijing warns of consequences*

TRIPOLI (AP), September 23 — A Pentagon spokesman confirmed that an American missile struck the Chinese embassy in Tripoli earlier today, calling it a tragic accident for which there was still no known cause. China's official news agency reported that the blast killed at least 25, with 18 wounded. Local volunteers are actively searching through the rubble for a number of embassy employees that remain missing.

Meanwhile in Beijing, unconfirmed reports tell of police standing aside as angry mobs form outside the American Embassy. The embassy is currently on lockdown.

Addressing reporters at the Pentagon, Secretary of Defense Dexter P. Jackson said that the intended target of the strike was a jihadist group threatening American personnel in the city. The disaster follows several months of heightened tensions between the U.S. and China, and is likely to further complicate planned de-escalation talks at the upcoming Group of Eight (G8) summit, where the world's most populous country was scheduled to celebrate its inaugural membership in the exclusive club of nations.

Jackson declined to name the specific group targeted, but added, "The Chinese embassy was not the objective. We are bringing all available resources to bear in order to identify the root cause of this tragedy, and will release more details as they become available."

In a recent cyber attack on the U.S. State Department, China was accused of accessing an estimated 43,000 sensitive diplomatic files. Jackson said there was no connection between the two events.

A senior Department of Defense source speaking under the condition of anonymity said that a hack into the drone's weapons guidance system could have caused the mistargeted strike.

Beijing has yet to issue an official response to the incident, but Chinese President Kang indicated that the act would result in unspecified consequences for the United States.

**Travel Warning for U.S. Citizens**

As of press time, the U.S. State Department has advised American citizens to temporarily avoid traveling to China. Citizens currently in China are urged to remain indoors and take reasonable security precautions.

*This story is developing.*

# FOUR HOURS EARLIER

## Tripoli, Libya

Kyra Javan raced the bicycle through the city as if she were fleeing the dawn itself. As the horizon bled orange behind her, the 25-year-old American intelligence operative steadied the handlebars with one hand and held her hijab in place with the other. Beneath the black linen that flapped over her mouth and nose, revealing only brown deep-set eyes, she allowed herself a pensive smile. The sweet exhilaration of escape flowed through her like a drug.

It was 6:15 a.m. on what was to be her final day in Libya. Two hundred and thirteen days after she had initiated Operation Trojan Horse, the moment had finally come to kill the Butcher of Bahrain and his top commanders in one decisive blow. And with it, she would finally erase the persona she had so skillfully inhabited these past seven months.

She whizzed by sand-colored apartment buildings and parked cars and a whiff of open sewer. Down a straight stretch of road, she picked up speed, glancing over her left shoulder, checking to make sure that she had not been followed. She saw no vehicles behind her. Just the usual streams of early risers heading to sunrise prayer like so many pilgrims beginning the same quest anew day after day. The *adhan*, the Islamic call to worship, blasted from the loudspeakers of every mosque in the city. *Ashadu an la ilaha ill Allah. Ashadu anna Muhammadan rasoolullah.* Although the slow, twisting melodies were hauntingly beautiful, it was perhaps this sound more than any other that Kyra looked forward to leaving behind.

For the past week, she had been blessed with the most amazingly vivid dreams. Running amongst blooming cherry blossoms in Washington D.C. Eating strawberry sorbet with the sun beating down on her head. Her *entire* head, uncovered by the hijab. Unfiltered sunlight on her face, ears, scalp, hair. For her, that simple pleasure now represented freedom more than any other.

And yet even in those sweet dreams of Washington, the voices of the adhan played in the background. It was everywhere. Like a bad omen.

The mission to eliminate Saif Al-Mohammed, the so-called Butcher of Bahrain, had started nearly a year before Kyra first set foot in Libya. Al-Mohammed's involvement in the Allied Jihad – at first as a financier, and later, as its chief strategist in North Africa – had gradually moved him up near the top of America's target list. He had been wanted in connection with several attacks on Western targets, but he had become truly infamous after planning the abduction of an American journalist for the *Washington Post*. After repeated viewings of the gruesome video, in which the journalist was beheaded, analysts later confirmed that the man who had wielded the sword had been Al-Mohammed himself. He had followed that ghastly spectacle by organizing a suicide attack at the Formula One Grand Prix of Bahrain, in which 10 bombers had killed a combined 137 spectators. A moniker, and a Jihadi legend, was born.

Last year, a CIA-led strike missed the Butcher of Bahrain in the Sudan. American Intelligence later discovered his residence in Tripoli, where they hoped to get not only the Butcher himself, but his top lieutenants as well.

The administration was betting that the political blowback of a drone strike in Libya's capital city would be minimal. The war torn country had not truly seen peace since the revolution. Officially speaking, the current government had the backing of the United Nations, but how much longer could it realistically hold out against the various warring groups vying for control?

The strike had White House approval so long as two conditions were met, the first of which was ensuring the Butcher was actually present in his compound. Kyra had reported that he was to be in closed-door meetings with his top leadership all day.

He had given his wives explicit instructions that they were not to be disturbed until lunchtime.

The second condition: Make sure no children were killed in the attack. No problem there, either. By the time the missile hit, the children would all be in school.

She had done her job. There was just one task left: Escape.

Her handler was waiting for her in the marina, where he had hired a boat to take them to Sicily. His name was Blake Carver. Kyra would never forget how her boss had described Carver on a crisp D.C. night nearly a year ago. "If you need someone to infiltrate a mountain fortress in the middle of the night," he had said, "Carver is your man. And if you need someone to find out if we even have the right fortress in the first place, Carver is also your man."

# Tripoli Seaport

Blake Carver stood on the deck of a 28-foot trawler with the Sicilian Prince emblazoned on the aft. A mild current slapped rhythmically against the hull. As the boat rocked gently under his boots, Carver's green eyes searched the inlet road where he expected Kyra Javan to appear momentarily. To his right, a small fishing vessel left its mooring and headed out to the Mediterranean, its three-man crew waving as they passed.

He waved and smiled. Enjoy the day, Carver thought. Really. Because by the time you get back, the city will be awash in smoke and its entire population will be out in the streets. And when news of the Butcher's death gets out, some will quietly celebrate, and others will kill the first infidel they can get their hands on.

The phone buzzed in Carver's hand. The caller ID read "mom," the name he had spoofed for the National Counterterrorism Center in McLean, Virginia.

He answered. The encrypted voice on the other end belonged to Haley Ellis, who was Carver's eyes and ears via satellite. "Trojan Horse is approaching the old city," Ellis said, using Kyra's codename.

So Kyra was en route. The Butcher and his regional commanders were gathered in his Tripoli compound. And the strike drone was poised in the sky above. Everything in its right place.

Carver had begun his career as a member of the Joint Strike Operations Command (JSOC) – a paramilitary spy, capture and kill force that had seen heavy covert action in Afghanistan. Afterwards, he had been a CIA strategist and operative before having been drafted into America's most secretive intelligence organization. He and 26 others, including Kyra Javan, reported directly to Julian Speers, the Director of National Intelligence.

The agency had recently been named Guardian, although as a hard rule, it was never referred to as such in writing. The secretive, direct organizational structure minimized the bureaucracy that sometimes hobbled the flow of information and speed of operations across agencies. It also enabled Speers, who had 16 entire intelligence agencies reporting to him, absolute oversight of key missions.

Among America's spy community, Carver was either a legend or a pariah, depending on who you asked. Rumors of Carver's adventures still floated among the various intelligence agencies, growing more mythical with each retelling. But since the day he had voluntarily resigned from the CIA to join Guardian, those who knew his exact duties were limited to Speers, the president, his immediate colleagues and a few in congress charged with intelligence oversight.

He scratched his beard, sorely missing the chin that was buried under a three-inch layer of wiry fuzz he had grown for the operation. When they retreated to Sicily this afternoon, the first thing he was going to do was shave. And if there was time before they hopped on the plane back to Washington, he was going to eat a bucket or two of Pasta alla Norma. There was a cafe near the Guardian safe house that had the most mouth-watering basil and ricotta he had ever tasted.

To his back, an L-shaped seawall protected the 300 or so docked boats from rogue waves. He had noticed that there were no longer any leisure boats moored here. The sailboats and yachts that had once inhabited these docks were now on dry land on the other side of the road, some of them with bullet-riddled hulls, scattered about like enormous bathtub toys.

Aldo Rossi, owner and skipper of the Sicilian Prince, sat before a backgammon board. In Carver's intelligence briefing, he had described Aldo as a walking jack-o-lantern, noting his hairless scalp, tan, round face and gap-toothed grin.

"Sit and play," Aldo urged Carver, gesturing a leathery hand to the board. "A watched pot never boils."

Aldo was a career fisherman based out of Sicily, the football-shaped island at the tip of Italy's boot, some 300 nautical miles north of here. But these days, fishing was no longer Aldo's sole source of income. Since the Arab Spring, he had built up a lucrative side business ferrying smugglers and occasional American intelligence agents in and out of Libya. His biggest paycheck had come when U.S. Special Forces had embarked on a nighttime mission to abduct a known terrorist in the capital.

But Aldo's window of opportunity in Libya seemed to be closing fast. The Italian people had enjoyed favored nation status here for decades, traced back to a phone call in 1986 between Italian Prime Minister Bettino Craxi and Libyan dictator Muammar Gaddafi. The call had come just moments before American bombers reduced Gaddafi's resident to rubble, an act that enabled the dictator to hold onto power for another three decades. But to the Allied Jihad, who now occupied 30 percent of Libya, old favors meant nothing. To them, an Italian was just another infidel. The poor ones were beheaded on sight. The rich ones were held for ransom.

Now Aldo rapped a knuckle on the wooden backgammon board and looked up at Carver. "Your move."

Irrational anxiety welled up within Carver like a cramp. But why? All indicators were green. And yet deep inside, he knew that something was awry.

He replied without taking his eyes off the inlet road. "Aldo, you should start the motor."

"The boat will start just as fast when your friend gets here."

"Now, please."

The skipper sighed, grumbling as he went to the controls. "You Americans never relax."

Aldo had been told nothing about the drone strike, nor had he been told that Kyra would be fleeing one of the most wanted terrorist organizations on earth. He knew only that they were to smuggle an American out of the country, and that they would need to leave in a hurry.

For added insurance, Carver had rigged some IEDs along the road to the marina. If Kyra was pursued, he could set them off remotely to buy them some time. And below deck, he had stashed a couple of MP-4s and some RPGs. If he had to resort to using any of those things, then they were probably doomed anyhow.

Guardian had entertained various scenarios for Kyra's extraction. One such plan was to have Carver lead an assault team that would have taken Kyra by night and killed the Allied Jihad leadership by hand, similar to the one that had killed Osama Bin Laden in Pakistan. But unlike Bin Laden's quiet suburban existence, the Butcher's both vigilant and well armed, having not only the U.S. to worry about, but also opposing militias in Libya. The civil war the country had been plunged into after the overthrow of the Gaddafi regime had never quite ended. At the end of the day, the drone strike was deemed the best option.

Now Carver's phone buzzed. Ellis again. "Be advised. We may have a problem."

"What problem?"

"A white truck just exited the target area at high speed."

# The Old City
# Tripoli

Kyra pedaled faster now, counting down the blocks until she would reach the fishing marina where her handler, Blake Carver, would be waiting. Then they would sail for Sicily. She imagined watching the drone strike from the safety of the Mediterranean Sea.

By the time the missile hit, the children would be safely on their way to school. The men would be starting the daylong strategy meetings they held once a month at the compound. God willing, each and every one of them would be reduced to dust. To nothingness. As if they had never even been born.

She caught a fleeting whiff of someone's breakfast, pastry dough frying in olive oil. Much as she hated to admit it, she was actually going to miss the food here.

The bike jounced and wobbled as Kyra navigated a rugged street. The Old City district truly was a time machine to a bygone era, and the condition of its roads was no exception. She gripped the handlebars with both hands.

Her hijab caught air and flew off her head, parachuting into the street. *Seriously?* She had used no less than a dozen hairpins.

Kyra braked, skidding a bit in a patch of loose gravel, and turned back to retrieve it. Even with her hair covered, traveling the streets of Tripoli alone was a risky endeavor. In recent times, the city had become infested with gangs of frightening young extremists whose sole purpose in life seemed to be harassing women.

The previous week, a girl from the neighborhood had been severely beaten for walking unaccompanied by a male relative. Were Kyra to be caught this morning, especially without a hijab, a beating wouldn't be all she would get. The punishment for leaving her husband could be death by stoning. Or worse.

Her husband was not above administering such punishments, either. Especially now. Having expanded his pool of wives to four, he was expected to keep them in line.

It hadn't always been that way. Among Islamic terrorists, the Butcher of Bahrain had been a rare monogamist during his first 31 years or marriage. But some years after the Arab Spring had brought revolution to the country, it had also brought a strict interpretation of Sharia law, allowing him to take up to four wives.

He did not do this immediately, for fear of upsetting his first wife, Farah, who was notoriously jealous. But where the Butcher saw a jealous woman, American Intelligence had realized a once in a lifetime opportunity.

A CIA operative who had spent years establishing himself within Saif's inner circle planted the seed one day over tea. "I hesitate to bring this up, but people are talking. They see you have just one wife, and they worry something is wrong. Does he not truly believe in Sharia law? Or is he secretly ill? Is he so sick that he does not experience the normal desires of a man?"

Soon after, the Butcher told Farah of his decision. After more than three decades of matrimony, the idea did not sit well. But she was not stupid. Realizing that she had virtually no rights under the country's new climate of intolerance, she agreed to abide by her husband's wishes, but with stipulations.

The first was that she alone would share his bed, at least until such a time when she was no longer able to please him physically. The second demand was that he was not to marry anyone they knew. No one from Africa or the deserts, she had told him. The other three wives had to be imported from abroad. Otherwise, the shame would be too much to bear.

The Butcher relented to Farah's demands. The second and third Butcher Brides came via the commanders of rival groups, and he used the new bonds to form critical alliances. As for the fourth wife, he wanted someone more exotic. For help, he turned to his most worldly friend, the undercover CIA operative who had urged him to embrace polygamy in the first place.

Within days, the Butcher was presented with several videos of women interested in marrying a rich man living under a strict Islamic code. Despite the terrorist leader's extreme ideology, he was known to be obsessed with Western sports, entertainment and women. As such, they were confident that he would fall for the lovely, athletic blond Canadian. The Trojan Horse.

In real life, Kyra Shireen Javan had been born in Dubai to Iranian refugees who had left their native country after converting to Christianity. She spent her formative years in the United Arab Emirates before the family moved to Canada, where she became a citizen and attended the University of Toronto. After graduation, she was immediately recruited into the CIA's clandestine service as a linguist and translator.

At the age of 24, she had imagined that the CIA would move her abroad. Somewhere that was not particularly dangerous, but was quietly simmering, like Indonesia. Instead, they had her sitting behind a desk in Washington D.C., listening to scratchy surveillance audio. It was a cage. She decided to push for a transfer to field operations.

She never imagined that becoming a field operative would entail becoming a mail order bride for one of the world's most wanted terrorists. Nevertheless, when the opportunity presented itself to join Guardian and do just that, she jumped.

Thanks to her nomadic formative years, Kyra already knew what it was to be a chameleon. To be born of one world in which she had to pretend to survive, then adapt perfectly to another, and still another. But the art of betrayal was something she had to learn.

Until recently, she had thought of herself as a spy. But she wasn't just a spy. A female Judas was what she was. And she would gladly betray the Butcher with a kiss.

The only difference between Judas and me, she thought, is that the Butcher is no Jesus. He is the devil.

She dismounted the bike and bent down to pick up the hijab. It was then that she saw the white Toyota pickup truck turning onto the street. She knew that white truck all too well. It belonged to Mohy Osman. Unless she was very clever, Mohy's white truck would be her hearse.

# Tripoli Seaport

"The truck is speeding toward the Old City," Ellis said over the encrypted audio connection. Carver visualized Ellis's angular face, framed by a blond boy cut, premature feathery lines sprawling across her cheeks. The 31-year-old had racked up a lot of miles for someone so young. She had started her career as an Army medic, earning a purple heart in Iraq before transitioning to the Defense Intelligence Agency. She never stayed anywhere long. From there, she took a position at the National Intelligence Council and later, the CIA before her recruitment into Guardian.

It was nearly midnight at the National Counterterrorism Center in Virginia. Carver imagined Ellis and her team huddled before the satellite imagery as if it was a roaring bonfire.

"How far from me now?" Carver asked her.

"About two miles."

"You mentioned a white Toyota truck. Is the license plate 15-2754932?"

"Stand by." Ellis did not ask Carver how he had known the license plate number. His ability for total recall was well known within the team. The scientific name for Carver's condition was hyperthymesia, better known as super-autobiographical memory. Carver was able to evoke the details of past experiences with perfect sensual clarity and run them backwards and forwards in his head.

Carver had first seen the white Toyota during the week that Kyra and two other women had wedded the Butcher in a flurry of separate ceremonies. It had been a blustery 112-degree afternoon. As Carver observed the matrimonial caravan leave the Butcher's compound, he accumulated sand in body parts that he never thought possible. The white truck had a vibration that sounded like a cicada. It also had ridiculously oversized tires and, welded into the truck bed, hardware indicating that a heavy gun or missile launcher had once been mounted there.

He had then observed the truck's owner, Mohy Osman, following the newly formed group of sister wives as they made their way through a crowded local food market for the first time. Mohy was no garden-variety jihadist. He was a muscular man with a scar below his left eye and a skunk-like streak of premature silver hair on the left side of his beard.

Carver had planned for that day well in advance of the wedding. Because the Butcher's family was huge – 12 biological children, four others he had adopted, and various nieces and nephews – the wives had little choice but to divide and conquer the shopping list. Those scarce minutes of freedom had been Carver's only chance to communicate with Kyra, and was, as Carver had hypothesized, the only time going forward that she would be able to report in.

The trick had been finding her a safe place in which to do so. The answer was found in an elderly shopkeeper who specialized in importing Japanese rice, ginger, seaweed and other goods. As the Butcher was a well-known fan of Japanese food - a taste he had been unable to quench since the revolution, at which point Japanese restaurants became just a memory - it was decided that a professional sushi chef should train Kyra prior to her arrival in Tripoli. As such, she would be able to visit the Japanese import shop alone without question, and then please the Butcher with her culinary skills.

After losing Mohy in the winding aisles of the market, Kyra had introduced herself to the shopkeeper by asking for a rare form of sea urchin. He had then invited her into the shop's back office to look at his "special inventory," a ritual he would repeat again and again in the coming months as he made his ancient computer and phone available to her.

But that first time, Carver had been waiting for her. She fell into him, hugging him so hard he could scarcely breathe.

"How bad is he?" Carver asked.

Kyra straightened up and composed herself, pulling the hijab off, momentarily freeing her blond locks. "The Butcher is the least of my worries. He's rarely home. And when he is, Farah won't let him touch me.

"Who then?"

"That creep who followed us here. Mohy Osman. He's the Butcher's second cousin and a first-rate freak. I'm telling you, the evil coming off that guy is palpable."

"If you're in danger, we can still call this off. It's not too late. We can leave together right now."

She immediately dismissed the offer. "No. I can do this, just like we planned. I'll be embedded until the time is right. Then we take them all at once."

That had been more than seven months ago. Now they were less than an hour away from killing the Butcher of Bahrain and his top leadership. Over the past 24 hours, Carver had watched the NCC footage on his phone. The contingent of cell commanders from the Sudan, Syria, Tunisia, Pakistan, Egypt and Palestine had arrived at the compound just as Kyra had said they would. They had gorged themselves on mutton and couscous and butter cookies in the inner courtyard, some of them falling asleep for the night there on the cushions around the table.

This morning, the weekly delivery trucks had arrived just before daylight, right on schedule. The guards had opened the gates wide, and as always, the compound had fallen into joyful chaos. The Butcher and his men gathered to inspect the crates and chat with the drivers to get news from the other territories. They would be invited inside for a leisurely breakfast, where they would be fed fried pastry dough topped with sunny-side up eggs, followed by apple spiced tea. Meanwhile, the children screamed for fruit and candy. Farah chased after them to get them ready for school.

The weekly ritual, starting from the time the drivers entered the compound gates to the time they left, typically lasted more than two hours. Kyra had timed it over and over. She had practiced hiding within the compound to see whether her disappearance was noticed. It wasn't. And this morning, nobody seemed to notice as Kyra slipped between the trucks with a broom, sweeping this way and that until she mounted the bike she had parked by the sand-colored walls and rode off into the orange-hued dawn.

But now that careful planning seemed to be quickly unraveling. Carver had to make sure Kyra's months of sacrifice wouldn't be in vain.

Ellis voice crackled to life in the phone. "We're zooming in on the truck. Okay, I can see it now. Affirmative on that plate. The number is 15-2754932."

Carver nodded and told Ellis what he had already been certain of. That the truck belonged to Mohy Osman, and that he had discovered Kyra's absence.

He muted the phone and turned to Aldo, who was peeling off a layer of clothing as the morning sun warmed the boat. "Get ready. This could get bumpy."

With the phone still pressed to his ear, Carver stepped off the deck and walked up the marina toward a supplies shed, where Aldo had stashed an AK-47 and a motorbike for him. He left the rifle behind, considering it too conspicuous. While the sight of heavily armed men walking the streets of the capital was common, they traveled in groups and were members of organized militias. A lone traveler with an assault rifle would stand out. Besides, he wasn't completely unarmed. As usual, his trusty 9MM SIG Sauer was tucked into his ankle holster.

As for the bike, the tires were nearly bald, but it would do. He rolled the old Yamaha out onto the pavement and started it up. The motor growled.

"What was that?" came Ellis's voice in his ear.

"I'm going in after her."

"Negative. Let's discuss options."

But Carver knew there was no time for chitchat. It was now or never.

# The Old City

Kyra's body thrummed with dread. The bike pulled left and right with each pump of the pedals. She had lost sight of the objective. Her only thought now was Mohy.

Mohy's white truck was something of a legend among the Butcher's inner circle, many of whom had fought alongside him during the Arab Spring. It had a reputation for speed despite a smoky engine and visible war wounds, including a dozen bullet holes in the rear fender. Once, Mohy showed her a photo of a freakishly large artillery cannon mounted in the truck bed. "My truck killed so many," he had said with pride and genuine amazement.

Now Kyra entered an intersection and jerked the handlebars left, narrowly missing a group of children. She heard them yell, pointing at the mane of blond hair now flowing freely behind her. She looked over her shoulder. The truck veered around a group of men and onto the sidewalk. The front bumper clipped a pastry cart, flinging it to the curb like a toy. Then the truck plowed into a fruit cart that had just been set up for the day. Hundreds of oranges catapulted into the air.

And yet the truck kept coming. An unstoppable force.

Kyra turned west. The old thoroughfare was nearly empty. There were no obstacles. And soon the truck's rattletrap engine roared just behind her. Louder than the adhan, even. Louder than her own panting.

As the truck bumper came alongside her wheels, she glimpsed Mohy's glare through the window. The window was down, but he did not yell. He didn't need to. Kyra was sure she already knew what he was thinking. *I'm going to punish you. I'm going to make you scream.*

An alley opened up to the right that was far too narrow to accommodate a vehicle. She cornered and pumped the bike into it, unsure of what she would find on the other end. It was mercifully empty at this time in the morning, and as she traveled toward the light at the other end, she realized that it was not a street, but rather, a specialty market where she and the other wives came perhaps once a month. She swerved, nearly clipping a vendor pulling a red wagon full of pistachios. This was the rear entrance, she realized. Maybe she still had a chance.

She imagined Carver waiting at the marina for her. If only she could call him now. She had left her phone at the compound so that she could not be tracked, and due to the Butcher's regular security sweeps at the compound, she had considered stashing a burner phone far too risky.

Now Kyra dismounted the bike and tied the hijab over her hair. Inside, the market was not yet bustling. Most of the stalls were only now being set up for the day. It would be difficult to hide until the crowds came in an hour or so.

She decided to abandon the bike. She ran up a stairwell, racking her brain for a way out. She imagined Mohy had parked by now. Would he call the others to come looking for her on foot?

Something told her that he wouldn't, and the thought of that was even more frightening. Farah had once said that Mohy kept a jewelry box full of souvenirs from the women he had killed for disobeying Allah. At the time, Kyra had thought it was just a lie to keep her in line. But now she believed it with all her heart.

Through a break in the ceiling, she caught sight of a minaret. It was attached to an old mosque from the Ottoman era that was rumored to have a separate entrance for women. If it was full, perhaps it would be a good place to hide. If Mohy had decided she was an unrighteous whore, then a house of worship would be the last place he would look for her.

# Coastal Tripoli

Carver navigated the motorbike onto Al Shat road, which - to Carver's great amusement - came out as *I'll shit* in Ellis's mild southern twang. The parkway ran along the edge of the city. The marina was to his right, and beyond that, the Mediterranean. The relative safety of Sicily was a mere 300 miles across it.

Ellis was still in his ear, and her message now was unambiguous: "Turn back."

"That's not going to happen. Now tell me where Kyra is."

"We're off script," Ellis replied, which was shorthand for an operation where the cover of the primary operative had been blown. And that meant just one thing – Ellis wanted to cut her losses by striking the compound now.

"That's speculation. If we were off script, more people would be exiting the target area. There's one maniac chasing her. *One.*"

"The decision has been made. We hit now, before we lose our opportunity."

What Carver wanted to say next was something that should never be said over open communication lines. He hoped Guardian's latest call encryption technology was solid, because he needed to invigorate whatever humanity might be left in Ellis's cynical soul.

"There are kids in that compound," he said. "They leave for school in 30 minutes."

"We don't know that for sure. Turn back."

At times like this, Carver wondered if he had ever really known Ellis at all. Last year she had suffered a head trauma in the line of duty so severe that she didn't know her own name for days. Months of therapy had eventually resulted in a clearance for active duty, but Ellis was different now. Altered.

And there *were* kids in that compound. Carver didn't have children of his own yet, but he was an uncle to two young boys in Arizona for whom he had already started college funds. The rare moments he had spent with them were pure magic. In Carver's mind, the only thing separating the Western world from the jihadists' was the commitment to protecting innocent life. *All* innocent life.

"Is Julian in the room?" he said. "I need to hear it from him."

Julian Speers, the Director of National Intelligence, was a good man. He had two kids of his own. But with 16 intelligence agencies reporting to him, plus Guardian, he couldn't be everywhere at once.

"Negative," Ellis replied. "Your orders stand."

"Then put me on the room mic. I want everyone to be accountable for this decision."

"Carver – "

"Our operative is going to be caught and tortured, spilling so many operational details that we'll never replicate a mission like this again. Then he'll rape her. He'll cut her head off and put the video on the Internet. That's all going to be on you, plus the murder of a dozen or more kids."

There was a click, then silence on the other end. He hoped that was a sign that Ellis was conferring with the others. Al Shat road stretched out before him. Carver could see the old city now. Kyra was close. He could feel it.

Seventy-three seconds later, Ellis returned to convey the verdict: "You have 29 minutes."

# The Old City

The mosque's magnificent domes were intricately carved with floral motifs. It was a truly astounding architectural achievement, built during the Ottoman Empire's nearly four-century occupation, which had never failed to inspire. On the floor beneath, 60 women moved in carefully choreographed movements. Their prayers were drowned out by what was bound to be hundreds of men worshipping on the other side of the enormous partition separating the two sexes. She had always found the deep reverberation of their collective incantations oddly stimulating.

Her lips moved in sync with those of the women around her, but no sound escaped them. Over the past several months she had become quite skilled at appearing to venerate Allah while mentally praying to the God she had grown up with.

*Our Father who art in heaven, Hallowed be thy name. Thy kingdom come. Thy will be done on earth, as it is in heaven. Give us this day our daily bread. And forgive us our debts, as we forgive our debtors. And lead us not into temptation, but deliver us from evil.*

Yes, evil. Despite all those hours of Sunday school, had she ever truly believed in the existence of evil before meeting Mohy? She thought not. Now she shivered as her mind drifted to the image of his face behind the wheel of his truck. Her bowels lurched. She feared she might need to find a restroom.

She tightened her abs, trying to bring her body under control. She needed to hide here a little longer. At 7:15 a.m. local time, the drone would strike the compound. She had to make it to the marina by then.

Kyra moved in unison with the other women. The chanting within the great mosque grew louder and more feverish by the minute. The collective passion was contagious. She felt energized. She was going to do this. She was going to make it. Sometimes, it seemed to her that God had abandoned this country, its people and even Kyra. Maybe loudness was what was required to be heard above the mostly senseless noise of greater humanity.

On a subconscious level, she sensed Mohy's presence a millisecond before she knew for sure. Maybe it was a whiff of the musky cologne that always masked his abhorrent body odor. But when he pulled the hijab from her scalp, sending her frizzy blond hair askew, she was not surprised. She closed her eyes, knowing that she was in God's hands now.

# Mohy Osman Residence
# Tripoli

Kyra woke in a cramped one-room apartment that smelled like dirty laundry. She was on her left side, her wrists and ankles bound behind her. She heard running water. The morning sunlight coming from the room's lone window warmed her face.

The back of her skull throbbed. Her mind flashed back to the mosque, to the euphoric sensation of intense group prayer. Then shock. Then an instant of fear. Then darkness.

The weight of the moment came rushing back to her all at once. This was the 213th day of her life as Kyra Al-Mohammed. And one way or another, it would be the last day of that life.

Suddenly Mohy stood over her, filling her vision. He grinned lewdly, the way he had when he showed her the picture of the truck with the ridiculously oversized gun mounted in the back bed.

"I always knew," he said now, jabbing her shoulder with the index finger of his right hand. He poked her again, his finger punctuating every syllable. "Al-ways-knew."

"Knew what, Mohy?"

He slapped her. "You were going to betray him. Anyone could see that. Except Saif. He was a fool for you."

*I am definitely not at the compound. Mohy would have never called the Butcher a fool if he thought he might be overheard.*

Behind him, she saw a broken-down single bed with rusted posts. Beside it, a brass table and an ancient LED clock that read 6:54 a.m. Searing fear gripped her.

*I'm in Mohy's apartment. And there are just 21 minutes until the strike on the compound.*

She had to stall for time. If Mohy called the Butcher, he might be tempted leave the compound before the drone attack. If that happened, the entire operation – everything she had sacrificed – would be wasted.

"You've got this all wrong," she lied. "I simply wanted to ride my bike. Like a normal – "

He slapped her again, catching the edge of her mouth along with her cheek. It stung. Her top lip began to swell instantly.

"Like a normal woman? Is that what you were about to say? You are not normal. And you are not in Canada, or wherever it is you really come from. Saif Al-Mohammed chose you for his wife!"

She had to keep him talking. "Mohy, where in the Koran does it say that a woman cannot ride a bicycle by herself?"

And suddenly he had a blade at her throat. A serrated kitchen knife, pressing dangerously close to her larynx.

"Shut up about the stupid bike. Just admit what we both know to be true."

"Admit what?"

"You are not a Canadian from Iranian parents. That was all a fake. You are in fact an American spy. CIA."

"How could that possibly be true? Saif's best people performed an extensive background check on me. Are you really questioning my husband's judgment?"

"Even a lion sometimes has sheep in his army."

He removed the blade from Kyra's neckline and plunged it into her thigh. She yowled in pain as he withdrew it, the serrated edges tearing muscle tissue. Blood flowed from her leg at a frightening pace.

He regarded his handiwork, grunted approvingly, and left her. As Kyra bled, she heard a squeaky sound. The turning of a valve. The gush of running water slowed to a drip.

Mohy returned with a long piece of plywood, which he placed behind her back. Using a belt, he secured her legs to it. Then he used a second belt and began securing her torso until it was impossibly tight. Blood now poured from the open wound in her thigh.

Rogue Empire

"Mohy," she said, begging now. "Listen to me. I'll tell you anything you want. But you've got to stop the bleeding. If you don't, I won't be awake long enough to tell you anything."

"Blood is the least of your worries."

Kyra had always heard that Mohy possessed superhuman strength, but she had not witnessed it until now, as he picked her and the board up so easily, tucking her under one arm, as if she was no heavier than a surfboard. She screamed hysterically as he carried her to the bathroom, set the edge of the board over the tub, and tilted it backward so that her blond mane fanned out over the water's surface.

Suddenly, Mohy's face was calm and collected. Easily wielding the board with one hand, he raised his left index finger to his lips. "Shhh. Shhh." He waited several seconds until she had calmed herself. "Now then. What is your real name?"

She considered telling him. But what if the madman was just testing her? Even the CIA staged mock abductions of some of its new operatives and subjected them to intense interrogations to test their loyalty. She herself had been subjected to a similar test in training. Would the Butcher not do the same?

"Still refuse to talk?" Mohy said. "Then you better be good at holding your breath."

He tilted the board further, until her mouth and nose were plunged into the water. She tried to kick free, but it was impossible. She managed to hold her breath for nearly 40 seconds before water rushed into her airways.

Mohy tilted the board back up so that her face was up out of the water. She coughed uncontrollably. At some point, she became aware of Mohy's laughter. He was enjoying this.

But just as she caught her breath, he tilted her back into the water again. Her stomach twitched and spasmed. She soiled herself. The indignity of filling her pants in front of this monster seemed almost worse than the prospect of drowning.

Again, she kicked her legs against the board. Her arms struggled uselessly against the belt. The board bowed slightly, touching the small of her back. She no longer felt the sting of the knife wound in her thigh.

Seconds later she was back out of the water. "Your real name," he said again.

"Kyra Al-Mohammed."

Her head plunged back into the bathtub. Kyra knew that she would die now, either by drowning or bleeding to death, or some combination of the two. She prayed silently. *God, at least let me live long enough to hear the explosion! Depending on where we are in the city, I might even be able to feel it. At least then I will die knowing I completed my mission.*

And then she was visited by the recurring dream. Washington D.C. Cherry blossoms on the National Mall. Her hair hot from direct sunlight. Only this time, the call of the adhan was nowhere to be heard. It seemed so real. As if the past 213 days had never happened.

Suddenly, the dream was ripped away. Plunged deeper into the tub, her neck and shoulders engulfed by water. A sickening gurgle escaped her as water entered her lungs. A shadow came over her. The shadow of death, she assumed. The grim reaper.

Kyra seemed to float free from her body, watching from above. And what she heard seemed distant now. As if it wasn't through her own ears, but rather, through underwater microphones.

Then a second man entered her vision. He was familiar, but she could not place him. He wasn't local. She knew that much by the quality of his teeth. He was bearded, and thin around the waist, with large shoulders and thick forearms stretching out from his rolled-up shirtsleeves. And his eyes, green and intense.

*Blake Carver. He found me.*

He swung a lamp at Mohy's head, missing badly and sending him off balance. Mohy slammed a wooden chair against Carver's side, shattering the cheap piece of particleboard furniture into pieces. A chair leg splintered and flew free. Carver caught it in his right hand before it hit the ground, and in one deft motion, plunged it squarely into Mohy's chest. The Libyan fell backwards. Carver was suddenly on top of him like some crazed vampire killer. He pressed the stake deeper with both hands until it stopped against Mohy's backbone. A lake of blood bloomed around him.

Kyra watched as Carver turned his attention to the tub. He lifted her from the water and set the board on its side. Fingers invaded her mouth, stabbing at her throat. Her gag reflex triggered. A tidal wave purged through her mouth, and then she was coughing, gasping for breath.

And suddenly she saw the room through her own eyes. Heard Carver speak with her own ears. Carver crouched behind her, his calloused fingertips untying the braided ropes that had been wrapped around her wrists. The belts loosened. He eased her to the floor.

"You're going to be okay. I'm going to stop the bleeding on your leg. I want you to stay awake, okay? We have to get out of here. I have a boat waiting. Just like we planned."

# The Sicilian Prince
# Mediterranean Sea

As the Sicilian Prince left its mooring, Carver knelt on deck, rummaging through the boat's ancient medical kit. Kyra lay unconscious beside him. A burlap canopy on either side hid them from view from passing boats in the marina.

At Mohy's apartment, Carver had ripped the sleeve from his shirt, wrapped it around Kyra's thigh and tightened his belt around it. It had been better than nothing, but it was no substitute for a proper tourniquet. With more time he could have done far better, but they had a narrow window with which to leave the city before all hell broke loose.

Kyra's pulse was getting weaker. She needed blood. Carver was O negative, making him a universal donor at least in theory. Realistically, Carver knew there was far more science to blood compatibility than simply aligning O with A, B and so on. But based on how much blood Kyra had already lost, he couldn't wait until they got to Sicily to find out for sure. That left just one option.

The medical kit contained several syringes. Now he just needed to find some sort of tubing.

Suddenly, he heard the distant boom and saw the black smoke rising from the city. Carver looked skyward, where the attack drone was no doubt circling at high altitude, photographing the aftermath of its mission. Carver allowed himself the luxury of a celebratory fist pump. It was then that he noticed the searing pain on his left side for the first time. He replayed the blow in his mind – the chair legs thwacking against his ribs – suffering the full sensory experience all over again.

Aldo returned to the deck, dazed, like some bear whose hibernation had been rudely interrupted. "What is *this*?" he said, pointing at the smoky horizon. "You said this mission was to rescue the girl. You said nothing about *bombs*!!"

"We're off script," Carver said, borrowing Ellis's language.

"What does that mean?"

"It means they're going to be coming for us. *All* of us. So just get us to Sicily, and fast. Okay?"

Aldo grunted, went back inside and doubled the trawler's speed.

Carver refocused on the task at hand. There were syringes in the medical kit, but he still needed tubing. He would simply have to hack something together.

Then it came to him. He suddenly rose, darted below deck and returned with the backpack he had brought onboard yesterday. The pack, designed for hikers who loathed carrying bulky bottles or canteens, contained an internal bladder and a clear plastic tube that allowed for hands-free sipping. It was a far cry from the medical grade equipment he wanted, but he figured it might be good enough to keep her alive for a little while longer.

Fifteen minutes later, Carver's blood was flowing into Kyra's body. Behind them, the Tripoli skyline grew gradually smaller. Aldo brought some ice up from the freezer and held it against the back of Kyra's head. Her eyes fluttered open. She gasped and struggled to sit upright.

"Relax," Carver said, but she ignored him, propping herself up so that she could see the city skyline in the distance. Then Kyra spoke, but her words were hard to understand. Her top lip was busted and swollen, like some grotesque purple grub.

Carver bent closer, so that his ear was close to her mouth.

"This is all wrong."

All wrong? Regret was the last thing he had expected to hear. When they had met in the market after the start of her mission, she didn't seem to have had any misgivings about the mission at all. And based on the reports passed through her contact in the months afterward, her conviction seemed to have grown over time.

"You lost a lot of blood," Carver told her. "Things will look different tomorrow."

"No," she insisted, pointing to the Tripoli skyline. "You see? The smoke. It's in the wrong part of the city."

Carver looked again, finding his landmarks along the city's coastline – the Port, the big hotels downtown. Then he saw that she was right. The smoke *was* in the wrong part of the city. The Butcher's compound was much further east.

His phone buzzed in his pocket. It was Ellis. This time, her voice was full of despair. "We have a big problem."

# PART II

# BREAKING: Chaos in China

—*Violent anti-American demonstrations in Beijing*
—*American Embassy sacked*
—*U.S. State Department diplomat among dead*

BEIJING (AP), September 24 — Hours after the destruction of the Chinese Embassy in Tripoli, angry crowds stormed the U.S. Embassy in Beijing, killing a U.S. diplomat and wounding several others. Elsewhere, mobs chanted anti-American slogans and damaged American-owned businesses. The U.S. State Department has directed Americans working in China to stay home and keep a low profile until further notice.

Washington's claim that the attack was accidental has done little to soothe civil unrest in China, where demonstrators were estimated to number at least 16 million across Shanghai, Chengdu and other cities. The residence of the American Consul General in Beijing was set ablaze in the hours following the initial reports, and two McDonald's locations were also heavily damaged. Buses packed with students headed out of campuses across the city, attempting to enter the city's embassy district. Eyewitnesses said local police stood by while the violence continued unabated.

Meanwhile in Tripoli, authorities continue to search for survivors in the embassy ruins. None have been found thus far. The dead are said to now include 27 Chinese and at least four Libyans, with others still unaccounted for.

Fueling skepticism over the American apology is the sense that history is repeating itself. American missiles destroyed the Chinese embassy in Belgrade in 1999. Despite American claims that the strike was a mistake, conspiracy theorists claim that the bombing was intended to silence broadcasts originating from within the embassy, which communicated directives to Yugoslavian troops fighting United Nations peacekeepers.

The disaster is only the latest in a series of incidents that have fueled tensions between the two superpowers this year. Over the summer, U.S. intelligence officials openly accused China's military of hacking into the U.S. State Department. Subsequently, China went on the diplomatic offensive over the U.S.'s sale of missile defense weaponry to Taiwan. Recent tensions over the disputed Japanese Senkaku islands have further soured U.S.-China relations.

In an official letter of protest sent to the United Nations, the Libyan government condemned the attack and detailed a long list of American military operations against the country. Cited among them were the 2013 incursion by U.S. Special Forces to snatch an Al Qaeda operative, cruise missiles fired into the country during the 2011 civil war, and the 1986 bombing of Libya that targeted the residence of then-President Muammar Gaddafi.

*This story is developing.*

# The White House
# Washington D.C.

At four a.m. Eastern, Director of National Intelligence Julian Speers entered the Situation Room. He carried *The Morning Book*, a collection of classified briefings including National Intelligence Daily, the State Department's Morning Summary and other reports. Today's edition was slim and incomplete, as the final wasn't typically completed until 6:00 a.m.

Today, Speers hadn't even bothered to skim it on the way from McLean. Only one thing mattered at the moment: China.

It had been less than four long hours since Speers had watched the embassy disaster unfold in real time on the gargantuan monitors at the National Counterterrorism Center. Even now he felt short of breath. His legs still felt rubbery. Crow's feet had seemingly appeared around his eyes overnight.

In the 18 months since he had left his post as White House Chief of Staff to become the nation's Director of National Intelligence, he had never felt such a profound sense of failure and embarrassment. It wasn't just what the entire world now knew, which was that the drone had blown up the Chinese embassy. It was that they had missed a rare opportunity to kill the Butcher of Bahrain and his top commanders all at once. But in light of what was now unfolding in Beijing, their failure to kill one of the world's top terrorists would be quickly forgotten.

*That* was how bad this was. It wasn't just an intelligence or military failure. It was a diplomatic catastrophe.

Speers felt as if he had woken half of Washington with the sobering news. His first call had been to the president, who had quickly asked for an emergency meeting of her security council. En route to the White House, he woke the press secretary and worked with him to create a statement that was later delivered by Defense Secretary Jackson. Speers then sought advice from former Secretary of State Madeline Albright, who had served during a U.S. attack on the Chinese embassy in Belgrade way back in the 1990s. "There is no blueprint," she said though he had clearly woken her from a deep sleep. "You're not dealing with the same China."

He knew she was right. During that first embassy bombing, China had hardly been a superpower. The 1990s China had no advanced technological capabilities to speak of. Despite its great size, its rival Japan had dwarfed it economically. This was a different era.

Now the Situation Room smelled like French roast coffee. The National Security Advisor, the Secretary of Defense and the heads of the CIA, FBI, DIA and NSA were already seated at the main conference table, comparing notes and complaining about the global reaction to the disaster.

FBI Director Chad Fordham watched as Speers sat and poured himself a cup of coffee. He reached for the crystal candy dish on the table that contained a small mound of Hershey's Kisses. Speers had always been a stress eater, and recently, it had only gotten worse.

"Wait," Fordham said as he pulled the dish just out of the reach of his boss's chubby fingers. He pulled an expensive-looking chocolate bar from his satchel and pointed to what was written along the packaging: *95% Cacao*. He slid it across the table. "My dad always said when things are the worst, fortify yourself with the best."

Speers broke off a piece. "Good advice." It was probably the only kindness he would experience all day. He savored three seconds of bliss as the chocolate hit his taste buds and began to melt. Then the door opened as the president entered. Everyone stood in near unison.

President Eva Hudson had her hair back in a tight ponytail, as she often did on mornings when she had only to see those in her inner circle. But this was no ordinary morning briefing. Those happened later, at a more reasonable hour.

The president took her seat and peered over her eyeglasses at the group. "So how did this happen?"

All eyes turned to Speers. "All I can tell you at this stage, Madam President, is what we've ruled out. Pilot error, for one. So far, we can find no fault with the drone pilot's actions or behavior. Remember, this wasn't a moving target. We've had the target coordinates for the Butcher's compound locked into the system for weeks."

At that, the president held a marked up version of the statement Defense Secretary Jackson had made earlier. "See this? The original language you drafted was, and I quote, 'an unspecified drone guidance systems error.' You retracted it before press time. Why?"

"As your press secretary pointed out, we gain nothing by releasing too much detail prematurely."

"The idea came from somewhere, did it not?"

Speers' face was hot. He realized that he was blushing. He was accustomed to handling incredible levels of pressure, but he wasn't used to the president putting him on the hot seat. They had been through a lot together. In private, he still called her Eva, and she called him Julian. So why was she acting like this was all *his* fault?

He never asked for this job. She had practically begged him to take it. After sacking the heads of 14 of the 16 major intelligence agencies, she really had no other choice than to convince someone she knew to rebuild what she had destroyed with a few phone calls.

He took a breath, containing his rage. "We're working on a theory that the weapons guidance system was remotely compromised."

"Meaning what?"

"Meaning the drone, or its associated targeting systems on the ground, were compromised."

"So you're saying someone hacked into the drone, took control of it, and what – intentionally attacked the Chinese embassy?"

"Again, it's a theory. They would likely need a way in at root level. That might take cooperation from someone on the inside, either to infiltrate the system or at least to provide detailed system specifications. We're taking a long look at that possibility."

The president was rendered momentarily speechless. Speers could understand. The idea that this had been a simple accident would have been much easier to accept. It was easy to learn from accidents, to fix the things that had gone wrong. But this theory, if they were correct, would be far more difficult to defend.

The country's chief executive leaned forward, resting her elbows on the long rectangular table. "What are the chances that something like this could happen again right now?"

Speers glanced at Chad, then at the heads of the CIA and DIA for help. Each shrugged in turn. He directed his attention back to the POTUS. "We have no way of putting a probability on that scenario."

The president's voice raised an entire octave. "Stop telling me what you *don't* know, and tell me what you *think*."

He folded his hands before him to stop himself from fidgeting. "All right. This wasn't an accident. We have far too many safeguards in place. I think someone wanted to bomb that embassy, and they wanted it to look like a deliberate act by the United States."

FBI Director Chad Fordham grunted approvingly. "Madam President, there may be something to this. Within an hour of the strike, I spoke with one of our field agents who has been investigating a Chinese operative right here in D.C. He is convinced that the Chinese themselves did this, and I have to say, the case he laid out was intriguing."

The President squirmed in her seat. "You're suggesting that the Chinese may have somehow manipulated our drone to bomb their own embassy?"

"I'm just saying the idea has been floated. Again, this is a field agent who I had never spoken to until this morning. We're looking into it."

The President leaned back from the table and crossed her legs. It was her favorite power position, broadcasting that she not only owned her own space, but also the space all around her.

"The German chancellor called a little while ago. It seems that the UN Security Council will call an emergency session today and vote to condemn the embassy bombing."

Defense Secretary Jackson clasped his thin, dark fingers before him. He was the longest-serving cabinet member, having held the same position in the previous administration. "This is an outrage. They should be *supporting* our effort to find out what really happened."

"It gets worse, Dex. As you know, the American drone program has been under intense criticism, even by our own allies. Some have even floated the idea of sanctions against the United States in the past. The idea of that happening in the past was ludicrous. But now it seems that they may have the votes."

"Madam President," Jackson said, "I hope you're not suggesting that we voluntarily ground the drone program."

"I'm saying we may have no choice. We've all seen the devastating effect of sanctions to the economies of Iran, Russia and North Korea. Now imagine that happening here."

"The only thing we have going for us right now is the ability to vaporize the lunatics of the world before they do the same to us. Make no mistake, we are under attack. Public blowback has already cost American lives in Beijing. We've got to assume a defensive posture and move our forces in the Pacific to REDCON 3."

"REDCON 3?" the president said, her voice laden with irritation. "Is that what the China Playbook calls for in this situation?"

"This situation is unprecedented. There *is* no play for it. But we have an algorithm that measures the hostility level between our two countries, and REDCON 3 is the appropriate stage of military readiness for what we're seeing."

"Dex, this crisis will be managed by human beings, not algorithms."

"Understood. But –"

"Any increase in troop readiness status will be seen as a serious provocation."

Speers nodded in agreement. The riots in Beijing aren't just a reaction to the embassy bombing. The American relationship with China had been slowly deteriorating for years. In the past 12 months alone, the U.S. had been on the receiving end of five million cyber attacks from Mainland China. They probably weren't all state-sponsored, but the Chinese government wasn't exactly trying to stop them, either.

The hostilities weren't strictly limited to espionage. In recent months, American Navy aircraft had regular visual contact with Chinese pilots in the vicinity of Okinawa, the site of America's closest base to the Chinese mainland.

"Julian," the president said, "I'd like to show the group why, from an economic security perspective, we need to de-escalate the crisis as quickly as possible."

Speers stood and dimmed the lights. Then he powered up a massive screen on the far wall. A graph showing U.S. debt over the past two decades appeared.

The president spoke first. "As you all know, I had the pleasure of serving as Treasury Secretary in the previous administration. I worked with my predecessor to come up with an aggressive plan to decrease the federal deficit. When I became president, I continued to execute that same plan. It has failed. Although our exports are up, GDP is growing and we've been able to raise interest rates, we are in more debt than ever."

The next slide was a simple pie chart showing countries that owned significant amounts of American debt. The largest slice, which was shown in red, was attributed to China. "It should come as a surprise to none of you that China is our biggest debt holder. I realized that this made us vulnerable, and so I directed my team to try to find a way to at least reallocate some of the debt load to our allies. Two years later, they have achieved only a small fraction of our goal. Julian?"

Speers took control of the presentation and advanced to the next slide, which showed three graphs, with captions written in Hanzi. The first showed Chinese holdings of U.S. treasuries plummeting by $1.5 trillion in the span of a week. The second chart showed the cost of U.S. borrowing skyrocketing. The third showed a stock market crash that looked even more severe than The Panic of 2008.

"What you're seeing comes directly from a plan that was obtained by one of our operatives in Beijing. We believe it was written by one of China's top tacticians."

"Translation?" SECDEF Jackson said.

"This is what would happen if China dumped all its American debt on the open market, combined with an intentional drop in the Chinese Yuan and targeted cyber attacks on the NASDAQ and New York Stock Exchange."

"A perfect storm," the president added. "Of course, this plan poses risks to the Chinese economy too, but I think the ramifications for us are certainly worse."

Speers turned the room lights back up and took his seat at the table. "When we caught wind of this, we created a defensive plan of our own that would result in mutually assured economic destruction. And through our assets in Beijing, we made sure President Kang saw a leaked version of it."

The president held up a neatly manicured hand, the purple nail polish gleaming under the room lights. "Let's not get overwhelmed in operational details. Suffice to say that until now, our strategy seemed to have paid off. The result was an invitation to negotiate an economic treaty at the upcoming G8 in Tokyo that would provide economic safeguards and insurance for both our countries."

SECDEF Jackson winced. "That's just 11 days from now."

"*Was* 11 days from now. President Kang cancelled the meeting. The more hawkish elements of the Communist Party are obviously seizing this moment to influence him and grow anti-American sentiment." The president stood and gathered her things. "That's why I want all hands on this. Our focus will be finding out who is responsible for this drone attack, and proving it to the satisfaction of not only the Chinese, but the United Nations as well. Our livelihood is riding on it."

# Somewhere Over the Atlantic

In Carver's dream, he was at his parents' ranch in the Arizona high country. It was a gloriously chilly morning. The mountaintops in the distance looked as if they had been dipped in white chocolate, and the scrub in the valley was bitten with frost. Carver was on horseback, searching for a lost calf, knowing that when he came home with his prize, he would be rewarded with chili made with tomatoes from his father's garden and venison they had killed together.

There would be blackberry pie. And a few games of backgammon before a roaring fire.

*Agent Carver.* The voice seemed to float, as if contained in a bubble, from somewhere deep within the endless layers of the white noise that enveloped the aircraft. *Agent Carver.*

He forced his eyes open and saw the medic's face bending toward him. She looked almost angelic in the pale blue light of the cabin. The painful touch of her hand against his side, however, was all it took to usher him back to reality.

And reality was far from ideal. He was aboard a Gulfstream jet en route to Washington, where he and Kyra would have to answer for an epic failure they did not yet understand. They had missed an opportunity to knock out the entire North African Allied Jihad terror command structure, and the world was a far more dangerous place today than it had been yesterday.

"Good morning Agent Carver," the medic said. "I measured your vitals while you were sleeping, but I need to have a closer look at that wound."

"I'm fine," Carver said. He went to scratch his beard, but it was gone. He had erased it from his face with a straight blade on Aldo's boat, leaving just his gentleman's haircut and trademark two-inch sideburns.

The medic unbuttoned his shirt and pulled it back, revealing a massive ink-colored bruise running from his left armpit to his waist. She prodded it with her fingertips. "Does that hurt?"

"If I say no, will you stop?"

She gestured to the back of the plane, where Kyra was attached to an IV. "Your colleague back there is lucky to be alive. I heard you rigged up a workable field blood transfusion kit from a backpack. That's a new one."

"You're welcome."

"For what?"

"All the mileage you'll get out of that story."

She smirked. "Nobody would believe it." She pulled a bio scanner out of her pocket. She waved it up and down his side. Then she set it aside and probed again with her fingers. It felt as if she was actually trying to wedge her fingers between each individual rib. "It's probably just a bad bruise, but they'll take a closer look in Washington. In the meantime, I'll give you something for the pain."

"No thanks." Painkillers dulled the senses. There had been times in Carver's life when he'd had to turn to medication to manage his hyperthymesia, but those were dark days, and he had sworn them off forever.

As the CIA recruiters had hoped all those years ago, total recall had been extremely useful in Carver's line of work. His life experiences lived in his head like an enormous library of movies. To see, smell, touch or taste something was to document it. His remembrances were fully sensory. Recalling a moment in time was nearly the same as reliving it. On his better days, he was a walking dictionary with the ability to retrieve even minor details from his long-term memory at will. But that power could also be exhausting, and at times, even crippling.

Carver was vulnerable to flash floods of past experiences and unrestrained mind chatter. The psychiatrist who had first treated him as a teenager had called them "torrents." Back then, those torrents were so intense that Carver would sometimes hyperventilate and lose consciousness. There was no known drug or procedure that would cure it. During one particularly rough stretch, the psychiatrist had prescribed a combination of potent antidepressants and central nervous system stimulants. The cocktail stopped the torrents, but the world became a fog through which Carver could barely function.

Over the course of his life, and with the help of specialists, Carver had gradually learned to control it. The key was cultivating narrow mental focal points to help quiet the extraneous noise. The technique was like meditation, except Carver was unable to actually conjure nothingness. Instead, the trick was focusing on one tangible thing until the torrent splintered into pieces, like an asteroid burning up within the atmosphere of his mind.

Now, as the medic stood and went back to check on Kyra, Carver pondered his dream. His sister and her boys. His parents and The Two Elk Ranch. He had scheduled a trip out to Arizona to see his family this week, thinking that he would take a well-deserved recharge after killing the Butcher. But he could forget about all that now. Finding out what had happened in Tripoli, and who was behind it, was going to thoroughly consume him.

His parents were going to be crushed. His sister was going to be irate. Better to deliver that bad news now, he figured, before touching down in Washington. Carver reached into his pack, booted up his laptop, connected to the satellite, and used an IP mask to make it appear as if he was logging in from Geneva, Switzerland. Then he logged into his personal email.

He chewed gum as he started going through his new messages. He opened one from his sister with a photo of the kids, ages four and five, making a scarecrow out in a pumpkin patch. He missed them like crazy.

The next message was from his mother.

*Son,*

*We are so looking forward to your visit! So you know, the main ranch house is under renovation, so you'll be staying in the old cowboy quarters. Very rustic! But if you're lucky, you'll arrive just in time for the birth of our new horse.*

Carver replied, typing out a quick apology to his parents with a sufficiently vague explanation about urgent business dealings. They still thought he was a contracting specialist for the State Department with an office on K Street. He hated the lies, but had grown accustomed to them. The charade was for their own protection. Or at least that's what he kept telling himself.

Just as he pressed the send button, a new message came in. It was from his ex-girlfriend, Eri Sato. Memories of their time together — the scent of Eri's shampoo, the feel of her breath on his cheek — flooded his mind. Goosebumps broke out across his forearms. The blood below his waist flowed a bit faster, too.

It had been almost 12 years since Eri had left the apartment they shared in D.C. together. After their relationship hit a rough patch, she had moved back to Tokyo to take a job with Japan's Public Security Intelligence Agency. Banged up as Carver was, traumatized as he felt, the mere thought of Eri *still* caused a palpable chemical reaction.

In a section of the multiplex theatre in his mind, home movies of Eri were always showing. If Carver was being honest, she was more than just an ex-girlfriend. He had come within a few weeks of popping the question. Even now, when he thought of someday having children, it was still Eri that he imagined having them with.

But contact with Eri was infrequent these days. The last message had been 93 days ago, and it had contained just three businesslike lines:

*Blake,*

*Hope you are well. I have a colleague headed to Washington on business. Can you recommend a good American soul food restaurant?*

*XOXO, Eri.*

This new message was even shorter:

*Call me. Need your professional opinion on something. Tried your phone — looks like your number changed again. XOXO*

That was odd. It wasn't like Eri to ask for advice. She was far too competitive to ask his opinions on career topics. Maybe she was finally going to be promoted? He hoped so. Even after they had broken up, he had always rooted for her.

Carver connected his phone to the satellite and dialed the last number he had for her. A twinge of nervousness rattled through his chest as he heard the phone start ringing. It had been more than a year since he and Eri had an actual voice conversation. The last time, she had asked him to look up some federal travel records for a Yakuza leader who had flown to Los Angeles to buy a kidney.

Before Eri could answer, Carver received an inbound call. It was Julian.

Speers got right to the point: "Whatever plans you had today, cancel them."

"The debrief. I know. Ellis told me."

"Debrief? No. That's not going to happen today. I need your every waking moment focused on finding out who blew up that embassy."

"Fine by me. But you might want to talk to Ellis. I got the impression she's out for blood."

"She can get her pound of flesh later. You two are going to crack this together."

Just like old times, Carver thought. But he didn't believe it. Ellis had changed. And way down deep, he knew that there was no going back.

# Washington D.C.

At half past five, Speers' driver pulled the car up to one of his boss's old Adams Morgan haunts, The Diner. He shook his head in dismay as he peered out the window at a couple of chubby patrons exiting the 24-hour eatery. "You promised you were through with this place, boss. What if your trainer finds out?"

Before becoming a father of twin girls the previous year, Speers had eaten here four nights a week, usually after leaving the White House between midnight and three a.m. It had been one of the only places in the city where he wasn't bound to run into someone from the Hill. At that time of night, Speers just wanted to eat a plate of French toast bread pudding, surrounded by tipsy strangers, and maybe watch stupid cat videos on his phone.

The Diner visits had stopped on the insistence of his new fitness trainer. Late night restaurant visits, in particular, were off limits. Speers had negotiated an exception in the case of business meetings, arguing that food was a central component to getting anything done in Washington.

So far, he had lost 18 pounds. That was still 60 pounds short of his goal weight, but it was something.

Now Speers' driver cleared his throat. "Mister Director?"

Speers gestured to the car behind them, which contained his security detail. "Tell the others to wait outside. I'll be quick."

A frigid wind caught him off-guard as he exited the vehicle. Global warming my ass, he thought. It isn't even October yet.

Inside the restaurant, he spotted the blond boy cut worn by Haley Ellis. As Speers had asked, she was seated in the back of the room, near the kitchen, away from windows. In Speers' estimation, she was a little dressed up for government work, in a black sleeveless dress, stockings, two-inch heels and pearl earrings. A *persuasion* outfit. And Speers had to admit that Ellis was infinitely more persuasive when she looked like she did now.

Lately, he hadn't been able to shake the sense that he had given Ellis too much responsibility. He had never thought of her as brilliant, but she had been relentless and loyal. He had texted her just a half-hour ago, when most sane people were still asleep, and here she was. What more could he ask? Still, since the brain injury, something had been a little off. He couldn't quite put his finger on it.

Speers sat without taking off his coat. "The week that won't end."

"I ordered the French toast bread pudding and coffee for you," Ellis said. "When's the last time you were home?"

"Three days ago."

"Your wife must love that."

Speers shrugged. "She knew what she was getting into. So did you look into that China lead?"

"I did. And it's interesting. He's a third-year FBI analyst who thinks he found the Pink Dragon."

Speers leaned back and folded his hands, tapping his index fingers together. The Pink Dragon was the codename for a spy rumored to be working for China's Technical Reconnaissance Bureau. Her ongoing mission was, allegedly, to steal technical documents from American defense contractors that would enable China to match America's military capabilities without going to the expense of research & development. Her target seemed to be anything and everything related to the defense industry. Through an intermediary, the Pink Dragon had paid a dockworker $15,000 for some photographs of a nuclear aircraft carrier under construction. Weeks later, the assistant to the Defense Secretary had been offered $10,000 to disclose her boss's travel itinerary. She had once managed to seduce a DIA engineer, and while he was sleeping, used his phone to introduce vulnerability into a key Pentagon firewall.

The secret to her success? As far as they could tell, she lived a remarkably low-tech lifestyle. In an era in which the NSA had access to every conceivable communication from each man, woman and child in America, the Pink Dragon rarely sent or received anything electronically. She wore an analog watch. When she did use phones, they were disposable handsets tossed within 24-hours. She always paid in cash, and in turn received hard copies of data and files.

Ellis powered up her phone and pushed it across the table. "The Pink Dragon may have bought information on the drone's weapons guidance system from this man."

Speers regarded a photograph of a white male in his late 30s. "Who is he?"

"His name is Jack Brenner."

"Brinner? As in breakfast for dinner?"

Ellis smirked. "Someone's hungry. It's Brenner, with an E. He's a senior engineer working for LithiumXI. They're a boutique defense contractor specializing in weapons guidance systems"

"Like the one we had in the drone over Tripoli?"

"Exactly."

Speers sighed. If this was true, Brenner would have been the latest in a long line of defense contractor employees to have sold information to the Chinese. The FBI had made seven so-called insider arrests in recent months.

"Did Brenner have financial motivation for doing this?"

"We don't know. These are all just allegations. Nobody's dug deep into this yet."

"Look, maybe Brenner did it, and maybe he didn't. But can we just admit that this is a crazy theory? Can we do that? This is China we're talking about. They don't want a war. They've got plenty of land, money and resources. They just want to steal all our intellectual property and then take the kids to Disneyland."

Ellis held up her hands in deference. "You're preaching to the choir. But we know that there are factions in the communist party that want to cut ties with the West. Every time they wake up, there's another Starbucks in Beijing, another kid who's found out how to access Google, another washed up NBA player dominating the Chinese Basketball Association."

"What's your point?"

"If you wanted to stoke enough anti-American sentiment in China to change foreign policy, can you think of any better way than staging an American attack on a Chinese embassy?"

Speers shook his head. "I'm skeptical. But since this is the only thing we have at the moment, I'm going to give you the resources to chase this."

Ellis stopped just short of grinning, but looked triumphant nevertheless. "Thank you. I appreciate your confidence in me."

"Blake Carver lands in a few hours. You two will team up on this." As soon as he said it, he could see that all the wind had left Ellis's sails. "Is there a problem?"

She paused, choosing her next words carefully. "If you don't mind, Julian, I'd like the opportunity to choose my own team."

There it was. The reason she had put on pumps, perfume and the dress. Speers reached into his pocket and unwrapped a lollipop. He did so slowly and purposefully, letting the silence build until Ellis could no longer stand it.

"Considering what happened in Tripoli," she said, "I can only assume Blake's debrief will be exhaustive."

Speers shook his head. "We don't have the luxury of time. Besides, with Carver's memory, the team could question him 10 years from now and get the same answers."

"What about disciplinary action?" she said, searching Speers' face hopefully for some confirmation. "Carver disobeyed a direct order. He's going to have to answer for that, right?"

"He questioned your directive, Haley. And thank God he did. He's the only reason Kyra is still alive."

"Carver is toxic. Trouble follows him. And I for one am sick and tired of getting caught up in it."

So that was it. Ellis was referring to an ongoing investigation by the House Intelligence Oversight Committee into Carver's operation to disrupt and destroy a secret society called The Fellowship. In Speers' judgment, Carver had eliminated a substantial threat to domestic and international security. But left in the operation's wake were 29 bodies in Rome, including an MI5 operative and the worldwide leader of the Jesuit Order. He had also, in committee-speak, "Made unauthorized use of a fugitive asset." That asset was Nico Gold, a notorious hacker who was still wanted in a dozen countries.

Ellis had been Carver's partner on that operation. She herself had barely escaped death, requiring months of rehab for a traumatic brain injury before being reactivated. After recovery, she had to deal with a very nosy task force put in motion by the House Intelligence Oversight Committee.

It had all taken a toll. Despite Ellis's recent medical clearance, Speers knew there were still doubts about her mental health. That was just one more reason why he wanted Carver on the case.

"So you're going to give Carver a pass again," Ellis said. "No offense, Julian, but do you even realize how many times you've saved his ass?"

"Haley, I'm going to say this just once so you're clear about my view on this. Carver is the best we have, and I have nothing but confidence in his judgment. And if anyone asked me about you, I'd say the same thing."

He stood and buttoned his coat.

Ellis looked up. "What about your French toast?"

Speers plucked a 20-dollar bill from his pocket and laid it on the table. "You eat it, Haley. You could use a little sweetness in your life."

# Joint Base Andrews Maryland

The Learjet carrying Blake Carver and Kyra Javan touched down and taxied toward its hangar, wings gleaming in the mid-morning sun. Two black SUVs and an ambulance were on hand to whisk them to their respective destinations. Julian Speers stepped out of the lead vehicle and waited as the plane was secured for disembarkation.

Speers had a smidge of scrambled eggs in his beard. He watched as the door to the Learjet popped open. Kyra emerged first, leaning on a medic for support as she descended the stairs. Carver came down right behind them.

"Glad you made it back safely," Speers told them.

It was a line he had actually given a lot of thought to. *Congrats* was out of the question. *Welcome back* seemed far too celebratory given the circumstances. *Thank you for your* service sounded final.

But it was Kyra, not Carver, who replied first. "Mister Director, I'm flattered that you came in person. But do you mind telling me what the hell happened over there?"

The quiet outrage in her voice caught him off guard. *Nobody* spoke to him that way. But given all she had been through, he decided to cut her some slack.

"We've got all hands on deck trying to figure it out. But I want you to know that your sacrifice won't be in vain. We'll have another shot at the Butcher, and the things you learned about him and his operation are going to help us do it. "

She sobbed violently and uncontrollably. Speers went in for a hug, but the paramedics that had been waiting to take her to Bethesda Naval Hospital were faster. They led her to the ambulance three abreast, where she would no doubt get something for her nerves.

Now Carver was beside him, watching as the ambulance pulled away. "I don't envy her. They're going to want to be sure she wasn't the leak. I've had some pretty hostile debriefs in my time, but this is going to be one for the record books."

Speers sighed. "At least she can rest assured that Mohy Osman is dead. You made damn sure of that."

Minutes later, the black SUVs – Speers' vehicle and his security detail – merged onto the Beltway. Speers sat opposite Carver, relaying the finer details of what some were calling The China Theory – the idea that fringe elements within China's communist party had in fact hacked into the American drone and destroyed their own embassy.

"So," Speers said at last. "What do you think?"

Carver pulled no punches. "Dead wrong. There are all kinds of problems with that logic."

"I tend to agree, but we have to consider the possibility. In a few minutes, you'll meet up with Haley Ellis. I believe she already sent you a dossier on a defense contracting engineer named Jack Brenner."

"Already read it."

"Just curious. You don't have a problem working with Ellis, do you?"

Speers' phone buzzed before Carver could respond. The intelligence czar absorbed the message with a grimace, and then lowered the vehicle's privacy glass.

"Turn on the radio," he said to the driver. "Any news channel will do."

RADIO BROADCASTER: "I just received word from our New York bureau. We have confirmation that the markets are back online after approximately 18 minutes of unexplained dead time, where the NASDAQ and the New York Stock Exchange were effectively knocked offline. This is looking a lot like the flash crash of 2010 that caused an estimated trillion dollars of damage to the U.S. economy, so it will be very interesting to see who or what has actually caused this."

Speers turned to Carver. "I'll tell you who or what caused this. It's payback for Tripoli. And it's just the beginning."

# The East Room
# The White House

The broadcast producer stood next to the teleprompter, checking to make sure that the last-minute additions to the president's speech had made it into the live script. She turned to President Hudson, who stood behind the podium in a blue dress, going over her remarks.

"We're live in 15 seconds, Madam President."

President Hudson cleared her throat and sipped hot lemon water from a silver thermos. Then she turned toward the camera and remained standing with her hands gripping both sides of the podium. A practiced posture that conveyed the right balance of power and determination.

An aide patted her brow and moved off screen. The producer put up his hand and initiated the silent five-second countdown. Then he pointed, indicating that she was broadcasting live.

"Good morning. Today, the world woke up to the news of a tragic accident in which one of our drones struck the Chinese Embassy in Tripoli. I have already extended our deepest apologies to the Chinese president, as well as to the Libyan prime minister.

As you may know, Libya is a nation experiencing extreme instability, including an ongoing civil war. It's no secret that it has also become a hotbed of terrorism. Our intent today was to protect a group of brave Americans operating in the area from a known threat. Obviously, that operation did not go as planned, and we're still working to identify exactly what went wrong. As of this morning, we have ruled out pilot error. We have not ruled out cyber attacks as a possible cause.

Now I want to take this opportunity to personally apologize to the people of China for the grave loss of life. However, I must caution President Kang against taking retaliatory action. Just hours ago, our embassy in Beijing was sacked by protesters, and one of our own diplomats, whose name has not been released out of respect for the family, lost his life. I urge Beijing to do everything in their power to ensure that the situation does not spiral even further out of control.

About an hour ago, the NASDAQ and the New York Stock Exchange were effectively knocked offline in what we believe to be a cyber attack. The American people and the world can rest assured that we are taking all possible measures to minimize our vulnerability and prevent another attack of this magnitude.

While our investigation is in its early stages, know that we will consider any deliberate state-sponsored attack as an act of war. Out of respect for the tragedy in Tripoli, I am effectively grounding the American drone program pending a full investigation into the incident. I have every expectation that the program will resume in due course.

In the meantime, the American military is on high alert. Any threat on the ground, on the seas, in the air, on the Internet and even in space will be dealt with swiftly and without hesitation. We will protect American citizens at all costs, whether they are at home or abroad, using the full power of the American arsenal.

To Americans everywhere, I say do not be afraid. Instead, let us find strength in who we are as a people: one nation, under God, indivisible, with liberty and justice for all.

Thank you. May God bless you. And may God bless the United States of America."

# Fairfax, Virginia

Two black SUVs powered through the neighborhood of two-story colonial homes and red maple trees, kicking up autumn leaves that rose and fell behind the convoy like confetti. The vehicles parked before a stately home with a white picket fence and a red front door. On the porch, a startled elderly couple steadied their swing, their lunch ritual ruined by the sudden presence of federal agents.

The convoy wasn't here for them. All attention was focused on the home across the street. A white commercial van was parked in the driveway with the words CAPITAL HOME HEALTH CARE printed in cursive on the side. The lawn hadn't been mowed in about two weeks.

A cool breeze hit Blake Carver as he stepped out of the lead vehicle. He buttoned his coat and watched Haley Ellis step out of the second vehicle. She wore a gray knee-length coat over a plaid skirt, a black blouse and black pumps. A bit upscale for fieldwork, Carver noted.

Carver gestured to four men in FBI jackets. They fanned out across the front lawn. Two entered the backyard through the side gate. The others would await Carver's signal to come inside and begin searching the place.

Ellis joined Carver as they crossed the street. "I need a word before we go inside."

"About?"

She folded her arms across her chest. "The operation in Tripoli. You disobeyed my direct order. Do you have any idea how embarrassing that was for me?"

Carver stuffed his hands into his pants pockets. "It was the wrong call, Ellis. And Kyra is alive. That should count for something."

"We all have to follow rules, Blake. If we don't, the whole system falls apart. This is my investigation, and I need you to show me the respect I deserve."

Carver leaned close to her, his nose confirming what he had suspected by the recent congestion in her voice. "When did you start smoking?"

Her lips pursed. "I swear you're more canine than human."

"So I'm a werewolf. You're ruining your complexion and your lungs with cigarettes. Why?"

Her face tightened until it resembled a fist. She started a rebuttal, and then pulled it back. "Let's just focus on Jack Samuel Brenner, shall we?"

The two started walking toward the Brenner home. "He was a senior developer on weapons guidance systems for LithiumXI's latest generation drones," Ellis said. "Parents are both dead. He has a sister with cerebral palsy that lives with him here. Late last year, he fell behind in the payments for his sister's home health care. He liquidated his assets and converted them to Bitcoin. A hacker stole all the Bitcoin from his account, and a week later, the Pink Dragon allegedly approached him."

"Any big money transfers?"

"We're working on that. But two months ago, the bank had been ready to foreclose on this place. Today the mortgage is paid in full."

"So Brenner had financial motivation for selling out his country." Carver peered into the van's front windshield. "Is this his van?"

Ellis shook her head. "It belongs to the nurse who cares for the sister. Brenner drives a BMW, but we don't know where it is. I put out a BOLO with local law enforcement."

Carver tapped the van's hood en route to the front door. "You know what I can never figure out? Why anyone would own a creepy white van."

"Not everyone thinks of white vans as creepy."

"Like who? That's like saying clowns aren't creepy."

The front door opened. A woman in white coveralls emblazoned with the Capital Home Healthcare logo stood in the doorway. "Can I help you?"

Ellis presented her ID, which identified her as an employee of the Office of the Director of National Intelligence. "We're looking for Jack Brenner."

The nurse looked about as puzzled as Carver expected. In his experience working white-collar espionage cases, those close to the perpetrator were rarely aware of the crimes being committed.

"He's not here," the nurse said.

Ellis was quick with a follow-up. "Is Jack's sister home?"

"Heidi? Yes, but what's this about? Is Jack all right?"

Carver left Ellis to present the search warrant and deal with the nurse. He slipped past her and began exploring the home. The living room was tidy, with a large TV, two cloth-covered chairs, a white couch and a few family photos. Carver opened the French doors to the back yard. He whistled and waved at two FBI agents who had been stationed in the backyard in case Brenner tried to flee out the back.

He headed upstairs. "Federal agent coming up," he announced as he went. The railing next to the stairway was outfitted with a mechanized wheelchair lift. Judging by the lack of wear on the rails, it looked to have been installed recently. That had to have been expensive.

Heidi Brenner was waiting for Carver when he reached the second floor landing. The 26-year-old was in a wheelchair. She was pretty. The hair was bad, though. A square-shaped brown mop of a haircut. Carver figured the nurse was to blame for that. Any beauty school dropout could have done better.

He noted Heidi's legs. She was wearing yoga pants, and the outline of her left leg was considerably smaller than the right one.

"We're with the Office of the Director of National Security," he said. "Jack is your brother?"

"Yes." Porcelain hands were folded tightly in her lap. "What's he done?"

Considering that Brenner had no criminal history, Carver found the question odd. "I don't really know, and that's the truth. But I'd like to talk to him."

"Good luck with that. I've been trying to get hold of him all day." She wheeled just past Carver to an antique mahogany desk that was situated in the hallway. She opened the top drawer and pulled out a stack of legal papers, then handed them to Carver. "He left all this on my pillow this morning."

The document on top was the deed to the home, which by the looks of it, Brenner had signed over to his sister. The second document was a generic will that he had printed up from an online legal site and signed that morning.

She was on the verge of tears. "I've been so worried. He takes anti-depression meds. He's been stressed lately. Unusually so. I thought maybe..."

"Maybe what?"

"He brought a gun a couple weeks ago. He wouldn't say why."

Carver called for Ellis. She was better at dealing with emotional people than he was. Or at least she used to be. She hadn't been quite the same since the injury.

He refocused on the sister. "Heidi, what time did your brother leave?"

"Must have been just before midnight." She nodded to a pad of paper on the desk. "Do you need to write this all down?"

"That's not necessary. You said he left before midnight. Are you sure?"

"Yes. He was here at eleven, which is when I went to bed. I got up a little after that to go to the toilet. I saw those documents and went into his room. He wasn't there."

That meant Brenner left about the same local time as the drone strike in Tripoli. "Did he take anything with him?"

"His entire supply of insulin."

"He's diabetic?"

She nodded. "When I saw it was all gone, that gave me hope that he wasn't going to, you know, harm himself."

"How often does he take it?"

"He wears one of those insulin pumps. Oh, also, his computer was gone. He took Molly, too."

"Molly?"

"His boa constrictor."

"Ah. Can I see Jack's room?"

Carver followed as Brenner's sister rolled down the hallway to the master bedroom. It could have easily passed for the room of a 15-year-old, decorated as it was with framed superhero posters.

On one wall, several shelves were filled with Marvel, Dr. Who and Game of Thrones action figures in their original packages. On other shelves, he had several gaming consoles from the 1970s and 1980s, all in mint condition under plastic.

In a corner sat an empty 20-gallon aquarium. The snake must have fed recently, because there was a significant amount of dung in the enclosure.

There were books, too. Mostly educational texts about programming. *PBASIC Essentials, Intro to LabVIEW, Programming with C++, Advanced Ruby on Rails*. And amidst all the technical books, a little something for Brenner's financial life: *The Ultimate guide to Gaining Wealth through Fantasy Sports Betting*.

"Your brother likes to gamble?"

Heidi's lips pursed. "Mother said that would be the end of him. Isn't that why you're here?"

Ellis appeared in the doorway. "Found these downstairs." She held a cluster of papers with the CarMax logo at the top. It was a bill of sale. "He sold his car."

The sister threw her hands up. "He told me the BMW was getting repaired. I should have known. He probably sold it to bet on some games. And that explains the Subaru."

"Subaru?"

"He's been driving a Subaru these past few days. Real piece of work."

"Can you be more specific?"

"One of the side mirrors was actually held onto the car with duct tape. He said it was just a loaner from the shop while his BMW was getting fixed. I asked him what kind of shop would loan out such a terrible car?"

They wouldn't, Carver thought. The question was, what kind of dealership would *sell* such a terrible car?

# Manassas, Virginia

Hullman Brothers Used Auto was a family-run dealership at the edge of a strip mall. Ellis and Carver pulled into the four-acre lot, which seemed to be populated with cars from every conceivable make, model and decade. While there had been no evidence on Jack Brenner's credit card or banking statements linking him to Hullman Brothers, the dealership had reported the recent sale of an old Subaru with the state department of motor vehicles to a Robert Wallace. The associated mailing address led to a post office box, increasing the possibility that the buyer had used a false identity. And the sale price — just $1,200, paid in cash — suggested that the car was probably wretched enough to fit Heidi Brenner's description.

As the two federal agents exited the vehicle, Carver noted Ellis's shaky hands. She hadn't been out of his sight all day, which meant that she probably hadn't had a cigarette. Earlier, he had discovered a package of Newport Lights she had stashed in the storage bin between the seats. He had no idea how long she could hold out, but he certainly wasn't going to give his blessing to smoke in the car.

The showroom smelled of popcorn and instant coffee. Carver lingered beside a vintage Ford Mustang with 10 helium balloons tied to its passenger-side door handle. "I spent the summer of my junior year in high school fixing up one of these," he said with pain evident in his voice. He recalled with remarkable vividness how he had, in frustration, hurled a wrench across the garage with such velocity that it punched through the drywall. For that, his father had grounded him for three months.

A grey-haired salesman closed in, grinning, hand outstretched. The sight of Ellis's federal ID cooled his charm.

Ellis cut right to the chase, handing the salesman the last known photograph of Jack Brenner. "You recognize this man?"

The salesman nodded, stroking his mustache with his thumb and forefinger. "Yeah. Fastest sale I ever made."

"How so?"

"That guy had only one thing on his mind. Privacy. He wanted a completely unconnected car."

Carver whistled at the audacity of the request. "That rules out GPS, navigation, anti-theft and remote diagnostics."

"Yup. The only thing I had for him was a super old Subaru. I would have to look up the file to even tell you the year."

"We're going to need everything you've got."

The salesman handed the photograph back to Ellis. "I don't mean to be a pain, but do you guys have a warrant?"

Carver looked at the salesman sideways. "Sir, this is a very fast-moving federal investigation. Your swift cooperation would be considered a patriotic duty. People at the *very top* are watching this one."

"The very top?"

"That's right." Carver winked, for added effect.

The salesman nodded furiously, as if he had been inducted into a secret brotherhood. "I'm with you! My daughter looks up to President Hudson. She's a role model." He hustled toward the office, waving for the two feds to follow him. "That car had no plates, but I can get you the VIN number out of the file. And full disclosure, I want you to know that I was honest about that car with him. Completely by the book!"

"Honest about what?"

"I told him straight up I didn't even know if that car would pass emissions testing. It had just come onto the lot. Bald tires. Hadn't even been washed yet. But for someone that paranoid about privacy, an old car like that is about the only thing you can buy."

"Makes sense," Ellis said. "I think we can guess the answer to this question, but I just have to ask. How did he pay?"

The salesman grinned. "All cash. Of course."

# Rural Virginia

Carver drove the lead vehicle as the convoy powered down the two-lane highway and the sun dipped near the horizon. They were only a little more than an hour away from D.C., but it was another world out here. Vineyards, horse farms and road kill that looked almost fresh enough to eat.

Every little bump in the road felt like a knife in Carver's bruised ribs, but he had reason to smile. He and Ellis had just caught the break they needed. AAA had received a call for roadside assistant for a Subaru matching Brenner's. The car's left front passenger tire had blown out. Carver smirked at the irony. The escape plans of such a gifted engineer, entrusted to work on one of the military's most advanced technological achievements, had been derailed by the failure of something as ancient as a wheel.

Ellis rode shotgun, driven mad by her desire to suppress her nicotine craving. She fidgeted endlessly, first with her phone, then with her hair. Carver drove wordlessly, watching out of the corner of his eye as his reluctant partner eventually reached into the storage bin between the seats. Her fingers did not locate the package of Newport cigarettes she had stashed there. They instead found a book with a yellow cover and black letters called *The Power of Habit*.

"What the...?"

Carver allowed himself a smug grin. "I took the liberty of ducking into that bookstore next to the dealership. I promise you, that book will help you quit smoking."

Ellis's face filled with disgust. "You actually threw out my smokes?"

"There's a twenty-dollar bill inside. You can use it as a bookmark, or to buy a new pack of Newports. Your choice. But I do hope you'll at least check out the first couple of chapters. I'm worried about you, Ellis."

"Mind your own business."

The onboard navigation announced their destination coming up in a quarter mile. Carver feathered the brakes and pointed to a stone building that appeared like a mirage in the fading daylight. An old-fashioned roadhouse. If they were lucky, Brenner would be inside waiting for AAA.

Following Carver's lead, the convoy slowed and pulled off the highway, squeezing into a clearing between the roadhouse and a grove of locust trees. Through the foliage, Carver could make out the old Subaru.

He shut off the engine, pulled his SIG out of its holster, and chambered a round into the barrel.

"Easy," Ellis said. "Brenner may be a traitor, but there's nothing to suggest that he's violent."

"His sister *did* say he had bought a gun last week."

"I'm saying use restraint. The mortality rate tends to spike when you're around, and I'm sick of internal investigations."

Carver knew he didn't have to justify his body count to Ellis, but the remark bothered him all the same. He had no regrets. He had been put in difficult situations and had done what had to be done. Nothing more.

He tapped a button on his coat, activating the closed communications system he shared with the team in the other vehicle. "I'm going in solo while you cover the rear exit. I want to try talking to him before we take him into custody. I'll leave my mic on, so just listen for my cue."

He exited the SUV, pulled his weapon and held it low at his side as he passed through the locust grove and slowly approached the sedan. Just as the car salesman in Manassas had mentioned, there were no plates on the car.

He approached with caution, half-expecting Brenner to be sleeping in the back seat. Instead he spotted a nylon duffel bag that was stuffed too full to be zipped completely. And next to it, a white pillowcase tied in a knot. Something inside it was moving in a slow, insistent rhythm. It had to be Molly, the boa constrictor Brenner's sister had mentioned.

"Hello Molly," Carver said. "We'll find you a good home. I promise."

He holstered his weapon, buttoned his coat to cover it, and headed inside. The scent of barbecue filled him with hunger. Dale Watson was playing on the bar's sound system.

*I lie when I drink,*
*and I drink a lot.*
*I only drink when I'm missing you...*

Brenner was one of just six customers in the place. He was seated at the bar, sipping a pint of some urine-colored beer. A plate of pulled pork sat before him. He was a portly fellow, with a bushy beard resembling the one Carver had just shaved off. His t-shirt rode a little too high on his back, and his jeans rode a little too low in the seat. His crack was showing.

Carver sidled up on the stool beside him and picked up the menu. He turned to Brenner. "What's good?"

Brenner shrugged without making eye contact. "Coors Light."

"Amen to that. But I'm hungry. You tried the pulled pork?"

Brenner shook his head. "No offense, buddy, but I didn't come here to chat."

"Then why come to a bar?"

Brenner turned his droopy-eyed gaze toward Carver. "If you must know, I'm waiting for roadside assistance. Had a blowout."

"Bummer." Carver motioned to the bartender. The redhead wore a half-shirt to show off a stomach tattoo that bore some smudgy resemblance to the Seattle skyline. She took his order – fish, chips and Coors Light – and walked it into the kitchen. Although Carver had been raised in a culture of complete alcohol abstinence, a recent global study on longevity in so-called blue zones – regions where people live unusually long lives – had convinced him that drinking moderate levels of alcohol would be good for his health.

Brenner kept his eyes fixed on the game on the TV mounted above the bar. Despite the efficiency of the bar's air conditioning, he was sweating. His phone chirped, signaling an inbound text message. Must be a prepaid phone, Carver thought, because they had found Brenner's primary phone in a neighbor's dumpster a few hours ago.

Brenner cursed when he read the text message.

"Bad news?" Carver said, although he already knew the answer. He had talked to AAA personally and composed the message Brenner had just received.

"They're running late. Could be another half hour."

"I can think of worse places to wait." Carver signaled to the bartender. "Another beer. My tab."

Brenner nodded appreciatively. "Thanks."

ESPN Classic was showing an NBA finals game from years gone by.

"Cavs versus Warriors," Carver noted. "Game seven. One of the best."

"Meh."

Carver motioned toward the screen. "Hey, check this out. LeBron's about to take a hard foul from Bogut. He's actually going to *bleed* from this one."

Brenner gave Carver an annoyed glance, and then watched in amazement as a cut opened up on Bogut's head.

The bartender delivered two beers. The two men toasted. Brenner drank a third of his beer immediately.

Carver pointed to the screen. "Watch this. Now he's about to make an incredible two-handed tomahawk dunk. Camera's going to zoom in on LeBron, and he's going to make the craziest face, like a cartoon character. Sometimes I think his head is actually going to explode into a ball of mist."

Brenner watched as the scene unfold on TV just as Carver described it. He was clearly astonished. "You a super fan, huh?"

"Nah," Carver said. "Casual at best."

"The Cavs played more than 100 games that year. How many times you seen this one?"

"Once."

"Seriously?"

"Yup."

Brenner scratched his beard. "Either you're lying, or you've got a photographic memory."

"You're warm."

"Seriously? An honest to God photographic memory?"

"That's not the clinical name for what I have, but you're in the right neighborhood."

"Wow."

"Yeah, I know," Carver said. He put on a smug smile, and it was genuine. Brenner was taking the bait, just as he'd hoped.

"So prove it."

"What?"

"Prove it."

"How?"

"You see the 2015 Super Bowl?"

"Of course."

"A hundred bucks says you can't tell me anything detailed about that game. And I mean *meaningful* stuff that nobody else would remember."

It figured that Brenner was itching for some action. The bookshelf in his room had contained several books on game theory, and the most dog-eared of them all was *Mastering Texas Hold'em for Fun and Profit*. Carver suspected his money problems had less to do with his sister's illness, as Ellis had speculated, and more to do with a gambling addiction.

Carver called the bartender over. "Two shots of Jose Cuervo." He turned back to Brenner. "Loser pays $100 and drinks two shots."

Brenner put his money on the bar. "You're on."

"Super Bowl forty-nine," Carver said. "That was February first, a Sunday. In the hours before the game, the Vegas odds closed from 2.5 points favoring the Seahawks to a toss up, which eventually proved remarkably prophetic in light of the evenness of the game itself."

Brenner shook his head slowly. "Not impressed. Anyone could say those things."

"There was a full moon that night, but nobody at the game saw it, played as it was in University of Phoenix Stadium, a domed arena, which is actually in Glendale, Arizona. The Seahawks were penalized seven times for 70 yards in all. Neither team fumbled. New England's Ryan Allen tied a Super Bowl record for the longest punt with 64 yards. The Patriots' Edelman caught nine passes for 109 yards and a touchdown, but he was only their second most prolific catcher of the game. The first was Shane Veeran, whose longest catch was 16 yards. The Patriots players made $189,000 each as a bonus for the win, which was –"

"Hold up." The fugitive picked up his phone and began looking up game stats. Moments later, he drank both shots and slid the money across the bar top toward Carver. "Buddy, you just blew my mind. What do you do for a living?"

"Play cards," Carver lied.

"That figures. For a guy with your mind, counting cards must be easy. What's your game? Blackjack?"

"Yeah mostly."

Carver figured his mark was sufficiently warmed up by now. "Hey," he called to the barkeep. "Would you mind switching to a news channel for just two minutes?"

She did as he asked, and as he had figured, the network was covering the crisis. They were replaying footage of anti-American protests in Beijing while pundits offered a play-by-play analysis.

"This China situation is pretty crazy," Carver said.

Brenner sipped his beer. "Yeah, you don't know the half of it."

And there was the conversational segue Carver had been building toward. "What do you mean?"

The fugitive shrugged. "Nothing, man. I'm just talking."

Carver swigged his Coors and nodded amiably. "Didn't sound like nothing to me."

"I've said too much already."

Carver turned and focused all his attention on Brenner. He flashed a sly grin. "I think you know something. C'mon, one gambler to another. You work at the Pentagon or something?"

The fugitive put a finger to his lips. "Shhh."

"I knew it!" It was time to double down. "Give me a hint!"

"Nah, I better change the subject, buddy."

The way Carver saw it, this was the last opportunity to get something unbiased out of Brenner. Once they had him in custody, he would get an attorney, and they might be stuck for months on end. "I'm a nobody, okay? What am I going to do? Who am I going to tell?" He slapped another hundred bucks down on the bar and watched as the fugitive, who was getting a bit buzzed, eyed the cash on the bar. "Come on. Double your money back?"

Brenner took the cash to shut Carver up if nothing else. He leaned close enough so that Carver could feel his breath. Then he lowered his voice to a whisper. "Keep your voice down. They might be listening."

"Who are *they*?"

"The Chinese," Brenner whispered. "They did this. Mark my word."

Brenner grabbed the cash off the bar and winced, realizing he had said too much. He checked his watch. "I better get out to my car and wait for roadside assistance." He whistled to the barkeep. "Check please."

Carver put his hand on Brenner's shoulder. "Hey friend. Last bet while you wait for your check. Fifty bucks says the next person to come through that front door is not with roadside assistance."

Brenner grinned wearily. "Dude. *Always* looking for action. You just can't help yourself, can you?"

"Takes one to know one."

"All right. You're on."

A ray of late afternoon sun flashed across the bar as the front door opened behind them. The two men turned. Ellis stood the doorway. "Excuse me, ma'am?" Carver shouted over the music. "I'm wondering if you could come over here and settle a bet." Ellis did, resting her right hand on her purse. "Ma'am, would you please tell my friend here who you are here to see?"

Ellis focused her attention on Brenner. She could still turn on the sex appeal when she really wanted to. "I'm here to see you, Jack."

Brenner looked her up and down. "You're with roadside assistance?"

"Nope." She nodded to Carver. "I'm with him."

The fugitive reached for the handgun in his ankle holster, but Carver was faster. He knocked Brenner off his stool with a forearm shiver, and then pounced, pinning his head against the ground with a knee. "Sorry, Jack. You lost the bet. Now put your hands behind your back. My friend here is going to cuff you. Then you're going to tell us where we can find the Pink Dragon."

"I don't know anything. I *swear* I don't."

Ellis disarmed Brenner and moved in with the cuffs. Then she flashed her federal ID to the bartender. "Make sure nobody leaves, okay? We need to talk to everyone."

Carver pressed his knee harder, squeezing Jack's head. "I get it, Jack. You needed money. You were desperate to pay your debts. All we want is the buyer, Jack. We want the Pink Dragon."

"I'm telling you, just shut up. They might be listening."

Ellis stole a glance at Carver. "*Who's* listening?"

The fugitive shut his eyes. He winced, as if someone had pinched him. "I don't feel good."

Carver squeezed his arm. "Focus, Jack. Who's listening?"

"You already know."

"Where is the Pink Dragon?"

"Please. I'm serious. I feel really sick all of a sudden."

The door opened again. Sunlight flooded the place as the FBI team entered. Ellis's hand pulled at Carver's shoulder. "Blake, ease up!"

But Carver didn't let up. He pressed harder. "You know, Jack, you could get the death penalty for treason. Unless you help us. *Right. Now.*"

The fugitive's voice was weakened. "There's a final drop. I sent a message telling her where to pick it up."

"Where? Where's the final drop?"

Brenner's eyes closed. Ellis dropped to her knees. "I think he's unconscious!"

Carver turned him cautiously. Brenner would hardly have been the first fugitive to feign illness.

The paunchy hipster's body convulsed so violently that Carver's doubts instantly vanished. The seizure hit again and again, as if Brenner were a human lightning rod. The room suddenly smelled of urine. Brenner's shirt rode up, revealing a small device attached to his belt. The insulin pump Brenner's sister had spoken of.

A small indicator on the device was flashing red. Carver touched it, and pulled his hand away. It was insanely hot, and a warning message indicated the pump was completely empty. This was far from normal. Carver's own mother had a pump just like it. He'd never heard of anything like this.

Ellis swooped down and wedged the edge of her jacket into Brenner's mouth to keep him from biting his tongue.

"Ellis, I think this thing just shot its entire load of insulin into Brenner."

"What? Why would it do that?"

"It wouldn't. Not without help."

He recalled reading, years earlier, about a hacker who had demonstrated his ability to hack a pacemaker before a live audience. It stood to reason that an insulin pump could be hacked too, and with fatal consequences. But could lightning really strike twice? Could the insider who had helped someone hack into the attack drone also be the victim of a hack?

Carver pointed at one of the FBI team members. "Search the parking lot and the pub for anyone with a computer. Confiscate all phones and personal devices."

Brenner's seizures continued. While Ellis treated him, Carver caught notice of the fugitive's burner phone, which had slipped off the counter and fallen onto the floor. The screen was cracked, but the device came to life quickly in Carver's hands.

He scrolled through Brenner's text messages until he stopped at a terse directive he had sent earlier in the day: *drop is at Verizon center. go to will call tonight. the ticket is in your name.*

Tonight? Carver knew the Washington Wizards were playing the Knicks tonight at home. Tip off was in 91 minutes.

Meanwhile, Ellis was still furiously working to save Brenner's life. Carver whistled for one of the other agents to come assist. "Take over," he said. "We have to go."

Ellis looked up, incredulous. "He could die! I'm a trained army medic!"

"I know where the Pink Dragon is headed. But we have to leave right now."

# Verizon Center
# Washington D.C.

Carver stood on the concourse in Verizon Center, wearing a Washington Wizards hoodie that he had purchased moments earlier. Tip off was in less than 10 minutes. Highlight footage of eye-popping dunks played on the overhead screens, and the enormous crowd seemed to sigh with each new video clip. *Ahhhhhhhhh. Ahhhhhhhhhh. Ahhhhhhhhh.*

He watched as basketball fans swarmed the arena like ants over a hillside, looking for the shortest route to their seat while shouldering all the pizza, popcorn and beer that they could carry. Carver figured that the Pink Dragon would indulge in no such luxuries. She would be businesslike in her movements. She would get what she came for and exit the game as quickly as possible.

Ellis was stationed at Will Call. Fifteen others in plainclothes surrounded the arena. Everything in its right place.

The ticket office confirmed that Brenner had indeed made the purchase, and that the envelope was left for someone named Jessica Wu. Was Jessica really the Pink Dragon, the spy the FBI had been chasing all these months? Could she be the link that proved China's Technical Reconnaissance Bureau was not only behind the massive intellectual property raid on American defense industry, but also the bombing of their own embassy?

Beneath the seat reserved for "Jessica," a small copper key had been taped to the plastic underside. A photo of the key had been sent back to McLean. But what did it unlock? Was it the key to a bathroom or utility closet within the arena itself? A locker somewhere in the team's facilities? A safe deposit box in a bank in another country? The possibilities were endless. Guardian's best people were working on matching the key against a vast database.

Still, barring some miracle, it would take days to find the answer. And that would be far too late.

One thing was for sure – Jack Brenner would be of no help. Ellis's attempt at CPR had been vigorous, but it was too late. The seizures had wracked his body with blow after blow of electrical energy until his heart stopped.

With Brenner dead, the Pink Dragon was their next best hope to unraveling the mystery of the errant drone strike in Tripoli. This boiled down to an old-fashioned stakeout, and there were 18,000 crazy Wizard fans in Carver's way.

Suddenly Ellis voice crackled in Carver's ear. "It's a go. She picked up the ticket at Will Call, and she's coming in now."

"Who am I looking for?"

"Asian female. Five-foot-five. Gray coat, fur collar. Black hair in a braid. Earrings, golden-backed studs with some sort of small gemstones. Black converse sneakers. Red clutch handbag." In his mind, Carver created a virtual mashup of Ellis's description and the grainy image the FBI had taken of the woman in oversized sunglasses.

Carver had a bitter taste in his mouth. Was it possible to actually taste adrenaline? Although his face was stone cold, his skin felt alive. The hair of his arms stood like 10,000 tiny antennae.

There she was, just 30 feet away now. The Pink Dragon. Jessica Wu. The unicorn. Carver had expected her to be taller, somehow, and more striking. Someone who could get people to say yes with a single look. She wasn't ugly, but she was no beauty, either. The kind of woman that would easily blend in with a crowd. "I have a visual."

"Maybe we should go ahead and take her," Ellis suggested.

"Absolutely not," Carver replied in a tone that was intended to discourage further debate. "We need to catch her in possession of the package. We need conclusive evidence."

"This is a big place, Blake. We could lose her."

The fact that Ellis was technically running this op did not elude Carver. But damned if he was going to see history repeat itself. Among the dozens of suspected spies nabbed in the U.S. on

Carver's watch, too many had been used as pawns to be traded in backroom diplomatic negotiations. Carver wasn't about to take any chances with this one. Capturing the Pink Dragon could be the game changer they needed.

"Negative," he said. "We will take her when she is in possession."

"As you wish. But my objection will be documented in the operation brief."

*Only if this is a complete failure. If it turns out to be a stunning victory, you'll take full credit, of course.*

He fished a white capsule out of his pocket. He opened it and removed a tiny tracking chip that looked and felt exactly like a piece of gray lint. Then he positioned himself behind the Pink Dragon as she made her way around the concourse. As he drew closer, he saw that the outer layer of her coat was a quilted nylon shell. The lint-like tracking chip wouldn't stick to it, nor would it likely take to her clutch. His only option was the fur collar.

He moved quickly, touching the soft chip to the collar as he brushed past her, pretending to look for someone. The lint-like tracking chip clung readily to the fur. From the texture and color, he guessed it was rabbit.

Carver broke away quickly, melting back into the crowd before speaking again. "It's done. Did she make me?"

"Not from what I can see," Ellis said. "She's still en route to her seat."

Carver descended the stairs, making his way to the landing below the Pink Dragon's section. The app on his phone displayed a detailed map of the facility. A red dot displayed the Pink Dragon's location. A blue dot showed Ellis, who was behind her. Fifteen other dots marked the location of the other agents, who covered the exits in case someone else picked up the key and slipped it to the Pink Dragon.

The red dot entered Section 404 and turned into one of the upper rows. Carver moved into position at the bottom of the section. He watched the Pink Dragon sit, rest her elbows on her knees and with her left hand, reach underneath the seat and retrieve the key. She balled up the packing tape that had attached it to the seat and dropped it to the floor. Then she dropped the key into her clutch. Now she flattened her right palm and patted the top of her head twice.

"Did you see that?" Carver said.

"Yeah. She flashed some sort of hand signal. She's working with a partner. Maybe she's going to pass the key to a contact here at the game."

"Then we need to take her now."

"Agreed."

The arena was suddenly plummeted into near darkness. The Wizard faithful that had been milling about the stadium suddenly scrambled for their seats. Thunderous music played as the jumbotron near the ceiling began flashing a highlight reel of gravity-defying dunks. The crowd sighed. *Ahhhhhhhhh.*

A voice boomed over the PA system. *Introducing your Washington Wizards. Starting at point guard, in his second year from the University of North Carolina, Demetrius Ferrera.*

Carver traversed the stairs two at a time now, squeezing past fans going this way and that. He was closing in. She was up in front of him, no more than 30 feet away. He glanced down at the tracking app. The red dot showed the Pink Dragon moving straight up the stairs.

*At shooting guard, Matt Wessel.*

As Carver neared the concourse, he stepped on something. He nearly slipped. The texture of the fabric - nylon shell - resonated, and he picked it up. It was the Pink Dragon's jacket.

*At power forward, Jacob Longley.*

"We lost tracking," Carver said as he leapt up the final series of stairs. There in the silhouette of the lit corridor that led out to the concourse, he spotted the figure slumped over the landing. The Pink Dragon was down.

*Starting at small forward, DeShawn Turner.*

He approached with caution. Out of instinct, his hand reached inside his jacket for his SIG. Not here, he thought, realizing that no matter how much he wanted the Pink Dragon, there would be no forgiveness for shooting her before 18,000 witnesses. That wasn't how the spy game was played. If brute force was necessary, it would be done quietly and swiftly, with his bare hands, here in the dark.

*At center, Derek Wiggins.*

He saw the gemstone earrings now. He was close enough to touch her. She was shaking. A sudden surge of vomit flooded from her mouth. And he knew from the telltale odor of the vomit - burnt almonds - that there would be no saving her.

*And your coach, Jake McCall.*

"Target is down," Carver said. "At the top of the stairs."

"Copy that. Heading your way."

The crowd cheered one last time before the house lights popped on and the announcer's voice suddenly broke into a different tone entirely.

*Ladies and gentlemen, due to a security issue, we ask that you proceed in an orderly fashion toward the nearest exit. Again, please proceed in an orderly fashion toward the nearest exit. Do not run.*

The energy in the arena abruptly shifted. Eighteen thousand people seemed to say, *what*? *Did he just say what I think he said?* Words on the jumbotron confirmed it: PLEASE PROCEED CALMLY TOWARD THE EXITS.

This was the last thing Carver needed. He hailed Ellis. "Did you inform security?"

"Negative. I'm as surprised as you are."

A bomb threat, Carver deduced as the crowds snaked around him. Whatever organization had conspired to kill the Pink Dragon had played this just right. Thousands of people rushing for the exits would make finding the perpetrators impossible.

The crowd did not proceed calmly. As thousands swarmed the aisles - shouting, elbowing and stepping past one another - the Pink Dragon's body went still. Carver's eyes searched the floor around her for an instant before it was covered in foot traffic. The clutch she had slipped the key into had disappeared.

He pulled the Pink Dragon's body into the aisle seat to keep it from being trampled by the mob making their way to the top of the concourse. A woman in heels stepped and slid in the puddle of vomit, but the throngs behind her kept her from falling.

Carver refocused his attention back to the Pink Dragon. Something sticky in the wispy ends of her hair. He brushed it away, revealing a small puncture wound in the neck. The spot where they had injected the poisonous solution.

There was very little time now. Arena security would be here within seconds. He quickly searched the pockets of the Pink Dragon's jeans. They were empty.

Ellis was suddenly next to him, ready to apply CPR.

"Don't," Carver said, holding her back before she could perform mouth to mouth with the poisoned spy. He pointed to a tiny injection mark that bled from her neck, then to the white substance foaming around her lips. "It's cyanide, Ellis."

# National Counterterrorism Center
# McLean, Virginia

The insulin pump that Jack Brenner had been wearing at the time of his death sat on a white table in the middle of the lab. Carver and Ellis watched as Arunus Roth, one of the Guardian's top geeks, powered up his laptop at the end of the table and connected to the pump wirelessly. The 22-year-old Roth had been expelled from a community college in Albuquerque for infiltrating and modifying the school's vocational aptitude software.

"I think this is how they snuffed him," Roth said. "I've never even seen one of these pumps before, and it took me all of five minutes to hack into it."

Ellis crossed her arms. "The ER doctor's preliminary diagnosis was a massive heart attack."

Carver snickered derisively. "At 31 years old?" He put on a pair of latex gloves and picked up the pump, examining it at different angles. Carver had read all about insulin pumps in a magazine while visiting his general doctor more than four years ago. A Tuesday. He had been there to get a physical, and he had been cranky because he had been fasting for 12 hours. At least he had apparently learned something useful while he waited.

"Brenner was poisoned," Carver said, "just like the Pink Dragon. The only difference was the method." He pointed to the device. "This tiny tube is called a cannula, and that's what connects the device to the body. It automatically detects how much insulin to put into the body at regular intervals throughout the day. The thing it's absolutely not supposed to do is shoot its entire load into you all at once."

Roth took the pump from him. "I think that's right. This pump is dry as a bone. When the tox report comes back, they're going to find that Jack Brenner has enough insulin in him to kill an elephant."

Ellis rested her face in her hands for a moment before coming up for air. "Okay, so who killed him? And were they planning to kill Brenner all along to tie up loose ends, or did they only kill him when they knew he was going to be caught? And how did they *know* he was going to be caught?"

"All the right questions," Carver said. "A minute before you walked into the pub, he said he thought *they* were listening. Apparently they were, somehow."

Roth shuddered. "That's spooky, bro."

Ellis shook her head. "The FBI interviewed the six other customers at the roadhouse at the time of Brenner's death, plus the kitchen staff. We can rule them out as suspects."

Roth bit his lower lip. "Yeah, but Brenner just takes a dirt nap right before he's taken into custody? Whoever hacked into his insulin pump could have just as easily hacked into his phone and used the mic to listen to every single word of your conversation."

"Brenner was using a burner phone."

"So? The Pink Dragon had the number. And she had just received the location of the last drop from Brenner."

The three of them exited the lab and went down the hallway to the National Counterterrorism Center. Carver loved standing at the second floor landing and looking out at the massive screens tracking enemy movements and operations in theaters across the world. So much data. So much brilliant technology with which to parse it.

He turned to Roth. "What are the odds of finding a digital breadcrumb linking the insulin pump to the hacker?"

Roth's answer came quickly. "About the same as capturing Bigfoot."

"So let's focus on finding the person that killed the Pink Dragon at the game."

"Already on it. We have people going through the footage in the arena surveillance cameras, matching the crowds against profiles in our database. Just to set expectations, the cameras aren't great quality. We might get nothing."

"That won't work. We need an answer by noon."

"If you've got a better way, I'd like to hear it."

"Sure. We are probably looking for a relatively fit man between the age of 25 and 55. Odds are he'll be foreign-born."

"This is D.C., bro. You're describing a huge portion of the population."

"For the thousandth time, don't call me bro."

"Sorry, Agent Carver."

"Blake will do. Now let's assume that the person who killed the Pink Dragon did not sneak into the arena. That would have introduced unnecessary risk."

"Agreed. So he paid to get into the game, just like 18,000 other people. And there are a ton of ticketing outlets. No way to segment the ticket buyers by age, ethnicity or nationality."

Carver walked to a whiteboard. Ellis and Roth followed. He picked up a purple marker. "So let's narrow further." He wrote the word TIMING in caps. "The suspect couldn't have bought his tickets until Jack Brenner told the Pink Dragon that was where he was making the drop, which was just two hours before the game." Carver wrote 120 MINUTES on the board. Then he wrote RESALE TICKET OUTLETS ONLY. "Besides, the Wizards are actually good this year, so the game was likely sold out well ahead of time. That means that the number of last-minute ticket sales within the final three days will likely be confined to resale ticket sale sites."

Roth brightened. "Hey, that's good!"

Carver wrote SINGLE BUYER. "And how many of those last-minute ticket buyers would purchase just a single seat?"

"Right! Loners go to the movies, not NBA games."

Next, Carver wrote PAYMENT TYPE. "And the person buying the ticket likely paid with a stolen credit card."

Ellis nodded wearily. "So we're looking for a single buyer who purchased within 120 minutes of the game."

"Scalper?" Roth said.

She frowned. "No. Too risky. The killer would have purchased online to make sure of getting in on time."

Carver agreed. He checked his watch. It was 3:35 a.m. "Now if you'll excuse me, I've been asked to explain this mess at the White House."

With that, Ellis's entire demeanor flipped. "*You've* been asked to explain? This is *my* op!"

Carver paused and turned. Due to the rigors of the past 48 hours, he found himself emotionally threadbare, unable to mask his frustration. He took a deep breath. "You're right, Haley. It is your op. I'll make sure to remind the president."

"Good luck. She tends to shoot the messenger."

# The White House
# Washington D.C.

Speers sat in a burgundy chair outside the Oval Office, hands folded in his lap like a choirboy who had been told to stop fidgeting. The president had summoned him for a sidebar prior to the daily intelligence briefing, which was scheduled for 6:30 a.m. The meeting request had elevated his already sky-high anxiety levels. As presidents went, Eva was a famously late riser. She needed seven to eight hours of sleep per night, and she often ran late to early morning meetings, keeping the agency heads waiting. And yet, Eva needed to speak with him *before* the daily briefing. No reason had been given.

Did she want his resignation? To fortify himself, he had forced himself to consider the possibility. He imagined the words coming from her lips. *A major international incident happened on your watch, Julian. It's nothing personal. I'm sure you understand. Someone's head has to roll.*

He had never been fired from a job in his life. Nor had he ever seriously pursued one. He had been lucky, he supposed, having simply fallen into one thing after another, the steps of his career appearing before him like a magic staircase. But unlike most of Washington politicos, Speers was far from wealthy. He had been raised by a single mother in Washington who lived check to check. Speers had taken out loans to go to law school. What little net worth he had now was tied up in his mortgage, and if he was fired, it wasn't like he could just take some time off to spend with his family. He would have to hustle for his next meal ticket.

Sometimes, Speers fantasized about landing on the board of some private intelligence firm that would pay him handsomely for his connections. *But I would hate that. They would want me to lobby the Hill for them. And I hate lobbyists.*

Rogue Empire

The door to the Oval Office flew open. "Morning, Julian," Eva said without slowing her forward momentum. "Walk with me."

For a big man, Speers got to his feet quickly. He noticed that Eva was fully dressed for battle this morning in a black power suit with rounded shoulders that looked, to Speers' eye, like the armored fenders of the Batmobile. The attire did nothing to soothe Speers' worries. On the day Eva had canned the directors of 14 intelligence agencies all at once, she had worn a similarly severe black outfit. As if mourning the executions she had herself carried out.

"I was shocked to hear Blake Carver will deliver the briefing."

Speers had expected to be on the defensive, but not about this. "Well considering that Carver was on the front lines both in Tripoli and Verizon Center, it seemed like a natural choice. He's also in the best possible position to answer our questions."

The president picked up speed as she rounded the corner. "You didn't read it, did you?"

"Read what?"

The president stopped. She pulled a memo from a leather folder with the presidential seal and handed it to Speers. "I always assumed you approved these memos before they reached my desk."

It appeared to be a simple operational brief. Authored by Haley Ellis. And no, Speers had not read it. He surrounded himself with people he trusted so that he didn't *have* to read everything.

According to the time stamp on the document, Ellis had submitted it at 4:53 a.m. That was just seven minutes prior to the deadline, making it impossible to be screened in time for inclusion in the Morning Book.

Speers blushed as his pupils danced over the incendiary text, all of which was directed at Blake Carver. Speers struggled to remember his conversation with Ellis at the diner. The look on her face when told that she would have to team up with Carver again. Hadn't she called him *toxic*?

"I need a moment to digest this," Speers said.

"Read and walk." The president resumed her march to the Situation Room. Speers did his best to keep up.

OPERATIONAL BRIEF 26A-47

AUTHOR: Haley Ellis, Sr. Counterterrorism Analyst

After analyzing Agent Carver's behavior over the past 48 hours, I recommend a full investigation into his activities, with the goal of identifying any possible leaks or compromises as they pertain to Operation Trojan Horse. In general, Carver's actions have become increasingly erratic and counterproductive to agency policies and procedures. There is sufficient reason to believe that he may be obstructing the investigation or even involved in sabotage. Examples:

9/23: Carver disobeyed a direct order and entered Tripoli alone, purportedly to extract the operative in question, Kyra Javan. Carver claims that he killed Allied Jihad soldier Mohy Osman, but no proof exists. In her initial debriefing, Ms. Javan has no recollection of Carver's entering the Osman residence where she was purportedly rescued. It should be noted that the drone target objective coordinates were verified by the NCC just prior to the time that Carver entered the city, and mysteriously changed during his time in the city itself, when he was unobserved. More needs to be discovered about Carver's activities within the hour before the drone strike hit the embassy.

9/24 (a): Carver insisted on meeting suspect, Jack Brenner, one-on-one, instructing the team to delay its entry into the pub where he was drinking. While we have audio of the exchange, we have no direct visual knowledge of the encounter. Brenner died suddenly after consuming alcohol with Carver. Afterwards, Carver was oddly quick to cite the cause of Brenner's sudden death as an insulin pump hack (many hours before it was confirmed by lab analysis). We need to learn more about why he was so certain about Brenner's cause of death. In addition, Carver failed to protect the crime scene. The suspect's glass and utensils were promptly washed by the restaurant's dishwasher, making additional analysis impossible.

This was all nonsense. Carver was one of the few people brilliant enough to make such a keen observation on the spot, and he had no doubt that the toxicology report would confirm Carver's suspicions about Brenner's cause of death. Speers flipped to the second page, where Ellis's attack continued:

9/24 (b): At Verizon Center, Carver was alone with Jessica Wu [AKA The Pink Dragon] for between 30 and 60 seconds under low-light conditions. He radioed that she was down almost immediately. When I arrived on the scene, Carver blocked my attempts to perform CPR. He pulled me away from the scene, proclaiming that the suspect's death was due to cyanide poisoning by injection, despite having no actual evidence.

The president's voice interrupted his focus. "Julian, we're here."

Speers looked up. He and the president stood just outside the Situation Room. He realized that in addition to the president having read Ellis's memo, the morning briefing had also been distributed to the heads of all the federal intelligence agencies. And now Carver was waiting to present to them in the Situation Room. And whether he knew it or not, there was a huge knife stuck in his back.

"Julian?"

"Madam President, I strongly disagree with the way Carver has been characterized here. I think this may be a straight up case of professional jealousy. The warning signs were there. I should have –"

"You may be right. But I think this warrants an investigation into Carver's activities."

"You can't be serious! We both know Carver is brilliant. You yourself offered him a job as your National Security Advisor."

"And he turned me down. Why?"

"Because he hates politics."

"Or is it because he's working some other angle? Carver was just on the ground in Tripoli, an unmitigated bloodbath. Now that he's back home, two more people are dead right here in Washington, in two separate incidents. That's a coincidence?"

"We use our best operatives in the most dangerous situations."

"After this briefing, I want him grounded pending a formal investigation. And another thing. You're too close to this. I want a multi-agency team to handle this, starting with a formal debrief on his activities in the past 48 hours."

"You are making a huge mistake. We need him, now more than ever."

"Noted. But this is my decision, and I expect you to get on board."

# The Situation Room

Carver stood as the president entered, with Speers walking three steps behind her. "Let's get started," the president growled, as she – along with the heads of the CIA, DIA, FBI, NSA and other intelligence agencies – took their seats. "Agent Carver, you have our attention."

"Thank you, Madam President."

Carver had rarely felt as physically spent as he did right now. In the past 48 hours, he had extracted Kyra and killed Mohy Osman and witnessed the mistargeted drone strike. He had found Jack Brenner and the Pink Dragon, and watched both die. Nevertheless, the show had to go on.

He dimmed the room lights and displayed a large image of two people on one of the room's screens. "The suspect on the left is Jack Brenner, an engineer who worked for LithiumXI until his death last night. We suspect Brenner of selling sensitive information about the weapons guidance systems on LithiumXI's fleet of attack drones, one of which was used in the attempted attack on the Butcher of Bahrain in Tripoli. The suspect on the right is the alleged buyer, known commonly as the Pink Dragon. This morning we discovered her true identity. Her name is Jessica Wu. She's a 32-year-old Chinese citizen."

The president put her glasses on and took a good look at Wu's profile pic. "And how long has Jessica Wu been operating in the U.S.?"

"At least three years. She operated a textile manufacturing business that sold to American manufacturers, giving her plenty of legitimate reasons to go back and forth between the U.S. and China."

The president twirled her pen in her left hand. "Agent Carver, we've all read Haley Ellis's report in the morning brief, so I'll just go ahead and ask you what we're all wondering."

Carver had not read Ellis's brief. He had spent every moment since leaving the NCC formulating his presentation. "Yes, Madam President."

"There have been more than 200 confirmed incidents of Chinese espionage on American soil in the past year. We have apprehended 32 of these spies and 10 of their American counterparts. And in the only such incidents handled personally by you, both suspects ended up dead. Why?"

Carver was aware that the decision to turn down the president's generous job offer had not endeared him to her. But until now, he had only suspected that she held a grudge. Now he knew for sure.

*Don't take this personally. Stick to the facts. Focus your thoughts. Everything in its right place.*

"In both cases, cause of death is still preliminary, pending further investigation. But we suspect that Jack Brenner's insulin pump was hacked, delivering a fatal dose of insulin. I don't think it's a coincidence that he was killed just as he was about to tell us vital information. This was a man who had root access to the guidance systems of the same drone that attacked the Chinese embassy."

The president leaned forward. "Are you suggesting that before his death, Brenner was about to implicate the Chinese in the bombing of their own embassy?"

"He said as much. But we can't jump to conclusions."

"And why not?"

"Jessica Wu was a Chinese citizen, but that doesn't necessarily mean she was working in the Chinese government's intelligence program. There are any number of terrorist groups or foreign states that might benefit from a loss in American credibility, and there would be nothing to stop any Chinese operative from acting as a free agent."

"It's pretty thin, Agent Carver."

Carver paused for a sip of water before resuming. "Let's assume for a moment that Wu really was working for the Technical Reconnaissance Bureau or some other spy agency. That means that some Chinese official with knowledge of the buy would have ordered her death to tie up loose ends."

"What's so hard to believe about that? It's Occam's razor. The simplest theory is usually the right one."

"If you'll indulge me." Carver switched to a new slide. In the photo, a much younger Jessica Wu was seated at a formal state dinner party with two much older men.

The president immediately recognized the tall man at the photo's center, with one arm around Jessica Wu. "Is that President Kang?"

Carver nodded. "President Kang, of the People's Republic of China, to be exact. It seems that Jessica Wu came from a very connected family." Carver pointed his laser toward the second man in the photo. "And that's Li Wu, Jessica Wu's grandfather. He was only a teenager in 1967, but he volunteered to go to North Vietnam and help the war effort. He slipped across the border and started running intelligence back and forth from Vietnam to China. According to the intelligence supplied by NVA defectors, Wu was personally responsible for coordinating the supply of over 1,000 Chinese anti-aircraft batteries into North Vietnam." Carver looked around the room. "I'm sure everyone here knows how that turned out for the United States."

Defense Secretary Dexter P. Jackson leaned forward, silver eyebrows closing ranks over his blue eyes. "It was a bloodbath, Agent Carver. Those Chinese batteries were responsible for shooting down 1,700 American planes."

"That's right. And when the U.S. pulled out of Vietnam in the 1970s, Li Wu was heralded as a hero in China, and quickly rose up in the Communist Party at the same time that Kang was named Vice Chairman of the Central Military Commission. Our sources inside the Communist Party tell us that he's now the head of a secret intelligence bureau that answers directly to Kang."

Jackson groaned. "Sweet Jesus. Next you're going to tell us that President Kang is Jessica Wu's godfather."

"I don't know if they even have godfathers in China. But if they do, then yes, Kang would be hers."

A dour silence settled over the room as the president leaned back, staring at the ceiling. No words were necessary. The spy that had just been killed on American soil was practically a blood relative to President Kang, the most powerful Chinese premiere in recent history. Not only had Kang assumed the Chinese presidency, but he had also made the office – which was, like the American presidency, designed to be limited in power – a truly elevated position. Kang had consolidated power by simultaneously fulfilling the role of President, the General Secretary of the Communist Party and the head of the country's Central Military Commission. Kang was King.

Carver brought the room lights back up. "The point is that considering her ties to Kang and her uncle, Jessica Wu would be considered untouchable. Nobody's going to order a hit on her just to tie up loose ends. Therefore, I think it's highly unlikely that the Chinese blew up their own embassy."

The president slipped her glasses off. "Do you have any more actual evidence to back up your assertion, Agent Carver?"

"Nothing hard just yet. But if you'll indulge me, I'd like to –"

"Thank you, Agent Carver. That will be all."

"If you please, Madam President, I'd like to —"

"That will be all."

The silence was deafening as Carver gathered his things.

Had he failed? It sure felt like it. Perhaps he had underestimated the momentum that the China Theory – the idea that the Chinese were somehow provoking the U.S. into war, or at lest manufacturing a reason that would justify economic sabotage – had already gathered within the administration. And that was a truly frightening proposition. If the president was wrong about this, she could end up doing something they might all regret.

The investigation had to move faster. But how? Carver could think of only one person with the skills to help him quickly enough: Nico Gold, the infamous hacker who had spent several years in a federal penitentiary for "redistributing" wealth from the International Monetary Fund and various other Robin Hood crimes. As cybercriminals went, Nico Gold was in the Hall of Fame.

Unfortunately, Nico wasn't just someone you could call in a pinch. He played hard to get. Last Carver had heard, Nico was living in a Las Vegas hotel. Carver was going to have to show up in person. And he would beg if he had to.

# The Sofitel
# Washington D.C.

Speers entered the hotel lobby wearing the look of a desperate man who had been wandering in the desert. In reality, he had walked just two city blocks from the White House, having come immediately upon getting Ellis's call. "We already have a suspect in Jessica Wu's murder," she had told him. And so he had come without asking any further questions, clearing his schedule or even notifying security of his plans.

After the licking he had just taken from the president, Speers hoped that the fresh air would do him some good. Despite the security tensions, the streets of the nation's capital were still crowded with tourists and residents alike. Speers walked alongside a class of 7th graders fresh with excitement after a tour of the FBI building. He crossed the street alongside a retired veteran and his spouse who were heading to the Vietnam War Memorial. Closer to the hotel, he walked behind a Hungarian couple who, as evidenced by the brochure in their hand, had just been to the International Spy Museum. In just two blocks, he had heard Hebrew and Greek Russian and Korean and the strongest Kentucky accent he had ever heard. And unlike the rest of the grumpy old men and women working in Washington, Speers actually liked tourists. They invigorated him. They were a reminder that he was privileged to work and live in this city.

I needed that, he thought as he stepped inside the elevator, pressed the button for the 5th floor and prepared to see Ellis, who had revealed herself as a backstabber of the highest order. Thanks to her, Speers was going to have to exile the best intelligence operative he'd ever had.

When the elevator opened on the 5th floor, Speers was surprised to find that the hallway was already crowded with feds. He wandered out as if in a dream, barely registering the greetings from a dozen or so ODNI and CIA employees. *Good morning, Mister Director. Right this way, Mister Director.*

Ellis stood in the doorway of a suite near the ice machine. She was wearing a white HAZMAT suit with the headpiece pulled back from her face like a hoodie. She motioned him inside. Speers wanted to choke her.

The first thing he noticed was the transparent plastic barrier that sealed off the entrance to the bathroom. He skipped the pleasantries. "You said you had a suspect?"

Arunus Roth stepped out from behind Ellis. "We do. Or at least what's left of one."

Ellis set about zipping her boss into a HAZMAT suit. "We decided to focus our search on the person who killed the Pink Dragon, thinking that would lead to bigger fish. We went on the assumption that the killer was a foreign-born man between the age of 25 and 55 who purchased a last-minute Wizards ticket at a resale outlet."

"Gotta give Agent Carver credit for the profiling," Roth said. Ellis shut him down with a withering look.

She led Speers through the plastic bubble to the restroom, where they stood overlooking a bathtub filled with water the color of beef stroganoff. Four limbs — the hands and feet had been hacked off — stuck out of the tub at odd angles. The head and torso, however, were barely recognizable as human. It was one of the most disgusting things he had ever seen.

Roth piped up behind him. "Looks like the killer tried to make Mexican Stew."

Mexican stew. Speers was familiar with the term. Although the practice was hardly unique to Mexico, the term was derived from Mexican drug lords' solution of heated sodium hydroxide that would chemically liquefy a body in a matter of hours. The cartels typically boiled the lye in large cooking pots, then hacked the bodies up and put them in one piece at a time.

"Do we know who he is?"

"According to his passport, he's a 31-year-old Chinese man. Arrived in D.C. four nights ago and prepaid the room for an entire week. Flew in via Hong Kong, routing through Tokyo

Narita. And he was sloppy. Used the same credit card to reserve the room here as he did to purchase the Wizards ticket 51 minutes before game time."

"Do we have his computer? His phone?"

Roth shook his head. "No such luck. Whoever got to him before us broke into the room safe. Perhaps they stole it. We did find a few smoking guns, though. A Verizon Center map, a game ticket stub and the Pink Dragon's clutch."

"Was there a key inside?" Speers said, referring to the key Carver said he saw the Pink Dragon drop into the purse.

"No. And that isn't all that's missing." Ellis held up a package for a single disposable syringe. It was empty.

Speers nodded, remembering Carver's theory that the Pink Dragon had been injected with cyanide, a fact that had yet to be confirmed by the lab.

Roth gestured to what was left of a hand on the counter in a sealed bag. "We might still get some DNA, and a few x-rays, but forget about fingerprints or dental records."

A wave of nausea coursed through Speers. He turned and went back into the room, frantically unzipping his headpiece as soon as he cleared the plastic bubble.

He knelt before the room air-conditioner, inhaled the filtered air gushing from its vent and closed his eyes. Roth peeled the HAZMAT suit from him as if he were an oversized banana. Then the young fed gave him some water, helped him up and into a chair in the hallway.

Speers gathered himself. "Thanks Arunus."

Moments later, Ellis appeared. "You all right there, chief?"

He nodded. "Tell me the rest. Just the broad strokes."

"Everything we have so far supports the theory that Jack Brenner sold the drone's weapons guidance system specs to the Pink Dragon, a.k.a. Jessica Wu. She then sold that to someone who used the information to hack into the drone that took out the Chinese embassy."

"What else?"

"The theory is that the killer sought to tie up loose ends. Including Jack Brenner, Jessica Wu and whoever's in that stew."

Speers could no longer hold his rage. "Have you thought about blaming Carver for this, too?"

Ellis turned to Roth. "Give us a minute." She waited until Roth was out of earshot. "I take it you're referring to my memo suggesting that Carver be investigated."

"Congrats, Ellis. The president actually read it. You must have known that I wouldn't have time to review it prior to putting it into the morning briefing."

"I followed protocol. I operate on the assumption that you approve anything that the president sees."

"Well I don't. It's not humanly possible. I simply have faith what you will write isn't an embarrassment to yourself and your colleagues. You took advantage of that trust for personal gain."

Ellis folded her arms across her chest and lowered her voice. "When you asked me to join Guardian, you said you wanted my, quote unquote, *unfiltered* opinions. I told you I didn't want Blake on my team. You ignored me."

"Rationalize it all you want to. You're wrong about Carver." He gestured to the crime scene. "You wouldn't even be here without him."

She wiped her mouth with the back of her hand. "So what now? Am I fired?"

"Unfortunately not. I need you to find out who really did this." Speers stood and buttoned his suit jacket. "But rest assured, Ellis. What goes around comes around."

# The Four Seasons Hotel
# Las Vegas, Nevada

Scarcely 48 surreal hours since he had left Tripoli, Carver stepped into the hotel elevator along with a couple of tall bottle blondes in sleeveless fur vests, wrap skirts and high heels. Russian escorts, he decided. But when they began arguing about money, Carver's rudimentary knowledge of eastern tongues told him that they were in fact Ukrainian.

The sheer amount of perfume coming off these ladies was suffocating. And that was unfortunate, since Carver needed all the oxygen he could get at the moment.

The elevator ratcheted ever skyward. 10th floor. 11. 12. 13. 14. *Just. Breathe.* 35th floor. 36th. 37th.

If there was one thing Carver hated, it was heights. Not much else got to him except for that. And given Carver's super-autobiographical memory, just the thought of it could give him vertigo.

Years ago in Paris, while pursuing a suspect, he had leapt across a chasm between two 10-story buildings, rooftop to rooftop. He had done so without thinking. Only later did the memory of what he had done — and how far he would have fallen had he missed his mark — drive him to his knees.

The Ukrainians exited at the 38th floor, leaving behind the veritable perfumery. Seconds later, the elevator reached the 40th floor. As the doors opened, Carver regarded the view. A sheet of floor-to-ceiling glass was all that separated him from a 530-foot drop to the Las Vegas strip.

He beheld a magnificent garden of neon. Far below, a monorail car left the neighboring Luxor hotel with families and gamblers. And further down the strip was the High Roller, Las Vegas's 550-foot-high Ferris wheel. To someone like Carver, the idea that people actually paid to experience such heights was nauseating.

The sight triggered an explosion of light in his neural pathways. A torrent of unbearably vivid memories. Eleven years, four months and 23 days ago. The Sikorsky UH-60 Black Hawk his team had boarded in Anbar Province had been hit by a SAM, and the aircraft and was listing in a smoky death spiral. His JSOC team sprung into action around him, doing precisely what they had trained to do — leaping one after the other into the blackest night he had ever seen, and pulling their chutes nearly as soon as they had cleared the chopper.

But the fear of falling overtook Carver. He heard no sound. He could not feel his hands. He was paralyzed.

Then he was suddenly propelled, as if a great puppet master were making him fly. He had the sickening sensation of free falling for an instant before feeling the jerk of the parachute. He plunged in darkness toward the cold desert floor of Afghanistan.

His legs dangled below him. His left boot was gone. His sock was gone. His foot shivered in the void, a hopeful signal that at least the flesh remained.

Only the sporadic click-clack of small arms fire proved that the earth awaited him below. He heard someone shout in the sea of black, although the direction of the disembodied voice eluded him. Then the chopper exploded, distant enough that his chute didn't catch fire, but close enough that he still felt heat on his face.

Something large and sharp whizzed by him in the night, slicing his left pant leg. A rivulet of blood opened up below his knee, down his ankle, his foot, and dripping from his big toe into the never ending black.

Now Carver collapsed, half in the elevator, half out. The elevator door closed on his gray suit, growling and jittering in place as the LED indicator blinked the number 40 over and over again.

A woman appeared. Or was he hallucinating? She was a vision straight out of ancient Rome, clad in a sleeveless white linen stola that covered the entirety of her legs, the hem brushing the tops of her sandals. A woven wool belt encircled her waist, and another strapped her breasts firmly in place. Her hair was a spectacular assemblage of tight brunette curls.

*This isn't a memory. I must be hallucinating.*

The woman grabbed Carver by the arms and dragged him out onto the 40th floor landing. She tried lifting him into one of the armchairs overlooking the view, but he was more substantial, more muscular than he looked underneath the finely tailored suit.

In an enormous glass pitcher, alongside an arrangement of autumn flowers, sliced cucumbers floated in ice water. She took a plastic cup from the stack, filled it with the cold water, dipped her fingers into it, and gently applied it to Carver's forehead. In his half-consciousness, he heard her baby-talking him in a language that he had never heard before. His eyes darted to the elevator doors. And then to the view of the Vegas strip that had started the torrent in the first place.

*This might be really happening.*

Now she spoke in English. "That was quite an episode, Agent Carver. Can you walk?"

*She knows my name.*

"I think so. Who are you?"

"Octavia the Younger. You can call me Octavia."

Carver laughed. "As in Marc Antony's wife? I think you might be lost, Octavia. Caesars Palace is a little further down the strip."

She held her hand out to him. He touched it. It seemed real enough. "Come with me. Nico is expecting you."

He got to his feet and followed her to the northwest corner of the floor, suite 40404. A series of locks unfastened rather loudly, one at a time. He stepped onto a marble floor and into a fully enclosed foyer facing yet another intimidating set of locks.

Octavia came in behind him, shutting the outer door.

"Empty your pockets," she said pointing to a white steel box. "Place your belongings in that safe, including your weapon."

Carver chuckled. "There's been some misunderstanding. I'm –"

"Blake Carver. I know. If you want to see Nico, you'll leave your personal belongings here. So what's it going to be?"

Then the door before him opened. A second brunette entered the foyer. Like Octavia, this one was dressed like it was a balmy day in Rome circa 100 B.C.

"If I had known this was a costume party," Carver said, "I would have at least worn a bed sheet."

The second woman spoke in a voice that was like black velvet, deep and distinctly southern. "Hello Blake."

He knew that voice. A new flood of memories unleashed. *Madge?* Yes. Madge Howland. The North Carolina programmer who had become engaged to Nico during his time in prison. The last time Carver had seen her, they had been in South Africa. Carver had traveled to their hideout in a tiny hamlet on the Western Cape to offer them a deal. Nico was to assist in a sensitive operation in exchange for the forgiveness of his domestic crimes. In addition, Madge would not be prosecuted for aiding a fugitive. But it seemed that Madge wasn't in a trusting mood, as he soon found himself looking down the barrel of a sawed-off 12-gauge. Carver had managed to disarm her, but he had taken his lumps in the process. Madge was incredibly strong, and not in a muscular, I've-been-pumping-iron kind of way. Rather she was blessed with the kind of inexplicable strength that strikes like lightning, enabling grandmothers to suddenly lift cars and manic-depressives to overwhelm cops twice their size.

Now Carver noted the Taser gun she held in her left hand. "Is there a problem?" He had no desire to tangle with Madge again.

"It's nice to see you, Madge." He emptied his pockets, unable to get over Madge's transformation. She had once been downright frumpy. Slovenly, even, with bad skin. Now her T-zone was spotless and tan. Gold ringlets encircled her toned, muscular upper arms. Even her toenails looked freshly manicured. "Who's your friend?"

"My sister."

Octavia knelt to frisk him, starting with the ankles, and moving up both pant legs. In front, Madge began probing him with some sort of wand.

"He's clean," Madge soon declared. She opened the double doors that led into the suite, which was lit entirely by ancient looking gas lamps. "Leave your shoes here."

Carver slipped out of his loafers and entered the suite wide-eyed. Immediately before him was an enormous white statue depicting Pan – the half-man, half-goat god of the wild – copulating with a she-goat.

*Okay. Now I know I'm dreaming.*

The next voice Carver heard was a familiar one: "Has our guest arrived?" Nico Gold stepped into the room barefoot, clad in a toga. He sported a curly beard and a Roman-era Afro. The superstar hacker had always been eccentric, as well as a chameleon, but this was an unprecedented level of reinvention. When Carver had first met him, he had been an imprisoned activist who seemed quite content to be martyred for his cyber crimes, which he considered noble. A year later, he had transformed into a deeply religious and reclusive fugitive. Carver wasn't quite sure what to make of this latest incarnation of Nico Gold.

The hacker embraced him in a bear hug. "My dear Agent Carver, I watched the entire episode at the elevators over my surveillance cameras! Are you quite all right?"

"Fine," Carver said pulling away from Nico and his massive perm.

"You're lucky those Ukrainian peasants didn't rob you. This hotel has plenty of charm, but the riff raff still manages to get in."

In Rome last year, Nico had escaped from Carver by digging a tracking chip out of his arm. He later appeared at Carver's D.C. condo to throw himself upon the mercy of the federal government. It had come as no surprise that Nico's DIY surgery had left him with nerve damage, but the fact that Nico had voluntarily surrendered was still a shock. "This nerve thing is making me sloppy," he had explained. "The Saudis almost had me last week. They want to cut off my hands! Then my head!"

After two surgeries at Bethesda Naval Hospital and several weeks of rehab, Nico made a full recovery. Meanwhile, Speers, who had given his blessing for Carver to solicit Nico's unique talents in two prior operations with dire security implications, was able to persuade the president to grant him a non-public pardon for his longstanding crimes. There had been just three conditions for his freedom: that he remain in the United States, stay out of trouble, and that the Guardian be aware of his whereabouts at all times. The last condition wouldn't be a problem so long as the new tracking chip remained in his body.

Carver only wished that they had set a fourth condition: owning a phone. Communicating with Nico required an in-person meeting, arranged in advance via a set of complex security protocols.

Now Nico stepped behind the statue, mugging, holding his face alongside Pan's. "What do you think of my new trophy?"

"You do realize that possessing stolen antiquities would violate the terms of your pardon?"

"Stolen? *Please*! Pan is legitimately mine. A few months ago, some gentlemen from the Italian government came to me with a very serious security threat. They said if I solved their problem, I could name my price."

"And your price was a *priceless* work of art?"

"You know how people are when they learn about my particular set of talents. They feed the crocodile in hopes that he will eat them last."

Octavia and Madge took up positions on a pair of oversized recliners, watching him like birds of prey.

Nico seemed to float to the bar. "What are you drinking, friend?"

"Nothing, Nico. I'm here on business."

The hacker's face was suddenly serious. "Oh. Weren't you told? I'm not going by Nico right now."

"Excuse me?"

"I will answer only to Titus."

"Titus?"

"Yes. As in the Roman emperor Titus. Only I have given it an American twist. Written, it is spelled T-I-T-U-$. That was Madge's idea. Because if Titus were alive today, he would certainly be a celebrity."

There was no point in arguing. Besides, Carver reminded himself, I'm here to beg for Nico's help. If he wants to be Titus, let him be Titus.

"So, Titus, are you going to tell me what's up with the Roman theme, or do I have to guess?"

Nico's face brightened. "Yes! Terrific idea! I've told Octavia here how brilliant you are. Go ahead, Agent Carver. Show your stuff."

Carver pretended to be irritated, but he was in fact pleased. It was rare that he had the opportunity to flex his substantial intellect with others. "If memory serves," he said, "when we met at Lee Federal Penitentiary, you were studying Cornish, Muskogee, Aramaic and Coptic. All dead languages. And when I came in tonight, I couldn't help but notice several sheets of handwritten paper in a script that I had never seen before. Therefore, I'm going to guess that you have sequestered yourself here for some sort of language immersion exercise. A very *dead* Roman language immersion, to be precise."

His three hosts clapped. "Bingo on the *linguam immersionis*," Nico said. "But can you deduce what dead Roman language we are in fact studying?"

"Hmmm. Despite the fact that you just used Latin, it's far too pedestrian for your taste."

Nico threw his head back in a hearty laugh. "Guilty as charged! Go on!"

"Hellenistic Greek would technically fall under the geography of the Roman Empire, but again, being a stickler for languages that are truly dead, not just sort of dead, you would disqualify it since it is *still* used as the liturgical language of the Greek Orthodox Church."

"Correct. And yes, it's really more of a zombie language than a truly dead one."

"And if I know you, you're also going to snub most languages from lands that the Romans conquered and occupied, such as Coptic, or Biblical Hebrew. If you go Roman, you're going to go all the way."

At this, Octavia applauded. "Are you psychic? I proposed that we study Coptic, and that is exactly what Titus said to me!"

Carver acknowledged her with a slight bow before returning his gaze to Nico, who now hung on Carver's every word. "For the sake of authenticity, you're going to use a language that was purportedly developed in what became the Roman heartland before the birth of Christ. For example, Oscan was an indigenous tribal language near what became the capital city, Rome, last spoken around 100 AD.

Nico grinned. "You're getting warm. Go on..."

"So Oscan would have been tempting. But since it was not as widely spoken as other languages, opportunities for study material would not be as plentiful as, say, *Etruscan*. The Etruscan civilization occupied what is now Tuscany and Umbria, and was absorbed into the Roman Empire around the 4th century B.C."

Nico whooped and turned to the ladies. "*Bing*! See? I told you. Agent Carver is nothing less than a walking Wikipedia!"

The ladies clapped once again. Carver bowed theatrically, then turned to Nico. "Now then, is there somewhere we can talk business?"

His host turned to the ladies and asked in what he presumed was Etruscan if they would clear the room. They rose, disappearing to one of the suite's rear bedrooms. Nico reclined on a flat cream-colored couch with gilded legs.

"You look at home here in Vegas," Carver said.

"Where God has his church, the devil has his chapel."

"Does the devil's chapel have television?"

"No. While TV is wonderful for garden-variety language immersion, it is counterproductive to *dead* language immersion. Still, I have been following your little crisis on the Internet, if that's what you're getting at."

"It is."

"I see no logical reason why the U.S. would attack the Chinese embassy, though of course logic does not always prevail in matters of war. And although I find the conspiracy theorists entertaining, I don't buy for a second that the Chinese bombed their own embassy."

Carver nodded. "I'm with you, but there are certain people in Washington who feel otherwise."

"And how is Eva holding up these days?"

"The president is extremely concerned, of course. She told me to express her thanks in advance for your help."

"Balderdash. It was you and Julian who convinced her to give me a pardon. Eva wants nothing more to do with me, although I imagine she might be quite desperate right now. At any rate, now it comes out. What is it that you want from me?"

"Some of the evidence suggests the bombing was the work of a hardline group inside the Chinese government. The theory is that they did this to force President Kang to move more aggressively against the U.S."

"What kind of evidence?"

Carver reached into his coat pocket and removed a small flash drive. He handed it to Nico. "That contains everything we know. You'll find a leaked proposal to dump American debt on the open market and tank the economy. There are also dossiers on four key Chinese government officials who may have knowledge of it. Home and office street addresses. Digital addresses and handles. Known associates and family members. Organizations they belong to. Online accounts."

"And what exactly am I supposed to do with all that?"

"We need to know what they're thinking."

Nico laughed. "Oh, you *just* want me to *read their minds*?"

"You know what I mean. Get inside their phones. Their computers. Their offices. Surely you've got an application that can analyze speech and text."

"That's the NSA's job. And one that they seem to do quite well, I might add."

"That was before Edward Snowden exposed their bag of tricks. Look, Nico – "

"Titus!"

"Whatever. The reality is, if you don't help me, we could all be speaking Mandarin by this time next year."

"I might actually prefer that. It's a gorgeous language."

Nico stood and went to a corner table, picked up a bottle of Roman wine, and poured it into a glass. Then he reached into an earthen bowl and pulled out several green grapes. "I suppose the head of China's Technical Reconnaissance Bureau is one of the four people on your list."

Carver nodded. "Yes. His name is Li Wu. And there's also someone above him."

"Naturally. Let me guess. President Kang."

"Kang is easily the most powerful figure in China since Mao. Not content to be president of a mere billion people, he had also managed to appoint himself the General Secretary of the Communist Party and the head of the country's Central Military Commission."

"Oh, so you just want me to spy on the leader of the world's largest country. And you want it done yesterday."

"In the name of preventing a third world war. Yes."

"Well that won't be easy."

"You owe me."

"Oh *please*! I earned that presidential pardon. The terms don't include working for free."

"All right. So you want to be paid. How much?"

"Well, let's see what we know about the federal contracting pay scale. During the Iraq and Afghanistan wars, the CIA paid its torture gurus $80 million to teach the CIA how to waterboard prisoners."

"That was a fluke, and you know it."

"Perhaps, but it *was* paid. Would you say that preventing war with China is at least as valuable as teaching the CIA how to waterboard prisoners?"

Only a fool would answer that question directly. And yet Carver couldn't afford to turn him down. Not now. He would agree to whatever he needed to, and deal with the consequences later.

"If it's money you want, I can make sure you're well paid for this. But you'd have to deliver proof positive the United States is not responsible for the embassy bombing. Something so bulletproof that the president can present it before the United Nations, and the entire world will believe her."

Nico pushed a button. The fresco on the wall glided upward, revealing an enormous screen. A photograph of an enormous ancient goblet appeared on the screen. Engraved on the goblet was a bearded man entangled in grapevines.

"You're looking at an artifact known as the Lycurgus Cup. It's an ancient Roman goblet estimated to be 1600 years old. That man immortalized in the artwork is King Lycurgus. He's being attacked by nature for evil acts committed against Dionysus, the Greek god of wine. Isn't it amazing?"

"Get to the point."

"This isn't just any goblet. It's an ancient chameleon. It appears jade green when lit from the front, but it turns blood-red when lit from behind."

"An accidental byproduct of the ancient manufacturing process?"

"*Oh please*! The effect was most certainly *deliberate*. The Romans employed glass infused with tiny particles of silver and gold, 50 nanometers or so."

"Why are you showing me this?"

"This is my price. After I deliver the proof you require, I want to hold that goblet in my hand and drink out of it."

"Nobody in their right mind would drink out of something that old."

"Let me worry about that. Do we have a deal?"

Carver sighed. He had no authority to negotiate something of this magnitude, but he had to get Nico working. "Where is the cup now?"

"The British Museum in London."

Now it was time to start bluffing. "As it happens, the president is close with the British Prime Minister."

"So the tabloids say. I thought Eva would always remain a widow, but the gossip is that after she was his guest in his Wimbledon box, they spent three days at Camp David."

Carver winked. "No comment."

Nico grinned hopefully. "So you think it's actually possible? Eva can get me the cup?"

"Given what's at stake, she'll do whatever she has to."

"Then it's settled. I will help you. But first, to consummate our deal, I ask that you stay for dinner."

"Sorry, but I'm not really comfortable with the words *'consummate'* and dinner in the same sentence."

"I really must insist, Agent Carver. I have something special planned. In celebration of our language immersion exercise, Madge and Octavia have been marinating dormice for hours."

Carver's stomach flipped. "Dormice? As in a *dormouse*, on a plate?"

"Imported from Europe, of course. They were considered a delicacy in ancient Rome." He stood, gripping Carver by the shoulders, his Afro wobbling to and fro. "Come on, Agent Carver. It's just a little rodent between friends."

# University of Maryland
# Greater Washington D.C.

"And finally," Speers said, addressing the distinguished crowd of business leaders, scholars and government officials who had assembled for the black tie gala, "I will leave you with this. It's only natural to be concerned by the crisis that has dominated our headlines this week. But let it also inspire us into action by funding scholarships for the next generation of cyber security leaders."

Thunderous applause enveloped the Director of National Security as he left the podium. Speers smiled in gratitude at the standing ovation. But just as he had expected before he had gone onstage, there was no time for glad-handing now. Arunus Roth waited for him in the wings, and he was tapping his watch face.

Speers' security detail led them toward the rear exit, through a backstage area cluttered with boxes and set pieces. "Nice speech," Roth said.

"Thanks. You're probably wondering why I asked you to come here."

"Yes sir," Roth said eagerly. Until now, the scope of Roth's work had been largely limited to working under Carver, who had taken the green analyst under his wing.

They emerged into the chilly autumn evening, where Speers' SUV and that of his security detail were waiting. He and Roth got into the back seat of the second vehicle. Speers shut the privacy glass and fastened his seatbelt as the SUV sped off toward the National Counterterrorism Center in Langley. Then he made eye contact with Roth, whose pupils were set behind thick black-framed eyeglasses.

"I have teams across many agencies working on the embassy bombing," Speers said. "But as for Guardian's piece of it,

I want you to be my eyes and ears on this and report to me directly."

"Thank you, sir. But what about Carver and Ellis?"

"I asked you here, not them."

"This is a lot more responsibility. And I'm still just a GS-8." Roth referred to the federal pay scale, which ranged from GS-1 for administrative assistants, to GS-15, for senior administrators and other highly qualified federal employees."

"If you show results on this, you will be rewarded."

"But I've been showing results. Isn't that why you're giving me more responsibility, sir?"

Speers shrugged. Roth had a point. "Fair enough. I'll have my assistant draw up the paperwork. You're a GS-9."

Roth flashed a pained smile. "With all due respect, sir, my background, limited as it may be, is in *cyber* security. I have Silicon Valley recruiters calling me day and night. Until now, I haven't been returning those messages. I wanted to give you at least two full years of service as a thank you for all the things Agent Carver has done for me. But now that window is closing fast."

The director's brow furrowed. He hadn't expected the kid to negotiate a raise at a time like this. But Speers needed him. "GS-11, then. And that's my final offer."

They shook on it.

Speers' phone rang. It was FBI Director Chad Fordham. "You're not going to like this," Fordham said.

"What?"

"We just got a so-called courtesy call from CNN. They're going live with a story about Kyra Javan."

# The Four Seasons Hotel

Carver stepped out of the Four Seasons elevator, relieved to be back on the ground floor. He felt upbeat about his meeting with Nico Gold, the one person in the world with the talent to get the level of intelligence they needed quickly. It wasn't just Nico's intricate knowledge of programming languages and breach tactics that set him apart from the hackers working in federal cyber security. It was the fact that he understood that behind every machine was a flawed human being. His ability to exploit human weakness was what made him great.

Now, taking every precaution, Carver avoided the Four Seasons lobby, where he might have been seen coming in. He instead turned left, following the walkway until he entered the adjoining Mandalay Bay casino. His face twisted into a scowl as he entered the casino's smoky atmosphere.

Slot machines stretched as far as the eye could see. So too did every imaginable type of human being. Thin fat, old, young, gray, purple and blond – all were welcome here. Carver quickly changed course, checking his six as he went. Just one person crossed the casino floor behind him – an Asian male in his late 20s with camo-patterned jeans and shaggy brown hair that reached his earlobes. Again, Carver changed course. The guy followed.

Carver didn't believe in coincidences. He turned and stopped, observing, mentally recording, pretending to look at his phone while sizing up the possible tail. The man was perhaps five-foot-seven and trim, with a slightly effeminate gait. The oval face, low cheekbones and accentuated nose suggested Japanese heritage. But without seeming to notice Carver, he made a beeline for a Texas Hold'em table, where he sat and plucked down a neat stack of chips.

Hmmm. Maybe his sleep deprivation was making him paranoid. The three hours he had snatched on the plane to Vegas had been the only rest he had gotten in 48 hours.

With that settled, Carver cut through the grid of machines and blackjack tables and continued walking through the mini-mall that bridged the Mandalay Bay and the Luxor, where he intended to get ground transport to the airport. He took out his phone – which had been off in the hours since Octavia had confiscated it – and powered it up.

The device shuddered as messages flooded in. One was from Eri, containing just three words: *are you ok?*

I'm the worst ex-boyfriend in the world, Carver thought, realizing that he had never returned her latest message. There were also multiple texts from both Speers, demanding that he report in.

As Carver walked past an Irish pub, the TV mounted over the bar seized his attention. It was tuned to CNN. A photo of Kyra Javan — aka Kyra Al-Mohammad, the CIA's Butcher Bride — was onscreen. In the pic, Kyra was wearing a headscarf, which meant the pic had most likely been taken when Kyra was embedded in the Butcher's Tripoli compound.

The ticker across the bottom of the screen: *Libyan government seeks alleged CIA operative in connection with Chinese embassy bombing.*

Carver ducked into the pub and slid a $10 bill across the countertop to the bartender. He pulled up a stool. "Sparkling water, please. And would you mind turning that TV up?"

The camera cut to CNN newscaster Veronica Dutton. Unbeknownst to Dutton, Carver happened to have found himself behind her in a D.C. grocery store the previous summer. He had been struck with how much thinner and paler the waifish TV personality looked in person. It was no wonder. Her shopping cart had been full to the brim with cactus water, kale, pine nuts, beets and radishes. Food fit for a tortoise?

DUTTON: We're devoting today's program to the stunning turn of events that has the world on edge. A senior official in the

Libyan government claims that the woman on your screen, Kyra Javan, is in fact a CIA operative who had taken up residence in Tripoli sometime in the past year, presumably to surveil the Chinese embassy. Libyan local police are reportedly searching for Javan due to mounting evidence suggesting that Kyra Javan actually coordinated this week's drone strike from the ground. With us to explain the implications is Gavin Riley, an expert on U.S.-China relations from Stanford University. Dr. Riley, welcome to the program.

RILEY: Thank you, Veronica. Glad to be here.

DUTTON: This development isn't bound to please the White House.

RILEY: Quite the opposite, Veronica. It appears to be just the latest in a series of diplomatic missteps. First the White House denied involvement over the attack. Hours later, they admitted responsibility only after the Libyans produced evidence that an American attack drone was operating over Tripoli, claiming they had in fact intended to target a terrorist threat.

DUTTON: But they have refused to name the terrorist or terrorist target they were going after, correct?

RILEY: That's right. And the outing of this alleged CIA operative, Kyra Javan, seems to place doubt on the original story. What's going to be interesting is how China responds to these allegations.

DUTTON: Some analysts have suggested that the embassy attack was retaliation for China's continued espionage operations against American companies. Based on what you know about the relationship between the two countries, do you think there's truth in that?

RILEY: We may never know for sure, but we are definitely seeing real world consequences of the frayed relationship. The American stock exchanges were knocked offline this week, and while Beijing did not claim responsibility, they didn't deny involvement, either. And let's not forget that just a few weeks ago, we had an incident where Chinese planes reportedly came close to firing on American ships patrolling the East China Sea. That, of course, was in the vicinity of islands that are the subject of a territorial dispute between China and Japan.

DUTTON: Let's touch on that. Japan's Prime Minister actually called the U.S. out for not taking a tougher stance. He actually suggested that the Americans should have shot the Chinese planes down.

RILEY: That's right, Veronica, and I have to think that given what has transpired over the past few days, that's exactly what might happen the next time there's a showdown. And that's a real problem, because the Americans need China to come back to the table over economic issues, as they were scheduled to do at the G8.

Carver picked up his phone and dialed Speers, who answered on the first ring. Carver didn't have to ask if Speers was also watching the broadcast. He could hear it playing on the other end.

"We have a leak," Speers said with spice in his tone. "The question is, which part of the plumbing is leaking?"

"We can rule Kyra out," Carver said. "Mohy Osman almost killed her trying to get her to confess to being a spy. I was there."

Feeling the bartender's eyes on him, Carver took his leave and went back out into the mini-mall that bridged the two hotels. Speers sighed into the phone. "I've been trying to reach you for hours. Where have you been?"

"In Vegas. Eating a rodent cooked by Nico Gold's wife."

"Come on."

"That's the truth. And Nico agreed to help us, by the way. You're welcome."

"I'm not so sure getting Nico involved is a good idea. You have a bigger problem on your hands."

"Like what?"

"Haley Ellis."

"What do you mean?

He listened quietly as Speers described the scathing memo Ellis had written, in which she cited examples of what she deemed as Carver's "erratic behavior" and recommended that he be investigated in connection with the circumstances of the past three days. Speers continued his monologue, but by then, Carver was no longer paying attention.

A visceral memory of something Ellis said at Verizon Center surfaced in his consciousness. When he had refused to arrest the Pink Dragon before she had picked up the drop. *My objection will be documented in the operation brief.* Later, she hadn't concealed her jealousy when Carver had been tapped to brief the president. *The president tends to shoot the messenger.*

"Blake?"

"I'm here. Just reeling."

"Me too. This is garbage as far as I'm concerned, but for my own satisfaction, you'll have to indulge me on one thing. The other night at Verizon Center, how did you know Jessica Wu had been killed with a cyanide injection?"

"The scent, Julian. It was clear as day."

"But how would you recognize the smell of cyanide?"

"Document number DK11044781PF2. Look it up."

"Good Christ, Blake. I don't have time to go looking up old case files. Just tell me."

"I was with JSOC back then. We were on a mission to capture a Taliban warlord, but we were a few minutes too late. He had vomited up everything in his system. Some foul smelling stuff, again, like burnt almonds. We found a cyanide injection mark on his butt. That was later confirmed by an autopsy, of course."

Speers exhaled heavily. "That's helpful. I'll direct the Office of Security to the file you mentioned and make sure they include it in the investigation."

"Investigation?" Carver said. "Wait, can't you just make this go away?"

"I'm afraid it's out of my hands."

Carver couldn't believe his ears. He'd been in hot water more or less continuously throughout his career, but nothing had come close to this. "Who's running intelligence, Julian? You, or the president?"

"Contrary to popular belief, we live in a republic, not a democracy. I have to do what the president says."

"And what exactly is that?"

"She ordered a multi-agency task force to look into your activities. You have to report to them in 48 hours."

"Sounds like a witch hunt."

"Just don't do anything stupid. This thing is going to blow over, I promise. In the meantime, it won't be fun. You just have to show up, talk to these people, and play ball. Just tell them the facts. If you aren't transparent, then they're going to dig in even deeper."

A bench in the middle of the mall beckoned Carver. He sat down and caught his breath. "When and where?"

"Two days from now. FBI headquarters. Can I count on you to show up?"

FBI headquarters. Well at least there was that. Carver had always liked FBI Director Fordham. Not the sharpest knife in the drawer, but competent and fair. "So in the meantime, I have two more days to find out who hacked into the drone?"

Speers let out an astonished chuckle. "You're kidding, right? These are serious accusations. As of this moment, you're on administrative leave. With pay, of course."

So that was it. He was out. *Exiled.* How was Carver supposed to simply step away? The biggest firestorm between the U.S. and China was ablaze. His nature was to run *toward* fires, not *away* from them.

"Blake, you didn't answer the question. Can I count on you to meet with the task force? Think about your answer carefully."

He thought for a good long moment. "Sounds like I have no choice."

"Good man. Now as your friend, I have some advice, which I hope you'll take."

"I'm listening."

"Don't fly straight back to Washington. The Arizona state line is an hour's drive from Vegas. Spend some time with your family. While you have the chance."

# PART III

# Two Elk Ranch
# 35 Miles Outside Flagstaff, Arizona

Carver stood before the corral and inhaled a lung full of mountain air. He was conscious of his own breathing. He wasn't winded, exactly, but the 7,000-foot elevation was going to take some getting used to.

A storm was blowing in. The afternoon sky was bruised purple and black with intermittent streaks of lightning so far away that he could not yet hear the thunder. On either side of the valley stood gently sloping hills of volcanic rock, dotted with junipers and scrub oak. To the east, a kettle of turkey vultures screeched as they circled over some unseen animal in distress. And to the north, the peaks were blanketed with early season snowfall.

He wasn't all that surprised to find a sun-bleached mountain lion skull nailed to one of the tall posts marking the corral entrance. There was always a new skin, antler or bone nailed up somewhere. If his father hadn't become a rancher, he would have made a fine witch doctor. Carver vaulted himself up on the fence so that he was high enough to peer out at the dusty cattle corral through the cat cranium's hollow eye sockets.

His father's Springer Spaniel, Duke, spotted Carver and let out a trio of hearty barks. The liver and white hunting dog sprinted without fear through the phalanx of bovine legs, causing several guttural complaints from the startled cattle. The impeccably trained dog wagged furiously at the sight of him, but did not jump.

"Duke!" Carver said. He jumped down into the corral, roughhousing with the dog as it swirled around him. "How are you, buddy? You staying out of trouble?"

Now the herd parted, revealing his father's sturdy figure in green flannel, sneaker boots and a Stetson hat. He held an orange irrigation kit in one hand. In the other, a Winchester rifle.

At this distance, Carver couldn't tell whether the old man was happy to see him. He loved his children, but he did not like surprises. He preferred to see people on his own terms.

The two men met halfway across the corral. His father waited to speak until they were within spitting distance of each other. "Your mom said you weren't coming."

"Everything worked out at the last minute."

Speers' advice had weighed heavily on him. *Go see your parents. While you have the chance.*

Why not? The truth was that with Carver's work suddenly taken from him, he had little else with which to occupy his time. He had carefully curated a life that often found him disappearing for weeks or months on a moment's notice. He had no pets, no kids, and at the moment, no girl. The only living thing in his condo was a miniature pipe organ cactus that his sister had named Marty Robbins.

Now he took the heavy irrigation kit from his father and carried it toward the road, where his Dad's one-ton truck and his own rental were parked.

Worry creased the old man's face. "Business all right?"

"Fine," Carver said, but didn't elaborate. Unable to tell his family what he really did for a living, he'd told them he was a federal procurement consultant and left it at that. He had spent months crafting that cover before his boss had finally signed off on it, complete with an office down on K Street. Procurement consultant was one of those put-you-to-sleep job titles that naturally quelled all desire for follow up questions.

"Well you just missed your mom. She'll be up at the old place until the weekend, getting it ready to sell."

The original family ranch was a hardscrabble, postage-size piece of real estate near Joseph City, a Mormon settlement located more than three hours to the east. Earlier this year, his parents had sunk their savings into the 10,000 largely forested acres where Carver now stood. For how long was anyone's guess.

Most of his parents' friends had left the high country by now, retiring to one of many hilly desert communities with names like Saddlebrooke and Surprise.

Carver pointed at the mountain lion skull mounted on the post. "You kill that cat yourself?"

"Yup. End of summer. Caught him eating one of the calves. Shot him not 10 feet from where he's strung up now."

"That's some real wild west justice, Pop."

"That old boy's kept the predators away, that's for sure." He slid his rifle into the back of the truck. "Say, you want to make a little money tomorrow?"

"Business is fine, Dad, I swear. I don't need money."

He could tell his father didn't quite believe him. "Sure it is, sure it is. But all the same, I had a ranch hand leave me high and dry this week. I need to get three hogs over to Ash Fork tomorrow by half past five."

Carver didn't need money, but he had to admit that he was in dire need of distraction. It might take his mind off the task force that was no doubt gearing up to tear him limb from limb.

"All right then. You're on."

"Good." He gestured toward the dog. "Might as well take Duke here with you and do some hunting while you're over in that neck of the woods. You know those ducks will be flying at daybreak."

Carver knew a pond in that area that had never let him down. He and his father had been duck hunting there since he'd been old enough to walk. A rancher had once given them a key to a gas pipeline road that, to their great surprise, gave them near-exclusive access to a wide swath of wilderness.

"How about we go together?"

His father shook his head. "Too much to do and not enough time to do it. But if you bring a few ducks back, I'll make a good dinner for us."

# Las Vegas

Nico Gold hunched over the computer as he browsed the Beijing Premiere Western Talent Agency website, which billed itself as the leading supplier of Caucasian actors to Chinese corporate and media production companies. Further down the page was this: *Our actors earn an average of 5,000 RMB/day. If you're an attractive person from the USA, U.K., Ireland or Australia, and are of at least average height, apply now and we will make you a star!*

He browsed the website's talent portfolio, scanning rows of headshots for an actor who would help him penetrate Zhongnanhai, the central headquarters of the Communist Party.

The plan – which was magnificent, in Nico's humble opinion – had come to him last night like a thunderbolt from Jupiter. Carver had left soon after dinner, and his ladies had gone to bed early, leaving Nico alone with his excitement at getting the Lycurgus Cup. Sleep was out of the question.

But how could he possibly deliver on what he had promised Carver? He hadn't been simply playing coy when saying that eavesdropping on China's leaders was far easier said than done.

If the NSA hadn't found a way back into Zhongnanhai, how could he pull it off in just a matter of days?

Many of his best tricks no longer worked on the Chinese. In the past, he would have simply logged into a daisy chain of proxy servers, activated a legion of zombie computers from across the globe, and launched a mammoth denial of service attack on the Zhongnanhai network, taking the system down just long enough to place a Trojan Horse inside that would allow him to monitor internal email and VoIP communications.

And if he had more time, he could have simply phished some poor party underling with an email link, waited for him to download malware, and then watched for the target to login to something sensitive. But even if time had been on his side, there was no guarantee that such a plan would gain him the everywhereness within Zhongnanhai that he needed.

As he often did these days during his bouts of insomnia, Nico took off his wig, put on some mainstream clothes, and ventured downstairs. He prowled the casino floor, surveying the blackjack tables in search of the most anti-social blackjack dealer. He hated yappy dealers. They distracted him from counting cards.

As usual, the predictable rhythm of blackjack calmed him. The cards came to him easily tonight. Within 45 minutes, he was up $800.

In the midst of his hot streak, an extraverted American entertainment executive joined Nico at the table. He was a big drinker as well as a big talker. Between hands, and with little prodding, he disclosed just how badly his company, MassiveStreamz, wanted to seize the Chinese entertainment market. How the company was willing to do *anything* to get permission to launch an unrestricted version of their TV content in the country.

*Anything*?

That sparked the idea he had been searching for. Nico cashed his chips in and raced upstairs. Now, browsing the talent agency profiles at the Beijing Premiere Western Talent Agency website, he came at last to a distinguished looking American male.

Jasper Blick was his name. Caucasian, in his late 40s, with salt and pepper hair and a clean-shaven face. Blick had appeared in a number of Chinese commercials.

Curiously, his reel also showed him standing in for a physician at what looked like a real medical conference, where he presented a lecture on contemporary prostate surgery technique. It was a bit weird, but it demonstrated the kind of ethical elasticity that Nico would need for this operation.

Blick was no male model, but his vibe emanated success and authority. In a suit, Nico figured, he would be a believable

American executive who would do anything – *anything*! – to establish his content network in the world's largest economy.

Nico leaned forward and kissed the monitor screen. "Jasper Blick, you and I are about to make history together."

# Two Elk Ranch

It was no wonder his father had purchased the ranch for a song. A monster spring snow had caved in the roof of the main ranch house and flooded most of the second floor. Although it was just September now, winter had already come to the mountains, and it was going to take a miracle to get the remodel done before snow hit the valley.

Carver watched as five exhausted workers bid his father good night, got in their trucks, and disappeared down the pebbly road toward Highway 89. The construction zone left them with just one room in the main house that wasn't in complete disarray – the kitchen.

His father lit an iron stove that warmed the room with impressive speed. Carver was actually grateful that there was no cell or Internet coverage in the house. Every part of him wanted to call Arunus Roth and check in on the investigation. Every part of him wanted to watch the news, to see if there had been any new provocations between the U.S. and China. Now he couldn't. And that was a good thing.

*Yeah, keep telling yourself that. Maybe in a day or two, you'll actually believe it.*

"That's your luggage?" his father said, eyeing the leather bag that held his computer.

Carver shrugged. "Like I said, this trip came together at the last minute."

"Must have." He regarded Carver's suit. "Well you can borrow some of my clothes."

The two men washed up and played a couple of hands of Gin at the pinewood table. His father beat him soundly, then got to his feet and set a skillet on the gas range. "Hope chicken-fried steak is all right."

Carver checked his watch. "It's wasn't even five p.m. yet. "There's a steakhouse out on I-40. I'm buying."

"Save your money. "

"Pop, business is fine. "

"Chicken fried steak. End of conversation."

His father got up and began pounding the steaks into thin cuts flecked with rock salt. Carver pitched in, cracking eggs into a bowl before whisking them into a gooey yellow mass. Then he combined the eggs with a flour and crumb mixture, dipping the steaks into the goop before laying them into a skillet that had grown black from decades of use.

He watched as his father stood at the stove, whistling bluegrass standards as he prodded a pan of sizzling home fries this way and that. The quiet, familiar rhythm of the work was comforting. Soon enough, the smell managed to rouse his hunger.

His father spoke without looking at him. "So how's your health these days?"

"Normal blood pressure, low resting heart rate."

"C'mon wise guy. You know what I mean."

Carver knew all right. He meant his brain. The hyperthymesia. Back when he was 14-years-old, the family doctor thought he was just another kid with severe attention deficit disorder. He had been prone to migraines and extreme inability to focus. His mind was constantly blooming with running replays of all that had come before. He had explained it to the doctor like this: "You know how they say your life flashes before your eyes before you die? That's what it's like for me all day, every day."

It got worse. Carver spent much of his sophomore year of high school at home, doing his assignments in the privacy of his bedroom, living in isolation as his specialist in nearby Flagstaff prescribed one ADHD medication after another. The drugs didn't work. Mostly, they just made him worse.

His father, meanwhile, had sought to heal him with prayer. He hosted several gatherings in which the other priesthood holders in the community bestowed their blessings on him. The ritual made Carver feel better, but it wasn't a cure.

One time they hired a healer out on the Navajo reservation. They spent an entire night in a sweat lodge with five of the healer's cousins. At one point during the various incantations, Carver thought he felt an otherworldly presence, but there was no noticeable improvement in his condition.

His junior year of high school, they drove down to Phoenix to meet with a Mayo Clinic psychiatrist. After just 15 minutes, the shrink told him that he would never need to take another pill. The diagnosis? Hyperthymesia.

Over the course of the next two years, he taught Carver meditation techniques to help him learn how to compartmentalize and control the constant torrent of memories. His favorite method involved focusing on the beating of his own heart, which he imagined as a huge bass drum and a unifier of the visions in his head. The visualization technique had worked well for a few years before inexplicably losing its magic one day.

After that, Carver went back on meds for a stretch. The pills slowed down the mind chatter, but they also dulled his thoughts. Convinced he had lost his analytical edge, he went off them again and spent the next two years as a metaphysical journeyman, seeking the world's great visualization experts. At a yoga retreat in Chiang Mai, a guru taught him to imagine the actual removal of his head, his thoughts fizzling out as if short-circuiting, until the torrent was under control. It worked, but it was impractical when he was in the field.

His latest coping mechanism had come to him in the gym this past summer. He had been working with his fencing coach, when Radiohead's mesmerizing song *Everything in its Right Place* had come over the speakers. The song's simple chord progression rendered him spellbound. He immediately added it to the playlist on his phone. Later that night, he listened again, studying it. Visualizing the notes on a song sheet along with the insanely simple lyrics:

*Everything. Everything. Everything.*
*In its right place.*
*Right place.*

*Right place.*

The result was pure focus. Go figure. It was like a miracle. Most days, replaying the song in his head was enough. But the torrent he had experienced in Vegas was something else. That was worrisome. Powerful enough to knock him out. He was fortunate not to have split his head open.

Now his father laid the plate before him and sat opposite. He said grace, and then picked up his utensils. "Here's to getting some of your mom's good cooking very soon."

"Don't be modest. This is delicious. I forgot how good actual butter is. When I get back to D.C., I'm throwing out all my coconut oil."

His father swallowed. "So. Have you met my future daughter-in-law yet?"

"Not yet, Pop."

"What about Eri? You ever see her any more?"

"No. She moved back to Tokyo years ago. You know that."

Twelve years ago, in fact. His parents had met Eri during their one and only trip to the nation's capital. Carver had given them the grand tour. Fourteen museums in nine days. The Lincoln Memorial, the Capitol Building, the White House. But Eri Sato was the one thing they talked about afterwards. How perfect they were together. How they were going to give them beautiful grandkids. If only Carver would make an honest woman out of her.

He didn't blame them. He and Eri had been good together. He had never felt as close to anyone. But he had lost her for one very simple reason – he had loved his work more than he loved her.

It was the work he had ended up marrying all those years ago. And now, it seemed, the work had left him too.

# Beijing, China

Jasper Blick peered out the window of his 10th-floor apartment building and slipped on his eyeglasses. He was still utterly unable to see the buildings on the other side of the road. This was the fourth day in a row that the city had been under a toxic gray haze, and the 30th air quality alert of the year. The fit 41-year-old ran his fingers through his salt-and-pepper hair, then over his face, pulling at his cheeks.

Cabin fever was creeping in.

Once again, the government had ordered major factories to suspend production and non-essential vehicles to stay off the road. And as it always did on days like this, the economic consequences rolled downhill. This morning, his phone's insistent ring had woken him at 6:03 a.m. It was the agency. It seemed that his gig playing an English butler for a department store opening ceremony had been postponed due to hazardous air quality.

He needed that money. The Yuan had been tanking in recent months, and he was getting absolutely crushed when converting his money to USD. At least he wasn't paying any income tax. All his gigs were paid in cash.

Still, if this kept up for long, he was going to have to go back to his career as a nurse in Oregon. God forbid. Beijing was where all the action was these days. Until the currency crash, he had been completing acing the ex-pat lifestyle. He had more girlfriends than he could keep up with, and until recently, the easy gigs had flowed like a river.

And to what did he owe this screaming success in matters of love and money? Was it because he was a great actor? Nope. Mostly, he figured, it was because he had been born white and male and American. He was blessed!

As he saw it, that was the critical difference between China and the states. Back home in Oregon, it seemed like all anyone could talk about was the need to increase diversity. Northwesterners were constantly complaining about how "white" it was up there. Some of his best friends lived in a constant state of white guilt. To make matters worse, the whole gender equality thing was really picking up steam. His friends back home told him that the system was literally taking money out of men's pockets and reallocating it to women. One of his buddies back home was actually considering faking a transgender move so he could qualify for one of those women-only small business grants! Had America really been sissified to that extent? Having to switch genders to get ahead? The lunatics were running the asylum!

But not in China. The government might be wary of American foreign policy, but man oh man, the girls *loved* white guys from the states. In China, he was special. So if Blick was being honest, this kind of life just wasn't going to happen for him back home, *ever*.

His phone chirped. He didn't recognize the caller ID, so he answered in his most professional business voice, hoping the caller would know English. Despite having been in Beijing for three years, he still didn't know much Mandarin.

"Is this Jasper Blick?" the caller said. He sounded American.

"Yes it is. With whom am I speaking?"

"Your next client."

Blick grinned. "Did the agency give you my number?"

"No. I need to deal directly with you, Jasper."

Well this was a first. Blick was at a loss for words. He sat at his tiny dining table, absentmindedly tapping the goldfish bowl that served as its centerpiece. The fish spooked to the other side of the bowl. "What did you say your name was?"

"You can call me Titus. Are you in front of a computer?"

Blick's machine was within easy reach. He pulled it off the counter and set it on the table, next to the goldfish. "Sure am."

"If you'll check your bank account, you'll see that I've already made the down payment for the job."

Blick let out a nervous laugh. "Sorry, Titus, I didn't quite catch that."

"You heard me. I paid in advance. Go ahead. Log into your bank account. I'll wait."

Blick set the phone down and put it on speaker. He pulled up his banking app, logged in, and checked the balance. OMG. The balance was *$10,000 USD higher* than it had been last night. It was like money had fallen from the sky!

But it was also weird. And a little creepy.

"Okay," Blick said. "Be straight with me. Is this some reality TV show about expatriate life in China?"

"On the contrary. You will never speak of our agreement to anyone. I demand strict confidentiality."

"Look, Titus. If this isn't a gag, and the agency didn't refer you, then I really have to know who you are and what's going on."

"I found you in the slush pile of humanity. Then I put ten G's in your account as a down payment for your services. That's not so bad, is it?"

"No. It's just – "

"There's at least another ten Gs in this for you if you just work with me, and you won't have to share a penny with the agency. But again, I demand a high degree of confidentiality in return."

Blick stood and held the phone tight against his ear as he went to the window. The haze outside was still thick. "Mister Titus or whoever you are, I don't mean to be ungrateful, but I feel a little *violated* right now. I don't understand how you could have gotten my direct deposit number unless you hacked into my account. I hope I'm wrong about that, because I would hate to have to call the authorities."

The voice sighed. "The pig accustomed to dirt turns his nose up at rice."

"Excuse me? Did you just call me a pig?"

"I think the real thing you have to ask yourself, Jasper, is this: What happens if I *don't* take this job? If this mysterious person can magically make money *appear* in my account, can he also make it all *disappear*? Could he even make my work visa disappear? Would I have to move back to Oregon? And if I did, would he find me there too?"

There was a long pause before Blick spoke again. "What do I have to do?"

"I need you to play the role of an American executive this week. It's a 20-hour commitment. And Jasper, I'll know if you tell anyone about this. You believe that, don't you?"

Blick cleared his throat. "Yes."

"Good. First, you're going to go out and have a bunch of business cards printed up. Your name will be David Stone, and you'll be playing a Senior Vice President of Entertainment Content for a company called MassiveStreamz."

# Two Elk Ranch

After Carver had eaten his fill of chicken-fried steak, he bid his father good night and retired to the staff quarters just behind the main ranch house. A row of 10 units had been built for the property's first ranch hands back in 1907. Each contained a single bed, a nightstand, a lamp and a foot locker. A shared bathroom — which had been fitted with indoor plumbing and a shower in the 1960s — stood at the end of the hall.

He entered the first unit, then moved on to the next, hoping it was in better condition. It wasn't. He sat on the edge of the mattress and imagined the endless succession of sun-weathered vaqueros over the past century that had once sat where he was now. Their messages to him had been engraved into the yellowing wall before him.

*Manny era aqui '59.*

*God bless all who enter*

*Te amo Gloria*

*John freaking Wayne!*

*Nixon is a crook.*

*¡Eh,... Macarena! Aaay!*

Carver slid the drawer of the nightstand open. Inside was an emergency sewing kit and a dog-eared, leather-bound Bible that had been placed there in 1947. He could think of no use for the sewing kit, but he was fascinated by the old Bible. He picked it up and flipped through, astonished by the thousands of highlighted and underlined passages. The margins were filled with handwritten notes in English and Spanish.

His eyes danced over chapter and verse, finally resting on key passages that had been cited so many times that it was nearly impossible to read the original text. But that did not matter. Carver knew them all from memory.

*Proverbs 27:23: Know well the condition of your flocks, and pay attention to your herds; For riches are not forever, nor does a crown endure to all generations.*

*Romans 12:2: Do not conform any longer to the pattern of this world, but be transformed by the renewing of your mind. Then you will be able to test and approve what God's will is—his good, pleasing and perfect will.*

*Matthew 11:28: Come to me, all you who are weary and burdened, and I will give you rest.*

Rest. That was a good idea. He had not had anything resembling peaceful sleep for weeks.

He put the Bible back into the drawer and shut the light off. He reclined on the bed, but his bruised ribs wouldn't let him get comfortable for long. He tossed and turned. Jack Brenner's insulin pump pestered his thoughts. The image of the WiFi-enabled device sitting under the lights in the ODNI lab, the clear tube that had fed Brenner's body disconnected, inert. If Arunus Roth's theory was right, even while Carver was busy plumbing Brenner for information, someone had hacked into the pump, releasing a fatal dose of insulin. His death had come at the precise moment when Carver was about to take Brenner into custody.

He did not believe in coincidence. Brenner had seemed paranoid in the pub, claiming that "they" were listening. Minutes later, he was dead. Someone had planned this all very carefully and was executing it to perfection. Were they, in fact, watching him right now? Or were they inside him, the same way they had been inside Brenner, at this very moment?

He rose and went to the window, scanning the darkness for flashlights, car headlights, movements in the shadows. Carver was no stranger to nighttime paranoia. He accepted the fact that he had accumulated many enemies over the course of his career in intelligence, and realized that some day, one of them might go to extraordinary lengths to exact vengeance. He just hoped his professional life would never follow him back home to Arizona.

*Relax. There is no cell coverage here. There is no Internet. There is just one road in and out of this place. No one can track you. Not tonight, at least.*

Never satisfied, he opened his suitcase and took out the computer he had taken with him to Libya. He booted it up and, with a few keystrokes, wiped its memory clean. All applications, all data, everything. Then he slid the sheet off the corner of the bed and, using the keys of his rental car, cut a slit in the mattress. He shoved the computer deep inside until he felt its metal come against the springs. Then he stitched the fabric back up with the sewing kit in the nightstand and forced himself to lay back down.

He focused on the sound of a train in the distance. The Doppler effect of its horn as it wound through the nearby canyon, and the predictable syncopation of its wheels against the tracks. *Ch-ch-chaff. Ch-ch-chaff. Sha-hoosh. Sha-hoosh.*

And at last, Carver slept.

# The White House

Julian Speers headed toward the Map Room, an elegant parlor that had once served as President Franklin Roosevelt's wartime communications center. He felt that the room's history was well-suited to the stated intentions of his guest. At the president's insistence, Speers was to meet with the Japanese ambassador to the U.S., Kai Nakamura, who had promised to deliver classified information that would shed light on the crisis with China.

This was highly irregular. To the best of Speers' knowledge, a foreign ambassador had never had access to anyone from American Intelligence, to say nothing of its chief executive. But Nakamura had snubbed his meeting with the Secretary of State, claiming that the sensitive intelligence information he had to share was beyond her. He had demanded a meeting with the president. When she had refused, he indicated that Speers would be an acceptable replacement.

As he turned the corner into the Map Room, Speers found Nakamura standing by the fireplace. Steam rose from a teapot set on a nearby table. Nakamura was the youngest diplomat Speers had ever seen, slightly built and in an impeccably tailored navy suit with emerald cufflinks. Before his career as an ambassador, he had earned a degree in international law at Stanford.

Nakamura turned, unsmiling, and shook Speers' hand. "Mister Director," he said without any trace of accent.

"Ambassador," Speers said with forced warmth. "It's rare that I get the honor of meeting a diplomat of your stature."

"Indeed. I appreciate the symbolic gesture the president has made by holding this meeting in the White House. I trust that what I am about to share with you will be passed on to her without delay."

"The president obviously appreciates the importance of your request, as I do."

Speers gestured to a stuffed-back armchair that was said to have been built by legendary Philadelphia cabinetmaker Thomas Affleck. He waited for his guest to sit, then took the chair opposite.

Nakamura reached into his bag and pulled out a leather-bound document that was at least three inches thick. He dropped it on the mahogany table between the two chairs, and its weight against the wood registered an impressive thud that made both Speers and the teapot jump.

"That is a log of more than 900 sorties flown by Japanese fighter pilots intercepting Chinese J-31s over the past 12 months." He paused, raised his eyebrows for dramatic effect. "Go ahead. Examine it. I had it translated to English for you."

Speers kept his hands in his lap. "I'm aware of the situation. You're referring to Chinese planes buzzing the disputed Senkaku Islands."

"Not just the Senkaku Islands. As you'll see, these incursions are happening all over our territories with increasing regularity."

"I see."

"Did you know that China's J-31 is an advanced stealth aircraft?"

"Yes, Ambassador."

"And did you also know that our Japanese pilots fly American F-15s? A plane that has been in service since 1972?"

"Ambassador, if you're asking me to make a case for selling you more advanced aircraft – "

"For now, I simply ask you to understand what we are up against. The Chinese have been probing our defenses. By now they realize that they can get close enough to our bases to destroy our planes before they even leave the ground."

"Ambassador, this is a little out of my jurisdiction, but I believe I'm accurate in saying that we have approximately 50,000 troops in Japan that are ready to protect your country. That includes the Seventh Fleet and hundreds of fighter aircraft that could easily match up with anything China could throw at you. Not to mention our forces in the region at large."

"And yet China encroaches deeper into our territory each day, while the United States does nothing to defend our sovereignty."

Speers was starting to think this was a job for the secretary of state after all. The U.S. had, of course, lodged protests on Japan's behalf, but it hadn't done anything militarily. The U.S. wasn't about to risk a major conflict with a superpower over a few largely deserted islands.

Nakamura reached again into his bag and pulled out two folders. He set the first on the table and opened it, revealing a series of photographs.

Speers put on his eyeglasses. Some of the images were satellite photos, while others appeared to have been taken at close range. One depicted an enormous barge, big as an oil tanker. An army of bulldozers was pictured pushing sand from its open aft and onto a tiny island. The island's coordinates were stamped on the lower right-hand corner. There were several more photographs like these, all with different coordinates.

"What are they doing?" Speers asked. "Enlarging these islands?"

"There were no islands there to begin with. Those were just shallow reefs. First, they dumped rubbish on the reefs to raise the elevation. Then they brought sand and concrete."

The second series of photos showed construction crews installing what, even to Speers' eye, looked like missile defense systems. Other photos showed the construction of piers, harbors and in one case, an airstrip.

"We call it the Great Sand Wall of China," Nakamura explained. "At 16 locations in the East China Sea, they have added 8.5 square miles of land."

Speers set the photos down. Some months ago, the government of Malaysia had lodged a formal complaint when one such project encroached on international waters. China had claimed that they were trading hubs to help encourage shipping commerce among Asian nations.

"I gather you think this activity is provocative in nature," Speers said, although he himself had little doubt.

"Isn't it obvious? These islands are forward operating bases for the People's Liberation Army."

Speers stood. "I can understand your concern, Ambassador. You have my word that I will personally show these photos to the president. Now if you'll excuse me…"

"We are not finished. These photos are simply for context." He passed Speers a document dated the evening before. It was a transcript of a conversation that supposedly took place with a high-ranking informant within the Chinese government. "That document proves that China destroyed its own embassy."

Speers felt his mouth suddenly go dry. "Come again?"

"You heard me. China destroyed its own embassy. It's part of a larger plan they call Operation Ukraine."

"Ukraine?"

"We think it is a reference to Russia's invasion of the Ukraine in 2015. I think you will agree, as they clearly do, that it was the most brilliantly executed invasion in modern times."

Speers had to concur. While the Russians were hosting the Winter Olympics in Sochi and building goodwill through the illusion of peace, love and understanding among nations, it quietly began seeding the Ukrainian territory of Crimea with undercover Russian soldiers. Just weeks after the winter games closed, they began seeding civil unrest, with the embedded soldiers disguised as Ukrainian police, military and even civilian "separatists." They then staged a civil war within the country itself. Eventually, it followed with a visible occupation by regular Russian troops who entered on the pretense that they were protecting endangered Russian-speaking citizens in the eastern part of the country.

Still, Speers found himself lost. "How is the embassy bombing related to China's activities in the East China Sea?"

"You may have forgotten the most critical piece of Russia's invasion of the Ukraine. Russia had to ensure that its invasion would not be met with an immediate counterattack from U.S. or NATO forces. Tell me, Mister Director, how did they manage to invade a close American ally like the Ukraine without a fight?"

"By creating confusion. A series of carefully timed false news reports. Disinformation campaigns. Two-faced diplomacy. It all added up to a smokescreen that kept us off-balance until it was too late to act."

"Yes. Trickery. This situation with China is no different."

"Ambassador, are you actually suggesting that China is about to invade Japan?"

Nakamura nodded. "I suggest nothing. It is a fact. According to our source, Beijing has decided to take not just the Senkaku Islands from us, but expand upward, annexing additional territory in the East China Sea and perhaps even parts of Hokkaido."

He pointed to a location on the map.

Speers leaned back as if he had been slapped in the face. "Our base in Okinawa is right in the middle of the area you're talking about."

Nakamura smiled at Speers and shook his head. Pityingly, as if addressing a child. "To quote from *The Art of War*, victorious warriors win first and then go to war, while defeated warriors go to war first and then seek to win. As Beijing sees it, the consequences of their actions will be attending peace talks, which will naturally fail, and mild economic sanctions."

"They wouldn't dare."

The ambassador stood. "China seeks to neuter the American military into a confused, submissive state. And forgive me for this observation, Mister Director, but I do believe it has already succeeded."

# Two Elk Ranch

It was pitch black and 21 degrees out as Carver started the truck motor. Duke sat in the passenger seat, teeth chattering as the vehicle heater struggled to life. Carver's ribs were less sore today, and for that, he was grateful.

As they passed the corral, the truck headlights flashed over the lion skull Carver's father had nailed up. The ghostly image was a trigger. Something he'd seen when he was with the CIA in Afghanistan. Dead men dragged through a village by the Taliban. Strung up on posts as a warning to others that might collaborate with the Americans. Left to rot in the sun as the birds picked them down to the bone.

He braked as a possum darted out into the road. The animal froze in the headlights. Then it keeled over like a toy that had run out of batteries. And just lay there, motionless.

Carver had of course seen possums before. He had heard people refer to playing possum. But he had never actually seen a possum do such a thing.

He left the engine idling, stepped out of the truck and approached the animal. Its eyes, staring up at the still-starry sky, were convincingly glassy. A limp tongue hung out the corner of its mouth. Limbs were motionless. Carver started to wonder. Do possums have heart attacks? Do they have strokes?

Then he saw the animal take a very slight, nearly undetectable breath. "Well-played," Carver said, grinning. He got back into his father's truck and drove around the award-winning animal actor. He looked in his rear view mirror, but it was too dark to see the possum rise up and run away.

Fifteen minutes later, he was headed east through the town of Williams. A surge of nostalgia pulsed through him as he passed an RV park owned by a childhood friend. In the tiny downtown, a coffee shop was managed by his high school valedictorian. She still ran into Carver's parents every Fourth of July. Will you tell Blake to call me? She would say. Everyone is always wishing he would keep in touch.

*Not going to happen. I have to tell enough lies as it is.*

His old friends might be aghast at the lengths to which he had gone to keep up with their lives all these years. How he had looked them up on Facebook, lingering over their family photos. How he had read their blogs and lit anonymous virtual candles on their grandparents' obituaries. How he had donated anonymously to their causes. How he had cheered when the local church announced the births of their children.

He fully intended on reconnecting one day. In Carver's retirement fantasies, he showed up unannounced at a high school reunion, having scarcely aged since college, and apologized to the surviving members of the senior class all at once. *For your own safety, I couldn't tell you what I did for a living. Forgive me?* And in those fantasies, everyone did. They even thanked him for his public service. And he was deluged with homemade pie and invitations to Super Bowl parties.

At 4:45 am, Carver dropped the hogs off in Ash Fork. The young rancher purchasing them seemed happy with their size. Said he intended to crossbreed them with some sort of big Russian boar and make "a truly epic pig."

At half-past five, Carver started down the craggy forest road leading to the duck pond his father had mentioned. About two miles in, he came across the gate for the gas pipeline road, put the truck in Park, and got out. He thought about picking the lock just for fun, but using the timeworn key filled him with a delicious dose of fond memories from his youth.

He pulled through the gate and locked it behind them. From there, he put the truck in four-wheel-drive mode, babying it over the rough spots so the rocks wouldn't do much more than scratch the undercarriage. A half-mile further, he came across the rock pyramid they had made years ago to mark their personal parking space. Driving in much further risked spooking the ducks. *If* there were any ducks. The temperature on the dash read

29 degrees. That might be too cold for the shallow pond down the road where he had hoped to hunt.

He put on the hunting vest he had borrowed and chambered several shells into the old man's shotgun. The steel of the gun barrel was as cold as ice.

The bitter cold didn't dissuade his companion whatsoever. Duke's entire rear end wagged in anticipation. "Got a feeling the pond will be frozen over, bud. We'll check it anyhow."

The spaniel trotted out in front as they crept along the winding game trail, stepping gingerly over timber that the forest service had felled last season. They thinned these forests as a matter of routine now for fire prevention. Despite one or two massive storms, droughts had ravaged the high country in recent years. A couple years earlier, 19 firefighters had been killed in a massive blaze down in Yarnell. A few years before that, wildfire had nearly wiped out the town of Greer.

The dog's white and liver coat was luminescent in the pre-dawn light, bobbing this way and that, making almost no sound as they wound around the ridge that led to the duck blinds. He charged ahead 20 feet, then looped back over and over again in a constant flushing motion.

A hint of purple light was just beginning to crest the eastern mountaintops as they reached the duck blinds, two semi-circular masses of dead scrub brush overlooking a shallow cattle pond. He sat down, planting himself upon a wide stump that had no doubt been used by his father and every other hunter in the Williams area. It was too dark yet to see the pond, but if it were frozen, there would be nothing on it and nothing likely to come in.

Then Carver heard a vehicle. Or did he? Noise traveled far and wide at that time of morning.

He heard it again. The *whirr-whirr-whirr* of an underpowered gas engine struggling over a high spot in the road. Then the unmistakable grind of a vehicle undercarriage on rocks. There was only one road in and out of this place, and someone was coming in behind him.

Damn. He had hoped he would have this place all to himself this morning. He wondered how many keys that old rancher had given out over the years. Lots, probably. Or maybe none. Some people probably just picked it.

He listened intently as the vehicle drew closer. *Not a truck. No, something far smaller. A four-cylinder sedan.*

Carver figured there were just three types of people who might come back here before dawn on a Wednesday: hunters, ranchers and target shooters. And few of them would drive an economy car. This was truck country.

So what kind of idiot would come back here with a car like that? Even as he pondered the question, he feared he knew the answer.

# The White House

The president sat behind the Resolute Desk, so named for the fact that it was carved from the timbers of the H.M.S. Resolute, an abandoned British ship discovered by American sailors. The desk had been a gift from a grateful Queen Victoria to President Rutherford B. Hayes in the 1800s. Despite taking significant fire and water damage during an attack on the White House during the previous administration, Eva had kept the desk in the interest of executive tradition.

As they had done each day since the embassy bombing, the president's Director of National Intelligence, Defense Secretary and Secretary of State engaged in a mid-morning huddle. Aside from morning briefings, which were traditional sit-down affairs, Eva patterned her other meetings after the so-called "stand-ups" preferred in Silicon Valley. The basic idea was to come prepared to discuss what you had accomplished since the last meeting, what your next steps were, and obstacles the president could remove to help you accomplish your goals. The act of standing was essential, since it forced participants to focus on only the most important topics, thus shortening the meeting.

Now the beleaguered commander-in-chief stood across the desk from her charges with a mixture of anticipation and dread. Makeup concealed the deepening age lines around her eyes, but could not hide the dark semi-circles below them.

"Dex," the president began, "Where are we on the embassy bombing?"

Jackson cleared his throat before speaking. "We have learned additional details, Madam President, but nothing yet that would definitively point to a perpetrator. You'll be the first to know when there's any break."

"Keep me posted. Madam Secretary?"

"President Kang is still planning to attend the G8 in Tokyo, but so far, he refuses to come back to the table."

"What's it going to take?"

The Secretary of State laid a document on the table. "For one thing, a televised apology."

The president put on her reading glasses to have a closer look, but not before Speers plunked down the three-inch thick leather booklet Ambassador Nakamura had given him on the antique desk. He topped it with a slew of reconnaissance photographs. "I suggest that you look these over before deciding whether to apologize."

The president's eyes rolled up to meet Speers'. "Context?"

"Japan's official position is that Beijing framed the United States for the embassy bombing. This is their evidence, circumstantial as it may be."

"And China's motivation would be what?"

"To pave the way for an invasion of Japanese territories in the East China Sea," Speers said with skepticism evident in his voice. "Nakamura claims the embassy bombing was part of a wider campaign to weaken U.S. resolve so that we would be reluctant to defend Japan's sovereignty with military force."

"Damned right we would be reluctant. Risk war with the world's largest country over some islands that nobody but Japan cares about? Risk further scrutiny at the United Nations? Our back is up against the wall here."

SECDEF Jackson spoke up again. "Madam President, I think we should take this seriously. If the Chinese control the islands in the East China Sea, they would then control significant trade routes."

"This is one case where economics and defense go hand in hand."

"Exactly, Madam President. We have 50,000 American troops in Japan. Twenty-nine thousand in South Korea. Thousands more in the Philippines. The moment the Chinese take the first strategic objective unopposed, then any semblance of deterrent by our military presence evaporates instantly. And even if you don't believe that we have a moral obligation to defend our allies, we have a duty to keep China from choking economic activity in Asia."

Speers nodded reluctantly. "I have to agree. Nakamura says the Chinese are patterning this after the Russian invasion of the Ukraine. And one of those islands is just a few miles from our bases in Okinawa."

Eva stood, speaking as she stared out at the Rose Garden. "That would put the Chinese right on our doorstep. Dex, do we have a play drawn up for this situation?"

"We do. This scenario came up in our joint war games with the Japanese last year. The situation calls for deploying the Pacific Fleet into the area with a tactical geo-fencing strategy. A virtual perimeter enforced by ships, aircraft, subs and satellites."

"A kill web."

"Yes. But this strategy includes steady rotation of recon drones from our bases in Japan and Korea, and I think this may be another situation where we need an audible at the line of scrimmage. Our drones are grounded, and our carriers now appear to be vulnerable to the DF-21D. That's China's Carrier Killer missile, Madam President."

"I know what it is, Dex."

"Madam President, there is something else. Space weaponry. It's largely untested, but a conservative estimate is that we could take out 80% of China's satellite capability overnight."

Speers groaned. "What's stopping them from retaliating?"

"They'll hit back hard. They're going to hurt us bad. But in the land of the blind, the one-eyed man is king."

# Kaibab National Forest
# Arizona

Purple light crept over the forested valley as Carver hiked up around the pond bank, traversing a steep ridge that overlooked the road. Then he scurried up the hillside until he had found a high point. At last he could see his own vehicle, its white paint barely visible in the half-light.

Further down the road he spotted the sedan, the chrome of its grill glimmering briefly as it powered through a wash that looked, for a few moments at least, as if it might trap the little car in the sand. Carver found the vehicle in his binoculars. The driver, perhaps having had enough of the gut-busting road, pulled to a clearing. Two figures emerged from the car and stepped out onto the dirt. Both were slightly built, but the way they walked and moved indicated that they were men.

Maybe they were hunters. Except for that car. In a land of trucks, why would two hunters not drive a truck? Or at least an all-terrain-vehicle?

The driver walked behind the car and opened the trunk. The other man joined him. It was still barely light, and the open trunk blocked Carver's view, but something about their movements told him they were assembling something.

*Get a grip. At dawn, you can only trust half of what you see. The rest is imagination.*

Duke shivered by his side. Carver crouched, pulling the dog close. Soon the two began walking up the road toward the pond. As the light grew incrementally brighter, Carver could see that one of them carried a long rifle with a scope mounted on top. Maybe a .308 or a .30-06. There was no way to know for sure from a distance. Either way, the scope was telling. If they had come to hunt ducks or geese, they would have been carrying shotguns. Those were in season. A weapon like that was for shooting long distances. Elk or deer. Or people. But the man's sidekick carried a short-barreled weapon with a long clip. A short range machine pistol or assault rifle. An illogical choice for big game.

The serpentine road they walked took them in and out of view. Soon, Carver spotted the blue glow of a phone screen carried by the driver. He peered into it reverentially, as if consulting an oracle.

The landscape seemed to brighten all at once as the huge orange orb broke over the distant mountaintops, warming Carver's face. He drew back behind the foliage to ensure that the lenses of his binoculars didn't reflect the sunlight. He turned, checking the pond behind him. Now he could really see it. Sure enough, the surface was frozen solid. So much for duck hunting. Even if there were still a few flocks in migration, it would be a good three hours before the sun melted the ice enough for any birds to land.

Carver found the men in his binoculars again. They approached the section of road where he had pulled his father's truck into a clearing and parked it.

The point man leaned his rifle against a boulder. Then he straightened up and pulled a handgun from a shoulder holster inside his coat. He then screwed what looked like a muzzle suppressor onto the end.

The suspicious pair split up, crouching, arms at the ready, creeping up on the vehicle from both sides. They soon determined that the truck was unoccupied. The taller of the two pointed his weapon at the passenger-side tire. The muzzle flashed twice.

# Tokyo, Japan

Eri Sato emerged from the easternmost Shinjuku station exit and broke into a brisk run, or as close to a run as she could manage in heels. So as not to be ID'd, her hat was pulled low over her face.

Long black hair grazed her shoulders. Her scarf billowed up around her neck. And although it was well after dark, she wore sunglasses. The fact that she could scarcely see did not matter much. She knew these streets like the back of her hand.

One by one, the sensory guideposts came to her. The sweetly sickening smell of Mister Donut. Check. The rhythmic *ding-ding-ding* of the pachinko parlor on the next block. Check. The sweet potato cart whose owner sang the *yakimo* song over a portable karaoke system.

The Golden Gai neighborhood was home to hundreds of tiny specialty bars. She stopped before the entrance to Autograph – a little dive owned by her best friend – and pretended to look at the cocktail menu while she scanned the street behind her. There was only one way in or out of the tiny place, and before going inside, she had to be sure nobody had followed her.

Now satisfied, Eri descended the steps to the tiny basement-level drinking hole. Autograph was scarcely more than three meters wide, with seating for seven. The walls were filled with memorabilia scrawled with the signatures of movie stars. A color photograph of a young Ryan Gosling. A Beverly Hills Hotel napkin signed by Jennifer Lawrence. A poster of Ken Watanabe in full samurai garb.

*The Sound of Music* soundtrack blared over the speakers. Six college kids were chain-smoking and singing along. The fact that they knew the words to the decades-old classic did not surprise Eri. All the regulars did. The bar's owner, Taka, was an anglophile who played classic Hollywood soundtracks virtually every night.

Taka grinned as he spotted his favorite customer. He swept a hand across his unruly pompadour and then pointed to the end of the bar, where there was one stool remaining. Even if someone *had* been sitting there, he would have asked them to move for Eri.

"*Hisashiburi*," he shouted over the music. Long time no see.

"*Gomen*," Eri apologized before switching to English. "Kentucky Mule, please. A double."

Taka's right eyebrow bent into a boomerang shape. "Eh? It's *like that* tonight, huh?"

Like Eri, Taka had spent some of the best years of his young life in the U.S. before repatriating to Japan to open Autograph. A longing to return to the states one day was the pillar of their friendship.

He leaned in so close that Eri could smell his aftershave. "Everything okay?"

"I can't talk about it."

He pulled back and winked. "Ah. A work thing?"

Eri had never explicitly told Taka that she worked for Japan's Public Security Intelligence Agency. He had guessed one night after a couple strong cocktails. Fortunately for her, he was good at keeping secrets.

Now, as Taka mixed her drink, Eri pulled out the burner phone she had purchased on the streets of Akihabara earlier in the evening. She downloaded the *Age of Undead Ninjas* app, a vintage role-playing game. The basic idea was to slay zombie ninjas. Back in the day, when she first moved to D.C. to live with Carver, they had spent way too many late nights playing it together. Those were the good times. Before his career took over his life.

Tonight she logged into the game with the username "Fluffy." Following the emergency plan she and Carver had agreed to many years ago, she deleted Fluffy's profile description and replaced it with new text: *You are not safe. Meet me at Naked Fish. Tuesday. 1930 hours.*

Then she jammed out a quick nonsensical email. The body text was just a decoy. As Carver would surely remember, the subject line was all that mattered. In that field, she wrote: *Age of the Undead Ninjas.*

It was a message that only Blake Carver would understand. She just prayed that he would see it before it was too late.

# Kaibab National Forest

Duke shivered and whined. Carver bent down to comfort the dog. He used his other hand to slip the backpack off his shoulder and locate Duke's leash. "Sorry," Carver whispered as he fastened Duke's leash to his collar. "Gotta keep you close."

The two assailants had shot out one of his truck tires and continued their walk up the road. It wasn't yet light enough to see their faces through the binoculars, but as the sun continued to break over the mountain, sunlight fell across the road before them. The one on the left turned, giving Carver a view of his backpack.

He had seen it before. In Las Vegas. The Mandalay Bay Casino. On the Asian guy who had crossed the casino floor behind him.

He recalled the poker player's face. Oval, with low cheekbones and a prominent nose. Japanese, perhaps, but there was no way to know for sure.

But why come all the way out here? Carver had created a lot of enemies during his career, but if someone really wanted him dead, it would have been far easier to get to him back in Washington.

Unless it had something to do with Tripoli. Or Nico Gold. Or Jack Brenner. Or the Pink Dragon. Somehow, he had crossed an invisible line.

Even so, how had they found him? The only person who had known he was coming to Arizona was Julian Speers. A man he trusted with his life.

As he watched the men approach in the distance, Carver mentally retraced his steps. He had booked his own flight to Vegas at the counter at Reagan National Airport, just 40 minutes before flight time. And from Vegas, having made last-minute tickets, he had flown a tiny commuter plane to Flagstaff, where the airport was a single-airline hub that was scarcely bigger than a bowling alley. He had studied the face of every person on both planes. The assassin he had seen in Vegas wasn't on either aircraft.

Fast-forward to this morning. The only person who had knowledge of his plans had been...

...his father.

# Beijing

Jasper Blick stepped outside the print shop, holding one of his new business cards up to the scrutiny of sunlight. Or at least what passed for sunlight on a red alert day. The gray haze was thick and low to the ground for the fifth day in a row. He liked to say that if the ladies of Beijing didn't kill him, the air quality just might.

To his eye, the business cards looked authentic. *"I'm Massive!"* he said with vigor. He had purchased a good thick card stock. The MassiveStreamz logo looked authentic. If there was one thing Chinese manufacturers were excellent at, it was the art of forgery.

He checked his watch. Titus was due to call at any moment. Despite the ministry of environmental protection's warnings about spending prolonged periods outside, Blick stopped dead in his tracks while he still had a strong mobile signal.

What a crazy predicament he had gotten himself into. This guy Titus was both employer *and* blackmailer. He had – how had Titus put it? – *plucked* Blick out of the slush pile of humanity, and hacked into his bank account. As Blick saw it, his only choice was to roll with his strange new adventure and see where it led.

The phone rang right on cue, and his employer/blackmailer spoke even before he could. "Do you have the business cards?"

"I do. And they're ah-amaz-ing!"

"Pull that mask off. I can barely hear you."

Blick pulled the face mask down below his chin. "Yes, I was just saying that I have the cards. I'm officially David Stone, SVP Entertainment Content, MassiveStreamz, at your service."

"A car service will pick you up in an hour. The driver will take you to a warehouse, where you'll pick up five boxes. Each box contains 20 MassiveStreamz Sticks."

"Those things that people plug into their TVs to stream movies and stuff? Aren't those pretty much banned here in China?"

"Of course they are. Our entire plan depends on it."

"Okay then. Five boxes. Twenty sticks each. What then?"

"You're going to deliver them to a government worker named Zhang Wei at Zhongnanhai."

"Zhongnan-what?"

Titus sighed. "You've been in Beijing for three years, and you still don't know where the president of China works? Look it up. Listen, I sent a script to your email, and I'm expecting a top-notch performance from you."

"Not to worry. I keep the bar for my acting very high."

"I've already contacted Zhang Wei on your behalf, so he'll be waiting for you at the Zhongnanhai gate. Your job is to convince him that MassiveStreamz Entertainment will do anything – *anything!* – to get government approval to sell streaming content within China. As a sign of your goodwill, you are presenting him with a gift of 100 free streaming sticks, which he will personally deliver to the 100 most important officials in the Communist Party. Make a point to emphasize all the banned American TV shows they'll be able to stream."

"One question. What makes you sure he won't just sell these things out of the trunk of his car?"

"I hacked into his back account. That's the stick. Then I deposited cash. That's the carrot. Sound familiar?"

# Kaibab National Forest

A cold wind stirred as the sun crept over the horizon, further illuminating the forested valley before him and the purple-tinged mountains in the distance. The assassins came back into view. They were perhaps four football fields away, walking along a gulch that led in his general direction.

For professional hit men, they walked clumsily. They stepped heavily, trampling dried branches that broadcast their movement. Rabbits and squirrels that might have otherwise sat tight, waiting for them to pass, fled well ahead of their advance. It was clear that they had no formal military training. But that made them no less dangerous. If anything, they were less predictable.

The wind let up and it was suddenly very still. It was then that the dog heard it - a high-pitched whistling noise. Duke looked up and barked twice. Carver followed the dog's gaze.

A tiny low-altitude S33KR drone, scarcely 14 inches in length, hovered just 40 feet overhead.

The S33KR was essentially a bloodhound with wings. Carver had attended a private demonstration of its capabilities some two years earlier, at which time the drone had been marketed as a cheaper and more effective alternative to helicopter coverage during manhunts. One of its most impressive features was the ability to use thermal imaging to systematically sweep a predefined area, and relay live aerial footage back to law enforcement.

So *this* was what the assassins had been assembling in the pre-dawn light. They were using it to track him.

Carver pushed the stock of his father's 12-gauge shotgun against his right shoulder and raised the barrel. When he pulled the trigger, some three hundred birdshot pellets blasted forth, clipping the little drone and sending it into a death spiral.

Something hot nicked Carver's left ear. An instant later the thunderous report of a heavy caliber rifle shot erupted throughout the valley.

Carver grabbed Duke and slid down the backside of the ridge as fast as he could, determined not to give his assailants another distance shot. Once he had found cover behind the hill, he paused momentarily to remove the battery from his phone. Unreliable as cell service was in that neck of the woods, there was just one explanation for the fact that they had followed him there – the S33KR drone had somehow penetrated one of the location-based apps on his phone.

With Duke on the leash, Carver headed down a game trail heading due south. The typically obedient dog pulled obstinately. It was no wonder. He had been trained to retrieve waterfowl immediately after the blast of a shotgun. He couldn't understand why Carver was retreating from the kill area.

The trail meandered and narrowed as they went. After just 20 minutes, Carver, who ran three miles daily back in D.C. but wasn't used to the high elevation, was already winded.

He pushed on nevertheless. They ran for 15 more minutes until they came across a mountain spring that hadn't completely frozen over. Carver checked his six. Nothing moving. He dropped to a knee and let the dog drink, but not too much. Then he too drank. And then he splashed the frigid water on his face and hair.

They retreated to a nearby thicket where they had a partial view the valley to the south. Duke settled in beside him.

His left ear stung badly. Carver swatted it with his fingers, expecting to find a wasp or bee. Nothing flew. He then probed with his fingertips, and did not like what he discovered.

The top of his ear - the outer rim called the helix - was no longer smooth and contoured. He had been shot. Thanks to the assassin's bullet, blood oozed from a dime-sized semi-circle notch in the top of his ear. Had the bullet traveled an inch to the left, Carver knew, he would be missing far more than some skin and cartilage.

He tore off a piece of his shirt and applied pressure to the wound. The bleeding, in his estimation, was not bad enough to have left a blood trail. At least there was that.

The mind chatter started up again. Who were these people? Why had they followed him out here? How had they even known he would be here in the first place?

*Stop. Reign it in. Slow your heart rate. Everything in its right place.*

He focused on what he had seen through his binoculars that morning, assessing his adversaries. Replaying every image in his mind, looking for any detail he might have missed. Yes, they had technology and firepower on their side. But they did not walk like experienced outdoorsmen, or even men who had ever had military training. They had moved out in the open, sticking to the road, where they could have easily been picked off. They had worn sneakers, stepping clumsily on dried sticks and other noisy ground cover. They had walked continuously, never stopping to glass the hillsides for the glint of a metallic object or the reflection of a riflescope. They had instead relied entirely on the data from the drone, never changing course until it had located Carver and relayed his location.

Carver considered his options for escape. These were his old stomping grounds, and virtually every game trail and contour of these forests was etched in his memory. He and Duke could easily travel southeast, sticking to the brushy ridges, until they reached I-40. From there they would cross and travel the back roads, reaching the town of Williams before dark.

That wasn't a good option. Because sooner or later they would give up looking for him and head back to the truck. And when they did that, they would find his father's registration card, which had his address. Then they would surely head to the ranch. Unless, God forbid, they hadn't been there already.

Besides, Carver decided, he had to know who they were. And more importantly, who had hired them.

Since nicking him with the rifle shot, he reckoned that the assassins had likely split up, dividing and conquering the territory. They might hunt for two or three more hours before giving up.

Had Carver been alone, he would have taken them one at a time out here in the woods. Stalk, hit and run. But with Duke beside him, there was virtually no chance of success. The dog's natural instincts were to run, flush and circle back, over and over again, with his human companion the center of his universe.

*But the dog was also trained to wait patiently, hours at a time if needed, in a duck blind.*

It was settled, then. If Carver couldn't stalk these men, then he would ambush them.

# Kaibab National Forest

Carver tore off another piece of his shirt and used it to fashion a muzzle for Duke. "Sorry bud," he said as he wrapped it around the dog's snout, careful not to restrict his breathing. "This is the only way I can keep you from blowing our cover." The pair set out again at a slow pace, sweeping up and around the next ridge, circling back northeast toward the road they had come in on before dawn.

Fifty-seven minutes later they came full circle. Carver settled Duke behind some underbrush, and then topped a rocky crest overlooking both the road and the pond. He raised his binoculars and glassed the surrounding area. He saw neither the men nor any drones. He also didn't see any other people. He reckoned the gut-busting road and the gate might be enough deterrent to keep most people out.

A pair of ducks circled high above the pond. They swooshed in low, taking a close look at the duck blinds, and then disappeared over the ridge before circling back again. Carver found them in his binoculars as they made their final approach. Green-winged teal. Nice fat ones that would have made a good dinner.

The ducks spread their wings wide, arched their backs and extended their legs like fleshy landing gear. And when their paddles hit the layer of ice covering the little pond, they slid in what could only be described as a controlled crash before lifting off again, deliriously quacking and honking as they went back over the horizon in search of warmer water.

Looking out along the road, he saw that the Toyota sedan remained where he had last seen it this morning. That meant that the assassins were still out here, somewhere. Carver hoped they were still far afield. He needed more time to get into position.

He and Duke moved on, remaining high above the road, following a sheltered trail that gave him intermittent visuals on the canyon below. Soon he was directly above and across from his father's truck. The two-ton vehicle seemed to hunch painfully over the shot tire.

He spotted a pair of mature bucks grazing on the opposing hillside. That was a good sign. They would never be so calm with those clumsy bushwhackers tromping around. Deeming the immediate area safe, he did not linger, silently making his way to the hillside to his east until the Toyota sedan was directly below him. He inspected it with his binoculars. The license plate frame read FLAGSTAFF RENT-A-RIDE.

Carver found a flat piece of earth under a pine skirt with both a view of the car and cover on both sides. He took the Leatherman from his pocket, pulled out the little saw, and cut pieces of the pine skirt just enough so that he could bend them over him to form a canopy.

He tethered Duke's leash to the tree, then lay prone and waited as the dog slept.

The mind chatter came and went like ocean tides. Old combat experiences played endlessly in his head. He struggled to focus on the present.

*Everything in its right place.*

Around a quarter till noon, noon, the two men came ambling back down the road. Both were breathing hard, no doubt whipped by the altitude. One of them was actually limping. Neither spoke, but they walked with guns brandished, right in the center of the road, like they owned it.

Perhaps sensing Carver's tension, the dog shifted awake and let out a whine that was no more audible than the wind. Carver laid a reassuring hand on the animal's shoulder. *Shhhh.*

He felt the dog quiver with excitement as Carver held the butt of the Mossberg shotgun to his shoulder and peered down the length of its barrel. He would only have one chance at this. And given that he was packing birdshot, his targets would have to be at close range.

Carver waited until the two men were directly in front of the car, about 25 yards below him.

Suddenly, one of them spoke. *"Samui, ne?"*

"So desu ka."

Were his ears playing tricks on him, or were they speaking Japanese? Although Carver was inexplicably terrible at speaking foreign languages, he could understand several. During his year abroad in Japan, just after college, Eri had tried – and failed – to make him conversationally fluent. Nevertheless, he had committed more than 3,000 words of Japanese to memory.

Now Carver took aim. He fired two shots in quick succession. He hit the shorter man directly in the center of his back, the shot forming a jagged circle in his jacket about 20 inches in diameter. He aimed to maim the other man, blowing out his left knee, causing him to drop his TEK-9 machine pistol. When he reached for it, Carver fired again, blowing the weapon out of his reach, as if God himself had exhaled a mighty breath. The boulder behind him was a canvas of blood, tissue and bone.

Carver left Duke muzzled and tied to the tree for his own safety. Then he got to his feet and slid by the heels of his boots down the ridge, keeping his eyes and weapon trained on the one who was still alive.

The assailant's eyes were weepy and bloodshot. His right hand was a gooey mess. As he saw Carver close the distance between them, shotgun in hand, he defecated in his pants.

Carver braved the stench, pushing the Mossberg into the man's abdomen. "Who sent you?"

That was the most important question to ask in the moments before death. Discovering this man's identity would be relatively easy. Within 24 hours, the Guardian could likely learn his alias, his birth name, who his parents were and where he had gone to school. But finding a professional hit man's employer was exponentially more difficult.

The man glared at him and spat. Semi-transparent spittle landed in a gooey clump on Carver's chin. He wiped it with his jacket sleeve and then stepped on the man's blown out knee with the heel of his boot. The man howled.

"Tell me who sent you."

"Wakarimasen!"

"*Nihonjin?*" Carver said. You're Japanese?

The would-be assassin made a quick grab into his jacket pocket.

"Don't!" Carver yelled as the attacker reached for his secondary weapon. It was too late. Carver stepped back, blasting his chest with birdshot.

A loaded Beretta fell from the dead man's hand.

Carver dropped to a knee. His ears rang. Duke was barking now, having managed to work free of the muzzle, but Carver could barely hear him.

He needed a minute to think. And catch his breath.

Speers' words loomed large in his mind. *Don't do anything stupid. This thing is going to blow over, I promise.*

He had shot these men in self-defense, but it might not look that way to a judge. The intelligence community already thought of him as the grim reaper, and a task force was getting ready to burn him at the stake. Adding two more notches to his belt wasn't going to help at all.

*So there it is. No one can know about this. Not even Julian.*

Carver whistled. Duke stopped barking. He settled down again, watching Carver as he dragged both corpses behind the rental car, where both the vehicle and a cluster of pine trees would shelter his activities. Then he set about searching the bodies. Given that he had shot both at close range with birdshot, there was no way to avoid getting his hands sticky.

He pulled a game bag from his vest that he had intended to fill with ducks. Instead he filled it with the duo's personal possessions – rings, watches, miscellaneous paper from their pockets, phones, the remote control for the S33KR drone, and a hair sample from each man.

Their passports gave him pause. Maroon-colored passports from the People's Republic of China. They were also biometric, containing a microprocessor chip with the bearer's image and fingerprints.

And they were most certainly faked. After all, he had heard the two men speaking Japanese with native fluency. He was sure of it. It didn't add up. English, not Japanese, was the primary business language learned in China.

No time to dwell on that now. He had to collect evidence that might help him identify these men. He would then destroy anything that could tie him to the shootings.

Using a plastic bag over his right hand to avoid leaving fingerprints, Carver also searched the car, but found nothing of potential value except the rental agreement. He took it, along with the rental company's license and registration.

He heard the buzz of helicopter blades in the distance. He thought of the local hospital in Williams. Hadn't there been a helipad? Carver froze, steadying his breathing as he surveyed the skies.

*Relax. Nobody's going to come looking for these guys. Nobody even knows that they are in the country.*

The sound dissolved into the ambient tapestry of bird chatter. Carver relaxed and resumed his work.

He lifted the hood of the rental car and disconnected the battery, making the car nearly impossible to ping from a remote server. Then he removed the license plates along with the silver plate from the interior that was inscribed with the Vehicle Identification Number. Later today, he would dump them in a different location.

Now Carver broke off the rear view mirror from the rental car and pressed a fingerprint sample from both men onto it. He wrapped it in cloth and put it into his father's truck for safekeeping. Surveying the stripped vehicle, he considered setting it ablaze. *No. That might just draw unnecessary attention.* Instead he collected dead brush and laid the branches over the top of the vehicle, making it harder to spot from the air.

At last he would dispose of the bodies. He had observed long ago that shallow graves were the undoing of many killers. Better to leave them unburied, he knew, but away from the road. This country was thick with all sorts of carnivores. Mountain lions and bobcats and coyotes and bears. By dawn, he reckoned the bodies would be eaten to the bone, and within three days, the bones themselves would be scattered across several square miles of wilderness.

He lifted one of the corpses and carried it to a nearby wash where he had seen coyote tracks that morning. He began removing the man's clothes, which he would dump elsewhere. He used a hunting knife to cut the pants and shirt away from the body. Meanwhile he inspected the flesh for any tattoos or birthmarks that could help with identification. Seeing nothing on the man's chest, arms or legs, he turned the body, and in doing so, found more than he could have hoped for.

The symbol was imprinted on the man's lower back, just above the beltline. A symmetrical design about four inches in diameter. An orb with thick bands emanating from the center. The Rising Sun, the Japanese war flag that had first been used during the 1870s, and had become internationally notorious as the symbol of the Imperial Japanese Empire during World War II.

But it wasn't a tattoo. The Rising Sun had actually been *burned* into the man's flesh. He had been *branded*.

The only other time he had seen something like this was in college. Members of the Omega Psi Phi fraternity had the omega symbol branded on their arms or chests. It had always seemed to Carver like an unreasonably high price to pay for membership.

Now he sat up and took a deep breath, considering the significance of such body art. For decades, Americans had tattooed themselves with all manner of Asian imagery, ranging from dragons to Kanji. But this – a brand burned into the flesh – had to mean something more than just whimsical body art.

His curiosity piqued, he dragged the other body to the wash, turned the assassin, and cut the shirt away. And there it was. Four inches of raised scar tissue on the lower back. The Rising Sun brand.

These guys were part of the same club, all right. And he was betting it was no friendly frat.

# Tokyo

As Eri returned to Autograph for the second time in as many hours, the last drunks were just stumbling up the steps to the street. Taka was shuttering the place. He froze when he saw her, as if caught in headlights. He reached out and wiped a bit of her smudged eyeliner away with his thumb.

"Can I crash here at the bar tonight?"

Taka's typically jovial face transformed into one of pure concern. "You're in trouble?"

She nodded. There was no use in pretending. "Two of my colleagues are dead. Murdered."

"Did you try the police?"

"They think it was suicide."

"How – "

"It's complicated, Taka."

And it was. Just one thing was for sure – she couldn't go home again. Ever. She thought about leaving the country, but there was still one loose end. Blake hadn't responded to her message. She feared it was too late. But she had to hold out one more day at least. Just in case he decided to come.

"Taka…"

"Shhh. Eri, don't say another word. You can come to my place tonight."

"No. That's far too generous. I can just stay here."

He sported a wry grin. "And leave you alone here with my booze? No way. You know that American saying about leaving the fox in the henhouse."

# Kaibab National Forest

It took Carver longer to change the truck tire than it did to move the bodies. As he had predicted, no one else had come in on the pipeline road, and their only company was the turkey vultures that were already circling over the corpses. Now he used a tree branch to sweep up his tracks in and around the kill.

Satisfied, he opened the truck door and motioned for Duke to jump in. The dog looked at him sheepishly, wagging his tail.

"So I'm not the only one who's sore," Carver said. He bent down and scooped the dog up into his arms. He lifted Duke into the passenger seat. "Make yourself comfortable, bud. We're taking the long way home."

To minimize the chances that they were seen leaving the area, he would avoid the direct route back out I-40, where he knew there were both wildlife cameras and highway patrol. Instead he drove his father's truck deeper into the backcountry, navigating a series of logging roads that had devolved over the years into little more than muddy ruts. Eventually, he knew, he would get back to the main pipeline road and head out to the two-lane highway headed toward Flagstaff.

The slow crawl through the mountains afforded him plenty of time to think about his would-be assassins. The Rising Sun brands mystified him. Japan was a place where pristine skin was held in especially high regard. Most spas and gyms wouldn't admit anyone with a single tattoo, much less branded flesh. A notable exception was the Yakuza, for whom extensive ink was a rite of passage. But Carver, who had studied his fair share of Yakuza body art, couldn't recall a single instance of the crime syndicate branding their members.

The Rising Sun flag itself was associated with Japanese imperialism, having been the official Japanese flag from 1877 until

Japan's surrender to American forces in 1945. These days, it lived mainly on the ships of the Japan Maritime Self Defense Force.

Was it possible that Japanese sailors had taken to branding the symbol onto their backs? Maybe. But even if they had, it did nothing to explain why these two wanted him dead. The more he drove, the more convinced he became that there was some connection to the embassy bombing.

He switched on the radio for the first time today. Willie Nelson sang out in a surprisingly clear voice. Carver didn't follow country music, but as with any song he'd heard at least once, he knew all the words.

*You're like the measles, you're like the whooping cough*
*I've already had you, so why in heaven's name can't you just get lost?*

Around 2:00 p.m. they came to a utility road that took them out to a two-lane highway heading to Flagstaff. He thought of his sister and young nephews. Although he saw them twice a year at most, they talked often, and his sister sent lots of videos to keep Carver abreast of their development. Still, for them, each visit was as if they were meeting their uncle for the first time. In adults, he found memory loss highly irritating. With the boys, however, he found it cute.

He stopped at the first full-service auto repair shop he came across. His first order of business was getting a new tire to replace the one that had been shot up. He pulled his black beanie over the tops of both ears. The notched left ear stung like crazy, but at least it was hidden, and would not be a conversation piece for every person he met.

Out front, there was a dirty and disused public pay phone. To Carver's great surprise, it still had a dial tone. The phone rang seven times. At last, a wave of relief washed over Carver as his father picked up.

"Expected you back by now," the old man said.

"The pond was frozen over, so I decided to do some exploring. Hey, did you get any visitors out to the ranch today?"

"Nope. Were you expecting someone?"

"No, Pop. Okay then. I'll see you tonight."

Inside, the shop owner said he could have a replacement tire – and a matching mud flap – delivered within two hours. He pressed $20 into the man's grease-blackened palm to hurry things up.

While he waited, he tossed his would-be assassins' license plate and hand-shredded rental contract into a dumpster bin around back, along with his cell phone SIP card and the spent shotgun shells.

In the adjacent convenience store, he bought a first-aid kit and took it into the restroom. He disinfected the wound on his ear and slathered it in liquid bandage. It looked a bit worse than he had expected. A semi-circular piece of flesh and cartilage was missing. Not the kind of thing that would simply grow back perfectly. If he wanted both ears to be symmetrical again, he would have to see a plastic surgeon.

But not today. The best he could do today was keep it from getting infected. After that, he would try to find out who was trying to kill him, and why.

By the time he had tucked the bandaged ear under the beanie once again, he had decided that the easiest way to learn their identities was to log into the Guardian portal and plug his assailants' passports into the system. Given that Julian had put him on administrative leave, it was a risky move, and one that could come with additional repercussions. But if he could get a match, perhaps something from their profiles — however incidental — would trigger a revelation.

There was just one problem. His laptop was stitched into his mattress at the Two Elk Ranch, with neither an Internet connection nor a cell phone signal within miles of the place. There were presumably dozens of public computers up at the university in Flagstaff, but there would also be surveillance cameras, and his online activities might be tracked or even blocked by the university's IT department.

Then he remembered that his sister had a computer in the den of her home, where the kids did their homework. Her place was maybe 30 minutes away. Besides, it would be good to see the kids.

He put more change into the pay phone and called his sister. She answered on the first ring, sounding more relaxed than he had heard her in ages. "I decided to drop into town," he told her. "Mind if I stop by?"

Instead of an invitation, he received a scolding. "Why didn't you tell me you were coming? We're up at Lake Powell. Do you realize you missed Luke's birthday?"

Carver apologized his way through the rest of the call, deflecting pressure to drive several hours north and join the family up at the lake. He considered asking for permission to go to the house and use the computer anyhow, but arrived at the inevitable conclusion that common courtesy would bring more harm than good. What possible reason could he come up with? None. He would simply have to break in.

# Flagstaff, Arizona

His sister's family lived in a modest rambler on a half-acre lot near the Lowell Observatory. A smattering of early snow, mostly melted and dirtied over the course of three days, whitened the shadowy portions of his sister's front yard in the late afternoon sun. Carver parked down the road a bit behind some trees. Then, with Duke on the leash, he cut through the forest until he came to the back of the home. There was no fence, affording an unobstructed view of the snow-capped peaks in the distance.

He immediately set about looking for the hidden key. Not that she had ever mentioned hiding one. He knew her too well.

Sure enough, Carver spotted the fake rock hide-a-key from Walmart beside the back door. As if any fool wouldn't have noticed how different the texture was from the volcanic rocks around it. He made a mental note to give her an alarm system for Christmas.

He let himself in, and then went straight to the fridge, where he found several leftover sausages in a Ziploc bag. He fed one to Duke, and then ate one himself. Cold, so as not to smell up the place.

Carver lingered on the family photos on the fridge. The boys, all dressed up in their youth hockey uniforms. The boys, riding on Pop's tractor. The boys, snuggled up with Mom on the front porch. Man, they were growing up fast. He had to get out here more often.

He went the living room and sat before the family computer. The mammoth size of the screen felt luxurious. With Duke at his feet, he logged into an anonymous web browser and routed the connection through an IP mask that made it seem as if he was logging in from Washington. Then he inputted the 32-digit alphanumeric URL, and tried signing into the Guardian network.

It didn't work. Somewhere, Carver knew, an IT security person at the Office of the Director of National Security had just received an intruder alert. He severed the connection before it could be traced.

Julian's voice popped into his head. *These are serious accusations. As of this moment, you're on administrative leave.* Somehow, he had thought Julian wouldn't sever the umbilical cord so officially. But he had. All semblance of trust was lost.

What now? His ear stung like crazy. He rose, went to the freezer, and found a bag of frozen peas, which he strapped to his head with a jumbo-size rubber band that he found in his sister's kitchen junk drawer. The cold numbed the pain.

With access to his investigative tools now cut off, he was going to have to call in favors. Ellis was out of the question. So too was Kyra Javan. He decided to call Arunus Roth. The kid had only been at Guardian for a little over a year, but Carver had looked out for him during the initial probationary phase and later recommended him for a permanent place on the team. That should earn him some loyalty.

He went back to the machine, booted up the web browser's VoIP app and the IP mask, and put in the call. Roth answered on the first ring.

"It's me," Carver said. "Don't hang up."

"I got a visit by some very unpleasant dudes this morning," Roth said.

"Office of Security?"

"Yup. They told me not to take your calls. But seeing as how you always looked out for me..."

"What exactly did they tell you?"

"They wanted to make sure I knew you were persona non-grata. They scheduled a time tomorrow when I'm supposed to walk them through the investigations into Jessica Wu and Jack Brenner. Sounded kind of serious."

"What else?"

"They started rummaging through your office."

Carver leaned back in his chair. He wiped his hand from his face. Was this really happening? Until now, he had hung onto the idea that his exile from the intelligence community would blow over after the G8, when the president would no doubt smooth this whole thing with China over. But now, for the first time, he realized he could find himself on the outside looking in for a long time. Possibly forever.

He decided to put up a brave face for Roth. The kid idolized him. "It's worse than it looks, Arunus. I'll be back soon enough."

"I saw them talking to Ellis. Just saying, I don't think she's your friend right now, bro."

God, he hated it when the kid called him 'bro.' It grated on him like little else. But now was not the time.

"Julian will handle it. In the meantime, I need a favor."

"Name it."

Carver used his sister's scanner, uploaded the assailants' passports, and sent them over the encrypted network. Then he held the line while Roth went to work crunching their identities.

Ten minutes later, Roth was back. "Those passports were checked through Tokyo Narita Airport a little over a week ago."

"Where to?"

"Washington. Then they were checked again at Dulles yesterday morning for a flight en route to Las Vegas."

So the assailants *had* been in Washington when Brenner was killed. Maybe they had even been in the pub where they arrested him. If Roth was right that someone had killed Brenner by hacking into his insulin pump, what would stop them from hacking into Carver's phone as well?

"Good stuff, Arunus. What can you see prior to Tokyo? There was a customs stamp showing that they had flown into Beijing at some point."

"Weird. Nope. It's like these passports didn't even exist prior to that. Unless, of course, they came into Japan illegally."

Just as he had thought, the passports were fakes. This, coupled with the fact that they had been speaking Japanese even amongst each other, was just too strange to chalk it up to anything else.

"Thanks, Arunus. Keep this to yourself, all right?"

"Anytime, bro."

Carver disconnected and logged out.

The assailants sounded Japanese. Looked Japanese. *Were* Japanese. Unfortunately, that meant Carver was back to square one. He had no idea who these people were or why they wanted him dead.

The only thing he knew for sure was that he was exhausted. The frozen peas had thoroughly numbed his ear, and the absence of pain had made him sleepy. Duke's rhythmic breathing was hypnotic. Carver's own eyes grew heavy too.

As he reclined on the couch, he heard the train pass through downtown, the predictable syncopation of its wheels against the tracks. *Ch-ch-chaff. Ch-ch-chaff. Ch-ch-chaff. Everything. Everything. Everything.*

# Flagstaff, Arizona

Carver woke on the living room couch as night fell. All at once, his eyes shot open. The only illumination in his sister's house was the blue light of the computer.

*Eri!* In the madness of the past three days, he had neglected to call her back. And it just so happened that he needed her now. She worked for Japanese domestic intelligence, and as such, she might be able to pull up more information on his assailants.

He crawled to the computer, rose up on his knees, booted up the anonymous browser, and logged into his personal email. Spooky. A new message from Eri Sato was waiting in his inbox. The subject line: *Age of the Undead Ninjas*

He knew what he would find next before he even opened the message. It was the coded emergency message they had created way back when they were living together in D.C. Carver had received his first assignment abroad that year, and they had created the system as a way to communicate if everything went to hell in a handbasket.

*Everything that is, is not. Everything is, yet at the same time, nothing is. I myself am the emptiest of all. XOXO, Eri*

A quote from the Japanese artist and philosopher, Kawai Kanjiro. The quote itself was meaningless misdirection. The subject line was what really mattered. Age of the Undead Ninjas was an old first-person shooting game featuring zombie ninjas. He and Eri had created a profile within the game called "Fluffy," and the real message would be hidden within that profile.

Suddenly, Duke woke with a start. He growled, low and menacing. Headlights shot across the room. A vehicle had pulled into the drive.

Carver recognized the sound of his sister's old gas-guzzler.

*Oh God. They're home early.*

He could just imagine the look on her face as he quickly spun some completely improbable explanation for his presence in the house. He had to finish up and get out.

First, he slipped Duke's leash on and anchored it under his chair. He made the dog sit. "Shhh."

Returning to the keyboard, he frantically pounded out the URL for Age of the Undead Ninjas. Meanwhile in the background, he heard the car door open. Squeaky door hinges penetrated the otherwise blissful night. One of the boys was crying. Maybe he had gotten seasick. Or sunburned. Whatever the reason, Carver was out of time.

Duke whined. Carver tried to focus. He located the Fluffy profile. Sure enough, it had been updated just 58 minutes earlier. The new text in the character description section: *You are not safe. Meet me at Naked Fish. Tuesday Night. 1930 Hours.*

Two car doors slammed. Duke let out a startled woof. Again, Carver signaled for him to be quiet. He re-read Eri's message. *You are not safe. Meet me at Naked Fish. Tuesday Night. 1930 Hours.*

Well she was right about one thing. He *wasn't* safe. But how would she know that? Did that mean she had known the brand brothers were coming for him? And then there was the name, Naked Fish. It wasn't even the name of a real place. It was an inside joke that only they shared.

What they called Naked Fish was really a restaurant called Sushify, located in Tokyo's Shibuya ward. It had been a small, exclusive place located on the second floor of an otherwise nondescript building. It had but one item on the menu – the Chef's Special. Carver recalled watching in both horror and fascination as the chef plucked a fish straight out of a massive aquarium behind him, held the squirming fish on a cutting board, and using one of the sharpest knives he'd ever seen, expertly stripped the sashimi from the fish's side. He served it to them immediately. The fish's head, spine and tail were still on the plate too. The odd experience of tasting the still-twitching flesh while the "naked fish" peered up at him had been disturbing, to say the least.

Carver heard the metallic grinding of keys in the front door. He stood, re-reading the message one last time. *Meet me at Naked Fish.*

Eri was the opposite of a frivolous person. She had been, in fact, a little too practical and moody for Carver's liking. Eri wouldn't ask him to come to Japan unless it was a matter of life or death. Unless a face-to-face meeting was the only way to safely communicate about something of the utmost importance.

But there was the task force to think of. *Two days from now. FBI headquarters. Can I count on you to show up?* He had promised, but there was no way to be in both Tokyo and Washington at the same time.

He heard the front door open. Both nephews were crying now. Every part of him wanted to go embrace them.

Duke whined, but the kids were far too loud for him to be heard. Working at a furious pace, Carver clicked to edit the Age of the Undead Shoguns character description. He erased Eri's message, and replaced it with one word: *Banzai.*

His sister's voice, which had no doubt been soothing and supportive earlier, was shrill. *"Go to your room and take off your clothes! It's time for your bath!"*

Carver powered the computer down. He took Duke up into his arms and carried the dog out the back door. Hopeful that his nephews' wails would mask the sound, he locked the deadbolt behind him.

There was no moon tonight. Despite the full dark, he managed to replace the spare key in the hide-a-key rock from Wal-Mart. Then he put Duke on the leash. They fled into the forest just as the kitchen lights came on behind them. Carver treaded carefully, taking care not to sprain an ankle while traversing the woods back to the truck.

As they walked slowly, he calculated his options. Julian's words fully inhabited his thoughts. *Can I count on you to meet with the task force? Think about your answer carefully.*

It was what Julian didn't say that was more telling. *Don't make me send someone to take you into custody.*

The more he thought about it, the more he was convinced that the task force would be a kangaroo court. Hadn't Julian said as much? *Go visit your parents. While you still can.* In his most paranoid moments, he reckoned the president was fanning the flames because he had refused the National Security Advisor role. And if her task force didn't nail him, then the intelligence committee would. It was just a matter of time.

That settled it. He would not be boarding a plane to Washington tomorrow. For better or worse, he was going to meet Eri.

She wanted to meet at 7:30 p.m. local time. The time difference between Arizona and Tokyo was sixteen hours. The closest airport offering nonstop service? Los Angeles International. And that was six and a half hours by car, or three hours flying a shuttle between Flagstaff and Phoenix. Either way, once he got to L.A., he was looking at 10 more hours in flight time over the Pacific.

He would also need to drop Duke off at the ranch. And somehow find time to eat and hydrate. It was an insane schedule, to be sure. But if he left now, and pushed the speed limit, he might just make it.

# PART IV

# Tokyo Imperial Palace

The black Lexus carrying Prime Minister Akira Ito stopped over the moat at Sakashita Gate, just outside the imperial palace walls. The handsome PM, who was famous for conveying a contagious sense of confidence, sat pensively. His lips moved as he silently practiced the talking points he would use during his meeting with the emperor.

The palace guards surrounded the car and swept its undercarriage for bombs. Ito's left hand fondled the long, thin package containing the ancient sword that he would present to the old monarch as a gift. One that was sure to make a lasting impression.

A white-gloved guard on horseback escorted the vehicle to a circular driveway, where the emperor's chief of staff was waiting. Ito stepped out of the car and the two men bowed simultaneously. When he straightened, the chief of staff's eyes lingered on the exquisitely wrapped gift. "I assume that is for his majesty?"

"Just so."

"Excuse me, Prime Minister. May I please inspect it?"

"I think your men have kept his majesty waiting long enough, don't you?"

The chief of staff hesitated before relenting. "Very well. Please follow me."

He led Ito through the palace grounds, which offered a delicious taste of nature in the midst of the world's largest city. Gold and crimson maple leaves glistened in the breeze. The palace was a far cry from the PM's official residence across town – a shimmering, glass-covered cube in Tokyo's government district. The monstrosity had been built in 2002 on the site of the former PM residence, which although small, had featured a pleasing blend of Eastern and Western architectural styles heavily influenced by Frank Lloyd Wright.

Ito's wife hated the official residence even more than he did. Over dinner at an expensive eel restaurant in Ginza, she had informed him that the grounds were haunted by Tsuyoshi Inukai, the prime minister who had been assassinated on the property in 1932. The security guards that guarded the place had confirmed the rumors, she said, before informing him that she would not be moving in. What was the point, she had asked in a tone that was more pragmatic than cynical. After all, the average time in office for a Japanese PM was just 18 months.

She did not realize that her husband had no intention of leaving office. Not in 18 months. Not ever.

Ito looked no further than Vladimir Putin as a 21st century example of a democratically elected official who had managed to hold onto power long past the confines of his official term. And of course there had been many others. Muammar Gaddafi had held on for 41 years in Libya. Then there was Fidel Castro, who had served as Prime Minister for 17 years before switching to the title of President for several more decades.

But Ito had resisted the temptation to share this plan with his wife. His Restoration Party had survived largely due to their extraordinary ability to keep secrets. There was no sense in adding additional risk just to impress his spouse.

Now the imperial chief of staff led him to a small garden with brightly colored koi swimming in a reflecting pool. The chief of staff gestured toward a pair of brightly colored fabric slippers. "His majesty has tea overlooking the garden every day at this time. You may join him now."

Ito swapped his loafers for the slippers and ascended the short staircase. He found the white-haired emperor in an elevated, open-air tatami-mat room. He sat on his knees, straight-backed, wearing a practiced stoic expression. He wore gray wool pants and black tuxedo tails that were splayed neatly behind him. His skin was textured with age, as if it had been painted with an oil brush.

Ito stood before him and bowed. The emperor bowed in return, but did not stand. He then gestured to a pillow on the floor on the other side of a 14-inch dark wood table.

"Your Majesty," Ito said, "thank you for seeing me. I apologize for any inconvenience my request for a meeting has caused."

The irony of Ito's humility was not lost on either man. As prime minister, Ito now had what the emperor did not — real power. And yet social etiquette demanded that he show the throne the same level of ceremonial respect that had been maintained for over two thousand years.

The emperor's father had in fact been Japan's last true imperial ruler. These days, while the royal family remained extremely popular, and talk of royal weddings and babies dominated the tabloids, the office was, in fact, largely ceremonial.

Ito knelt before the table, holding the oblong present in his outstretched hands. The emperor thanked him, took it wordlessly, and passed it to his white-gloved butler.

"Your Majesty," Ito said. "If you please, may I have the pleasure of seeing you open my gift?"

An audacious and unusual request to be sure. The emperor considered it for a moment. Then he turned to the butler and asked him to unwrap the gift on his behalf. The act of peeling away the expensive rice paper was done with excruciating slowness and delicacy. Eventually, he revealed an exotic-looking sword that, despite its graceful curve, reached 70 inches in length.

"An *odachi*," the emperor said in genuine surprise. He touched the blade and found that it was sharp. "Very generous, Prime Minister. A remarkable replica."

"It is no replica," Ito said with pride, for it was indeed authentic. Although popular in feudal times, such massive swords had been outlawed by shogunate decree in 1617. "Your Majesty, this rare blade actually has an interesting story to tell."

"Oh?"

"Yes. The blade once belonged to your father."

The remark clearly confounded the old monarch. "My father held this in his personal collection?"

"Just so. I understand it was one of his favorites."

"Well, I must confess, I am sure you are right, but my memories of this particular blade are vague."

"Understandable. You were just a boy when the sword was last seen here at the palace. But it so happens that during the last days of the war, when Tokyo was under American bombardment, your father took it with him into his private bunker."

The emperor took the sword into his own hands now, lifting it gingerly up and down, as if guessing its weight. "But tell me, Prime Minister, how do you know all this? How did it come into your possession?"

"The explanation is quite simple. During the war, my grandmother was a servant here at the palace."

The old monarch's face relaxed. "Ah. Now I know you must be joking. I read that your bloodline is traced to a feudal aristocracy."

"True, my grandmother was a distant cousin to the royal family. But when her father was disgraced, she was cast out of the aristocracy and groomed for service."

The emperor grunted sympathetically. He handed the sword to the butler, who backed out of the room, bowing as he disappeared from sight. The emperor waited to speak again until he was sure they were alone. "Forgive me, for I am very old. I still do not understand how the sword came into your possession. Surely your grandmother did not…"

"Steal it? Certainly not, your Majesty. During American occupation at the end of the Second World War, the sword was confiscated by American General Douglas MacArthur, along with your father's other personal weapons."

"Ah, yes. I was just a boy, but I can still recall the general's visit to the palace. Very difficult." His mind wandered for several seconds. Then he refocused on Ito. "You were saying?"

"On that day, my grandmother was overheard speaking English to the soldiers. General MacArthur needed a translator, and she was taken to his new headquarters, where she worked under him."

"Ah, yes. The Americans employed several of our best, including the dear nanny who had raised me!"

Ito clucked his tongue. "The sadness you must have felt!"

"Indeed."

"Well, as for my grandmother. Years later, when MacArthur was ultimately summoned home to the United States, her employment was of course, terminated. But as a parting gift, the general presented your father's sword to her. You can imagine her predicament. How could she possibly accept something that did not belong to her?"

"Indeed! An impossible situation!"

"She decided to accept the sword in hopes of returning it to the palace. But by then, the new palace guards did not know her. Three times she came to the palace, and three times she was sent away."

The emperor grunted approvingly. "I admire her steadfastness and sense of honor. Well. Thankfully, those dark times are behind us. And now the sword has found its way back to the palace. It is truly an amazing story. If you don't mind, Mister Prime Minister, I am hosting a small dinner tonight, and I would like to tell my guests the story of your grandmother and the sword. I think they would find it highly inspirational."

"By all means."

The butler returned to pour tea into two earthen cups, then left the room again without turning his back to them.

The emperor sipped his tea before speaking again. "I was surprised to receive your request to see me. In the past 25 years alone, I have inducted 14 new prime ministers. You are the first to return to the palace for a social visit."

"Surely they did not wish to bother you while you were busy conducting state affairs."

The emperor nodded approvingly, but in fact, it was rumored that, apart from light ceremonial duties and occasional meetings with foreign ambassadors, the emperor spent most of his time writing poetry, bird watching on the palace grounds, and practicing Shinto.

Ito had practiced what he was about to say carefully, as the topic would be extremely delicate. The emperor had been just a small boy during World War II when his father, Hirohito, refused surrender despite the total destruction of his navy, a firebombing campaign that destroyed 67 Japanese cities, and the prospect of an imminent ground invasion of the mainland by both American and Soviet forces. Surrender came only after the second nuclear bomb destroyed Nagasaki. In the ensuing months, under pressure from the Americans, Hirohito declared that he was not a living deity, was stripped of power, and was reduced to that of a ceremonial figurehead. In addition, the country had been forced to renounce its right to war forever, and accept a constitution dedicated to pacifism.

Ito set his tea on the table. "Well then, I'll get to the point of my visit. Have you been following the protests on television?" He referred to the large crowds protesting Ito's push for a strong Japanese military and an amendment to the country's pacifist constitution.

The emperor sighed. "I have little choice but to follow the news. My guests expect intelligent conversation about the issues of the day."

"As you know," Ito said, "the Restoration Party is no longer content to be dependent on the Americans for security. We propose amending the constitution to allow for the creation of a proper military."

"I am aware. A somewhat unpopular point of view, from what I understand."

"The masses fear what they do not understand. And what is your opinion on the matter? Do you agree with the opposition?"

The old monarch rose to his knees. "Come. Let me show you something."

The two men exchanged their slippers for loafers and set out on a garden path. They stopped on the other side of a koi pond. The emperor pointed to a three-story castle keep. "That is called Fujimi-yagura. It is one of the few buildings that remain from the original citadel. There were many others like it when I was a boy. What fire did not take over the centuries, the American bombers destroyed."

"The original palace must have been beautiful."

"Yes. But during the bombing, I went underground for a long period, living with my family and the servants like well-fed rats. When the attack ceased, and I was at last allowed to see the sun, my nanny told me not to look at the smoking ruins all around us. She told me to instead focus on Fujimi-yagura, which was miraculously untouched. And that is what I did. For days, weeks even, I acted as if I wore blinders."

The emperor sat on a wooden bench, his eyes still fixed on Fujimi-yagura.

"I am sorry for your suffering," Ito said. "But as to my question about your view on national defense?"

The old monarch sighed. "The present situation was not what my father intended when he agreed to the terms of surrender. He never imagined the Americans intended to stay forever. And yet given our security situation with the North Koreans and the Chinese, are we not held by golden handcuffs?"

"Just so. Then you agree that we should militarize?"

"Prime Minister, you have missed the point of my story. I fear that your plans to build an army could backfire. We have enjoyed peace for many decades. Pacifism was not our choice, but this – " he gestured to the grandiose palace grounds around them – "has been our reward."

Ito sat on the stone bench. "True. But your Majesty, this security we enjoy is an illusion. May I tell you something sensitive? Information that you must not repeat to anyone?"

The prime minister delivered the same intelligence briefing that Ambassador Nakamura had given Julian Speers in Washington. He explained how China was building military bases in the East China Sea and preparing to take the Senkaku islands and other disputed Japanese territories. He told him that China had arranged the destruction of its own embassy in Libya in order to mute the Americans' response to aggression. Then he further explained that the activity was already negatively impacting Japan's economy by blocking trade routes.

The shocking news sent the old monarch into a coughing fit. Suddenly, the butler appeared with a glass of water. The emperor took it, drank several sips, and waved him away.

As the emperor's cough quieted, Ito resumed the conversation. "Surely now, your Majesty, you can see why urgent action is needed."

"My father always said the Chinese would seek revenge for what we did to them in the Great War. That is one reason he embraced the Americans. But in light of this, Mister Prime Minister, I am afraid I still do not understand the purpose of your visit to the palace."

"To ask for your help, your Majesty."

"*My* help? What could *I* possibly do?"

Ito smiled. Then he explained his proposal in detail. It was audacious, he knew, but if the emperor would do as he asked, there was little doubt that the nation would fall in line behind him.

Now the emperor silently digested all that had been said. For Ito, the wait was excruciating. His plan to reach this exact moment in time had been years in the making. A refusal would not deter him, of course. But it would simply mean that the country's transformation would require more risk and blood than he had hoped.

Finally his majesty pointed to a pair of large black birds cruising the pond. "The imperial black swans. Very rare. Gifts from the Prime Minister of Australia to my father decades ago. They nest here on the palace grounds. In captivity, black swans have been known to live more than five decades."

"Impressive."

"Yes, but there is one problem. To keep them from escaping the palace, the stable master clipped their wings."

The monarch's meaning was not lost on Ito. It was, in fact, a sign of progress. "Under my plan, your Majesty, the imperial throne will once again soar."

# Tokyo

Well after sundown, Eri Sato woke on the futon that Taka had rolled out for her the night before. She sat upright, blowing the hair from her face. Wiping the drool from the corner of her mouth. Fumbling with a burner phone that she had taken from the evidence room at work, one of hundreds seized in a Yakuza sting.

She squinted at the too-bright display. 17:57 hours, or 5:57 p.m. She had slept for nine hours. Nine *blissful* hours. It had been months since she had gotten even five.

Eri sat up, powered up Age of the Undead Ninjas, and logged into the Fluffy profile. She grinned as she saw Carver's reply: *Banzai!*

So Carver was alive. And he was en route. At least one thing had gone right this week.

She made her way to the bathroom to get ready. There, taped to the mirror, was a note written in Taka's fanciful handwriting, along with a key:

*Gone to Autograph. Please stay another night. Or 10,000 nights.*

*—Taka*

A sweet gesture. But time was one of the many things Eri had run out of. She was due to meet Carver at Naked Fish in less than two hours. That was assuming the *Kuromaku* had not gotten to him first. From there, they would travel south to Kyoto, where she would introduce him to her informant, Sho Kimura.

As she filled the bathtub with intensely hot water, she pondered the weirdness in preparing to see her ex after all these years. Sure, they weren't completely estranged. She had, in fact, made a habit of pinging him on some professional pretense every so often. Like some fool who kept touching her hand to the stove just to make sure it was hot.

And now, she feared, those misguided attempts to stay connected had put his life in danger.

After a relatively quick soak and scrub, she dried herself with one of Taka's monogrammed towels. It wasn't until the act of patting her face dry that she realized that she had no makeup except for a tube of lipstick. The horror of facing Carver like this was too much to bear. She would have to pick something up on the way over.

Twenty-five minutes later, she locked up Taka's apartment and headed out on foot through the narrow streets of Shinjuku. Soon she was back in the Golden Gai neighborhood. Her muscles tensed as she reached the stairwell leading down to the basement-level bar. The music was booming from Autograph, as it always did at this time of night.

But where was the laughter? Nobody went to Autograph for the drinks, much less his tiny collection of Hollywood memorabilia. They went to see Taka.

She reached into her purse and pulled out her Krazy Kisser. The device looked like an ordinary tube of black lipstick, but with a flick of the wrist, it expanded into an 18-inch stun baton, capable of delivering a 5-million watt jolt. So with the Kisser in hand, she crept down the stairs until, standing on the fourth step from bottom, she could see through the open doorway.

Five bodies were strewn across the floor of the tiny bar. Blood spatter freckled every framed autograph mounted on the opposing wall. They had been hacked to death.

Taka's body lay atop the counter. His eyes stared up at the ceiling at a t-shirt that had once been signed by George Clooney. He was missing two fingers from his right hand. They didn't even try to make it look like a suicide, the way they had done with Fujimoto and the others. They had tortured him.

And suddenly Eri was propelled forward. The realization that she had been kicked dawned on her before she hit the floor.

Only then did she feel the pain in the square of her back. The Kisser was behind her, the hot end still thrumming with voltage.

She sat up, gasping for air, and turned just in time to see the man who had booted her down the stairs. He wore a blood-spattered Issey Miyake suit. His head was topped with a prickly batch of purple hair above a perfect set of teeth. He held a 14-inch knife with an elaborate handle tipped with a sterling silver panther's head.

He was not in a hurry as he turned and rolled the metal shudder down behind him. He nodded, satisfied that the rest of his work would go uninterrupted. Then he cleared his throat before making an announcement. "I am not a killer of women."

It struck Eri as the most ridiculous introduction she had ever heard. "So...you're not going to kill me?"

"You must die. But I would prefer to preserve our mutual codes of honor. I mean *seppuku*, of course." He held the knife before him and turned it, mimicking the traditional Japanese suicide by disembowelment. "Do you agree to my terms? The alternative is far worse for both of us."

Just who did he think he was dealing with? Suicide was a popular way to go in Japan, but that didn't mean *everyone* was into it. Eri wasn't going down without a fight.

"You're Kuromaku?" she asked.

"Of course. Were you expecting someone else?"

"No. Well then." She knelt before him. "It seems I have no choice."

He dropped the knife on the ground and kicked it toward her. He then pulled another blade from a shoulder holster underneath his jacket. Just in case.

She collected herself, fighting tears as she positioned the blade with her left hand a few inches from her abdomen. With her right, she unbuttoned the bottom half of her blouse, exposing her stomach. At this, something shifted in her assailant's eyes. Was it lust, or bloodlust? Acting on instinct, she undid two more buttons until her bra was exposed. Now her would-be executioner was clearly staring at her cleavage.

His lack of focus wouldn't last forever. Eri lunged forth with her left hand, swiping at him with a motion that fell intentionally short. She fell back just as his repost came. She used her left hand to grab the Kisser and swing it around her body. The hot end connected with his right nipple. His lips peeled back in agony, revealing just how white, straight and expensive his dental work really was.

She then plunged the knife into his stomach, twisting it clockwise, scrambling his guts. Now it was he who sank to his knees as she stood before him. As he sat dying, she circled behind him, using the second knife to cut open the back of his suit jacket.

He was *Kuromaku*, just as he had claimed. The Rising Sun branded onto his lower back was proof enough.

All at once, her head was filled with visions of poor old Fujimoto. She looked up at Taka, whose unseeing eyes glared up at the ceiling. And finally she thought of Carver. He had to be warned. And maybe, just maybe, he could help set things right.

# Shibuya Crossing
# Tokyo

Shibuya Crossing was often called the Times Square of Japan, and it was cruel sensory overload for someone who had just flown in from rural Arizona. Carver reckoned the population density around his father's ranch was about one person for every 10 square miles. Here at Tokyo's busiest six-way intersection, he stood shoulder-to-shoulder with thousands of his fellow human beings.

He had seen all this before, but the massive video screens on the surrounding buildings still awed him. A 50-foot woman in a perfume ad strutted in sapphire stilettos while cartoon birds fawned over her. A tennis star walked on water while swinging a bus-sized racket. Demonic cockroaches were sprayed into submission by watermelon-scented bug spray. When the crossing lights flashed green, 3,000 people stepped off the curb, walking in every possible direction, like disparate armies clashing on some ancient battlefield.

Carver knew it was pointless to check his six. There was simply no way to spot a tail in a crowd like this. He was just a few blocks from Naked Fish now, where he hoped Eri would be waiting. Hope was all he had to work with, unfortunately. He was already 18 minutes late, and Eri wasn't answering her phone. Had she destroyed and ditched her phone just as he had? The lone communication they had was her cryptic plea for help on Age of the Undead Ninjas, and his coded response.

His bruised ribs were definitely on the mend, but his bullet-pruned ear throbbed. The pain had moved into a new dimension during flight. At the airport, he had cleaned the ear again, changed the bandage, and purchased a gray slouchy knit cap to replace the black beanie he had worn hunting. It was still not Carver's favorite look, but at least he no longer resembled a dockworker.

Carver's only luggage consisted of a leather bag just large enough to fit the new laptop he had purchased at the airport. He had deemed his work computer too big of a security risk to take abroad, and had left it stitched into his mattress at his Father's ranch.

Now he sliced this way and that through the fabric of the crowd until he had reached the other side of the intersection. Then he began navigating via a mental map of Shibuya that had been stored within his mind since he had first explored it years earlier. The sight of this place triggered a torrent of memories, showing at theatres across the landscape of his brain, all at once.

Carver had ended his collegiate foil fencing career ranked 27th nationally, and the idea of learning the Japanese way of the sword held tremendous allure for him. The summer after graduation, he arranged to study Kendo with a renowned club in Tokyo. By then, the CIA had already started recruiting him. They were intrigued with what a straight-A student athlete with hyperthymesia might be able to do for his country. He was on the verge of joining up, but he wanted to log at least three good months training in a real Japanese dojo before making his final decision.

He barely survived the first week in his host country. The Arizona homer found Tokyo's food, smells and sensory assault almost too much to bear. Simultaneously, his kendo training had been far more physically intense than anything he had ever experienced back home. His kendo *sensei* had been nothing if not patient and professional, but the club members showed him no mercy. During that first week, he amassed so many welts on his back, shoulders and arms that there was no way to sleep that did not hurt.

On his first Saturday in Tokyo, hurting and homesick, he had a full-on emotional breakdown. He called his father and tearfully informed him that his Japanese adventure was over. "This was a big mistake, Pop. I should have never come here."

The disappointment in the old man's voice had been evident. He had, after all, paid for half the cost of the trip as a college graduation present. But he was also reasonable. "All right, son. Go ahead and book your ticket home. But before you board that train to the airport, will you take a moment to get your mother a souvenir from Japan? She's got her heart set on a little something exotic."

Carver hung up and went to the train station. The orange line toward Musashi-Koganei ground past on the platform above him. The first available one-way express train ticket out to Narita Airport, where he planned to fly standby, was at seven o'clock that evening. He held the ticket in his hand, reading and rereading the platform and departure time, as if expecting some sense of relief to cleanse the loneliness and remorse he felt inside.

He gathered himself and hobbled down to the Marui department store in Shibuya, where he wandered the futuristic store floor by floor, passing acres of shimmery dresses and expensive perfume. There seemed to be nothing there for a rancher's wife.

A voice behind him spoke in near-perfect English. "Excuse me. May I help you find something?"

He turned and took in the stunning beauty of a 23-year-old Waseda university art student who, he would later learn, worked the perfume counter on weekends.

He botched an attempt to introduce himself in Japanese.

She giggled good-naturedly and responded in English. "My name is Eri."

"Blake."

"Are you looking for a present for your girlfriend, Blake?"

"Uh, no. I don't have a girlfriend."

"Well this is the ladies' department. Are you lost?"

Hell yes he was. He had never been more lost in his life. But something about the way she asked. Something about the look on her face. It was a bolt out of the blue sky. Suddenly the train ticket in his pocket seemed like yet another colossal mistake.

The next words from his mouth were a surprise even to him. "Eri, would you have dinner with me tonight?"

A complete roll of the dice to a perfect stranger. And to his great surprise – and hers, it seemed – she said yes.

# Office of the
# Director of National Intelligence
# Washington D.C.

Speers' assistant appeared in the doorway with apologies written all over her face. "FBI Director Fordham is here. I told him you were busy. "

Fordham barged into the office behind her. "It's urgent, Julian." The FBI Director folded his tall frame into a mid-century chair that put his rear end just 12 inches off the ground. With his long legs bent at sharp angles before him, and his green tie, he resembled a praying mantis.

"Carver boarded an American Airlines flight to Tokyo," Fordham said. "It looks bad, Julian. The task force is convening *today.*"

Inside, Speers was furious. Carver had promised he would return to Washington today. But he couldn't let his frustration show with Chad. He had to smooth this over. "Relax. He's not running from this, if that's what you're worried about."

"Obviously."

"Blake took the news hard. I was worried about his state of mind, so I told him to take some time off. I may not have been clear enough about his expected return date."

Fordham grinned knowingly. "You're a real piece of work. You'd do just about anything to protect him, wouldn't you?"

"Protect him from what? As far as I know, he's done nothing wrong. And listen. If a guy like Carver really wanted to run away, do you think he'd be dumb enough to fly commercial?"

"Well..."

Speers slowly unwrapped a lollipop and slid it into his mouth, letting the quiet seconds drip out like water from a frozen pipe. Chad was a chatterbox. Given enough time, he would reveal anything else he was concealing.

True to form, Fordham continued, unable to stand the silence. "There's more. Yesterday, Carver called one of your people, Arunus Roth. Of course Roth denied it, but we have the recording of their conversation. Carver asked him to run two passports on the sly."

So they were monitoring their calls. Speers hadn't authorized that, which meant the order had to have come from the president. This time she wouldn't be satisfied until she had Carver's head on a platter.

"I don't know anything about that," Speers said. "But if he did call Roth, then it says something about his work ethic, doesn't it? Who else is going to keep working for us after being thrown to the wolves?"

Chad stood, buttoned his jacket, and turned to leave. He paused in the doorway and looked back.

"You know I've always been a Carver fan, right? There have been plenty of times I stood by him when nobody else would. But this is different, Julian. We're going to have to bring him in."

# Tokyo

The neon signs on the Shibuya buildings were as big and garish as Carver remembered, although some of the names had changed. Much to his amazement, the immense nine-floor Tower Records was still here, having somehow survived the rise of cloud music services. Back when he had lived here, it had been nothing less than a temple of music worship, the likes of which he had never seen since. Now he grazed the building with his fingertips as he walked past, gathering flecks of flakey yellow paint underneath his nails.

A little further up, he walked west through a neighborhood of fashion boutiques and high-end eateries. The energy was somewhat less frantic over here, but it was no less crowded. The sidewalks were shoulder-to-shoulder, filled with young, carefree Japanese wearing trendy designer clothes.

Carver was in the same suit he'd worn to see Nico Gold in Vegas, having counted on a quick return trip to D.C. At least he had managed to buy a couple of new shirts at LAX between flights. Soon he would meet with Eri and find out why she had beckoned him here. If this was anything but an overnight trip, he was going to need to get to a men's boutique that specialized in Western sizes ASAP.

A black van rolled slowly past. Rising sun flags flew from the hood, and speakers on top blared nationalist propaganda. He'd called the van parked in Jack Brenner's driveway creepy, but it had nothing on this. His Japanese comprehension was a bit rusty, but he thought the lecture-on-wheels had something to do with the American military bases in Okinawa that had been in place since the end of World War II. To some, they were a much-needed firewall against Chinese aggression. To others, they were proof of a sinister American occupation without end.

The familiar odor of fishy garbage that was so unique to Asian cities met him at the next street. Sushify – the restaurant he and Eri had dubbed Naked Fish — was still there, all right. But it was no longer relegated to a tiny portion of the building's second floor. The eatery had since taken over the floor above it as well, displacing a motorcycle bar that had once blasted classic rock every night of the week.

A familiar voice called out behind him. "You're late."

Carver turned as Eri stepped out from the shadows. He squinted, reconciling the woman who stood before him with the one he had last seen five years ago. She had grown her hair out to shoulder-length and had added some color to it, making it more brown than black. If he had to guess, she still fit into the same jeans that she had the last time he saw her. He stole a glance at her hands. Still no diamond ring.

"It's good to see you," he said, leaning in to kiss her cheek. But she pulled back, leaving him to settle for an awkward hug.

"We can catch up later. *Ikimasho.*" She turned, motioning for him to follow her down the alley.

Carver's mood plummeted. He hadn't exactly expected Eri to jump in his arms after all the time that had passed, but he had at least expected basic pleasantries.

"I'm starving," he said. "What about Naked Fish?"

She did not look back. Instead, she led him to a red racing motorcycle with custom spoke wheels that was parked amongst a row of scooters. Since when did she learn to drive a motorcycle? When they had lived together in D.C., she didn't even have a regular driver's license.

She put her helmet on and spoke through the still-open face mask. "You can order food on the train to Kyoto."

"Whoa. Who said anything about going to Kyoto? I just got here."

"No time to explain."

Carver felt his blood pressure rising. The trip to Tokyo from Northern Arizona via Los Angeles had been 18 hours door-to-door. His back was killing him, and Kyoto was another 300 miles away.

His ex handed him a helmet and scooted forward to make room on the seat. "*Dozo.* I know you have questions. But we had better go while we still can."

Carver heard a screech of tires. He turned. The propaganda van he had seen earlier was rounding the corner at high speed. The voice over the loudspeaker was no longer shouting nationalist rhetoric. Instead, it was telling them to stay where they were.

"Friends of yours?" he said.

"Shut up and get on the bike."

The van picked up speed. It was coming straight at them.

"Eri?"

"Hold tight."

Carver wrapped the fingers of his right hand around Eri's shoulder, and put his left around her still-trim waist. The bike lunged forward just in time to avoid becoming a permanent part of the van's grill. The van swerved after them like a hungry beast. It flattened a street sign and punted a mailbox, sending hundreds of pieces of mail sailing high in the air.

The motorbike shot like a bullet down the dark end of the street, and then skidded to an abrupt stop as Eri realized she had driven them into a dead end. They were cornered. Even the storefronts were shuttered.

The only sign of life was a ramen vendor who was preparing his pushcart for the night shift. The vintage wooden cart would not have been out of place on a Japanese street a century earlier, when ramen had still been called "Chinese soba." An elderly ramen man stood beside it, patiently stirring an enormous vat of frothy soup. He either did not notice them or did not care.

Like a wolf that had trapped its prey, the van slowed as it came down the street.

"Who did you piss off?" Carver said.

"Long story. Hope I live to tell it."

Out of sheer muscle memory, Carver reached for his SIG Sauer. It wasn't there. The weapon was still locked in his father's gun safe at the Two Elk Ranch.

This was all Julian's fault. Being put on administrative leave meant Carver had been forced to fly commercial. Getting on the plane with the SIG at Los Angeles Airport would have been as simple as checking it into the cargo hold, but the odds of clearing security with a firearm in Japan were all but hopeless. Had he still been with the agency, they would have sent a local outfitter with a small arsenal for him to choose from. Given the circumstances, he would be completely dependent on Eri's resources.

"Are you carrying?" Carver asked her.

She rolled her eyes. "This is Tokyo, not Texas. Not even the Yakuza carry guns now."

"What?"

"Too risky. Life in prison."

Now the van came to a stop about 100 feet away. The side door rolled open. Three pear-shaped figures stepped out. It was still too dark to see their faces, but to Carver, it looked as if they were carrying wooden baseball bats.

He scratched the day-old growth on his chin. "If it's a street brawl they want, we had better find something to fight with."

Eri reached into her purse and pulled out her Krazy Kisser stun baton. With a flick of the wrist, the black weapon elongated to 18-inches in length. A pulse of blue electricity crackled at the tip.

Carver frowned and shook his head. Although it was better than nothing, it was no match for a baseball bat, which was much longer and heavier. They needed

He walked over to the ramen pushcart. The elderly vendor's face glowed red under the lantern.

"*Komban wa,*" the ramen man said. Good evening.

Carver knew what he wanted, and how to say it. He had, after all, learned to read the three Japanese alphabets during his first month in the country, and memorized more than 2,500 words. But his pronunciation was another matter. It had always been terrible, and a fair amount of private tutoring had done little to improve it. For this reason, he thought better of engaging the ramen man in what would surely be a frustrating conversation for both of them.

Instead he reached into his pocket and pulled out five 10,000 yen notes — the equivalent of about $500 U.S. dollars. He pressed the money into the ramen man's shirt pocket. Then he put his hand on the cart's roof, which served as shelter for hungry customers on rainy nights.

"Okay?" Carver said.

The ramen man gave him the thumbs up. *"Dai jobu!"*

As he walked back to the idling motorcycle, Carver loosened the umbrella coupling and expanded the pole to its full length of about twelve feet. He got on the bike behind Eri, mounting the pole under his right arm as if it were a jousting stick.

"Ramming speed," Carver said. He lowered his face shield and curled his left arm around Eri's waist.

The motorcycle roared like a lion and shot forth like a slingshot. Eri aimed the bike at the heart of the trio, with Carver's harpoon-like weapon protruding over her right shoulder. The baffled thugs broke ranks before her, tripping over themselves as they scrambled to get out of the way of the two motorcycle maniacs.

"Lean left," Eri said as she swung the bike at the last moment, bearing down on one of the attackers. He dropped his bat as he ran, and the tip of the massive umbrella caught him under his left shoulder blade, dislocating it. He tumbled against the asphalt in agony.

But as Eri sped toward for the gap between the van and the open street behind it, the vehicle reversed course, blocking their path.

Eri managed to brake and turn just in time. Carver managed to hang on, but just barely. Then she veered off again in the direction of the other two assailants, who had huddled around their fallen colleague. They straightened, eyes full of panic, as the motorbike bore down on them at a speed that was just barely controllable.

Carver tightened his grip on the ramen umbrella pole. One of the men took off running in the direction of a grid of fish crates that were stacked several feet high. "Lean right," Eri said as she guided the motorbike in pursuit. Carver did, but not before the third man swung his bat and let go. The slender end of the 42-inch Louisville Slugger struck the front tire spokes just right. The tire locked up. The bike's rear end took flight, and so did Carver and Eri.

Time seemed to slow down. In mid-air, Carver curled himself into a ball, hoping to minimize the inevitable damage to his body. They landed among the stacks of fish crates, the cheap plywood breaking underneath them. Carver's helmet struck something harder, though, that made him think of melons. He rolled over, seeing the thing that had ultimately broken his fall – the skull of one of their attackers. The man's head was bashed in. His right eye had popped out of its socket.

Carver rolled to his knees, then got to his feet. The bike had wrapped itself around a pole that appeared to be holding up enough electrical wires to illuminate the entire neighborhood. The rear wheel was still spinning, but the front wheel was badly mangled, rubber ripped away, snapped spokes protruding at unnatural angles.

In the distance, he saw the red lantern on the ramen man's cart as the old man hustled it down the street. Eri, meanwhile, was sprawled among the mess, unmoving. Her eyes were closed, but she was still breathing.

The last man standing was coming toward them, popping the slugger against the palm of his hand.

The wrecked bike triggered an idea from the recesses of his infallible memory. A former CIA colleague stationed in Beijing had told him that in China, sharpened motorcycle and bicycle spokes were common street weapons. He put the heel of his boot against the motorcycle wheel and wriggled one of the loose spokes back and forth until it snapped off.

He tested the jagged edge against the palm of his hand. It was sharp, all right, but had far less reach than a baseball bat. He was going to have to get in close.

Carver retreated further down the dead-end street, hoping to draw the lone remaining thug away from Eri. It worked. When he was within 15 feet, Carver whipped the spoke back and forth before him, testing its balance.

Just as he was ready to move in, the van turned its wheels until its headlights were fixed squarely on Carver, temporarily blinding him. He danced to the right, forcing the attacker to circle like a boxer in the ring.

Soon, his attacker's face was illuminated. He was just a kid, no more than 21, barely shaving. He was grinning like a fool, but it was obvious that he had never been more scared in his life. But unlike his colleagues, the kid wasn't actually holding a Louisville Slugger. Close up and in the vehicle's illumination, Carver could see that it was actually a *shinai* — a kendo sword made of bamboo. That figured. As Carver had learned during his year abroad in Tokyo, kendo drew disciples from all walks of life, but was particularly coveted by right-wing nationalists.

Gripping the shinai at the base with both hands, the kid pointed the shinai at Carver's throat just below the helmet faceplate. The kid was stupefied. Who was this white guy, mimicking his kendo stance, holding this tiny motorcycle spoke?

In kendo, Carver recalled, every defensive move triggered a nearly automatic offensive response. Sure, there were an infinite number of ways to attack an opponent. But the dojo masters, almost without exception, emphasized tradition and perfection of a set number of actions and reactions until they were second nature.

Carver decided to use that to his advantage. He assumed a classic defensive position, hoping to induce his opponent into Katate Waza, a one-armed strike to the throat.

But when Carver lowered his right arm, as if he was going in for a torso strike, his opponent's muscle memory kicked in. He leaned forward in a classic thrust, aiming for Carver's jugular. Carver ducked left and threw himself forward in a classic flying lunge from the Western fencing tradition. The spoke entered the soft flesh of the kid's neck, just left of his Adam's apple, into his windpipe. Carver withdrew it and sidestepped left, watching as the blood spurt out forcefully in the white gleam of the headlights.

The kid fell to his knees, palm to his neck, trying to slow the gush of life from his body. Carver also put pressure over the wound, but it was no use. The kid was choking on his own blood. Forget speaking. He couldn't even breathe.

The kid caught one rattling last breath before his eyes fixed on some object in the great beyond. Carver turned the kid over and pushed the shirt up his back. As he had suspected, the Rising Sun was branded into the skin above his waistband.

Up the street, the thug that Carver had maimed with the ramen umbrella limped to the van and climbed inside. The vehicle made a hasty U-turn and squealed tires as it sped away into the night.

Carver went to check on Eri. He was relieved to see that she was awake and slowly testing her limbs. "Anything broken?"

She sat up and rolled to her knees. "I am okay."

Carver helped her to her feet. "Suppose you tell me who these people are, and why they're trying to kill me?"

She checked her watch. "*Ikimasho*. We can still catch our train."

WILLIAM TYREE

# Shinjuku Train Station
# Tokyo

The bullet train sliced through the gleaming heart of the Tokyo metropolitan area like a rocket struggling to break free of earth's atmosphere. At 198 miles per hour, it was astonishingly quiet save for the white noise that seemed to wrap every sound in a magic envelope, lulling its sleep-deprived city dwellers into a collective nap. All except Eri, who had insisted on sitting in the aisle seat so that she could see who was coming and going from the other cars.

Carver leaned close and whispered in her ear. "This is the part where you tell me why I'm here."

"I don't know where to start."

"When was the last time your life was normal?"

"A few months ago. I was leaving work. It was late, and I stepped into the elevator and found myself alone with Fujimoto, one of the old-timers in the agency. He helped catch the Aum Shinrikyo cult back in the 1990s. Remember them?"

Carver did. The cult had been responsible for a sarin gas attack on the Tokyo subway system that had killed 12 and injured nearly 5,000. "Yes. Go on."

"Fujimoto is a legend around that place. I had never actually seen him in person. Just in old news clips. The rumor was that at some point, he had been moved to a basement office, where his work rooting out domestic terrorism groups continued in secret. Others said he had gone insane, and he refused to retire."

"Eri, what does this all have to do with me?"

She snorted dismissively. "Same old Blake. You never had any patience for context."

"This is different. I've been attacked twice in two days, in two different countries. Can you blame me for wanting answers?"

213

"Yes. But I'm going to tell this story my way, or not at all."

"Just like old times." Carver leaned his head back and gazed up at the ceiling, as if he were asking God for help. "Fine. Go ahead."

"So I was in the elevator with Fujimoto. I was too nervous to say hello. And out of the blue, he says my name. Eri Sato. Just like that. And he tells me he has been watching my career. And he asks me out for a drink."

Carver felt the old jealousy pangs reactivate. "And just how old is Fujimoto?"

"Seventy-seven. But it wasn't like that. He said he had a case he wanted to discuss. Of course, I jumped at the chance."

"He took me to a noisy place where no one could hear us. He told me he was investigating the Restoration Party. Fujimoto thought they had been fixing elections."

Carver didn't know much about the Restoration Party apart from what he had seen in the news. It was a nationalist movement created by Akira Ito, who had recently become Prime Minister. Ito's critics called him a fascist, but no figure in modern Japanese politics had ever become so popular so fast. His party had been the first to seriously challenge the country's Liberal Democratic Party (LDP) in decades. In speeches, the party often referenced Japan's golden eras, including the Edo Period, in which the country was closed to the outside world, as well as the 20-year period before World War II, during which it was the lone Asian superpower. Prime Minister Ito sought to clamp down on immigration and limit foreign participation in traditionally Japanese sports such as Sumo wrestling. Also, in an attempt to halt the country's declining population, he had redoubled incentives for couples to marry and have children.

More controversially, he had recently called for an end to Japan's pacifist constitution. He advocated for a strong military as a deterrent to China and North Korea.

"Ito invited me to join the investigation," Eri continued. "There were two others involved as well. They worked in secret."

"What do you mean, in secret?"

"Without the authorization of the agency. Ito suspected corruption at the highest level."

"Was he right?"

Eri nodded. "We worked to build a case for months. We were getting close. Fujimoto was tapping the communications of several of the Restoration Party leaders. But then last week, something unexpected happened. One of Ito's closest advisors mentioned the attack on the Chinese Embassy."

"What's strange about that? It was the biggest news story in the world."

"They were talking about it the day *before* it happened."

Carver felt his arms break out in gooseflesh. "How is that possible?"

"I don't know."

"Is this why we're heading to Kyoto? Is Fujimoto there? Does he have the recording?"

"No. Fujimoto is dead. Disemboweled. They made it look like a suicide."

Carver saw the fatigue in her eyes. She looked as if she had been awake for days on end. She grazed the fingertips of her right hand across the top of his shirt. The familiar intimacy of the gesture threatened to burst the dam of memories Carver had spent so many years locking away. "I'm so sorry."

"They got to the others, too. When I discovered that they had hacked my phone and email, I realized I had called and emailed you. I feared they might assume you were involved. That's when I reached out on Age of the Undead Ninjas."

"You were right. It didn't take them long to come for me."

Her throat was suddenly full of emotion. "Did they hurt you?"

Carver pulled his beanie off and pointed to the notch in his left ear. Eri ran her fingertips over the wound. Now Eri was crying. She buried her head into Carver's shoulder. He petted her hair. In the highlight reel of his mind it was twelve years earlier, June 6th, 10:13 pm. He was holding Eri on a beach blanket as a bonfire raged before them, and she tried s'mores for the first time.

July 28, 7:12 a.m., kissing her goodbye before work, relishing the scent of the perfume she had worn the night before. Three days later, taking in a matinee horror film at a decaying downtown theater, uttering, "I love you" during the movie's most terrifying scene, as if it was some trial run for an actual declaration, knowing his words would not be heard over the film's bombastic soundtrack. And 19 minutes later, heading home in a rainstorm, fighting about something petty. By the time the night was over, he would be called to board a military transport headed for a covert JSOC operation in Islamabad, and things would never be the same again.

# The White House

Speers was summoned to the president's personal fitness center, where he found the commander-in-chief running on a treadmill. She was a wellness fanatic. She had banished vending machines from the building, replacing them with refrigerators and shelves stocked with organic snacks.

The staff had appreciated the gesture, but the act had merely driven their junk food cravings underground. Reese's Peanut Butter Bars were still devoured by the truckload, only now they were snuck in like contraband, eaten behind closed doors, all remaining evidence packed out each night.

The president slowed the machine to a walking pace, and then wiped the sweat from her neck with a towel emblazoned with the presidential seal. "Thanks for coming," she said before switching on the television, where she had a recording queued up. "This aired 20 minutes ago."

Network pundit Veronica Dutton appeared onscreen. With the backdrop of the D.C. skyline behind her, she looked across her desk at a pear-shaped man in a dark navy suit.

DUTTON: How will the breaking news out of Tokyo affect the United States? My guest is Gavin Riley, an expert on U.S.-Asian relations from Stanford University.

RILEY: It's a pleasure to be here, Veronica.

DUTTON: For those that don't know, Japan's government is a constitutional monarchy. The sitting emperor is the country's 125th in an uninterrupted line that dates back to 600 B.C. As I understand it, Japan's parliament decided today to actually return limited power to the Japanese Emperor.

RILEY: Yes, the move was unprecedented, Veronica. The Japanese National Diet met in a closed session that lasted nearly 11 hours. When they emerged, the emperor had been granted limited involvement in government affairs for the first time since World War II.

DUTTON: Fascinating. How is this news being received in Japan?

RILEY: Given the immense popularity of the royal family in Japan, I'd say the reception is a mix of thrill and shock. No one saw this coming. On the flip side, analysts are saying that Prime Minister Ito must have been quietly planning this for some time, since nothing happens quickly when it comes to Japanese parliamentary procedure. Legal analysts are scrambling to make sense of whether this move was even constitutional.

DUTTON: How much power has the emperor actually been granted?

RILEY: Quite a bit, relatively speaking. As a basis for comparison, the Danish constitutional monarchy gives the throne, and I quote, "the right to be consulted, the right to advise and the right to warn." That might not sound like much, but the Japanese model now does all this and more. The emperor will now be a de facto part of the prime minister's cabinet, and will be expected to participate in periodic meetings. Also, the emperor will now have what they are calling 'reserve powers.' And that is a big deal, since it means he can unilaterally make executive decisions in extreme circumstances, such as if the prime minister wasn't available during a national crisis.

DUTTON: At the risk of sounding insensitive, the emperor is a very old man. Why do this now?

RILEY: My guess? To shore up Ito's own popularity. Realize that Ito was not directly elected, so the public has mixed feelings about having a right-wing nationalist leading the country.

DUTTON: Tell our American viewers how that is even possible.

RILEY: In the Japanese election system, Ito first had to win a seat in the National Diet, the country's parliament. Then his party surprised everyone by quickly gaining a majority, which was a shock. As president of the Restoration Party, he was then appointed head of government. So while Ito's supporters love his efforts to protect Japanese culture, his call to aggressively build a large military has been met with sizable public opposition and protests. So if you want to restore a sense of patriotism and nationalism, aligning yourself with the royal family is one way to do it.

DUTTON: But does this move really align the emperor with the prime minister politically?

RILEY: So far, the answer seems to be yes. The emperor delivered a speech saying that the country faced imminent threats, that he had full confidence in Prime Minister Ito, and that the Japanese people should do everything in their power to support his efforts to quickly scale a military.

DUTTON: I'd like to ask you about a specific part of that speech. He said the country had been, quote, "sleepwalking in a state of false security for so long, that it should behave as if it is already under attack." Was he referencing Chinese aggression on the oceans?

RILEY: That would be my interpretation. Understand that China has pursued a very aggressive foreign policy, in some cases claiming disputed Japanese territories. Critics of the White House, including many in Japan and in our own Congress, say that we have done absolutely nothing to counter that aggression. I think Ito may be using this strategy as a way to get America to step up to the plate.

The president switched off the television and stepped off the treadmill. "How did we not see this coming?"

Speers took a towel from the stack and wiped the sweat from his own forehead. "Didn't we? I relayed Ambassador Nakamura's intelligence brief. His view is that we are the sworn protectorate of Japan, and it's our responsibility to push the Chinese back from their sovereign territory."

The president sank into a chair. "So you did."

"My guess is that Ito saw no tangible response from us, so he forced our hand."

"He succeeded. This makes us look weak, and that's one thing we can't afford right now." The president picked up a black handset. Moments later, she had Secretary of Defense Dex Jackson on speakerphone. "Dex. How's the China Playbook coming?"

"My team is still refining it. The fact that our drone fleet is grounded doesn't make reworking these scenarios easy."

"I want a full briefing with options within 24 hours. We're going to need a major show of force in the Pacific."

# Gion District
# Kyoto, Japan

The narrow street was lit with paper lanterns. Wooden-fronted shops lined both sides and the sweet scent of grilled eel filled the air. Up ahead, a Geisha flitted out of one of the ancient establishments, shielding her customer from the drizzle with a red bamboo-and-paper umbrella.

Carver and Eri walked through the rain with purpose, turning down a side street that was little more than a cobblestone path. Kyoto's Gion District had been built during the Middle Ages to serve travelers visiting Yasaka Shrine. Even tonight, in the face of a cold wind and even colder rain, the area was undeniably magical.

A scooter suddenly blazed out from behind them, handlebars barely clearing the lanterns on either side of the street. Carver pulled Eri into the doorway of an izakaya to let it pass. He held Eri's arm a moment longer than was wise, taking in her scent, which had always reminded him of citrus.

A little further up, she pointed at a ramshackle wooden structure. The sign bore no letters – just a blue-colored monk carved in the style made popular in the Edo Period.

Eri slid the wooden door on its track until it was fully open. The tiny restaurant was candlelit and featured just a handful of seats clustered in a half-circle around the kitchen. The restaurant's proprietor stood behind the counter, a muscular figure sharpening an enormous cleaver. John Coltrane's brooding jazz classic, Equinox, oozed over the sound system like simmering lava.

"*Irrashaimase,*" the proprietor said as Eri and Carver stepped in out of the rain.

A party of nine had just settled their tab. Reeking of sake, they helped each other to their feet, laughing drunkenly as they stumbled out into the night. The proprietor followed them out. He locked the flimsy outer door and then pulled down a secondary barrier that reminded Carver of the steel doors at American drive-up storage units.

Then he embraced Eri. The hug was warm and familiar. Carver felt a pang of envy, sharp enough to hurt. Eri broke away and gestured to Carver. "This is Blake Carver, the American I told you about. Blake, meet Shoichi Kimura."

"Hi Shoichi."

"You can call me Sho. I hope you are hungry."

Carver took off his jacket and sat on a stool next to Eri. He gestured to a mounted deer head on the near wall with a truly massive rack of antlers. "Is that a red stag?"

"Yes."

"Twenty-two points. Impressive. Did you take him down yourself?"

Sho nodded. "Deep in the woods in Bulgaria. Very difficult to pack out. But my customers enjoyed him for many weeks."

"You actually kill your own venison?"

Sho looked to Eri, then back to Carver, grinning. "I see that Eri did not tell you anything about me. She is good at keeping secrets. That is why we are still friends. Now, if you will excuse me. Tonight the main course will be wild boar from the Nagano prefecture."

As their host disappeared into the cramped kitchen, Carver caught a glimpse of a second person. A junior chef, perhaps.

He turned to Eri. "You're a little too good at keeping secrets for my taste. Why are we here?"

"Like I said on the train. I will tell this story my way." She pointed at the wall filled with recent culinary awards. "Sho normally serves just one meal each night. A very expensive meal. It takes months to get a reservation here. Everything Sho cooks is caught, killed and cooked by him or his brother. He is a true *shokunin*."

Carver had not heard this word, shokunin, for years. There was no single-word equivalent in English. It described an artisan that single-mindedly dedicated his life to improving his craft. It seemed to also imply a social and spiritual obligation to do so.

Sho dashed out from the kitchen, reached over the counter, and set before them a blue-and-white dish filled with what looked glazed nuts. "For an appetizer, candied grasshoppers."

Up close, the candied grasshoppers did not look anything like glazed nuts. They looked more like cockroaches. Carver decided he'd rather talk than eat them. "Sho, what's the name of this place?"

"The Blue Monk."

"Oh. Named after the Thelonious Monk song?"

Sho grinned broadly. "So you are a jazz man. I think we will get along fine, Carver-*san. Itadakimasu*!" He then disappeared back into the kitchen.

Eri rolled her eyes. "You don't even like jazz. Little does he know how full of useless trivia you are."

She was right, of course. He *really* hated jazz. But he could, if needed, replay Monk's 10 most famous tracks at will in his head. He had found that knowing a little bit about everything made it exponentially easier to chat people up. That led to bonding. Bonding led to trust. And trust led to actionable intelligence.

"Speaking of the arts," Carver asked Eri, "Are you painting?"

He could tell by the look on her face that he had touched a nerve. "I have not picked up a brush since I left D.C."

"That's a shame. You were good."

She waved her hand as if clearing smoke. "All in the past." She nudged the bowl of grasshoppers toward him. "After you."

"No thanks."

He watched as she put one of the crusty insects into her mouth as casually as if it were a potato chip. "See? Not so bad."

"For me, insects fall into the category of survival food, not gourmet cuisine."

On the opposite wall hung several fierce-looking photos of Sho in competitive ski gear. His jersey from the 2010 winter Olympics was encircled in a wooden frame. "So your boyfriend is a gourmet cook *and* an Olympic skier? Wow. You really traded up."

She shot him a look. "He is not my boyfriend. He was Fujimoto's informant. Now he's mine."

"I stand corrected."

"But yes, Sho was in the Olympics. I can't think of the word for the event. That one where they ski, and then do some target shooting, and then ski some more?"

"The biathlon."

"Yes. That one."

Carver grunted dismissively. "Well the Japanese have never medaled in biathlon. In fact, the only non-European nations to medal in biathlon are Kazakhstan and Canada."

"Stop it."

"Hey, does Sho still have his shooting license?"

She nodded. "He is one of the few licensed hunters left in the entire country."

Then maybe he can hook me up, Carver thought. He would have felt naked without his trusty SIG under any circumstances, but especially after what he had been through the past two days.

The kitchen door swung open again. Sho set three pint glasses on the counter. "I sent my little brother home. Food is cooking. We can talk freely now."

"A picture is worth a thousand words," Eri said. "Go ahead. Show it to him."

"Now?"

"Yes. Please. He needs to know."

The chef stood and untied his apron, revealing a black V-neck t-shirt stretched over an impressively muscled torso. He pulled the shirt up several inches and turned around so that Carver could see the brand. A fleshy orb of scar tissue with thick bands emanating from its center. The Rising Sun. Just like the three before him.

Carver felt a tiny ray of light break through. Here, standing before him, was a living and breathing connection to the person who had ordered his own assassination.

"What does it mean? " he said. "Who did it to you?"

The chef sucked his teeth as if the question itself was painful. Then he sat on the stool next to Carver's. He cracked open a gigantic bottle of Asahi lager and began pouring it into one of the pint glasses.

"I will tell you what you want to know," Sho said. Then he took a car key out of his pocket and slid it across the bar to Eri. "But you drive me home tonight. By the time my story is finished, I will be very drunk."

# NINE MONTHS EARLIER

# The Blue Monk
# Kyoto

The night the Rising Sun had been burned into Shoichi Kimura's back had started like virtually any other. As usual, Sho stood behind the counter of the tiny restaurant he had inherited from his father. He was an athletic figure with long hair tied up in a ponytail, carving up venison with an enormous cleaver.

Miles Davis's trumpet blurted epic melodies over the room speakers. Sho whistled along as best he could, fantasizing about the day he would retire and learn to play jazz for real.

Several taxidermied stag heads adorned the south wall. Below them, a large photograph of Sho in the 2010 winter Olympics, where he had competed for the Japanese National Team in the Biathlon. He had no medal to show for it, but the memories of that magic year and the red-hot patriotism that had fueled him stayed with him always. He was a man who had always loved his country.

The opposite wall was filled with culinary awards. He had framed several reviews and certificates from two magazines that had named the restaurant to their list of top Kyoto restaurants. A blank space was reserved for the Michelin Star he hoped to earn one day.

The tiny space where the restaurant stood had been in his family for nearly three centuries, and had gone by many names, but it had never been as successful as it was now. But how could he take advantage of it? Franchising the field-to-table menu he had created would prove impossible. Nor could he translate the

Blue Monk experience to a bigger location without losing its intimacy.

He decided to go upmarket. His first step was to make the restaurant far more exclusive. He did so by cutting back to just one dinner sitting per night, with a lone item on the menu — the Chef's Special. The fixed menu gave him the absolute culinary control he had always desired.

But, of course, he needed some way to recoup the money he would lose by serving just nine customers per night. He therefore set his price at 30,000 yen per person, or about $300 USD.

His little brother said he was out of his mind. Was the price exorbitant? Yes, of course. Such a premium was far out of reach for most people. And yet it had been the smartest business decision he had ever made. The limited seating, plus the high price, made Japan's elite want to get in more than ever. He had not had a vacant seat since.

And so Sho had been at the height of his game that night when the wooden door to the street slid open. Three men in dark suits appeared in the doorway. The one in the middle, perhaps in his early 60s, wore expensive brown eyeglass frames and had the mouth of an eel, with large lips and narrow, pointed front teeth. The Eel walked in front, clearly the boss. Sho sensed that the two that followed him, despite their fine clothing, were just punks in their late 20s.

"*Irrashaimase,*" Sho shouted as they ducked into the dark restaurant. He gestured to the seats before him. "*Dozo.* When will the rest of your party be joining?"

"It's just the three of us," the one in the middle said.

Strange. Sho double-checked the reservation book. The name was Yamada Taro, for nine guests. An obviously fake name sometimes used by celebrity diners who desired discretion.

"And name on the reservation is…" Sho hesitated.

The middle-aged man crackled his knuckles. "Yamada Toro," the Eel said.

"I see. There must be some misunderstanding. The reservation was for nine guests."

"No misunderstanding." The Eel gestured to the man beside him, who removed 270,000 Yen from his pocket – enough for nine diners – and laid it on the counter. "We wish to have the place to ourselves."

There was something off about this trio. They didn't exactly look like Yakuza per se, but something about them made his blood run cold. Still, who was he to complain if his guests wanted the entire place to themselves? Sho thanked them graciously and poured them drinks. Then he went into the kitchen, working with his 21-year-old little brother to prepare the venison and side dishes.

Some 20 minutes later, dinner was served, and the trio ate heartily. The Eel grunted his enthusiasm as he chewed. The venison was from a buck Sho had taken just two weeks earlier in Nagano. After a story about the restaurant had come out in the Japan Times newspaper, he had been inundated with requests from farms to come shoot the pests that were eating their crops. In a country with so few gun owners, demand for his services had remained high. The free meat was also excellent for his profit margins.

At one point during the meal, the Eel held his hand before his face and snapped his fingers. His colleagues stopped eating immediately. Sho also felt compelled to pay attention. "I do not like jazz," the Eel said.

Sho bowed slightly and promptly lowered the volume on the song — an extended jam by a young American prodigy named Kamasi Washington — before stopping it altogether. For the duration of the meal, the only sound in the restaurant was the three men cutting and chewing and swallowing.

When the Eel had had his fill, he put his napkin on the table. The others had not yet finished, but they followed suit, and put their napkins on the table as well.

"I was skeptical about this place," the Eel said. "But it's true what they say. Your venison is even better than your father's."

The complement hit Sho like ice water. There had been a six-year gap between the time of his father's disappearance and the time that Sho had reopened the restaurant under the new name. For the most part, the old clientele had been left behind. The few old-timers that had come back had been repulsed by Sho's high prices.

Still, Sho's curiosity was piqued. "Did you know my father?"

The Eel flashed a grin of yellow, crooked teeth, with gold caps. "He was one of Japan's true unsung heroes."

The unsettling feeling that had come over him was suddenly stronger. A part of him wanted to run out the back door. "I better go put the finishing touches on your second course."

"No. The time for eating is over. I wish to talk."

"To tell the truth, I'm not much of a talker."

"Sit down," the Eel said. "I insist."

Sho's mouth was suddenly dry. His tunic was dripped with sweat. But in his experience, you had to stand up to bullies the first time, or they would run over you for a lifetime. His hands shook as he pulled the 270,000 yen they had given him out of the leather pouch underneath the bar and offered it back to the Eel. "The geisha houses here in Gion are full of lovely ladies who specialize in conversation. Take your money and go."

In response, the Eel's right-hand man set a .50 caliber Desert Eagle handgun on the counter. Even to someone like Sho, who was one of Japan's few licensed hunters, the sight of the veritable pocket cannon in his restaurant was nothing less than shocking.

"Let your little brother go home early, Kimura-*san*. You will live to see him tomorrow. I promise."

Sho called back to his brother. "Go home."

"*Honto?*" came the disbelieving reply from the kitchen. He was, after all, not nearly done cleaning up.

"My treat. Now get lost."

Moments later, he heard the back door open and slam shut.

The Eel removed a gold-plated cigarette case from his jacket pocket and plucked a cigarette from it. "Do you have a light?"

Sho removed a lighter from the drawer and leaned over the counter. His hands were shaking as he drew near the cigarette.

His face was suddenly filled with a clear mist. The room got hazy. He lost his balance, but the Eel's friends caught him before he fell to the ground.

Twelve hours later, Shoichi Kimura woke to the sound of rushing water. Tree-filtered sunlight warmed his skin. Somewhere up above him, a flock of geese honked.

He was lying on his stomach. He raised his head, fingers pulling the pine needles from his face and hair. As he raised up, he realized the hotness in his lower back.

The smell of incense and burning flesh was still fresh within his mind. He reached behind him, probing gently, raising the hem of his shirt. A large bandage was taped to his lower back.

And his back wasn't the only thing that was hurting. His head was pounding. The worst imaginable whiskey hangover. Only he had not been drinking.

A note was taped to the hairless skin of his chest:

*Do not see a doctor. Do not discuss our meeting with anyone. Do not discuss the ceremony with anyone. We will be in touch.*

Ceremony? He had no recollection of any such ceremony. But something did jiggle loose in the recesses of his mind. He had been at Blue Monk. A trio of men, acting strangely. The Eel had sprayed something in his face. Then they had taken him. He knew that much. All other memories were still beyond reach.

He got to his feet and opened his eyes fully for the first time. He was in a pine forest. Twenty paces to the left was a river. He hobbled to it, walking slowly so as to minimize the soreness.

A pair of does spooked as he found the tree line. Judging by the position of the sun, which was behind the hills east of him, it was no later than 7 a.m.

Up in the distance, he recognized the shape of Mount Sajikigatake. He had skied there many times. That meant that Kyoto was due south. And the brook before him was the Kamo River. At least he had his bearings. To get back to the city, he needed only to follow it, keeping the mountain to his back.

Sho began following the river as it twisted its way south. His mind flashed snatches of distorted sound and visions, a jumble of unreliable recollections that seemed to come and go in quick bursts, like flash photography. Still, there was very little to hold on to. A few fleeting glimpses. A burst of extreme heat and pain. Nothing more.

Eventually he came to a road. The sound of a diesel engine disrupted the otherwise soundless morning. He turned, watching the old fruit truck round the corner. Fear gripped him as it slowed beside him, fragrant with the scent of oil, and stopped. The passenger side window receded into the vehicle.

The driver looked to be a farmer. "Are you alright?" He said. Sho nodded without speaking, but the driver did not appear satisfied. "Headed to town?"

"Kyoto."

"Me too. Get in."

"Thank you."

Sho stepped up on the running board and entered the vehicle. When he leaned back against the seat, pressing the bandage against the wound on his lower back, pain coursed through him.

"What day is it?" Sho said.

"Monday."

Good. The restaurant was closed on Mondays.

The truck bounced over a pothole, and the pain jogged his memory further. A patchwork of memories from the previous night that made little sense. He had been in some sort of vehicle. Blindfolded. He recalled the sensation of driving up hilly terrain, the road suddenly rough, the vehicle swaying a bit from side to side as they cornered.

The hinges of a heavy, mechanical gate. Someone shouting orders. He had been led out into the night. It had been much colder there. The air was damp and smelled of freshwater fish. Perhaps in one of the villages surrounding Lake Biwa, he thought, imagining the massive lake east of Kyoto.

The blindfold was removed at the entrance to a massive shrine that was bordered by hundreds of paper lanterns that glowed yellow in the night. "Bow your head," a voice had commanded, and with his eyes downcast he was pushed forward, made to walk through immense torii gates.

"Leave your shoes." And so he had stepped onto the heels of his sneakers, feeling the frosty cedar planks beneath his feet.

He had been led barefoot up a stone stairway that had been worn smooth over the centuries. He climbed higher, the outside air growing colder with each succeeding set of stairs. Fox statuary, guardians of the shrine, sat on either side of the stairway. The wind blew, fluttering *omikuji* - folded strips of paper tied to the limbs of cherry trees. On each omikuji was written a bad omen that had been left behind by a believer. Better that bad luck waits by the tree than attach itself to the bearer.

"Disrobe," the voice had commanded. And so he had stepped out of his jeans and underpants and pulled the t-shirt and sweater over his head. The garments were snatched away as quickly as they hit the floor.

At the top of the next landing they came before a stone basin filled with water. A Shinto priest blessed it.

"Purify," the voice commanded. He had knelt before the basin, filled the immense wooden dipper and doused it over his head, neck and shoulders.

Now the driver's voice shook him from his thoughts. "Excuse me." Sho realized that the vehicle was stopped. The driver was looking at him. They were already in the city. "Are you okay?"

Sho regarded the intersection. He knew this place. The Blue Monk was just a few blocks away.

He peeled a 10,000 yen note out of the front pocket of his pants and handed it to the driver. He declined, of course, but Sho left it on the dashboard as he stepped out.

He walked the rest of the way. When he reached the Blue Monk, he immediately drank two bottles of water, followed by three shots of his strongest whiskey. Then he went to the bathroom and removed his shirt.

Sho peeled the bandage from his lower back. The stinging he felt was nothing short of sensational. But he could not look at what they had done to him. He *dared* not look. Not like this.

He went out to the bar and drank three more shots of whiskey. Then he staggered back to the bathroom as the alcohol went to his head. Then he turned, peering over his shoulder to see his reflection in the mirror. He gasped when he saw it, looking away, steadying himself against the wall until he caught his breath.

The mark on his lower back was ugly. It was already scabbing over. But even now there was no mistaking what it would look like when it healed. The Rising Sun.

He had seen this before. It was the brand his father had worn all his life.

# Shoichi Kimura Residence

Shoichi Kimura's secluded country home was situated within a heavily forested draw in the hills just outside the city. The structure, built in the style of a European ski lodge, was surrounded by a meticulously groomed garden, which was in turn encircled by a perimeter of bamboo and fir trees that shielded it from the road.

Carver woke out of habit more than will, groggy and jet-lagged, reaching for his SIG, wanting the cold comfort its grip provided. He soon realized that he was an ocean away from his beloved sidearm.

In the upstairs guest bedroom where Carver had slept, the pink light of dawn illuminated the edges of the shutters. How strange life was. Just a few days ago, he had been in Tripoli, seemingly on the verge of eliminating the Butcher of Bahrain. Eri Sato had been the furthest thing from his mind. Yet now they were in Japan together, sleeping under the same roof.

And he was in exile. Or as Speers had put it, on *administrative leave.* Carver permitted himself to say it – "administrative leave" — out loud for the first time. He knew that the term was supposed to indicate a sort of temporary purgatory, but it sounded more like a career death sentence.

He rose carefully, standing to the side of the window, peering through the gaps in the shutters, careful not to rustle them. Sho's Land Rover did not look as if it had been moved since Carver had parked it last night. He had taken on the responsibility of being the designated driver as Sho and Eri drank their way into what would surely be a memorable hangover.

His focus fell briefly upon the window frame, where he noted the triple-layered polycarbonate glass. Bullet-resistant. A home security feature that had but three types of buyers:

celebrities, politicians and criminals. Sho may not have started out as a criminal, but he had adopted the lifestyle rather quickly.

Sho called this place the Green Ghost, and not only because the surrounding shrubbery camouflaged the home within the hilly landscape so effectively. The property, which had been in his family's possession for nearly as long as the restaurant, had literally been ghosted. After his father's death, the transfer of ownership papers had somehow been lost in the clerical shuffle. In subsequent years, Sho had never once received a bill for property taxes. Nor had he ever been billed for utilities, as the home was self-sustaining, with its own private well and sewage. Camouflaged solar power panels were discreetly mounted on the rooftop.

And yet the seclusion the Green Ghost offered gave Carver little peace. His mind was reeling with all he had learned last night. For starters, Eri was convinced that members of Japan's Restoration Party had advanced knowledge of the drone attack on the Chinese embassy. Unfortunately, she had no evidence to back it up, nor did she have any motive. Fujimoto's rogue operation was both off the books and quite possibly illegal. Whatever evidence he had gathered had surely gone with him to the grave.

Then there was the small matter of the Rising Sun brand on Sho Kimura's back. "We are called the *Kuromaku*," he had said, which Eri translated as the Black Curtain.

As Sho explained it, the Kuromaku were said to be as old as the Japanese empire itself. A secret society that had purportedly controlled the course of the nation from behind the scenes.

Carver wasn't quite ready to buy into the mythology of the Kuromaku, but he had no trouble believing they were a militant force. That explained why the clan had recruited Sho in the first place. In a country with no standing army apart from a tiny self-defense force, and the lowest gun ownership rates in the world, a man with Sho's marksman skills was highly valuable. He would no doubt be a far better shot than the imbeciles who had tried to kill him in Arizona.

He had, of course, wanted to find all this out last night. But by the time Sho had finished telling the story of how the Kuromaku had abducted him from his restaurant, and imprinted their mark on his skin like some common cow, he had been blitzed out of his mind.

Now some movement out front caught his eye. Someone was moving out by the bamboo. Carver's pulse quickened. Had the Kuromaku found them already? Or had Sho turned on them? He pulled back from the window, bracing for attack.

# Julian Speers' Residence
# Arlington, Virginia

Speers woke to the sound of his driver's voice. "Mister Director? You're home, sir." He sat upright in the back seat of the SUV, rubbing the sleep from his eyes. The vehicle slowed before the four-bedroom colonial that he and his family had called home for a little more than a year. The car turned cautiously as the iron gate to the driveway opened. The vehicle came to an abrupt stop behind another armored SUV.

He recognized FBI Director Chad Fordham's security detail standing in the driveway. Oh, that was just great. Just when he got a chance to leave the office, the office came home to him. He had wanted nothing more than to kiss his sleeping kids on the cheek — assuming they were actually sleeping — and crawl into bed for a couple hours with his wife.

Speers unbuckled his seatbelt, slid out of the vehicle and waved at the guards as he went to the front door. Inside, the house still smelled like the pork loin his wife had made for dinner hours earlier. The house was dark except for the reading light next to the leather easy chair where Chad Fordham now sat.

"Ever heard of a telephone?" Speers said. He sat on the stool in the foyer and untied his brown wing tip shoes. His socks smelled sour and the balls of his feet were crying out for a pair of slippers.

"This is a conversation better had in person. Your wife was kind enough to let me in. Well, maybe *kind* isn't the word. She was, let's say, *tolerant* of my presence."

Speers leaned against the wall. "I suppose this is about Carver?"

"No, actually. He failed to show for the task force, but you already know that. But unfortunately, we're all spread pretty thin right now. Nobody has the resources to go looking for him."

"So why are you here?"

The FBI Director stepped into the shadows near the front door before he spoke, his face less than two feet from Speers'. "The Chinese are calling their people home."

"Pardon?"

"The Control Group."

"You've been in this game two decades, Chad. Sometimes I think I'm still getting up to speed. What the hell is the Control Group?"

"Twelve hundred very special Chinese citizens in the United States."

"Spies?"

"No. The Control Group members are here for perfectly legitimate reasons, or at least that's what we think. They are distinguished professors, students of high-ranking communist party members, business executives from Global 100 companies, and so forth. The Bureau has an algorithm that decides who the 1,200 most important Chinese residents are at any time. We use automation to track their movements. Unless, of course, the trail goes dark. Then we put boots on the ground, so to speak."

Speers knocked the back of his head softly against the wall behind him. "I see. So the Control Group is a sort of early warning system."

"Right. A kind of human barometer, if you will. We figure that if the Chinese were going to attack us in some meaningful way, they would make sure these VIPs were out of the country first."

"And this is happening?"

Fordham nodded. "We noticed the Chinese embassy staff slimming down in a major way about 36 hours ago."

"Well can you blame them? We blew up their embassy in Tripoli a few days ago."

"That might explain the first exodus, which happened a few nights ago. Students taking redeye flights out of the country. Since it was less than 20% of the total Control Group population, we thought maybe it was just normal skittishness, and not a direct recall from Beijing. Fast forward to tonight. We can't account for the whereabouts of any of the 1,200."

Speers stood up. "None of them?"

"Not a one."

# The Green Ghost

The creature Carver spotted moving out among the bamboo had four legs. The doe made its way around the rock garden, cutting between two shrubs. Carver didn't know how the deer had managed to get over the fence and onto the property, but if it wasn't careful, he wagered it would soon find itself on a plate at Sho's restaurant.

He put on a shirt and padded downstairs to the den, where Eri had passed out on the couch the night before. A pool table formed the centerpiece of the room underneath exposed beams of white fir. The wood-paneled walls were covered in antlers and vintage skis. A fire burned in a stone fireplace that seemed diminutive relative to the room's high ceilings.

Through the window, he spotted Sho Kimura in the garden, dressed in matching indigo jinbei top and bottom, his hand outstretched. The doe Carver had spotted from his upstairs guest room was eating a carrot from Sho's hand.

Carver went outside onto the porch. The deer wasn't spooked by his presence. Sho was stroking its neck.

"When you said you harvested all your venison, this isn't quite what I imagined."

"This is Aya. Last winter was very bitter. No food in the forest. Aya wandered in the gate one day as I drove in."

"Did you reach for your rifle?"

"Yes. Then I saw how thin she was. I thought maybe I should fatten this beggar up before I shoot her." He grinned. "Now, as you can see, my plan to cook her was a terrible failure."

He released the last of the carrot to the doe, rinsed his hands in a fountain at the edge of the porch, and waved them quickly back and forth to air dry them. "Eri is still sleeping?"

Carver nodded. Back when they had been an item, he had witnessed a lot of nights like the last one. Her tendency to drink until she puked had been the source of several arguments, especially after she moved to D.C., where public drunkenness was substantially less socially acceptable than it had been in Tokyo.

Sho turned, squatted on his heels, and pulled a hand-rolled cigarette from his pocket. "You two have a history together?"

Carver nodded. "Years ago I came to Japan to study kendo. I ended up studying her." Carver paused long enough to note a competitive glint in Sho's eye. "But that was a long time ago. And you?"

Sho took another drag of his cigarette. "Three days after the Kuromaku put the brand on me, I was very sick with a skin infection. I tried not to go to hospital, but I had no choice. I went to sleep in the emergency room. The doctor saw the Rising Sun brand and called the police. When I woke up, Eri's boss Fujimoto was there, waiting for me. He had many questions."

Carver pulled the red passports from his pocket – the ones he had taken off the Kuromaku in Arizona – and handed them to Sho. The chef opened both of them, examining the photos and names of each thoroughly. Then he shook his head and passed them back to Carver. "I do not know them."

"They were branded, just like you."

"The only Kuromaku I know is the Eel."

"Then why did they choose you?"

"Ancestry. My father was Kuromaku. And very good with a rifle. When dirty jobs had to be done for the party, they looked to him."

"What happened to him?"

"He disappeared."

Or *was* disappeared, Carver reckoned. "Sorry to hear that. But I still don't understand. The Kuromaku put a cattle brand on your back and just expected you to simply take his place?"

"The Kuromaku hold on to the old ways of living. Membership is not a choice. It is a social obligation."

"And your father didn't warn you?"

"He had been preparing me, but I did not realize. From a young age, he taught me to pray the old prayers. Then he taught me to hunt. Then, to compete. Shooting very long distances. He was very proud."

"But all the while, he was training you to serve the Kuromaku."

"It seems that way."

Carver sat down beside him. "Eri had told me you were an informant. She didn't say you were an assassin."

"You would not understand. They threatened my mother and my brother. I do what I do for them."

"Did you kill Fujimoto?"

"No. He was my only way out. Now, my only hope is Eri."

# Las Vegas

Nico Gold slept on the chaise in the living room, his toga welled up around his waist, now swollen with wine and pasta. The only light came from the blue glow of his computer and the neon glow of the Vegas strip.

He was dreaming again. Before a pagan priest, he and Madge were reciting their wedding vows in Etruscan. They stood in an ancient temple with Roman columns and an elaborate mosaic on the dome overhead. On an altar, the Lycurgus Cup glistened magically in the morning light.

He woke as his computer chirped with an activation alert. At last! It had been two long days since Jasper Blick had delivered the goods to Zhang Wei, the government worker who was to bring the streaming entertainment devices into Zhongnanhai as a gesture of MassiveStreamz' goodwill. The alert was a homing beacon of sorts, a signal that at least one of the devices had been activated.

"Come *on*," Nico pleaded, urging the beacon to hone in on a geolocation. "Let's take a ride on the Orient Express."

He sniffed a cup of old coffee on his desk. It was cold, and at least 18 hours old, but he decided to drink it anyhow. It was just fuel.

This was going to go one of two ways. Either Zhang Wei would do as he was told and install the damn thing on one of 70-some televisions within the central government headquarters, or he was a bigger fool than Nico thought, and he would simply sell them out of his trunk.

All he needed was one installation somewhere in the compound. That would get him behind the firewall. From there, Nico would be able to infiltrate any connected device in any of the associated government offices.

A map unfolded. The city of Beijing appeared. But there was no precise location yet.

Suddenly the map before him crystallized, showing the beacon location within China's imperial city.

"Yesssssss!" He was in.

# The Green Ghost

Carver held a cup of steaming tea as he stood before the kitchen window, watching Sho cut fresh herbs in the garden. His host was wearing a wide-brimmed hat and gardening gloves. Now that was a real renaissance man. Olympic biathlete. Chef. Assassin.

It was madness. *All* this was madness. What had he gotten himself into? He longed for the relatively simple reality that he had known just a few days ago. He'd had but one primary objective — extract Kyra Javan from Tripoli before the CIA drone rained hellfire on the Butcher of Bahrain. Now, days later, the U.S. and China were on the brink of war, Carver's career in intelligence seemed all but over, and he and Eri were being hunted by people that he scarcely understood.

Sho entered the kitchen with a handful of shiso leaves. He politely acknowledged Carver's presence before turning his back to wash them in the sink.

The American needed a favor, and he decided there was no sense in pussyfooting around. "I need a gun."

His host pondered the statement for less than a second, as if he had been expecting it. "The Kuromaku give me a clean rifle before each hit. They destroy it after."

"You expect me to believe you don't have another gun?"

"I am licensed for only a single hunting rifle. That would be a bit awkward for you to carry, yes?"

"I can pay you."

Sho laid the shiso leaves onto a towel to air dry. Then he turned. "It is not a question of money.

"You must know someone."

He shook his head. "The government's gun control program has been very effective. There is no black market."

"Thank God I wasn't born here."

"Only eight people were killed by guns in Japan last year. How about your country?"

"It was 13,000 last year, thanks for asking. But I'm not here to debate gun control. You're telling me that if the Eel showed up in the middle of the night, you're going to fend him off with a deer rifle?"

Sho exhaled like a man who was tired of fighting. He removed his gardening gloves. "Let me show you something."

Carver followed his host upstairs to Sho's bedroom. Sho opened the nightstand drawer next to his bed, where there was a thick poetry anthology. Or so it seemed. He opened the book cover, revealing a hollowed-out interior concealing a Glock 18 machine pistol. He lifted it from the drawer and popped in an abnormally long clip.

"Thirty-three-round magazine," he said.

Carver took the weapon into his hands. "This is a freak of nature." He inspected the hollowed-out text, finding a standard 10-round clip. He swapped it into the Glock. "It's a bit less conspicuous, don't you think?"

Somewhere, a phone buzzed. Both men reached into their pockets. The call was for Sho. He answered, spoke only briefly, and hung up. He was pale.

"The Eel has one last job for me."

"Who's the target?"

Sho shook his head. "I am always the last to know."

# The Kuma River

Crouched behind a dense tree line, and not far from the roaring Kuma River, Carver and Eri watched as the helicopter carrying Sho Kimura lifted off from within a heavily forested valley. Tracking him there had been a huge risk, but considering the circumstances, it was one he and Eri had found it necessary to take. If they had any hope of understanding the connection between the embassy bombing and the *Kuromaku*, they had to find the organization's base of operations.

Carver surveyed the dense terrain, but could not see a clearing, much less a helipad or a building. He didn't even see a road leading into it.

Eri stood, watching as the helicopter disappeared over the horizon. "Do you think he's coming back?"

"You heard Sho. He said they always take him to a remote shooting range to practice the hit."

"I know. But I have a bad feeling."

With the chopper now out of view, Carver refocused on the valley below. "How long do we have until they come back?"

"Two hours. Three max. *Ikimasho*."

They began down a path leading to the valley. The volcanic rock underneath was slippery. Minutes later, they used their hands to navigate a tricky outcropping with a view. At last they saw something through the forest.

Below them, a mountain spring spewed steaming water into a natural bathing pool. "Look," Carver said, pointing to what appeared to be a building from a bygone era. It was almost totally concealed by nature.

They moved on. A pair of monkeys scampered across their path. Down further, the game trail gave way to a narrow canyon surrounded by wet rock. Studs in the surrounding walls suggested there had once been a railing and a well-maintained hiking trail.

Down further, Eri parted the shrubbery, revealing a rusted sign with two arrows pointing in different directions. The first arrow pointed to the valley floor. SUPA BIWA LAKE RESORT LOBBY: 1.2km. The second pointed to a thicket of dense forest. ONSEN: 1Km.

"I *know* this place," Eri said. "Or at least I did."

She explained that the Supa Biwa Lake Resort had been an employee retreat owned by a large Japanese electronics firm. In the 1980s and 1990s, it had served as a weekend getaway for executives, who enjoyed its natural hot springs, mountain air and tennis courts. She and her father had been guests once, long ago, when she was very small. But when the Japanese economy's bubble burst, the company had been forced to slash spending. The mountain retreat had been among the first things to go. Unable to find a buyer for the immense resort, it had been turned over to a private firm that, for a time, sold *onsen* packages to travelers bound for Kyoto. The venture failed miserably. Despite the resort's rugged beauty, the location was simply too far from the ancient sites of Kyoto. It was even too far from Lake Biwa, the massive body of water for which it had been named.

"Looks like nature took over fast," Carver said. If there was anything left of the resort, it was completely invisible from the two-lane highway that cut through the mountains. If it hadn't been for the tracking beacon Eri had sewn into Sho's pants, they would have never found it.

They descended further until they reached the valley. They walked through jungle in the general direction of the building they had spotted from up top. Soon Carver tripped over something surprisingly solid, even and long. A six-inch-high concrete barrier now covered in moss.

"I think this used to be the parking lot," Eri said.

At last they came to the thick ring of jungle that separated the resort ruins from the rest of the valley. Carver intended to simply slither their way through it, but at close range he saw a perimeter of densely planted bamboo, much like what

Sho had used to fortify the Green Ghost. Without a machete, there was no way in, and no way over. There had to be another path.

They walked the perimeter to a flat area with grass that was just eight inches high. Carver spotted tire tracks leading from the main highway that seemed to simply disappear into the jungle. Upon closer inspection, they found it – under a cleverly crafted canopy of dense vines, an opening wide enough for even large trucks. Only there was no sentry box, no razor wire, and nobody taking tickets. That was part of the camouflage, Carver supposed. This place was impossible to spot unless you knew what you were looking for.

Carver pulled the Glock from the ankle holster Sho had given him and held it low as they inspected the entrance. Eri wielded the Krazy Kisser. Beyond was a tunnel that led to a vast underground parking garage. Carver counted no less than 12 black shuttle buses lined up in a neat row. Judging by the smell of freshly burned oil, at least some of them had been driven today.

Buses? Who was getting bused into this place, and why?

An open door led to a staircase. At the top, they found themselves looking out over a courtyard and what was left of the main resort building, which was half-swallowed by vegetation. Carver scanned the windows, looking for any signs of life. He saw nothing but shattered glass. Damaged, he imagined, by earthquakes or settling earth.

They entered the former clubhouse through a door that was barely on its hinges. They heard nothing except the crackling insect chatter in the surrounding forest. The only light streamed in from a row of south-facing windows that looked out over a pair of overgrown tennis courts.

Tree roots had pushed up some of the floor tiles. Vines were growing on the inside walls and ceiling. An entire crystal chandelier was now green with flora. Looking out on the back property, a pair of golf carts had been overtaken by vines. Somewhere out there in the thickets had once been a golf course.

They pushed on, finding themselves in a banquet room with a view of the spring-fed valley below. The carcass of a long-dead squirrel was stretched out on one of several long tables.

"Lunch?" Carver whispered. Eri punched him in the arm.

"Why no guards?" she said.

"That would attract attention. Besides, you don't need protection if nobody knows you're here."

Something skittered up the wall behind him. Carver turned. A reptilian tail disappeared into a crack in the wall.

Those buses had been driven today. Carver was sure of it. So where was everyone?

They slowly made their way through the complex, room by room, finding nothing of interest except a supply room full of sports equipment that Carver imagined was once loaned out to guests. Racks of rusted bicycles, tennis and badminton rackets, croquet mallets, fly fishing rods and golf clubs.

They moved into the next set of rooms until they came across a window overlooking another courtyard. Ivy covered a long rectangular building.

Suddenly, a set of massive double doors opened in the middle of the foliage. Carver and Eri crouched down, clutching their weapons tightly, watching. Two men in black jumpsuits emerged. They were rolling a cart with several black boxes inside. Behind them, Carver could see into the building. On either side of a narrow breezeway, endless rows of storage racks held matching black boxes, each blinking green, red and yellow. A child might have mistaken them for Christmas lights.

"A server farm," Carver whispered. "They're hosting their own data center."

The doors closed behind the workers, until once again, Carver's only view was of thick ivy. Meanwhile, the men rolled the hardware into one of the adjacent buildings. Carver and Eri moved on to an adjacent wing, through a back door that led to a spotless, white-walled kitchen. Its ample shelves were lined with plenty of canned food as well as some fresh vegetables. Judging by an industrial-size rice cooker in the sink with some intact grain floating inside, someone had already made a big meal today.

The next room was an empty cafeteria. Unlike the rest of the place, there was no decaying opulence here. It had been – and still was – an employee lunchroom.

Eri pointed to the far wall, where the Rising Sun flag hung. She snapped a photo, and they moved on. Further down in the valley was a building that, unlike virtually all others on the property, was newly constructed. Satellite dishes flanked the gleaming, windowless, monolithic building. Concealing the entire array was a thin layer of topsoil and vegetation – stretched across a net – that stretched from end to end. From the air, the dishes underneath would be virtually impossible to spot.

A high-pitched hum emanated from the monolith. Carver could feel it in his bones. He and Eri crept around the other side of a well-tended hedgerow. There they spotted a pair of young men chatting and puffing cigarettes. They were thin, even waifish. Stick figures in identical jumpsuits. They had the long, delicate hands of musicians. Or programmers.

Eri slowed her breathing and cupped her ears, trying to focus on what they were saying. The workers lingered only a moment longer before they stubbed their cigarettes into a planter and went inside the monolith. As the door swung open, Carver glimpsed rows of workers seated at gleaming workstations.

"Could you hear what they were saying?" Carver said.

"Yes. Why were they talking about Native Americans?"

"They weren't. They said 'Apache,' but that's a kind of software that runs on web servers. JSON stands for JavaScript object notation. The only people who talk about that stuff are programmers."

"Programmers? Here?"

"The Kuromaku have apparently created a cyber warfare team. The question is, were they behind the drone hack? And if so, why?"

# Somewhere Over Japan

Mid-morning sun warmed Sho's face as it shone into the low-flying helicopter. He remained blindfolded as the aircraft skimmed the mountaintops. The Eel sat behind him, exhaling cigarette smoke. He spoke in a voice loud enough to be heard over the buzz of the rotor blades. "The autumn leaves are spectacular today. Just a few more minutes, and I'll take off your mask so you can see them."

Sho was in no hurry. These little trips seemed almost routine now. In the nine months since he had been branded, Sho had terminated three targets on the Eel's orders. The preparation before each kill was always the same. First, Sho was directed to take a small local train to Ninose Station in Sakyo-ku, a tiny village in the mountains north of Kyoto. The trip took about 40 minutes. The Eel always pulled to the curb in a black Lexus sedan with dark tinted windows. The moment Sho got into the car, he was handed a cushioned black eye mask exactly like the one his mother slept in.

He was taken to a helicopter pad. Still blindfolded, he swore he could hear a sizable waterfall in the distance. Later, he had gone looking for it on Google Earth. Despite searching for hours, he couldn't find a big waterfall anywhere on the map near Ninose. Maybe it was smaller than he had imagined. Or maybe it was tucked within a dense forest. He had reported these facts to Fujimoto, who had promised to go looking for the landmark a few weeks before his untimely death.

From there, Sho was flown to a remote rifle range in a deforested valley. The nameless chopper pilot, whom Sho had come to think of as "Pizza Face," removed a hard-shell rifle case from the helicopter. Inside was a Sako TRG-42 rifle fitted with a muzzle brake. There were also several boxes of .338 Lapua ammunition and a tripod rest.

Then the Eel would watch through a small telescope as Sho sighted the rifle in on targets the pilot had placed downfield. Human silhouettes were placed at 50 meters, 100 meters and 150 meters. They would shoot into the evening using night vision scopes.

Although a relatively heavy weapon at nearly 11 pounds, the Sako was even more powerful than the Winchester .30-06 he hunted with. Both weapons were a world apart from the featherweight .22 caliber he had used on the Japanese biathlon team.

On each trip back to Kyoto, Pizza Face blindfolded him once again. Along the way, the Eel would make pleasant conversation. *How is business? Where do you grow your delicious herbs? How do you get the venison to taste so good?* And then there were the veiled threats. *Sho, I happened to see your mother in the grocery store last week. What a coincidence!* It wasn't a coincidence. His mother lived in Matsumoto, more than four hours away. *She looked well. But you should visit her more often. It would be terrible if something happened to her.*

Even if the rehearsals were routine, carrying out the actual jobs had been anything but. The targets were never disclosed until game time. Sho was shown photographs of each person, but he was never given a name, nor was he given a reason.

His first target had been a vacationing middle-aged man with a thick, graying mustache and tiny eyes. Each night, he liked to enjoy a cigarette after dinner on the balcony of his hotel room. On the second evening of his trip, Sho and the Eel waited in the tree line about 80 meters from the hotel. Sho was nervous. Despite the implied threats against his brother and mother, he wasn't quite sure that he would be able to go through with it. The Eel pointed out that it would be no different from shooting deer. "We are all mammals," he had reasoned. "If anything, the deer deserve to live more than we do. After all, a deer can't be wicked, can it?"

At long last, about two hours before midnight, the target emerged from his hotel room. He unzipped the fly of his boxer shorts, pulled out his equipment, and began urinating down onto a flower bed below. It was a small thing, but the primal act was all Sho needed to clear his conscience. He switched the rifle's safety switch to the off position. And then, just as the Eel had said, the man began smoking. The brand of cigarettes was called Peace. Sho wondered at the irony for a split second before pulling the trigger.

The next morning, Sho learned the man's identity from a television newscaster. He was Kosuke Ueno. An election official from Gunma with Yakuza connections.

The next two jobs had been handled in much the same way. Both were holiday killings. The second target had been a judge in Nagano. The third was a candidate running for the National Diet from Hokkaido.

Why not just kill them quietly? Make it look like suicide? He wondered all these things but did not ask. He reckoned that the Eel felt the high-profile political killings would serve as intimidation.

Eventually, Sho had reported these crimes to Fujimoto, although he did not confess to pulling the trigger himself. He merely confirmed that the Kuromaku had been behind them. The old detective knew the truth, of course, but he seemed neither surprised nor judgmental. "Fits the profile," Fujimoto had said. "Keep bringing me information like this, and I'll continue to keep your name out of my reports."

Sho had not liked being owned by Fujimoto any more than he liked being owned by the Kuromaku. But he had hopes that the man who had brought down one of Japan's deadliest domestic terror cults could give him his life back. For that reason, the old investigator's death had devastated him. Now, en route to the practice session for what would be his fourth and final assassination, he hoped Eri would be able to finish what Fujimoto had started.

WILLIAM TYREE

# The Exclusion Zone
# Fukushima Prefecture
# Japan

The Eel pulled Sho's mask off, exposing his enlarged pupils to the blinding sunlight shining through the chopper's Plexiglas windows. Slowly, his eyes adjusted so that he could see the magnificence on the rolling hills below them. The forest was tinged with red and yellow maple trees. He wished this was all a dream. He wished they could stay aloft forever, floating over the autumn leaves.

And yet something was different today. It wasn't just the colors of the season. "Are we going to the same rifle range?" he asked.

"A new one," the Eel said. He wore a Yomiuri Giants ball cap. "Farther away. But relax. You will still get back to the Blue Monk in time to serve dinner tonight."

But he could not relax. His mind was filled with doubt. Were they going to kill him? It was a question he had asked himself every time he did a job.

Twenty-five minutes later, he could see coastline. As the ocean stretched out to the east, he could no longer spot vehicles or people below. Then it dawned on him. They were entering Japan's exclusion zone. The area that had been abruptly evacuated after the 2011 earthquake that triggered the ensuing tsunami and disaster at the Daiichi Nuclear Facility, some 12 miles away.

The helicopter descended over a ghost town called Tomioka. Sho caught sight of a clock tower on a bank building. The hands were stuck at 2:46 — the exact time of the earthquake.

"No one will bother us here," the Eel said.

As the pilot touched down and cut the engine, the Eel distributed matching white disposable coveralls, complete with hoods and face shields. "Just a precaution," he said, stabbing a nicotine-stained finger at the universal symbol for radioactivity that was emblazoned on the uniform's left breast.

Sho pulled the uniform on over his existing clothes. A few moments later, as the three men stepped out of the helicopter, he noticed how nature had taken over the abandoned town. Weeds, some of them more than six feet tall, lined the streets. Bamboo was growing up and around a building that had caved in on itself during the earthquake. Across the street, a group of monkeys stood atop a boat that had washed inland.

"Wake up," the Eel said, clapping his gloved hands in Sho's face. "We have work to do!"

Pizza Face pulled the heavy rifle case from the chopper — the kind built to endure endless abuse by airport baggage personnel — and handed it to Sho. Then he began walking toward a field clustered with mannequins. A set of bleachers stood at the far end.

"Don't follow him," the Eel said, his voice muffled behind the face shield. "You and I are going up there." He pointed toward the only truly tall building in the vicinity, a hotel that looked to be about 20 stories. Broken windows dotted the building's south side like dental cavities.

They entered via the abandoned hotel lobby. Rays of sunlight shone through where the tinted glass was cracked and caved in. A flock of pigeons spooked from behind the marble check-in desk. The floor was dotted with abandoned suitcases and luggage carts and seashells. Sho briefly imagined the people who had left all these things behind so quickly. When the tsunami alert sounded, had they ran outside, seeking higher ground, or had they simply gone upstairs?

"Up here," the Eel said, shining a flashlight into a dark stairwell. "The elevator is broken. Pace yourself. We're going to the 18th floor."

Sho groaned. In his training days, such a climb would have been no big deal. But these days, the sole exercise he got was de-boning animals in the kitchen at the Blue Monk. "Why so high?"

"We must recreate the exact shooting conditions of the next job as much as possible."

By the time they reached the 10th floor, Sho had overheated in his radiation suit. The rifle case seemed several times heavier than it had when they had started.

"Save your strength," the Eel said. He took the rifle case and carried it for Sho the rest of the way up.

One word described the 18th floor: haunted. Room service trays remained on the same carts they had been ferried on years ago. A radioactive breeze came in through a jagged opening in a window opposite the stairwell, blowing the yellowing curtains in a ghostly fashion.

They went into Room 1804, a north-facing room that had once offered guests a view of the abandoned town. The window had been removed completely, and a chair was set up before a shooting bench that was exactly like the one at the government firing range where Sho was required to retest for his annual shooting license.

The Eel set the rifle case on the bed and unlocked it. "Dozo," he said before collapsing into an armchair.

He watched as Sho plucked the precious hardware from the rifle case, checking the chamber for obstacles before sliding the bolt in. Then he screwed the muzzle suppressor onto the end of the barrel. It would serve the purpose of both masking the sound of the gunshot and the flash of the muzzle.

Then the Eel pulled a pair of powerful binoculars and an old-fashioned walkie-talkie from his duffel bag. He cleared the radio channel and spoke. "Is everything in place?"

Pizza Face's voice came over the device. "*Hai, dozo.*"

The Eel smiled. "Go ahead, Kimura-*san*. Sit down." Sho sat at the shooting bench. The end of the rifle edged out the open window like a nosy neighbor. "See that park?"

Sho did. A set of baseball bleachers was attached to a tractor. It looked as if they had been dragged from a baseball field on the other side of the park. About 20 mannequins had been arranged on them. All standing, they posed as if they had been taken directly from the windows of a department store.

From there, two more lines of mannequins stretched out across the field in two neat rows. Like an honor guard on either side of a red carpet, awaiting some high-ranking government official. It was a preposterous spectacle. So many mannequins. There were at least 100 of them, maybe more. Had the Eel looted every abandoned department store in the irradiated zone?

Sho did not like the looks of this. The Eel had said he meant to recreate the shooting conditions of the upcoming job, and this looked like some sort of mock ceremony on a grand scale. This time, he feared, the target wouldn't be some small-time election. It might be someone truly important.

"The distance to the target," the Eel said, "Is approximately 320 meters, and we are now 65 meters from the ground."

That was a much longer distance than Sho was accustomed to. He would have to make allowances for distance and wind. He tried to slow his breathing. His clothes beneath the coveralls were now soaked in sweat. He pressed the ammunition clip into the rifle. Returning his eye to the scope, he took note of what the mannequins were wearing. They were all dressed conservatively. The males were in black suits or in Defense Force uniforms. His eye quickly found one of the targets wearing a red tie. Further down, there were others. Most were in between the rows of mannequins, as if they were walking the red carpet.

"Go on," the Eel urged, having too found one of the targets through with his binoculars. "Start with the mannequin in the suit standing on the bleachers."

Sho chambered one of the .338 cartridges into the barrel. After he fired, his handler grunted approvingly as the plastic head burst into a thousand pieces.

"Now hit the one standing between the rows, nearest the bleachers." Sho returned his eye to the scope. He squeezed off another round, blasting the figure through its neck.

The Eel took a stopwatch from his pocket. "Good. Now, on my mark, shoot as many as you can in 30 seconds. Get the females, too."

Sho lined up three spare ammo clips, setting them within easy reach. On the Eel's mark, he picked off eight of the mannequins wearing red ties, reloading just once.

"*Sugoi!*" the Eel squealed in amazement. Then he spoke into his radio. "Engage the moving targets, please."

At last, Sho's rifle found Pizza Face. He was driving a quad hitched to a wagon. Standing within it were five suited mannequins with red ties, wobbling this way and that. The spectacle reminded Sho of a clown car he had seen in an old movie.

Sho trained his crosshairs on its driver. How many times had he fantasized about this moment? Getting his freedom would be easier than he had imagined. They were all alone out here in the irradiated zone. He would waste Pizza Face first. Then he would whirl around and finish the Eel at point blank range. Unless, of course, Sho decided to beat him to death with the butt of the rifle.

# The Kuromaku Base

Having discovered the buzzing Kuromaku cyber warfare nerve center, Carver and Eri slipped into the building next to the monolith, where no one seemed to be around. The former resort conference room had been converted to a traditional office with an open floor plan containing nine workstations.

A large portrait of Prime Minister Akira Ito adorned the far wall. The other walls were filled with maps of what Carver assumed were election districts. At the head of the room was an elaborately carved desk, and behind it, a carefully drawn whiteboard listing dozens of political parties and the numbers of seats they currently held in the National Diet.

In the center of the room was a scale model of the Imperial Palace. Carver had never been there in person, but he recognized it from photographs. Detailed plans for renovations were annotated throughout the complex. Existing rooms were labeled with office numbers and official designations, the best of which had been reserved for the Prime Minister's office.

"It's not enough for Ito to simply say he's a nationalist," Carver whispered. "He's going to prove it by moving his government into the palace."

"Impossible. The royal family would never approve."

"Something tells me he won't be asking for permission."

Eri set the Krazy Kisser down and began rifling through a stack of papers on one of the desks. Carver left her side, gravitating to a corkboard mounted behind one of the desks. It was dotted with headshots. In what was perhaps the most ethnically homogenous country in the world, he noted that none of the people pictured were Asian.

As he got closer to the headshots, he was stunned to find that he recognized several of them. At the top of the hierarchical arrangement was Saif Al-Mohammad, the Butcher of Bahrain. On the row of headshots just below him, the Butcher's Allied Jihad lieutenants. And below that was Mohy Osman, the monster whose heart Carver had staked in Tripoli, unmistakable for the skunky streak of premature silver hair on the left side of his beard.

There was one other face Carver recognized: Kyra Javan. And it wasn't just Kyra's wedding photo, either. In the photo, she was younger. Her hair was uncovered. It must have been taken *before* she was embedded with the Butcher. Had they known who she was all along? Carver used his burner phone to snap a quick photograph of the corkboard.

Somewhere down the hall, two men laughed like hyenas. Carver raised the Glock and chambered a round. "Let's go."

"Just a sec." The voices were getting closer.

"If we're discovered, they'll link you to Sho, and that'll be the end of him. And us too, by the way."

Eri picked up a tidy stack of files and tucked them under her left arm. She held the Krazy Kisser in her right. They went back through the compound the same way they had come, traversing the ruins of the old resort to the parking garage, around the bamboo perimeter and through the monkey forest.

Once they reached the far ridge, Eri set the files down in the grass and hunched before them, out of breath. She looked out over the forested valley where the party's secret lair had gone undetected until now. Carver sat beside her as she flipped through the files. Pages upon pages of handwritten notes, some of which were bound to surveillance photographs.

"What is all this?"

"I recognized it immediately as Fujimoto's research. They must have taken it from his apartment. There might be something here we can use." She went on, but Carver was lost in the experience of sitting beside her.

*This feeling isn't real. It's just chemical. Adrenaline and pheromones.*

Still, instinct took over. Carver kissed her neck. She turned. Their lips met for only an instant before she turned away again.

"We should focus on the task at hand."

He pulled himself together. "Yeah." He showed her the photo he had taken of the corkboard, explaining who each of the headshots belonged to. "Fujimoto was right, Eri. I think Ito's inner circle had advanced knowledge of the embassy strike."

"But how could they have known?"

"They couldn't have. Unless they orchestrated it themselves."

# The Exclusion Zone

Sho found Pizza Face in his riflescope, tracking him as he towed the wagon full of mannequins. They seemed to jitterbug as they were pulled over bumpy ground.

The Eel stood behind him. He lifted the face shield of his suit and lit a cigarette. "What are you waiting for? *Dozo!* Shoot them."

But it was Pizza Face's head that he wanted to see explode. And then, the Eel's. But if he did so, would he really be free, once and for all?

He considered the practical matter of escaping from this wasteland. He couldn't fly the helicopter by himself. None of the abandoned vehicles on the street looked drivable. He would have to walk 20 kilometers through the irradiated zone to the next town. Even then, he could never go back to his condo in Kyoto again. Or the Blue Monk. Or even the Green Ghost. And even if he fled the country and started over somewhere, would he ever sleep soundly?

It was anyone's guess as to how many Kuromaku there were. Hadn't Carver said they hunted him even in Arizona? Even if he escaped, his mother and little brother would surely pay the price for his freedom.

Pizza Face erupted over the walkie-talkie. "What is taking so long?"

Sho shifted his crosshairs to the first mannequin in the wagon and drilled it with one shot. He wasted the others with similarly brutal efficiency. As the Eel looked on, Sho reloaded again and again until he had destroyed all 132 mannequins in the field.

At last, the Eel said, "That's good, Kimura-*san*. Very good. You may clean the rifle now."

Sho turned and looked up at him through the plastic face mask. "What about night conditions?"

The Eel sat in an armchair in the corner of the room. "Not this time. The next job will be in daylight, just like this. You will shoot from a hotel room window, down into a public area."

Panic gripped him. The other jobs had been completed at night, in semi-rural environments. Sho had simply done his work and melted back into the cover of darkness. "What about the police?"

"They will arrest someone else. It has all been taken care of in advance."

"Someone else will take credit?" The words surprised even him. Was that pride talking, or stupid arrogance? Either way, he regretted the remark instantly. "Forgive me."

But his handler actually looked pleased. "Not credit, Kimura-*san*. *Blame*. The future of our country depends on someone else taking the blame for this. I think you will find some pleasure in the person we have chosen." The Eel paused for a moment. As if deciding whether to say more. "You see, over the centuries, we Kuromaku have influenced politics from the shadows. And we have frankly preferred it that way. Even after the humiliation of war, we held our enemies close." He stood up now, pacing as he spoke. "As the Americans occupied our country and married our women, it was we Kuromaku who put a Japanese car in every driveway and a Japanese television in every living room in America. How the Americans feared our economic might in the 1980s!"

"My father said those were the good old days."

"How they suddenly looked up to our schools! To our work ethic! What we could not do with the sword, we would do with our economy, sucking them dry until they had no choice but to leave. But where are we now? The Americans once again have the best technology and the most innovative workers in the world. China has once again risen from the east, and they threaten not only our territory, but also our economy. And what has become of our people? The veterans who understood the old ways are dying out. Our young men care only about trivial things.

We Kuromaku are the only ones who still believe that we can be great again."

Sho shrugged. Mostly, he avoided politics, getting most of his news from the more opinionated customers at his restaurant. He had nothing against America. He loved jazz. And he even loved his Winchester. Still, the Eel's words struck a chord.

He watched as the Eel got to his feet, pacing as he continued to rant. "Where are the Americans when the North Koreans kidnap our women from our homeland, and then brag about it? Where are they when the Chinese block our trade routes?"

Sho listened in stunned silence. Then he realized the Eel's question had not been a rhetorical one. He was waiting for an answer.

"I don't know."

Pizza Face pilot radioed from the helicopter. "How much longer?"

The Eel continued his tirade unabated. "The Americans demand fair trade and low prices from our factories. They demand that our constitution remain that of a pacifist country, so that we may not rebuild our own military. Meanwhile, their sailors on their bases make whores out of our women in exchange for protection against the Chinese. What protection?"

At last, the two men gathered their things and began descending the stairs toward the hotel lobby. Sho no longer noticed the sweat gathering in his suit, or the chafing of the material against his waist. He thought of Fujimoto. Of how he had wept when he heard of the old man's death. *You are just a pawn in a dirty power struggle*, Fujimoto had once told him. *I am the light that will guide you out of the darkness.* Sho had believed him. And he had believed *in* him. But now Sho suspected that he was part of something bigger than Fujimoto and his obsession with the elections. A movement centuries in the making.

# PART V

# Capitol Building
# Washington D.C.

Julian Speers and Kyra Javan sat before the 13-member Senate Select Committee on Intelligence. The windowless conference room had been built with the explicit purpose of protection against audio or thermal surveillance. Kyra had returned to the United States seven short days ago, during which time the U.S. Intelligence Community had filled her every waking moment with physical and psychological evaluations, as well as debriefing sessions held by representatives of various federal agencies.

Speers had, to the greatest extent possible, shielded Kyra from hostile interrogations. She deserved the country's gratitude, not its judgment. She had, quite literally, slept with the enemy to protect American lives.

But he realized he wouldn't be able to protect Kyra much longer. Following the leak about Kyra's identity to *Al Jazeera*, Speers knew full well that this committee, which Speers was required to keep "fully and currently informed" of all intelligence activities, would pull no punches.

Karen Hernandez, the junior senator from Arizona, had been pecking at Kyra for more than an hour already. "Let me make sure I understand you," she continued. "You claim that while attempting to flee the city, you were captured by one of Al-Muhammad's men?"

Kyra nodded with as much patience as she could manage. "That's correct. His name was Mohy Osman. He was killed during my extraction."

"How exactly did he die, Miss Javan?"

Speers put his hand over Kyra's mic before she could respond. The last thing he needed was Blake Carver's name surfacing during another committee hearing. Carver's vampire hunter act would do little to improve his odds of being reinstated with Guardian. "If I may, Senator, Kyra was being waterboarded at the time. She never actually saw what happened to Mohy Osman"

"I find it hard to believe that she saw nothing."

"Really, Senator? It's a little hard to see when upside down in a bathtub. You should try for yourself."

The remark elicited gasps from the committee. Senator Hernandez remained unmoved. "Kyra, did Mohy Osman say anything that led you to believe that the mission in Tripoli had been compromised?"

Kyra leaned into the mic. "Just before he put me in the water, he said he always knew I was going to betray my husband. He asked me to confirm that I was working for the CIA. I refused, of course."

"So your cover *had* been compromised?"

"We may never know. Mohy thought everyone was working for the CIA. I mean, he murdered his 13-year-old niece because she was listening to rock music. He thought the recording was encoded with secret messages from America."

Speers' phone buzzed. He had programmed his phone to remain silent except for messages from his assistant, and she had been instructed to screen his communications and let no one through unless the message was time-sensitive.

Speak of the devil. The message was from Carver. He had sent a photograph of photographs. Headshots, to be exact. He zoomed in and immediately recognized one of the faces. It was the Butcher of Bahrain. And further down, an image of Kyra Javan. The caption:

*Found these in a covert government facility in the mountains north of Kyoto. Note the absence of a headscarf on Kyra. It was taken pre-Trojan Horse.*

There was also a question: *If we coordinated anything with Japanese intelligence, I never heard of it. Am I wrong?*

Speers leaned into the microphone, interrupting another of Senator Hernandez's questions. "Excuse me, Senator, I need a word alone with Ms. Javan."

The senator called a brief recess. Speers rose, led Kyra out into the hallway and down an emergency exit staircase. His security detail blocked off the stairs above and below them. "Give us some Metallica," Speers told the head of his detail. Soon, an onslaught of guitar, bass and drums roared from the man's phone. Metallica was always Speers' go-to ambient noise to mask a sensitive conversation.

Now Speers stepped close to the five-foot-eight-inch operative, their faces scarcely 10 inches apart. "While you were embedded with the Butcher," he said in a near-whisper, "how did you get messages in and out?"

"With all due respect, sir, I've already answered that question ten times this week."

Speers stiffened at her sudden insolence, but allowed himself a moment to breathe before responding.

"Of course you have," Speers said with as much empathy as he could muster. "But when you manage 16 federal agencies as I do, you can only be a mile wide and an inch deep on anything. Will you forgive me?"

She softened. Her shoulders sagged. "Yes. Sorry. I think I'm just exhausted."

"Now Kyra, as you said before the committee, you were not permitted to travel alone. So what tradecraft did you employ to report in?"

"At least two to three times a week, I would go to the market with the other wives. It was a big, sprawling place. We always had at least 24 mouths to feed, sometimes more depending on who was visiting, so we would divide up the shopping list. Divide and conquer. Then meet back in 30 minutes to head home. There was this Japanese importer in the market. The owner was on the CIA payroll. He'd arrange quick meetings or pass messages."

"A Japanese importer?"

"Yes. The Butcher loves Japanese food. Apparently there were once great Japanese restaurants all over Tripoli, but most went out of business during the revolution."

Alarm bells rang out in Speers' mind. If the Butcher had loved Japanese food so much, why didn't his first wife, Farah, just learn to cook it for him? She had been intensely opposed to his marrying three women half her age, but relented because the alternative was getting stoned to death by a village of her peers. Still, she wouldn't have risked giving Kyra any competitive advantages.

"Were you surprised that Farah let you go alone?" he asked.

"A little at first, yeah."

"How did it work?"

"The shop owner would offer to show me his reserve supplies. I would step into the back. The first few times, Carver was there to facilitate. After that, the shopkeeper would have a phone waiting for me. I used it to text with him."

That was all Speers needed to hear. Either Kyra was lying, or the intermediary was the leak. He signaled to his security detail as he began descending the steps. "Bring the car around."

# The Green Ghost

As darkness settled in, Carver gazed out from the second floor window that had served as his crow's nest. The firs surrounding the property swayed in the wind, but the bamboo held fast, nearly unmoving, as if strengthening its resolve to protect the home and its inhabitants. Aya grazed quietly on a vine that snaked down the garden pagoda.

Sho's Land Rover was still absent from the ivy-covered carport. It had been nearly 12 hours since he had left for his outing with the Eel. Carver could only hope that when he returned, he would come alone.

Time was running out. Carver could feel that in his bones. It was time to check in on Nico and see if he'd made any progress. He logged onto Sho's private server. Recalling the 63-character URL from memory, Carver logged into the encrypted messaging system Nico had built. He couldn't help rolling his eyes as he typed the hacker's profile name, Titu$. Several sweat-inducing images of the Lycurgus Cup – the priceless Roman goblet Nico had asked Carver to get as payment for his services – loaded onscreen.

When Nico had demanded the cup in Vegas, Carver had hastily agreed to the ludicrous request, thinking that his old friend would come to his senses before any payment was due. Apparently he had been wrong about that. Carver honestly had no idea how he was going to pull this off.

Putting that little task out of his mind for the moment, he did as Nico had instructed and inputted the 40-character encrypted messaging key. No context was needed. Nico would understand what the code meant, and the messaging system would erase the note within seconds of Nico's reading it.

The machine bleated an alert communicating that he had received an encrypted invitation to chat on a second channel. He accepted and opened the page, which was just an undesigned chat window – white text on a black screen.

TITU$: Hail Carver! Are you in good health?

CARVER: surviving. any progress to report?

TITU$: To what avail is progress if one can't savor and boast about his individual achievements? My dear Agent Carver, I realized that the challenge you put before me was going to require, shall we say, special effort. But what specifically? I was initially flummoxed by the problem. Then I read in an intimate interview with Chinese President Kang that he has several large televisions in his private office so he could monitor world news throughout the day. While pondering how I might exploit his TV addiction, I had the good fortune to go down to the casino and meet a rather loquacious businessman whose blue chip company had been trying to penetrate the Great Wall of China.

CARVER: is this going somewhere?

TITU$: Patience, friend. It's fairly easy to turn most any Internet-connected television into a hot mic. And TVs that are video-chat-capable can be turned into full-blown cameras without the knowledge of those on the other side.

CARVER: that makes me feel better about my old analog appliances.

TITU$: The question of course, was how to bypass Zhongnanhai network security? The obvious answer, as you might have guessed, was to hack in through the television provider. But not so fast. Most of the city gets its television courtesy of companies like Beijing Gehua CATV, but obviously, they intentionally block most international news like BBC or CNN. The President would of course need unfettered access to all those forbidden fruits and more. But who could actually provide that service in a way that did not royally suck?

CARVER: PLEASE get to the point.

TITU$: Spoil sport. Let's just say that I slipped the solution past the Forbidden City gates. For your information, there are 145 Internet-connected televisions within Zhongnanhai. It took time to locate the right rooms, but we're all set now. So far, I have recorded 13 conversations between Kang and his top advisors.

CARVER: anything useful?

TITU$: Nothing. As a language, Chinese has been much more difficult to learn than I expected.

CARVER: what????

TITU$: Kidding! I am fluent in Putonghua/Mandarin. But before I tell you what they said, tell me about the progress you've made on acquiring the Lycurgus Cup.

The request caught Carver off guard. He had hardly forgotten, but it was way down his priority list. Still, Nico was his only intelligence pipeline at this point, and he had to keep him happy. Even if that meant telling a white lie.

CARVER: i told you that the president and the british PM are tight. he promised Eva he would personally deliver the cup to the G8.

TITU$: Excellent! And when will I receive it here?

CARVER: working on that.

TITU$: Good. So here is what I know so far: President Kang is actually scared to death. If his inner circle was responsible for the drone strike on their embassy, he doesn't seem to know it. Nor does he know anything about the so-called retaliatory flash crash on the U.S. Stock Exchanges. However, Beijing is in full operational mode now. They have begun quietly pulling their people out of the United States in expectation of a full escalation.

Sweat ran down the inside of Carver's arms. Kang was *scared*? There was nothing more frightening than imagining the leader of a billion Chinese making decisions out of fear. He was the most powerful Chinese leader in modern history. To say nothing of the economic power he wielded, he was in charge of more than 400 nukes.

Scared people didn't make *rational* decisions. They usually made *rash* ones that put lots of people in danger.

TITU$: My larger point is that China feels they are threatened. My guess is that they will continue to escalate in hopes the U.S. will back down.

CARVER: the conversations you've recorded will be helpful. please send the audio transcripts directly to julian speers.

TITU$: With pleasure.

CARVER: here is what i want you to look into next:

He typed in the latitude and longitude of the old Supa Biwa Lake Resort, describing in great detail the monolithic structure, the camouflaged satellite dishes, and even the dialogue of the coders he had overheard talking outside. He gave him the license plate of the Eel's car – the lone piece of information they were able to get out of Sho. And finally, a name: Prime Minister Akira Ito. No return text appeared on the screen.

CARVER: still there?

TITU$: You want me to spy on the Japanese? Please! These are the people who brought us the Prius, Hello Kitty and the robotic cat that washes my dishes.

CARVER: trust me. Ito is behind this. i just need proof.

TITU$: Well, as you wish. But this is out of the scope of our agreement. I'm afraid the Cup alone will no longer be satisfactory compensation for my services.

CARVER: hilarious.

TITU$: Not joking, Agent Carver.

CARVER: ok. can we talk about this later?

TITU$: Now is better. I'd like some fine wine to accompany the Cup. Namely, a 1787 bottle of Château Lafite Bordeaux, once owned by Thomas Jefferson.

While not a wine drinker himself, Carver had, of course, read about the so-called Jefferson wines, which were purportedly discovered in Paris in 1985, more than 200 years after Jefferson had signed the declaration of independence. The bottles — which had no label, but were etched with the year 1787 and the letters Th.J — were of dubious authenticity. That mattered little when the first bottle went up for auction, fetching $175,000 dollars.

CARVER: fine. deal.

TITU$: May the light of Apollo shine on you!

# Tripoli

Smuggler Aldo Rossi, captain of the Sicilian Prince, suppressed his anxiety as he ventured into the market where Kyra Javan had once shopped with her fellow Butcher Brides. He walked under a white archway and passed a section of carpet sellers, their long geometric patterns hanging from the rafters like elaborate sports banners. He paused at the fish section, regarding a vendor with dozens of swordfish stacked with their heads pointed at the ceiling. From a distance, they looked like a company of soldiers carrying bayonets.

The look on Kyra's face as she boarded his boat in the marina had never quite left him. The woman had been through something terrible. What, exactly, he did not know. But he felt that there must be far more to her stories than the ones *Al Jazeera* had published in recent days.

Since the Chinese Embassy attack, he had planned on keeping his distance from Libya. But money talked, and here he was putting himself in harm's way again. Not that he could complain. The Americans paid well and on time. All he had to do was dock in the harbor, come to the market, go to the Japanese shopkeeper, explain that he desperately needed to send an email, and offer him a king's ransom for the quick use of his computer. And then, as his CIA contact had told him, all he had to do was connect to a specific website. The American hackers would do the rest.

At last he came to the stall he had been looking for. But its tables were bare, its doors shuttered. Aldo went to an adjacent fruit vendor. A young entrepreneur standing behind vast buckets of figs, dates, apricots and olives. Smoke wafted from a hand-rolled cigarette as he greeted Aldo with a grin.

"Ciao," Aldo said. He spoke some Arabic, as well as some French, but he found that many of the locals treated him better when he made it clear that he was Italian.

He asked about the empty stall. The fruit vendor told him he had not seen the shopkeeper in some time. "The day after the Americans killed all those Chinese. He is gone. The landlord came around yesterday, looking for his rent money."

"Could you call this landlord for me?" Aldo said. "I might be interested in renting the stall, but I want to see inside first."

Minutes later, the landlord showed up. Aldo introduced himself as a fisherman who was looking for a way to sell his catch directly. He watched eagerly as the shopkeeper rolled up the steel door. It was dimly lit, with just one working light.

"I apologize for the mess," the landlord said as the foul stench of spoiled seafood escaped the shop. "The previous occupant left everything behind."

Just as Aldo had hoped. Holding his shirt over his nose, Aldo feigned interest in the space as he made his way past unsold inventory to the back room. To his surprise, an ancient computer monitor still sat on an old desk. But his heart sank as he noted the CPU, smashed in several pieces, underneath it.

"Say," Aldo said, thinking on his feet, "I think the stall is too small for me. But my son is a computer repairman. He is always looking for spare parts. Would you sell me that broken CPU?"

Then he heard the steel door roll down behind him. "My friends here have some questions for you," the landlord said.

Aldo turned. A tall, rough-looking Asian man had joined them. Then a third man stepped into the light. Aldo would have recognized him anywhere. Saif Al-Mohammed. The Butcher of Bahrain.

# The Green Ghost

Carver sat on a kitchen barstool, watching as Eri cooked. Over the stovetop were six monitors showing live feeds from security cameras on the property's perimeter. All was calm, but it had been dark for two hours, and Sho still hadn't returned.

At least Carver had dinner to take his mind off his worries. Eri was making gyu-don, literally translated as beef bowl. In reality, it was gristle with onion over white rice, and topped with shaved ginger root. Carver inhaled the meaty aroma and groaned approvingly. "I ate this fatty stuff every day for lunch when I lived here."

Eri smirked. "I know. That was cute. At first."

"At first?"

She sucked air through her teeth. "To be honest, it was a little embarrassing."

"How so?"

"Remember when I first came to live with you in America? What if I had eaten a cheeseburger for lunch every day? And told your friends over and over how great cheeseburgers were?"

"Speaking as an American who actually ate a cheeseburger every day until he was 30, I would have seen nothing wrong with it."

Eri scooped the gyu-don into an earthen bowl and slid one across the counter to him. "Just eat. I'll talk." She had organized the stack of Fujimoto's investigative documents recovered from the compound into folders. "Fujimoto was careful not to upload to the cloud, where they might be hacked. He was far too smart for that, so he kept these hard copies around, with duplicates in a safe deposit box. I had the only spare key. But when I went to the bank to collect the files, his account had been closed."

Carver bet her visit to the bank hadn't gone unnoticed by the Kuromaku. He pinched one of the pieces of marinated gristle between his chopsticks and put it into his mouth. It was every bit as juicy and flavorful as he remembered. "*Mmm.* This brings back memories. If you would have cooked this for me when we lived together..."

"You would have stopped being such a jerk?"

"Most definitely." He pinched a piece of the fatty meat between his chopsticks and held it out for her. And when she took it into her mouth, he could have sworn that she lingered over the end of the chopsticks for a moment longer than necessary.

*A world war might break out at any second, but my ex is actually flirting with me. Here's to small wins.*

Eri set a paper map on the counter, unfolded it, and ran her index finger along a yellow line. "This is one of the maps Fujimoto had hung on his apartment wall. These yellow lines mark the border between Japan's election districts. Just two years after Ito formed the Restoration Party, they were already winning a significant number of seats in the Diet against the Liberal Democratic Party, or the LDP."

"And what were the odds of that?"

"Slim. The LDP has pretty much dominated Japanese politics since the 1950s."

"And they did it with a nationalist platform, no less."

"Right. Restoring Japan to its rightful place as a superpower. Standing up to China. Changing the pacifist constitution so Japan could build a strong military. Cutting back on foreign work visas to preserve our culture. Increasing incentives for women to have more children."

"And beyond speculation, how did Fujimoto actually figure out they were cheating?"

"Statistical anomalies in the voting patterns. Across three consecutive election cycles, Fujimoto noticed that the final vote tally was usually well outside the standard deviation when compared to voter exit polls. For example, if a race was too close to call based on exit polls, the Restoration Party candidate would typically win by at least seven percentage points. On the other hand, if a Restoration Party candidate was shown to be behind in the polls by less than seven percentage points, that candidate would nearly always pull an upset, edging his opponent out by only a few hundred votes."

"Then what happened?"

"When Fujimoto presented his evidence to his superiors, they shut him down. But Fujimoto did not stop. He was obsessed. He hired photographers to follow the candidates and their entourages."

"Why would he do that?"

"In hopes of documenting the relationship between election officials, judges and the candidates. Fujimoto's photographers went to fundraisers, weddings, sporting events, parties, you name it. They took thousands of pictures. And it cost him more money than I'll ever earn in my lifetime."

Eri began thumbing through a series of photos. The first one she showed him was of a shirtless middle-aged man at an outdoor onsen. He had the Rising Sun burnt into his back. "Here is an election worker in Nagano." She then flipped to a vacation shot of a younger man on a beach with his children. Unlike everyone else on the beach, he wore a t-shirt, but as he bent over, it rode up on his back, revealing the Rising Sun brand of the Kuromaku. "National Diet member from Chiba." Eri flipped to another photo, this one showing a man swimming freestyle in a narrow backyard lap pool. The next photo showed the same man backstroking. "The head of the Public Security Intelligence Agency. My boss."

That got Carver's attention. If Eri's boss was in the party, then he had to be considered the primary suspect in Fujimoto's murder. No wonder they had connected the dots to Eri so quickly.

Next, Eri showed him a photo that had been taken through the window of an apartment building. The man was changing clothes. Like the others, he had the Rising Sun burned into his lower back. But it was the second image - showing the man's face - that got Carver's attention. It was Prime Minister Ito.

"So Ito isn't just the head of the country's most powerful political party," she said. "He's Kuromaku."

This put new perspective on the political assassination Sho was training for. Carver swallowed his last bite of dinner. Then he rose and reached for his jacket. "Sho should have been here by now. I'm going to the Blue Monk."

"Want company?"

"Yes. But you should stay here. Just in case." He reached down and unbuckled the ankle holster. He set it and the loaded Glock on the counter. "You know how to use this, right?"

"I think so."

"Good. At least one of us has to survive to tell this story."

# The White House

On the East Wing of the White House, the Jacqueline Kennedy Garden was a field of grass framed on the north and south sides by a holly hedge. A row of linden trees and boxwood hedges provided additional privacy. Kennedy herself had been in the process of restoring it to resemble a traditional 18th century garden when her husband's assassination abruptly ended her residence. It was completed by her successor, Lady Bird Johnson, and subsequent first ladies had used it for events such as teas and award ceremonies.

President Hudson found the area ideal for playing fetch with her dog, Trapper, an eight-year-old Belgian Malinois. Speers stopped at the garden's edge, watching as the president tossed a rubber duck. She had personally adopted Trapper after his handler, a Special Forces officer, had been killed in action. The entire staff had been overjoyed by the move. Having never remarried after her husband's sudden death in a traffic accident years earlier, the president had lived a monastic life. There were rumors of an intimate relationship between Eva and the British PM, but Speers had a hard time believing it was true.

"Madam President?" Speers called.

Trapper broke from his retrieval pattern and turned, teeth bared, growling. Speers leapt to his right, putting a rosemary bush between him and the dog.

The president enjoyed Speers' discomfort for a moment before settling Trapper with a snap of her fingers. "What is it, Julian?"

"Sorry for the intrusion, Madam President, but this couldn't wait. We received a gift, of sorts."

"What sort of gift?"

"Audio transcripts of President Kang and his staff, discussing the security crisis."

She guided Speers to a more secluded area of the garden. They stopped under a trellis and sat on a bench. Her fear of foreign spy satellites was so great that this was the only place on the grounds where she felt comfortable discussing business.

She spoke in a whisper. "You're telling me that we've been bugging Kang's office?"

"Not us, Madam President."

"Who?"

"I think it's in your best interest to stay ignorant of that fact."

"Who, dammit?!?"

Speers sighed. "Nico Gold. I was unaware of his involvement until late last night."

The president's demeanor changed quickly from that of a stateswoman to of a sullen teenager. "Carver hired him, didn't he?"

"That's not important."

"I'll decide what's important. I'm told Carver failed to report to the task force."

"That is true. Whatever he's doing, he's doing it as a private citizen. As for Nico's audio files, we're not done transcribing them, but I've seen enough to be convinced of one thing — President Kang did not orchestrate the bombing of the Chinese embassy."

"How can you be sure?"

"President Kang has in fact demanded a full investigation into certain fringe elements of the Communist Party. He said he hopes they find something internally, because if they don't, then they have no choice but to" – Speers made air quotes – "punish the United States."

Trapper brought the duck and laid it at the president's feet. The president bent down, picked up the duck, swung it over her head and flung it to the other end of the garden. The dog galloped after it.

"So if China didn't do this, and we didn't do it, then who did?"

"I've got all hands working around the clock to find the answer to that question."

"It's not enough," the president said, taking the slobbery duck from the dog's mouth once again. "At this point, I have to accept that we may never find out."

"Meaning what?"

"Barring a miracle, war may be inevitable."

# The Blue Monk

In the narrow alley behind the Blue Monk, Sho Kimura angled his umbrella so that the wind and rain might better shield him as he fumbled with the keys to the service entrance. As he opened the door to the kitchen, the utter absence of carnivorous fragrance was his first sign that something was wrong. As soon as he turned the corner, he spotted the problem – Blake Carver sat at the carving table, grazing on a bowl of candied grasshoppers.

"I was wrong about these," Carver said. "Once you get past the texture, and the wings, they're actually delicious."

Sho frowned. "Where's my brother?"

"I told him to take a walk."

"You what?" He looked around the kitchen, noting the unattended pots of meat and vegetables. He imagined the nine guests that would soon arrive in the expectation of a five-star meal. "We open in less than an hour!"

Carver kicked the chair opposite him back from the table. "Sit. The faster you start talking, the sooner I leave."

Sho plopped down in it like an ill-behaved child, arms folded across his chest. "What do you want to know?"

"Let's start with what happened today."

Sho described the helicopter ride to the irradiated town in Fukushima prefecture. "The Eel made me walk to the 18th floor of an empty hotel. To practice the exact shooting conditions, including angle and distance."

"Go on."

"There were at least 200 mannequins," he said, shaking his head in disbelief. "They were lined up like it was some sort of department store parade. There was even a red carpet. Mannequins on either side, and on bleachers, facing the other mannequins on the red carpet."

---

Carver pulled a notepad off its hook above the stove, and pushed it across the table. "Sketch it for me. The hotel. The field with the targets. Every detail is important. What angle were you shooting at? How far away were the targets? How, specifically, were they arranged?"

"You want me to draw all that? Now?"

"This can't wait."

Carver sat quietly, watching as ink was committed to paper. Sho worked fast, recalling minor details. The precise distance. The precise angle. The kind of ammunition he had used.

Fifteen minutes later, he rested the pen on the paper. "Any questions?"

"The name of the target," Carver said.

"I told you. I'm the last to know. Usually, I don't know until I arrive."

"So where is it?"

Sho shook his head. "A hotel in a big city. In daylight. That is all I know."

Carver took the paper, folding the sketch into a neat square. "And what about the escape plan?"

"He said I will be gone only one day. I will travel by train there and back. He instructed me not to cancel dinner service that night. He said I must be back in time to cook."

"It's called creating an alibi. But what about the hours before? If you're stopped and questioned, what's your reason for traveling that day?"

"I will not need one. It seems that the Eel already has...how do you say it in English? Someone to transfer blame to."

"A patsy," Carver translated. "That can mean just one thing. You're going to kill someone truly important this time. And the Kuromaku will frame someone else for it."

Sho sighed. "Go ahead, Carver. Judge me. Call me weak. But what if it was *your* family they had threatened?"

Carver didn't take the bait. Instead, he pulled a photograph from his jacket pocket and set it on the table. Although the photo looked as if it had been taken some years ago, its subject - a thin, spectacled man who was relaxing with friends in an outdoor onsen – was all too familiar.

Sho stabbed the photo with his finger. "The Eel!"

"His real name is Maru Kobayashi. According to Eri, he and Ito went to the same private school growing up. Later, Kobayashi was Ito's campaign manager, and later, his chief of staff. He was said to have retired."

Sho felt the blood drain from his face. "So the Eel... works directly for Ito?"

"Your kill order comes from the very top." With that, Carver put the sketches and the photograph back into his pocket. Then he stood and headed for the door.

Sho stood. "Wait. What happens now?"

Carver paused at the service entrance door. "I have to end this."

"And if you fail?"

"Then you're the last hope."

"Don't say that. Maybe you should just kill me now."

"I would if I thought it would help. But they would just find someone to take your place. Maybe someone who shoots well enough to win an Olympic medal."

# East China Sea

Captain Todd Peters stood on the bridge of the Arleigh Burke-class destroyer that he had commanded for nearly a year. Through high-powered night vision binoculars, he surveyed the massive Chinese container ship on the horizon. God, it was huge. A Triple-E class. Longer than the Eiffel Tower was tall, and loaded with shipping containers. He counted 10 rows of containers above deck. There were probably another eight to 10 rows below as well.

Peters' orders were to prevent any further supplies from being delivered to objective SCS-13, the Pentagon-designated name for the man-made island directly north of them. Until not long ago, the bathtub-shaped island had been little more than a shallow coral reef 2.5 miles long.

He couldn't imagine how many ships full of garbage and sand had been dumped there in order to establish the port that existed now. Concrete sea walls had been erected to protect the island from tsunamis. An airstrip was close to completion. A harbor had been completed with industrial cranes and facilities large enough to handle Triple-E-size ships like the one heading his way.

Commander Shiba, the Japanese coast guard officer standing next to him, cleared his throat, but said nothing. Considering that Japan claimed these waters as its own, Shiba had been permitted to ride along as a Japanese observer. So far, he had been extremely patient and respectful of the American operations. But now, Peters sensed that patience wearing thin.

"Try again," Peters said, addressing the Warrant Officer on the other side of the bridge. The young officer had been raised in Taiwan before his family had immigrated to the United States. He spoke fluent Mandarin.

Their calls in Mandarin and English were again met with silence. The container ship simply continued its trajectory toward SCS-13. Yesterday, during his call with the Seventh Fleet brass, there had been talk of landing a Navy Seal team on the island itself. The idea had ultimately been vetoed by the Joint Chiefs of Staff, as it was considered too provocative. What if Chinese soldiers were already on the island? What if a firefight ensued?

The incidents of the past several days had put the U.S. in an untenable defensive position. Relations were on a hair trigger.

"Captain," Commander Shiba said finally, "The container ship has no weapons. With respect, I request that you fire a shot across the ship's bow."

"I'm unable to, Commander." Peters wanted nothing more than to comply with that request. He had been training his whole life for this kind of situation, and the destroyer was well-armed for anti-ship combat, with Harpoon missiles, 127-mm guns and several cannons. Should a submerged Chinese vessel escort the cargo ship, the U.S.S. Fitzgerald's anti-submarine weapons system was ready.

Shiba wasn't about to let this go. "As the official allied observer on this mission, I request that you inform your superior of my request."

"Very well." He picked up the phone and called USPACOM, the United States Pacific Command. He spoke to his contact, explaining the situation as succinctly and professionally as possible, and waited for a reply.

To his surprise, Admiral Bennington, one of the Joint Chiefs of Staff, appeared on the radio. It was the first time Peters had ever spoken directly to one of the Joint Chiefs.

"I just spoke with the president," the Admiral said. "You are now authorized to put your ship directly in front of the harbor. You may fire a warning shot if needed. The new objective is to prevent the island from being resupplied until a diplomatic resolution is achieved."

Suddenly, the boat Warrant Officer handed Captain Peters a note. He felt the eyes of the Japanese observer on him. He turned his back so that he faced the observation windows as he spoke.

"Admiral, we have two PLA planes inbound."

"I wouldn't worry about that, Captain. The Japanese get buzzed by a few hundred Chinese fighters every year. It's just intimidation."

Suddenly, the ship's missile warning indicator sounded. The Admiral was still on the line 15 seconds later, when the Chinese YJ-12 missile slammed into the ship's hull.

# Kyoto

The white-gloved taxi driver drove Carver along the Kamogawa River, skirting the glowing edge of Kyoto's nightlife district. Carver was oblivious to the bright lights whizzing by. He removed Sho's sketch from his pocket and held it in both hands, angling it toward the window as the ambient light morphed with each passing neon sign.

Carver had, of course, memorized every detail of the sketch upon seeing it the first time at the Blue Monk. But he hoped that the act of holding it — the texture of the recycled paper against his fingertips – might yield some useful insight. If he was being honest, he hoped that the conclusion he had reached was wrong. If his theory about when and where the assassination would take place was right, then the Science and Security Board that governed the Doomsday clock might as well move the second hand to one minute 'til midnight.

He went over the whole thing again, replaying Sho's exact words in his head.

*The Eel said I will be gone only one day. I will travel by train there and back. He instructed me not to cancel dinner service that night. He said I must be back here in time to cook.*

From Kyoto, Tokyo was reachable by bullet train in a little over two hours. Sho would have time to go up in the morning, pull the trigger, and get back by dinner service at the restaurant.

*They were lined up like it was some sort of department store parade. There was even a red carpet. Mannequins on either side, and on bleachers, facing the other mannequins on the red carpet. Very strange, isn't it?*

Carver closed his eyes. He had seen this layout before, at least in photos. Tokyo's Akasaka Palace, informally known as the State Guesthouse, built in 1909 as the residence of the imperial

Crown Prince. Unlike the traditional Japanese architecture seen in the Imperial grounds, the State Guesthouse was an oddity – a 160,000 square-foot, neo-Baroque monster.

The palace was the official location of the G8 Summit. The photos in Carver's mind always featured a magnificent red carpet. And the bleachers Sho had described could have been a stand-in for the palace steps. As for the rows of mannequins flanking the red carpet? Japanese soldiers flanked the dignitaries making their way from their cars to the palace.

*The Eel made me walk to the 18th floor. To practice the exact shooting conditions, including angle and distance.*

As the taxi careened along the winding road, Carver booted up his phone and summoned an aerial map of central Tokyo, zooming in on Akasaka Palace. There were several skyscrapers surrounding the palace grounds, one of which was the Hotel New Otani. At about 350 yards from the Akasaka Palace steps, it was the only hotel in Tokyo that could offer such a magnificently close view of the opening G8 ceremonies.

Carver had never been to the palace, but he *had* been to the New Otani. Long ago, in the heat of his first and only July in Tokyo, Eri had taken him for Sunday brunch at the hotel restaurant, Trader Vic's. *Home of the Mai Tai!* But neither of them actually had Mai Tais that day. He didn't touch booze back then, but Eri discovered that Sunday brunch included unlimited champagne refills – even if you asked 11 times, as she had. The drinking, combined with the warm weather, caught up with her. Seventy-one minutes into the meal, she slid off her chair.

He recalled with perfect vividness the embarrassment he had felt as he helped his giggling date to her feet. His neck was hot as he noted the wait staff watching, judging. Even with his help, Eri was wobbly as she took her seat again. I'm going to have to carry her home, he had thought, imagining the 12 sticky city blocks between them and the apartment she shared with her parents.

Bad plan, he had decided. His father wasn't wild about her dating a foreigner, and he would only make things worse by bringing Eri home sweaty and drunk. He ended up splurging for a hotel room, a luxury he could scarcely afford on a student's wages.

After a brief check-in at the front desk, they had gone up to the 15th floor with a north-facing view of the palace. They had just less than two minutes to enjoy the view before Eri fled to the bathroom. She puked up a vile-smelling concoction of pineapple and rice and eggs as Carver held her hair back behind her. Later, as Eri slept, he reclined on the couch and listened to the couple next door chatting.

Beautiful room, he had thought. Thin walls.

Now the cab stopped at a red light. Something in Carver's peripheral vision interrupted his trip down memory lane. He noted a crowd of people standing around a giant television in a sports bar. Only they weren't watching a sports highlight reel. Carver couldn't tell just what had captured their attention, but he could see footage of black smoke on a vast ocean.

The crowd looked typical for a sports bar anywhere in the world. Mostly men with beer guts wearing oversized jerseys. But he didn't like the look of shock on their faces. It was the way he remembered people standing around TVs on 9/11. Or the night of the ISIS attacks in Paris. Aghast. Disbelieving.

Carver pressed a wad of cash into the driver's white-gloved hand, stepped out of the cab and crossed the street. Inside, the stench of unfiltered cigarette smoke was only slightly outdone by the aroma of tempura-fried bar food. Baseball pennants and soccer jerseys hung from the ceiling. Somewhere in the back, a video game bleeped hysterically.

The largest TV was mounted high on the far wall. Carver edged his way past the crowd until he could see the image on the screen for himself.

An American naval destroyer in flames listed badly. U.S. helicopters lifted sailors from lifeboats.

Then the broadcast cut to footage of Chinese President Kang, who was about to make a statement. Kang was immaculately dressed in a dark suit and red tie, but he looked rattled, like a child that had been pushed onstage to perform.

Carver couldn't understand Chinese, but he understood body language. Whether Kang liked it or not, he was about to deliver an ultimatum.

# The White House

The president and her executive team gathered in the Situation Room as the live feed of President Kang's broadcast played on the room's main monitor. A translator furnished by the State Department stood behind President Hudson, translating Kang's statement in real time.

"The American Seventh Fleet created a dangerous situation by occupying waters and territories claimed by China. Our pilots responded appropriately. As a result, the sailors aboard an American destroyer have paid with their lives, and so have our pilots."

Speers, who had remained standing, scoffed. "Responded appropriately? It was needlessly aggressive!"

The president shushed him and focused on the translator's voice. "We ask that the United States prevent further incidents by retreating to its established bases in the region. In light of this military escalation, I have suspended plans to attend the G8 so that I might focus on my country's defense. Know that we will defend ourselves against further aggression, and I promise you, Madam President, our next response to aggression will not be limited to the oceans. "

Kang moved away from the podium, and the monitor cut to black. The president's chief of staff was next to speak. "Excuse me, Madam President, I have Admiral Bennington on the line."

The president thanked the translator and waited for him to leave the room. Then she swiveled her chair a half-turn. "Put him on speaker."

The Admiral's voice was tinny over the satellite phone. "Madam President," he said, "A few minutes ago, we intercepted a transmission that you should know about."

"Go ahead."

"China has a new forward listening station on one of those islands they built. We were able to intercept some of the chatter off an insecure line. Moments before we lit up the Chinese fighters, one of them radioed in that he wasn't 'hot' when he fired on our destroyer."

"Meaning what?"

"Meaning it might have been some sort of accident."

The president leaned back, arms tight against her chest. "Admiral, we all heard Kang say his pilots responded appropriately."

Speers stepped closer to the phone. "Of course he did. Whether it was or wasn't an accident, he can't show any weakness now. But if our drone weapons system was hacked, who's to say those Chinese fighters weren't hacked too?"

SECDEF Jackson sat forward. "Madam President, we can speculate about what happened all day. But I would like to remind you about the intelligence delivered by Ambassador Nakamura. Remember, Beijing is patterning their strategy after Russia's invasion of the Ukraine. First, they slipped behind Japanese territory. Next, they occupied the land overtly. After they were discovered, they offered peace talks at the G8. And what did they do then? Step up their activities to fortify their positions. Unless we do something, the next step may be an all-out invasion."

"Noted. So what do you suggest?"

"A surge. We should quietly put more forces into the region. Flood the East China Sea with submarines that will be in position to strike at the first sign of trouble. And get Special Forces on the ground on those contested islands. We can call them observers, if you want. We can dress them up as missionaries, for all I care. But we have to get into a defensible position before it's too late."

President Hudson looked in turn at Speers, the Secretary of Defense, and the Joint Chiefs. A silent poll. Each nodded reluctantly.

# Kyoto

After gleaning what he could from Kang's speech, Carver stepped outside the sports bar to call Eri. He felt sure of the time and place now. Ito had played his hand perfectly. An assassination at the G8 would be the tipping point.

If they were to stop it, they needed to leave for Tokyo tonight.

Eri answered her burner phone on the third ring.

"Hello, Agent Martyr."

Were his ears playing tricks on him? Agent Martyr was a rhyming nickname she had invented during their first few months living together in D.C. She had passed it off as a term of endearment for a while, but Carver had correctly suspected it was actually a psychological elbow to the ribs. Had she forgotten how it had blown up into a colossal argument one day? Or had she been drinking?

"If I didn't know better, I'd say you chased that gyu-don with a beer. Or three."

"No, but I had some shrimp after you left."

Shrimp? No. She had certainly not had shrimp. Eri was in fact deathly allergic to shellfish. To this day, she still carried an EpiPen in her purse.

It was a signal. She was in danger.

Carver pictured the Glock 18 he had left on the counter. His gut told him that she had never had a chance to use it. If she had fought them, she would be dead by now. And that meant just one thing. Sho had let them in.

Her next question sounded decidedly forced: "Where are you, Blake?"

A better question was, where was Eri? Was she being held at the Green Ghost, or had they taken her elsewhere? Either way, they had no doubt stationed a crew at the Green Ghost to welcome him back.

Carver had to think fast. "Did you see the news?"

"No. I've just been sitting here, playing Age of the Undead Ninjas."

Carver considered his choices. He was alone. And he was close to proving that the United States and China were being goaded into war. And only other person in the world that believed this story was Eri Sato.

He wanted to rescue her, but the odds of success were nil. His only chance was to lure them out.

"The Chinese sunk an American destroyer," Carver said. "I'm watching the news at a sports bar called…" He turned and looked up at the sign "…Free Ball." He decided to pronounce it in *Katakana* for any Kuromaku who might be listening: "Fu-ree Ba-ru."

There was a pause. Carver imagined they were feeding Eri lines. When she spoke again, she said, "You should just come watch here. With me."

"Thanks," he managed, "But they've got a huge screen TV at the bar, so I'm going to order something, maybe order a few beers, and watch the coverage for a while. Don't wait up."

The line was silent for a moment. Then she said what Carver hoped weren't her last words: "Take your time."

It was on. The Kuromaku were coming for him. Again. Only this time, he would be ready.

# Prime Minister's Official Residence Tokyo

The emperor, clad in a blue *yukata* with a thick squash-colored sash, paused at the entrance to the prime minister's private steam room. He looked in wonder at the newly finished stainless steel and glass construction. It seemed that no expense had been spared. The floor beneath the old monarch's feet was made of fine Italian marble, and the locker room smelled of oak imported from France's Loire Valley.

The steam room made up just a tiny portion of the PM's private spa. It also featured a Western-style Jacuzzi, a barrel sauna, an ice bath and of course, a traditional Japanese onsen. The old monarch sucked his front teeth until they hissed. Rather extravagant for a public official, he thought. Why not simply make it out of gold? At least then it could be melted down into something useful when Ito was forced to resign from office like all the others.

Nevertheless, the emperor loosened the sash around his *yukata*, slid the garment from his narrow shoulders, and handed it to the PM's valet. The servant handed him a fluffy white towel, careful not to make eye contact. He gestured to the steam room. "The Prime Minister is waiting for you inside."

The emperor stepped inside the humid chamber. "I can't see," he complained as thick clouds of fog unlike any he had ever seen enveloped his body. And as the transparent door closed behind him, the intensity of the heat hit him all at once. He gasped. The sudden intake of hot air made him sputter and cough.

The Prime Minister's voice called out, God-like, from somewhere above. "Good evening, your Majesty. I apologize for the extreme heat. You may wish to sit on one of the lower rows, where it is cooler."

Had he heard that correctly? Had Ito actually suggested that he sit *above* the head of the imperial family? The suggestion was an outrage! In fact, the invitation to meet here, in the PM's private steam room, was *itself* an outrage! He had agreed to come only because of social obligation. For the first time in decades, the PM had done the unthinkable – return power, however modestly, to the throne.

So yes, he was obligated to show Ito his appreciation. But he would not be humiliated. Still unable to see through the soupy fog before him, he stretched out with his right foot, using his toes to feel his way along the floor until he located the first of a series of tiered rows. Despite his advanced age, martial arts kept him reasonably limber, and he climbed to the top row, where he sat.

As he opened his mouth to speak, the intense heat seemed to burn his very insides. "I still cannot see you, Prime Minister."

Ito's voice boomed from somewhere on the far side of the chamber. "I apologize for any inconvenience," Ito said. At least now it sounded as if they were sitting at an equal height. "I'm afraid the engineers I hired to build this steam room were too ambitious. They promised that they could reproduce the thickness of an actual thundercloud. I told them that was fine, but that I wanted the clouds to be heated."

A cloud? It was more like air pollution. "How hot is it in here?"

"Fifty-four degrees Celsius, or 130 degrees Fahrenheit. A bit more heat than is customary, but a temperature that I find ideal for meetings. I find that the intense heat unleashes creative solutions to difficult problems."

The old monarch could only grunt. How long was he expected to sit in this torture chamber? He wondered how big it really was. He had imagined a steam room with seating for 10 or 12 people. Perhaps it was even larger than he had imagined.

Ito continued on, oblivious to his suffering. "This is actually the second spa I have had custom built. Years ago, I purchased an old resort that had fallen into disrepair in the mountains north of Kyoto. Very secluded. Some areas are a bit decrepit, but I purchased it for the natural saunas, which are carved into the rocks in the mountain. Very good for transmitting heat."

"Fascinating, Prime Minister, but I am not used to these conditions. I apologize in advance if our meeting is shorter than you are accustomed to."

"Then let me get right to the point. I wished to express my gratitude in person. Your speech did what my ambassador failed to do — provoke the Americans to deploy their fleet and protect Japanese territory."

"And to what end? It seems that my words have in fact brought the Americans and the Chinese closer to war than ever."

"Just so. At last the extent of Chinese aggression has finally been exposed. And just in time for the G8, where we will reestablish Japan in the eyes of the world."

The old monarch fanned the fog with his hands, but could scarcely see his own fingers. "Still, the Americans and the Chinese are like flint and stone. Wherever they meet, sparks will fly. And what is near them will catch fire."

"Did the war your father started not create great national pride?"

"National pride, yes. But nationalism is like a kite. Its ascent into the air is thrilling, but a sudden shift of wind may send it spinning out of control."

The prime minister laughed. "We cannot be guided by fear, your Majesty. The latest poll shows that public opinion has suddenly shifted on the issue of a strong Japanese military. We have almost enough votes to pass the constitutional amendment."

It seemed that the heat had fried what few brain cells the prime minister had been born with. The arrogance was galling. And to think, just days ago, the emperor had spoken from his heart about the destruction of the palace during the war.

"Prime Minister," the emperor said, "when two giants battle, it is the grass underneath that is trampled. With that in mind, perhaps postponing the G8 is prudent. Peace talks could be held somewhere neutral, such as Geneva. And they must be scheduled weeks from now, to give both sides a chance to de-escalate."

"On the contrary. We must fan the flames of war, not douse them. True, a few Chinese pilots may find their grave in the Sea of Japan. True, a few communications satellites may explode in space. There may even be an attack on the American naval base in Okinawa. But according to my analysts, the majority of the damage may not be seen in the skies or the oceans. The real damage will be done to the American and Chinese economies. Wall Street and the People's Bank of China will be crippled. For the first time in nearly a hundred years, Americans may know hunger, and the Chinese may know humility."

The emperor's cough returned. The heat was truly unbearable, but perhaps not as unbearable as Ito's insanity. And he still could not even see the PM. "Prime Minister, the steam is making me ill. I must retreat to the ice bath."

"Your Majesty, if you could indulge me for just a minute longer. Our conversation is highly sensitive, and this is the most private area of the residence."

The emperor sighed and slowed his breathing. He imagined ice cubes. Entire glaciers of ice. He held the white towel to his face and took several deep breaths, using it as a filter against the intense heat. "Very well," he managed.

"For the reasons I have discussed, I feel strongly that both Presidents Hudson and Kang must attend the G8. Tonight the Americans said that in the interest of peace, Hudson has committed to attend. Now you must persuade Kang to come as well."

Had Ito just issued an order? The emperor understood that with power, came duty. But the throne was not simply a whore to be used whenever and wherever the PM pleased. "I am flattered by your faith in my powers of persuasion, but I must counsel you to be patient."

Ito was silent for several seconds before speaking. "This is disappointing. I had certainly expected your cooperation."

"Prime Minister, I do not mean to be uncooperative. It's just that – "

"Then we must also discuss something else, your Majesty. The heir to the imperial throne."

"What does my son have to do with this?"

"It is not the crown prince that I am speaking of. Do you remember when I visited the palace and presented you with a gift?"

"Of course. The sword. The one that your grandmother recovered."

"Just so. The night I told you the story of the sword, you hosted a dinner party. Do you recall?"

The emperor removed his towel, folded it, and draped it over his head. Then he pressed the fabric against his face as a cool filter to breathe through. "Yes, Prime Minister. I am not senile."

"A journalist from the *Japan Times* was at your dinner party. Upon hearing the story from your lips, he contacted my office afterwards. He wanted to know if it was true that my grandmother had indeed worked in service at the palace during the Great War. I confirmed the story, of course. I had my assistant send over photos of my grandmother with your father. I also sent a photo of my grandmother with you, your highness."

The monarch felt dizzy. His mouth was dry. How was it possible to be so thirsty while completely enveloped by humidity?

"How is that possible, Prime Minister? Members of the royal family did not pose for photos with the staff."

"I may have failed to mention one detail about my grandmother's service to the family. She was, in her later years, your sweet nanny."

The old monarch grew silent. When he spoke again, it was nearly a whisper. "No. It cannot be."

"It was a natural job for my grandmother, considering the circumstances. As the imperial ruler of Japan, your father had 39 court concubines, and in her younger years my grandmother was his favorite."

"Your grandmother? A concubine?"

"They had known each other as children. She was your father's second cousin, an offshoot of the feudal aristocracy that had served the palace for centuries in the Kuromaku. And so she watched as your mother tried in vain for nearly 10 years to bear an heir to the throne. Barren womb, I'm afraid. I understand it was extremely embarrassing. You know how people talk."

"I ask with respect that you stop this blasphemy!"

"Eventually, my grandmother was chosen to become a surrogate. She was kept hidden during the pregnancy. And at last, your father was blessed with an heir."

"Nonsense!" The emperor half stood, crouching as he made his way down the rows of tiled seating to the floor. He tried to find his way to the door, but found a wall instead. He slumped to the floor. It was not, as Ito had indicated, any cooler.

Ito's disembodied voice continued to surround him. "The secret of your mother's infertility was never known. And on her behalf, my grandmother bore six more children in the coming years. So you see, your highness, you're not the only one here with royal blood in his veins."

Blood. *Royal* blood. The emperor felt his own pumping through his neck, past his ears. Impossibly loud. "Lies!"

"After the American General released my grandmother from his employ, she returned to the palace not once, but three times. And three times she was turned away in disgrace."

The emperor reached out, feeling along the wall, pulling himself along the floor. At last, his fingertips touched the glass door through which he had entered. And with some difficulty, he got to his feet. The sound of his own blood – *true* royal blood – rushing through his veins was painfully loud.

From somewhere high above, the prime minister continued his lecture. "Your father, on the other hand, took pity on her. He continued to deposit money into my grandmother's bank account each month until her death. The newspapers will print the records of deposit as evidence."

"No. This story cannot be public!"

The emperor lunged at the glass door. It did not move. He found the handle and pulled it. It did not so much as rattle. The seal was unnaturally tight. Unable to stand any longer, he sank to his knees, using the palm of his hand to wipe the steam away from the glass.

Looking up, he saw Ito's face. How was this possible? The PM was looking down at him from the other side of the glass. He spoke through a wireless headset, and his suit appeared to be dry as a desert.

"There will be doubters, of course, your Majesty. But DNA tests will confirm the story of my lineage. And that means the question of royal ascension is no longer clear-cut. Given that my party controls the National Diet, I feel there is an excellent chance that I will be chosen to rule Japan as not only Prime Minister, but also, as your rightful heir."

The old monarch could no longer speak. He could no longer move. He could only watch helplessly as Ito's face disappeared into the white void as the glass steamed over.

# Kyoto

The air was thick with the smell of rain. On a night like this, the televisions inside Free Ball typically showed nonstop coverage of soccer, tennis and baseball. But tonight the crowds huddled around the screens as a news analyst dissected key moments of President Kang's warning to the United States.

Carver watched Free Ball from the second floor of a bicycle parking lot across the street. It had been about 20 minutes since he had spoken to Eri. Her last words to him echoed in his mind. *Take your time.* Words that the Kuromaku had certainly fed her. What, he wondered, would she have said if they hadn't had a knife at her throat? Would she have told him to run? Would she have said she loved him?

At last, a red muscle car – unnaturally loud, its muffler having either been removed or modified – pulled up in front of Free Ball. Two tough-looking brutes got out of the back seat. One had the build of a retired sumo wrestler, with the telltale tree-trunk thighs, a huge belly and a non-existent neck. The other guy was older, a real rhino of a man, and all bulky muscle. What remained of his thinning hair was spiked with gel.

Something told Carver these guys weren't there just to watch sports and drink beer. As the car sped off, the Rhino reached under his shirt and adjusted a knife holster that he had tucked into the small of his back. At least it's just a knife, Carver thought. If this was Islamabad – or even Detroit – he would have been packing an AK-47.

Carver watched as the brutes went into the bar and started making their way through the crowd. The hordes of shell-shocked sports enthusiasts had little choice but to make way for them. Meanwhile, the red car continued down the street, looking for an open parking spot. He eventually found one in front of an all-night laundromat three blocks away.

Carver realized this was his best opportunity to find out where they had taken Eri. Even if he could isolate one of the Kuromaku thugs and inflict enough pain to get him to talk, that sort of human intelligence was unreliable. But the car's onboard navigation system was another matter. It would contain route history, which might reveal her location.

He walked the length of the bike garage and exited via the stairs at the dark end of the block. He could see the driver now. Young guy, no older than 25. On the phone, grinning, probably elated at getting to drive such an expensive car. And by the look on his face, he was talking to a girl. Better to take him now, while he was distracted.

Carver took the stairs down to the street, crossed a shadowy section of pavement, and ducked behind a vending machine that sold several varieties of tea and coffee. He would need a weapon. And at a cost of less than 200 yen, this would be one of the cheapest he had ever acquired.

The inspiration had come years earlier. On a snowy Tuesday morning, Carver had read an FBI report of the top 40 most common improvised weapons made by inmates incarcerated in the state of Texas. Item number 32 on the list: a shank made from an aluminum can.

He put two coins into the machine and watched as the robot arm gripped the can of cold coffee and placed it gently into the receptacle. Carver opened the can and poured its vile contents into a storm drain. Then, recalling the photograph of the weapon as clearly as if he was reading the article all over again, he twisted the can in his hands until the aluminum tore. He then used his fingers to fashion the jagged bits into a crude four-inch knife. Finally, he shaped the smooth part of the bottom into a handle. Now complete, he tested the shank against the palm of his hand. It was no Bowie knife, but it was good enough for government work.

Now armed, he slithered behind the car, waiting for the right moment. That came seconds later, as the driver broke into hearty laughter. Carver rushed the driver's side door, reached through the window and plunged the sharp edge of aluminum into his larynx. Carver ground and twisted the makeshift blade until blood spurted past him out onto the asphalt. Unable to speak, much less scream, the driver grabbed at his throat with both hands. Carver opened the door and shoved him into the passenger floorboard, where he bled out as the voice of a bubbly young woman continued to erupt from the phone. The poor girl, Carver thought. She probably had no idea her boyfriend was such a lowlife.

He hung up the phone and wiggled into the warm leather of the driver's seat. Scattered raindrops appeared on the windshield and soon transformed into a drizzle. Carver put the car into gear and sped off until he found a relatively dark residential area about a mile south. Then he parked and put both hands out the window to rinse them in the cold rain. He wasn't sure what was more disgusting – the sticky blood, or the smell of bitter coffee.

Then he searched the glove box, hoping for a gun. Instead he found a switchblade knife. A significant upgrade over the prison shank. He also found a pair of driving gloves, which he put on immediately. He then took the pocket square out of the driver's jacket and used it to wipe his fingerprints off the steering wheel and interior. Once he was finished, he surveyed the car's navigation console. As he had hoped, the nav was set to log the car's route history. Before pulling up to Free Ball, the car had come from what looked to be a large warehouse a few miles north of his present location. Before that, the car had been to the Green Ghost. Bingo. Eri was no longer at Sho's fortified country house. She had to be at the warehouse. He just hoped she was still in one piece.

# Kyoto

The warehouse was located at the dog end of an industrial street on the outskirts of town. The skies opened up as Carver approached, drumming the roof with an intensity that could even be heard over the engine. Carver switched on the car's bright lights, and he saw the sign out front that read Ito Gardening Supplies. Hundreds of potted plants were arranged in neat clusters around the yard. A row of garden statues near the gate. That figured. The Kuromaku seemed to value anything uniquely Japanese, and there were few things more uniquely Japanese than the country's immaculate gardens.

As a rule, Carver did not believe in frontal assaults. But in this case, he regarded the red muscle car with the booming engine as the world's most obnoxious Trojan Horse. The Kuromaku expected him to be at Free Ball, and they would expect the driver of the car to be one of their own. If he could just get inside the gate, he had a chance. Disorient, disrupt and destroy. That was the only way he was going to get Eri out of this place alive.

He drove up to the gate, shielding his face with the visor and his hand. *Bingo*. It opened.

He continued through the entry and past a row of pagoda garden statues, manipulating the angle of the vehicle as he turned into the driveway so that the car was neither head-on nor sideways. He braked about 40 feet from the nursery's front entrance and backed the vehicle up against a cluster of potted bonsai. Then he put the vehicle in park. It emitted a throaty growl, even in idle.

He belted the dead driver so that he was upright and behind the wheel. He cranked up the satellite radio station loud enough that J-Pop bass rattled the car windows. Then he crouched behind the car, waiting for someone to emerge from the nursery.

It took less than a minute until a pair of black leather loafers scurried toward him. They stopped next to the driver's side door. He heard yelling. The driver's side door opened. A man's voice bleated a bewildered sound of confusion.

Carver rounded the rear bumper and lunged at the man's ankles, driving the switchblade into his right Achilles tendon. He ripped sideways until the blade was free of the blood-soaked sock. His terrified victim went down fast, screaming hysterically, hands gripping his leg, eyes wide, not comprehending who or what had just assaulted him.

As Carver had hoped, the ruckus drew three more men outside. By the time they reached their wounded colleague, who grew ever more delirious with each passing second, Carver had made his way among the potted boxwoods and bonsai around to the side of the greenhouse.

He entered the building through an open service entrance built wide enough to accommodate delivery trucks. Judging by the lack of activity, and the lateness of the hour, the nursery workers had all gone home long ago.

There, among rows of potted apricot trees, sat Eri. She was bound to a chair with heavy gauge utility wire. As Carver drew closer from behind, he began counting appendages. He saw eight fingers and two thumbs. Both ears were still attached as well. Everything in its right place.

"Don't move," he whispered as he came up behind her. She drew in an astonished breath. Carver took the pair of wire cutters from the shelf behind her and began clipping the bonsai wire they had used to bind her wrists and arms to the metal chair. "How many are there?"

"Four."

"Make that three and a half," Carver said, counting the man he had cut out front.

Now the rumble of the muscle car's engine stopped abruptly, and he could hear his victim's gut-wrenching screams. Overhead, heavy rain pounded the greenhouse roof.

Once he had freed Eri's hands, he began working on the several layers of wires that bound her ankles to the chair. The screams of agony grew closer as they dragged Carver's victim inside.

He managed to free her hands just as a door slammed at the other end of the space. She tried to stand. "Can't walk," she said. "My legs are numb from sitting."

"Happens to me all the time," he said as he set her back down on the chair.

"You still read on the toilet?"

"I'm a pro. Just start moving your toes up and down to get your blood flowing. The numbness will go away within a minute or two."

The voices were getting closer. Then he heard footsteps on the concrete flooring. He took one of the gardening forks from the shelf behind him and gave it to Eri. The short-handled instrument with massive black iron prongs resembled the talon of an enormous bird of prey. "Use this if they get close."

"What about you?"

He took a gardening scraper – a hatchet-like tool with a handle that was about 20 inches long – off the shelf. Then he slipped his shoes off, and kissed Eri on the cheek. "Just sit tight. I'll distract them from the other side until you can get to your feet."

Now the men were shouting at each other. Judging by the direction of their voices, they had split up.

Crouching in his sock feet, Carver went deeper into the warehouse, careful to stay behind rows of vegetation, until he was at the far wall. Then he began working his way back, hoping to outflank them.

He soon came across a wheelbarrow full of volcanic rocks. They were several inches tall, jagged in shape, and typically used to symbolize mountains and Zen gardens. He took one. It was surprisingly light, due to its porous composition.

He kept moving until he could see the back of one of the attacker's heads. He was standing in the mulch aisle on his tiptoes, peering over a row of neatly stacked bags, wielding a dagger in his right hand. Carver cocked his arm back, raised up, and threw the stone. His aim was true, striking the man's scalp, knocking the thug off balance. Carver took three lunging steps and swung his gardening scraper. He wedged the blade into the man's neck, careful not to damage the larynx. He wanted to make sure this one could still scream.

Now having added a second voice to the chorus of agony, Carver left the wounded man in the mulch aisle, took the dagger, and moved quickly to another section of the warehouse. The others were shouting again now. But among the mostly indecipherable chatter, Carver heard something he didn't like: "Sato! Sato! *Ikimasho!*"

Dread welled up in him. They had realized that to flush Carver out, they just needed to threaten Eri. And how right they were. Carver stood upright and looked across the warehouse. Both men were heading toward the back, where Eri was still trying to get the blood flowing in her legs and feet.

He put his thumb and index finger into his mouth and emitted an ear-piercing whistle. An old trick he learned while deer hunting. Carver had been just 12 years old when he had discovered that the secret to stopping a running deer was to whistle loudly. Nine times out of ten, the deer would stop and look back. That was all the time he had needed to line up the kill shot.

But he had no rifle here in Kyoto, and when both of his prey stopped and looked – both were tall, lanky men with bad skin – they weren't taking the bait. They simply resumed their march toward the back of the warehouse.

It looked like checkmate.

Carver broke into a run, but they were faster. The lanky one was the first to reach her. He pulled a knife from his belt and grabbed her with his free hand.

He suddenly stiffened and straightened weirdly, stepped back and turned. Both hands were wrapped around the huge gardening fork wedged into his abdomen. He collapsed in a heap.

Eri ripped the iron talons from his abdomen and got ready for the hedgehog. Realizing he was outnumbered, he bolted for the service entrance.

Carver decided not to pursue him. Better that the survivor reported what he had seen here. If he could throw the Kuromaku into chaos, perhaps they would finally make a mistake big enough for the world to notice.

Now Eri stood over the dying man, seeming to enjoy the sudden reversal of power.

"Eri," Carver called out. He snapped his fingers. "We have to go."

"Can I kill him first?"

"He's already dead. He just doesn't know it yet."

# Julian Speers' Residence

As Speers' wife started the minivan and rolled the windows down, he leaned into the driver's side window and kissed her cheek. He then move to each of the back windows and kissed his children as they slept in their car seats. "You guys are going to have a great time with grandma, right?"

In the hours before dawn, Speers had convinced his wife to take the children to her mother's place down in North Carolina. It's probably nothing, he had told her, doing his best to mask the level of alarm he felt inside after Kang's speech. The incident in the Pacific had set off a heightened military readiness level. That, combined with the knowledge that the Chinese were already moving their VIPs out of the country, had convinced him that it was for the best.

Now he moved back to the driver's side window. "It's just for a few days. Promise."

"What about you?"

"I'll be somewhere safe. I can't say more."

She put on a brave face and put the car in gear. "Call me tonight."

He watched until the car was out of sight. Then he got into the SUV that had been waiting for him. "Upstate Maryland," he told his driver.

"Sir?"

"I'll disclose more information as we go. Take the 27 toward Westminster."

The driver's hazel eyes filled the rear view mirror. "Is everything okay, sir?"

"Good Christ. Will you please stop asking questions and drive?"

"Yes, Mister Director."

Speers was uncharacteristically quiet as they pulled out of the driveway. The various threads of the security situation swirled in his mind like so many pieces of shredded paper. As the car entered the freeway onramp, his phone rang. It was his assistant in McLean.

"Mister Director, I have Ambassador Kai Nakamura on the line. He says it's urgent."

Speers' stomach filled with butterflies. After Carver had sent photographs that seemed to imply the Japanese had some connection to the attack on the Chinese embassy, Speers had hoped to avoid further contact with the Japanese until they had more evidence. Unfortunately, the man they had sent to Tripoli to connect the dots, Aldo Rossi, was still missing. To make matters worse, Carver himself had gone completely dark.

"Okay. Put him through."

Nakamura's voice crackled over the line. "Julian, I apologize for calling you directly. Protocol would have me place this call to your secretary of state. But after our recent meeting at the White House, I felt most comfortable sharing this tragic news with you. I must inform you that the emperor has died."

"Oh," Speers managed. "I'm very sorry to hear that. I trust he passed peacefully."

"Suddenly, in fact. While conducting state business with the PM. A historic moment. And given his considerable age, and Ito's relative youth, it signifies a passing of the torch, don't you think?"

A passing of the torch? A curious turn of phrase, especially considering Ito had spearheaded a return of modest powers to the throne. "Uh, yes, quite," Speers agreed nevertheless. "Please, Kai, tell me how I can help."

"Well there is something. Typically, the death of a monarch calls for a long official period of mourning. But given the current crisis, don't you agree that the G8 must go on as planned?"

"I can't pretend to know what is best for the Japanese people at this time."

"What is best, Julian, is that the United States and Japan continue to cooperate to defend against Chinese aggression even while we de-escalate tensions. Therefore, we will hold the state funeral for the emperor on the first night of the G8, so as to make it easy for all heads of state to attend."

"I see. Does that mean that President Kang will attend the G8 after all?"

"Naturally. Considering the emperor's death, he now feels a diplomatic obligation to do so."

"Naturally."

"Also, I have a message for President Hudson."

"What is that?"

"The Chinese have agreed to private peace talks – so long as they are kept secret from the public. I am quite confident that they will be fruitful."

# Kyoto

10:20 pm. Carver and Eri were racing toward Kyoto Station, where he hoped that they might catch the last train to Tokyo. He felt decidedly conspicuous. There were few people on the road this time of night, and perhaps only one white intelligence agent driving a loud red muscle car.

Eri powered the window down and tossed their SIM cards out the window. One block later, she flung the phones themselves into a ditch. Still, she seemed to be having second thoughts about the plan. "We could leave the country. I know a marina on the coast that's full of smugglers. For the right price, one of them would surely take us to South Korea."

"No. The Kuromaku came all the way to Arizona to find me. They'd go to Mars to get you. We have to finish this while we still can."

"Tell me again. I don't understand how this can work."

"Ito has to be exposed. It's the only way. When we get to Tokyo, I want you to go to the American embassy. Ask to get a message to my old boss, Julian Speers."

"*Old* boss?"

"It's complicated. Just tell them I sent you. They'll pretend they don't know who I am at first, but they'll get Julian, and he'll listen. Tell him you have information about the embassy bombing, but don't give it to him until he agrees to grant you political asylum."

"You're not coming with me?"

Carver's face grew even more serious. "Sho is going to assassinate the president at the G8."

She pulled her legs down and turned sideways in the leather seat. "You have proof?"

"Not exactly, but I'm sure. I'll fill you in on the train."

As the station came into view, Carver pulled over and helped Eri out of the car. She was walking much better now, and that was a good thing, since they had just 15 minutes to get their tickets and get on the train. As they picked up the pace, their hands touched briefly. Then again. And then suddenly, they were holding hands.

Eri spoke in a tender tone that he had not heard in years. "I didn't expect you to come after me tonight."

"You would have done the same for me. Just promise me that if anything happens, or if we get separated, you'll go to the embassy and get a message to Julian."

"Promise."

At last they came to the station. Along the far wall by the turnstiles, Carver spotted a series of green pay phones. "I have to make a call."

"The last train leaves in six minutes!"

"This won't take long. Go get tickets. I'll meet you at the turnstile."

He fed money into the phone, then dialed the Four Seasons in Las Vegas and asked for Suite 40404.

The phone rang for what seemed like an eternity.

*Come on, Nico! Answer the phone!*

After the eighth ring, the call was kicked back down to the front desk. The hotel operator asked if he would like to leave a message. "Try it again," he said. "Suite 40404."

As the phone rang, the stationmaster's voice came over the PA system, announcing that the eastbound *Shinkansen* – a high speed cross-country train – was about to leave.

The phone rang five times. Finally, Madge answered in a language he assumed was Etruscan.

"It's me. Put Nico on."

"He stepped out. Can you call back?"

"I might not be able to. Just tell him that I was right. The robotic cat that vacuums his floors is guilty as sin."

"Come again?"

"He'll understand. But tell him he has to get proof. And he has to find a way to make it public."

He looked up. Eri was on the other side of the turnstile, waving her hands frantically.

"Be right there!" he mouthed.

Now she screamed and pointed. "Behind you!"

Carver ducked and rolled left, but he wasn't fast enough. There were simply too many Kuromaku. He nailed one of them with a forearm shiver to the neck before something hard and heavy hit him behind the head. The world faded to black.

# PART VI

# Somewhere in Tokyo

When Carver woke, he did not know if it was day or night. He blinked, seeing nothing but blackness. His hands and ankles were bound with zip ties. His skull ached. There was no way to hold his head that didn't hurt.

Where was he? How long had he been here? Five minutes? Five hours? Five *days*?

The throbbing in his skull triggered a vivid memory. He had been at the train station in Kyoto. Two blows to the back of the head had rendered him unconscious. He winced as the full sensory memory hurt all over again. As unpleasant as it was to relive the violence in such clarity, he was, for a moment, at least grateful that his mental faculties were intact.

After that, Carver's recollection of his journey was sketchy. He had woken once in transit. He recalled the vague sensation of flying – the unpleasant vibration of rotor blades – but he had been unable to stay awake. His inner compass told him they had traveled northeast, toward Tokyo, but he had no evidence other than gut instinct.

The more important question was this: why had he been allowed to live? After all, the Kuromaku had gone to a great deal of trouble to try killing him in Arizona. Why had they not simply finished him off at the train station when they had the chance?

Maybe they wanted information. And now that they had him, they'd stop at nothing to get it.

He thought of Eri. When he was attacked, she had been about to board the bullet train to Tokyo. She had promised him that if they got separated, or if something happened to him, that she would get to the U.S. Embassy in Tokyo and get a message to Julian. He hoped to God that she had gotten on that train.

*She did. She made it. She's heading to the embassy right now. You have to believe that.*

He rolled his head slowly from side to side. The notch in his left ear felt wet and spicy all over again. The wound must have been reopened during the attack.

They had taken his shoes and socks. Damn. Those were valuable in captivity. His CIA trainers had taught him a choice bit of tradecraft that he had always followed – to wear paracord as shoelaces at all times.

Paracord was available in every conceivable color, and the type Carver wore looked much like a standard shoelace. It had many uses. The tremendously strong, all-nylon strands did not rot or mildew, and could be utilized in any survival situation. Even in space, as NASA's 82nd space shuttle crew found when it had to make in-flight repairs to the Hubble Space Telescope.

Paracord could also be braided and frayed in such a way that made for a devastatingly effective whip. But now Carver had another use for it – as a saw. The zip ties that bound his wrists and ankles were industrial strength. Unlike normal zip ties, which could be snapped by bringing his wrists together and jerking them hard against his hipbone, that wasn't going to work with these. He needed paracord, metal or something else to saw them in two.

*Stop dwelling on what you don't have. Explore the space.*

Now he moved his bare feet left, feeling the edge of the futon mat. It was no more than two inches thick.

His right ankle was swollen. No wonder the zip tie was so incredibly tight.

It was coming back to him now. At the train station, the blur of hands and feet as he blocked blow after blow. The flash of pain in his ankle as he had twisted to fend off the attack from behind.

Despite the pain, he forced himself to stand. He needed to know whether he could put weight on it. With some difficulty, he got to his feet. The ankle pain was sharp, but tolerable. Good. It was sprained, but probably not broken.

And the silver lining? Now he scarcely noticed his bruised ribs.

He reached out in front of him in the dark, trying to find a surface. He groped and hopped blindly until he found a wall. It was some sort of rough-textured stone, without creases or tiles.

Carver dragged the futon to the edge of the room and laid on his back. He propped his feet up against the wall, elevating the ankle in hopes of making the swelling go down. He did so knowing that the Kuromaku would no doubt begin interrogating him soon, and a sprained ankle would be the least of his worries.

Still, he had to prepare himself. With that in mind, he began doing a set of crunches. Just like back home in the gym. He had to be strong. Escape was a moral duty, and so long as he was physically able, there was always a chance.

# Deep Anchor
# Rural Maryland

One by one, the president's war cabinet arrived in the new emergency command bunker, located six stories below a farm in rural Maryland. While the estimated 10-year construction project was far from completed, its basic facilities were ready enough to serve as a secure temporary haven for the government's executive branch.

Construction on the secret facility known as Deep Anchor had begun two years earlier when the farm, which had been run continuously by a single family for 71 years, was purchased by the Department of Agriculture. By all appearances, the vast grazing meadows, barns and around 300 head of cattle had remained essentially unchanged. The only difference was that now, the USDA researchers running it used the uncharacteristically rustic facility to research animal phenomics. None had any idea that far below the green facade where they worked, President Hudson and her advisors were preparing for war.

The move to a neutral locale in a heightened security situation was not without precedent. Four days after the 9/11 attacks, President Bush had formed a war cabinet that met at Camp David to outline the new war on terror. But unlike the security situation in 2001, the threat of cyber attacks was now dire. If someone like Nico Gold could infiltrate the Chinese president's personal network so easily, what was to stop the Chinese themselves from infiltrating the Oval Office?

Now, in a decidedly unfinished war room, the president addressed the newly formed war cabinet from the end of a long walnut table. The Director of National Intelligence, FBI Director, CIA Director, Homeland Security Director, Attorney General, Secretary of State and the Joint Chiefs sat before her.

WILLIAM TYREE

"Thank you all for coming to Deep Anchor. I realize the impact the additional travel has on your schedules. But due to the sensitive nature of our meeting, I felt the need to work from as secure a location as possible. Now, without further ado, I'd like to turn things over to Dex."

SECDEF Jackson passed copies of a printed brief around the table. "As you all know," he said, "Talks between the president and Kang have been rescheduled for the G8. But we should be skeptical. According to the intelligence passed to us by Ambassador Nakamura, China intends to use this time to strengthen its positions militarily and economically."

Speers scanned the document, which proposed a variety of specific proactive attacks against China's currency, satellite communications and its domestic energy infrastructure. It also called for the immediate roundup of remaining suspected spies in the United States. And finally, it required Special Forces to occupy several uninhabited islands in the Sea of Japan and the South China Sea. Those positions would be immediately reinforced by naval power.

"Wait," Speers said, looking up in disbelief. "This is real? Last time we met, our strategy was to shore up our positions. These directives go way beyond that."

SECDEF Jackson was ready with a response. "Upon further analysis, it's my belief that the Chinese have been playing an elaborate game of chess for years. The first phase was mass intelligence gathering, stealing our intellectual property, infiltrating our security networks and economic platforms. The second phase was trading pieces to gain a positional advantage. Each side has lost pawns in the game as they tested our defenses and exploited our weaknesses. Now they'll move in for the kill, unless we move aggressively first."

Speers combed both fingers through his wavy black hair. "Dex, this plan completely excludes the intelligence we've gathered from surveillance on Kang's offices in Beijing. Those recordings demonstrate that Kang himself is completely oblivious to the nefarious plan you describe."

"That information is hardly conclusive," the president countered.

"I realize that. But what we have now should at least constitute reasonable doubt. Dex's proposal is a serious escalation."

"Damn right it is," Jackson said. At this, he stood with his hands flat on the table before him. "We must escalate."

With this, the secretary of state spoke. "Dex, preparing to defend ourselves is one thing. But this..."

"Basketball coaches love to tell their players that defense wins championships. But we all know that's not really true. The team that scores the most points wins."

The president motioned for Dex to retake his seat, which he did reluctantly. "This is about ensuring the long-term safety of the United States. And the only way to do that is to check China's capabilities before they gain an even greater strategic advantage than they already have."

Speers laid his reading glasses on the paper and turned toward the president. "And what about the G8?"

"I will attend the opening ceremony, and the emperor's funeral, as planned. Afterward, I will call a press conference in which I will lay out a public case against Chinese aggression. The speech will last approximately 30 minutes. And by the time I read the last word, all the offensive initiatives on this list will be in motion."

# Somewhere in Tokyo

Carver woke as artificial light streamed in through an open slot in the door. A pair of narrow brown eyes appeared, followed by a voice in heavily accented English shouting, "Move back!"

He did so as quickly as he could. The swelling in the sprained ankle had gone down a bit, but it was still weak.

The door unlocked and swung open. Carver was surprised to see an elderly man appear with *negi-toro don* — minced tuna over rice. There was even a radish garnish on top. The sight and smell of the food sparked hunger pangs. The old man bowed – a shocking cultural quirk, given the circumstances – and placed it just inside the room along with a glass of hot tea and a pitcher of drinking water. Carver moved his head to the right so that he could see the open doorway. As he had expected, the old man had not come alone. A guard with a Heckler & Koch machine pistol slung stood just outside the door.

He closed the door behind him, leaving Carver alone with his meal. Carver held the dish to his nose and inhaled. For what little it was worth, he smelled nothing irregular. If they wanted to drug or poison him, he reasoned, they had a multitude of other options. Still, he had to wonder. Why were they feeding him?

*Don't overthink this. Just eat. You need your strength.*

He did. Afterwards, he once again surveyed the room with his hands, searching for possible weapons or tools. A wooden bowl. Chopsticks. A wool blanket.

Nothing of use.

The walls were utterly smooth. There was no way to scale them. That probably did not matter much. He had no proof, but his instinct told him that he was deep underground.

And apart from the two-inch futon cushion, there was no furniture. For a toilet, there was only a hole in the floor.

If only he could get his shoes back.

He lay on his back on the futon, gazing up at the utter darkness. The only way out of the cell, he feared, was through the door.

For that, his ankle would need to be stronger, and the swelling would need to go down. He again propped his feet up on the wall. Then he closed his eyes and visualized his escape.

# U.S. Embassy
# Tokyo

The CIA's Tokyo station chief entered the conference room, unsmiling, tearing his coat off. He tossed it in the general direction of the table, pinning his full attention upon the woman standing at the window overlooking the city. He saw that she was athletic, even pretty, but her eyes were hopelessly sad. Steam rose from a cup of freshly brewed tea in her hand.

Earlier this morning, he had received a call from an embassy staffer about the presence of a woman named Eri Sato who had appeared at the embassy gates that morning. She had apparently requested diplomatic asylum in exchange for what she called time-sensitive information about an ex-CIA operative named Blake Carver and a terror threat against the G8.

The station chief figured she was probably a waste of time. Her information was hopelessly outdated. Most everyone in in the intelligence community knew that Carver had resigned his post at the CIA years earlier. Rumor was that he was working in some capacity for the Director of National Intelligence, but there was nothing on file about that. Still, her status as an employee of Japan's Public Security Intelligence Agency had piqued his curiosity.

"*Ohayo gozaimasu,*" the station chief said.

"We can talk in English."

The station chief gestured toward a chair. They both sat down. His eyes danced over her rumpled appearance. "Is that blood on your scarf, Miss Sato?"

"Yes."

"Is that blood from an accident, or from a violent crime?"

"The latter."

"I see. Have you been to the police?"

"As I told your assistant, I need to get an urgent message to Julian Speers. It's from Blake Carver."

He leaned back in his chair. "So, you've seen Agent Carver recently?"

"Put me in contact with Director Speers, and I'll tell both of you everything you want to know."

"First, let me put a finer point on my earlier question. Is that Carver's blood on your scarf?" At that, she simply stared back at him. He let the silence simmer for a few seconds before speaking again. "Okay. Tell me why I should trust you."

"The same people who destroyed the Chinese embassy in Tripoli are planning something here at the G8."

He lit a cigarette. The freedom to smoke indoors was one of the many pleasures he had found during his time stationed in Japan. "According to you, or according to the agency you work for?"

"According to Agent Carver."

"I don't believe you."

She stood, turned, and gazed out at the window at the bustling city she had called home for most of her life. "Let's say you sit on this information, and President Hudson is killed at the G8. Is that something you're prepared to live with?"

# Somewhere in Tokyo

Carver woke as artificial light from the hallway illuminated the cell. He sat up, blinking through the glare. A guard entered and set a chair in the far corner.

A second man stood in the doorway. He was tall and thin, in a narrowly trimmed grey suit. A white silk pocket square puffed from his left vest. His eyes were small under a set of expensive brown eyeglasses. He smiled, revealing narrow, pointy teeth behind large lips.

The Eel. AKA Maru Kobayashi. Prime Minister Ito's longtime head of security.

"Agent Carver. Meeting a man of your reputation is truly an honor."

Carver had learned long ago that in most every adversarial conversation, the person talking the least would nearly always win whatever psychological battle was being waged. Of course, in this situation, *winning* was relative. If the situation between the U.S. and China escalated further, there would be no winners at all.

"I believe you came to Japan to look for the man who ordered your assassination. Congratulations, Agent Carver. He's standing right in front of you."

This came as no great shock to Carver. He had assumed as much. He had just one question. "Why?"

"We were already aware of you, of course. But when the embassy bombing happened as planned, you were of no real concern. But you can imagine our surprise when Eri Sato contacted you not just once, but multiple times. We could only assume she had connected the dots between Tripoli and Tokyo. And we could not have any loose ends."

"So why am I still alive?"

The Eel lit a cigarette. Then he pulled a phone from his pocket. "I want you to call your boss, Julian Speers. Tell him that you have located a Chinese defector here in Japan."

*So that's it. They want me to feed disinformation back to Washington.*

"And what did this defector supposedly tell me?"

The Eel handed him a slip of paper with an address: Lan Kwai House, 5-6 Lan Kwai Fong.

"That's in Hong Kong," Carver noted.

"Very good. An apartment. Upon arrival, your American colleagues will find evidence that Chinese hackers were responsible for the recent attack on the American stock exchanges."

Why were the Kuromaku so keen to fan the flames of war between the U.S. and China? Carver needed to stall for time. In another 24 hours, his ankle might be strong enough to bear weight. Maybe then he could figure a way out of this place.

He recalled his initial CIA training for situations like these. It was important to give your captor the impression that he was getting exclusive information. It created an unwritten bond that did not necessarily change the game, but could extend your lifespan a little while longer.

"There's just one problem," Carver said. "Julian doesn't know I'm in Japan. I came on my own."

The Eel reached into his other jacket pocket. Carver was careful not to wince or shrink away. In situations like this, it was important to seem neither threatening nor threatened. But even Carver could not keep his cool when he saw what was in the Eel's hand: a photo of his father.

It had been taken from a distance, but there was no question that it was him. Green coveralls, wide-brim hat.

The worst part? It been taken recently. His father was mending a fence near the Two Elk Ranch sign, and the aspen leaves had just started to show their fall colors.

Carver was suddenly conscious of his breathing. Of the sweat that had broken out on his brow. Of the almost irresistible desire to gouge the Eel's eyes out.

"Agent Carver, if you do as I say, I can guarantee your father's safety."

So much for creating a personal bond between him and his captor. Things were apparently moving far too fast for that.

Maybe he could use this to his advantage. He thought of how Eri had tipped him off without raising alarms during her brief captivity. Perhaps he could do the same. "Okay. But I want my shoes back. And a clean pair of socks."

The Eel folded his arms across his chest. "How strange people are. I would have expected you to beg for your life. Or ask to keep your father's photo. But shoes and socks?"

"It's freezing in here."

"Request denied. Just make the call. One slip, one trick, and I will make your mother a widow."

# Deep Anchor

Speers returned to his temporary office beneath the Maryland countryside. He shut the door and pulled the blinds. Then he answered the call his assistant had held for him.

"Blake?"

"I don't have much time."

"Where are you? You promised you would come in. They're looking for you."

"I can't talk about that. But I have a strong lead in the cyber attack on the New York Stock Exchange."

"Why – "

"I think we have a leak, Julian, and I can't trust anyone else."

This was weird. Something was wrong.

"Okay. I'm listening."

"You'll want to write this down."

Speers wrote nothing. He was recording the call. He merely listened as Carver relayed the address of an apartment in Hong Kong. Carver then offered a few broad details about a defector from China's cyber warfare division. From anyone else, it might have sounded semi-plausible. But it was hardly believable from someone as meticulous as Carver. Still, he had to be sure.

"We'll look into it right away," Speers said. "And Blake, I have a quick question for you."

"We need a linguist on something fast. I'm looking for the name of that guy you hired a few years ago to decode Muskogee."

"Which one?" Carver said. "We had dozens of them on that project."

That was true. But only one of them had been any good.

"I think he was a professor. Old guy. I'm thinking maybe he taught in Oklahoma, but I can't recall exactly."

"That makes two of us. That was a long time ago. I just can't remember."

That was the tell he had been waiting for. Carver couldn't remember? Like hell. Carver couldn't forget. Someone had put him up to it.

Speers promised to follow up on the lead and hung up. Then he called Arunus Roth over in McLean.

"We need to recon an address in Hong Kong," Speers said without preamble. He read the street and unit number to Roth twice. "Send a canary. Someone low-level with experience breaking and entering."

"Okay then. I'll see if we have any common cat burglars on the local payroll."

"Don't be a wise ass. Just get it done."

"Yes, sir. But if I may ask, what are we looking for?"

"Digital breadcrumbs linking the flash crash to China."

"Wouldn't a cyber security crew be more fitting?"

"Yeah, but I have a bad feeling about this. If our canary gets in, and he's still alive 30 minutes later, then send a crew. But use extreme prejudice with anything you find."

"Got it, sir. May I ask where this tip came from?"

"No. That's all for now."

# The Four Seasons Hotel

Nico Gold had tried and failed to infiltrate the Reformation Party network. He didn't understand. It shouldn't be this hard. It was as if they had an entire army physically shutting down every approach he tried.

Now he had resorted to an old matchmaking phishing scam. Crude as it was, he figured it might be the fastest way to earn the bottle of 1787 Château Lafite Bordeaux that Carver had promised him in exchange for his services.

The concept was simple. First, he accessed a public list of the most common male name combinations in Japan over the past four decades. Then he wrote a program that appended those name combinations to the Restoration Party email address format [lastname].[firstname]@restorationparty.go.jp., resulting in some 114,000 variations. Finally, he wrote an email, translated it into Japanese, and sent it to the entire list:

*Subject: Lonely? Meet single women in your area now!*

*Hi [firstname],*

*Women in Kyoto and Tokyo are getting tired of online dating services. That's why my 26-year-old twin sister and I left our modeling careers to start a new matchmaking service.*

*Our goal? To introduce attractive single women to successful men like you.*

*We only started 5 months ago, and we already have 103,000 women signed up! Click here to fill out your profile and start chatting with the woman of your dreams right now.*

So far, the email open rate was abysmal, at less than one-tenth of one percent. His spammy messages were getting filtered out by the truckload. What few broke through were probably arriving with an email malware warning.

Still, wasn't anyone over there lonely? All he needed was one person behind the firewall to click. He would still have tons of work to do, but that would provide his doorway into the entire organization.

In the background, he heard Madge rise from bed and exit the bedroom. She came to him and rubbed his shoulders. "You've been at this for 37 hours straight," she said in Etruscan, looking down at the dizzying array of code on his monitor. "Take a break. Come play with me and Olivia."

"What I need is for one of these stupid fascists to take an interest in the lovely single ladies who are waiting to meet them right now!"

"Come to bed," Madge insisted.

At last, a notification popped up on the screen.

*ALERT: user shinzo.kondo 97@restorationparty.go.jp clicked a link. File uploading onto target machine.*

Nico turned, took Madge's head in his hands, and kissed her noisily. "You're good luck, my dear! I'm in!"

# Deep Anchor

Speers, who had been pacing the floor since his disturbing conversation with Carver, answered the inbound call from Arunus Roth on the first ring. "The Hong Kong address Carver gave you checked out, more or less. The team went in about two hours ago. They've been transmitting a flood of files, and we're going through them as fast as we can."

"Anything promising?"

"We found exactly what you said we'd find. These people even hosted their own servers onsite, and the digital fingerprints linking them to the stock exchanges is clear as day."

"So the evidence is compelling?"

Roth sighed. "To be honest, no. You said I should be extremely skeptical when evaluating these files, right? It's too easy. I have a hard time believing that anyone who could actually do this would be so sloppy. Sir, I think we found exactly what somebody wanted us to find."

Speers had figured as much. "Sounds about right."

"And sir, if I may...I keep thinking about the way the second Iraq War started. I mean, I wasn't even born when that happened, but we studied it in school."

"You're making me feel old."

"That so-called evidence about Saddam having those weapons of mass destruction? Looking at the intelligence that's coming in from Hong Kong, I would hate for us to make a big decision like that based on this. Know what I mean?"

Speers did. He would hold this close to the vest. For now.

# Joint Base Andrews

As Speers' car pulled up to the second checkpoint, he was relieved to see Air Force One still on the tarmac. The massive Boeing VC-25 — which cost over $200,000 per hour to fly — would be leaving at any moment for the G8 in Tokyo. Speers rolled down his window and observed the security detail checking the underside of the vehicle for bombs.

He spotted Hector Rios, the president's Secret Service team leader, on the other side of the gate. "Hector!" Speers shouted. "I have to get on that plane!"

The former NFL tight end-turned secret service agent crossed through the gate, towering over the young soldiers working the checkpoint. "Sorry for the trouble, Chief. We don't have you on the passenger manifest. The inspection of your vehicle will take –"

"Forget my car!" He pointed at a Humvee parked just inside the gate. "Just drive me over there yourself!"

Speers got out, crossed through the checkpoint on foot, and got into the Humvee. Rios stepped into the driver seat. "No luggage?"

"Just me."

As he pulled away, Rios tapped his radio and called ahead. "Be advised, Supermodel is coming on board," he said, using the codename his old friend had chosen for him. "Again, Supermodel is inbound."

"Can we revisit that during a quiet moment?"

"I don't think so." Rios switched off his radio as they drove. The two men had been through a lot together, dating back to Speers' stint as Chief of Staff in the previous administration. "Listen, Chief, can you do me a favor when you get on board that plane?"

"Depends."

"They are expecting heavy street protests at the G8. Traffic will be choked off near the palace. My job is to keep the president moving at all times. But in a city with 35 million residents, with all those protesters, I can't do that."

"If I have my way, the president won't be going to the G8 at all."

Onboard, Speers found President Hudson in what was commonly referred to as the Oval Office of Air Force One, which amounted to a fully enclosed workspace. She removed her glasses and set them down on the wood, eyeing him with bloodshot eyes that told of a long night reworking her G8 agenda again and again.

"Had I known you were coming," she said, "I would have packed a case of lollipops."

"I'm not staying, Madam President. After you listen to what I have to say, my hope is that you'll step off this plane, cancel plans for offensive military action against China, and return to Deep Anchor with me."

The president leaned forward, folding her arms on the desk before her. "I know you disagree with our strategy, Julian, but I need you to get on board."

"Please hear me out. There are new developments you should know about. First, I'm convinced that Blake Carver is being held against his will in Japan."

The president leaned back. Her mouth was tight across her face. "How is that possible? After he failed to report in, I told Chad to take him into custody."

"He's still an American citizen, and he's being held against his will. Worse, they don't know he's been exiled. They are using him to feed disinformation that deliberately moves us closer to war with China."

"What? That sounds crazy. Who's feeding him disinformation?"

Speers took a deep breath. "I believe it's coming from Prime Minister Ito's government."

The president shook her head. "You realize how insane that sounds."

"Yes."

"And what if I were to call Ito right now and ask him about these accusations?"

"You would be putting us in a very precarious security situation." Speers reached into his pocket and retrieved three sheets of folded paper. "This letter arrived by fax from the embassy in Tokyo this morning."

"Fax?" She took the letter from him. "What century is this?"

"After the email hack last month, we brought a fleet of fax machines back from deep storage. They're only used for the most sensitive messages. And when you read it, you'll understand why I had to give you this message in person."

The president put her glasses back on and began to read.

*TO: Julian Speers, Director of National Intelligence*

*FROM: CIA station chief, Tokyo*

*This message is transcribed from a conversation with Ms. Eri Sato, which we have confirmed is an analyst with Japan's Public Security Intelligence Bureau. She purports to have been with a former operative of ours named 'Blake Carver' until yesterday. We confirmed that Carver is former CIA, although his personnel file is currently restricted from access.*

Eva's face twisted in incredulity as she skimmed the remaining letter, which in three pages, made a variety of incendiary claims against Ito's government, finishing with a specific threat of presidential assassination at the G8.

At last her eyes broke away, her pupils seeming to target her intelligence czar like the barrels of twin sniper rifles.

Speers swallowed hard. "I realize it's a lot to absorb, Madam President. I also understand that it is largely unsubstantiated. But I do think it's enough to warrant slowing things down."

"Please! Do you know how many death threats we get every year? *Thousands*! I'm beginning to think that maybe I've got the wrong person running American intelligence."

"Maybe you do, Madam President. But please. Call the trip off. For your own safety."

"We've been over this, Julian. We can no longer be motivated by fear or political correctness. We have to act. We have to play offense."

The president's desk phone buzzed. She answered. It was her chief of staff. "Madam President, we're behind schedule. We need to go wheels up."

"I'm ready." She hung up, and then looked across the desk at the person that had, as recently as last week, served as her most trusted confidant. "You have two choices, Julian. The first is to get off my plane and have your resignation on my desk when I return. The other is this – come with me to Tokyo and help refine our strategy. What's it going to be?"

# Somewhere in Tokyo

Carver ripped off a set of 100 sit-ups. Then he elevated his ankle once again. The swelling was finally going down. He was getting stronger.

Could he fight his way out of this hellhole and get to the 18th floor of the Hotel New Otani in time to stop the assassination? If he was being honest, the ankle was at less than 70%. He did not even have his shoes. And there was absolutely nothing in the cell to weaponize.

He decided to pray. It was the only freedom he had left.

Minutes later, the cell door opened. Bright white light blinded him.

The Eel stood in the hallway. "You have a dinner invitation," he said.

"With who?"

The Eel turned toward the guards. "Get him cleaned up."

They helped Carver to his feet and led him to a room that was empty except for a floor drain, a hose and a series of chains and hooks dangling from the ceiling. He imagined the room had once been used to butcher animals. The guards cut his clothes off. Then they hosed him down with a high-pressure nozzle.

They shaved the three-day stubble off his face before finally cutting his zip ties. He was given a new suit that closely resembled the one he had flown to Japan in. After dressing, he was, at last, given his shoes. Tying them, he recognized the weight and color of the paracord laces. Good. At least there was that.

Once dressed, he was blindfolded once again. The guards led Carver down a hallway. "Now we climb," the Eel said, and they ascended a staircase. They went up one flight, then another, and still another.

As they walked, he heard no other people. No city sound. Just the rustle of their clothes as they walked.

Before him, a set of heavy doors opened. Now they ushered him across a surface that felt smooth, like marble. The echo of their shoes on the floor told of a room with high ceilings.

Now he smelled food. Miso soup. Rice. Pickled vegetables.

At last they stopped. He was pushed into a chair. His blindfold was removed.

He was at a formal dining table. Candles provided the only illumination. And sitting opposite was a man he had seen only on television.

"Good evening, Agent Carver."

*Akira Ito. The Prime Minister of Japan. The leader of the Kuromaku.*

Ito snapped his fingers. A waiter appeared and poured sake into two glasses. Ito picked up his glass up and held it before him. "To the G8! *Kanpai!*"

The idea of drinking a toast with Ito was reprehensible. Carver imagined breaking the glass into shards and jamming them into Ito's eye sockets. For the victims of the Chinese embassy bombing. For the sailors aboard the American destroyer. For Jack Brenner. For Fujimoto. For Eri.

*But you wouldn't be killing him. You'd be martyring him.*

Carver raised his glass. "To the G8," he said before drinking. The strong alcohol burned past his gums and down his esophagus.

"Do you like the candles?" Ito said. "I prefer bright light, personally, but after your time in the dark, I thought this might be easier."

Another waiter appeared and placed an assortment of sashimi before them. Thick cuts of mackerel, shrimp and tuna.

"*Dozo,*" Ito said, gesturing at the premium *nigiri* before them. Carver watched as the prime minister pinched a piece of fatty tuna between the chopsticks, rubbed it lightly in the combination of soy sauce and wasabi, and put it into his mouth.

Ito swallowed, then spoke. "Are you a spiritual man, Agent Carver?"

"I'm a pragmatist. I choose to believe."

Ito smiled. "Let us weigh the gain and the loss in wagering that God is. Let us estimate these two chances. If you gain, you gain all; if you lose, you lose nothing."

"Pascal's Wager."

"Just so. But I do not need philosophy to convince me that the spirit world exists. I was brought up in the traditional way, practicing Shinto. Some say it's not a real religion because there is no book of rules."

"You strike me as the type who likes to make up his own rules."

Ito nodded. "Quite right."

"Prime Minister, would you mind telling me where we are?"

"Ah. Forgive me, Agent Carver. You were incarcerated when the news broke. I'm afraid the emperor has died." He gestured at the opulent dining room. "And this is my new home. The Imperial Palace. "

The American tried to mask his shock. If Ito was telling the truth, he had been held captive in an ancient imperial dungeon for two or three days. "I doubt the public will approve."

"As they will soon discover, I am the rightful heir to the throne."

Carver raised an eyebrow. He sipped his sake. "You're even more ambitious than I thought. Are you going to tell me why I'm here?"

"Destiny. The spirits have a way of bringing people together who, unbeknownst to each other, are working toward a common purpose."

"You must be confusing me with someone else. I came to Japan to find the person who ordered my death."

Ito smiled. "You greatly underestimate your role in history, Agent Carver. You are not famous yet, but you will be."

"And how's that?" Carver asked, although he feared he might already know the answer to that question.

"Patience, Agent Carver. This is a great honor for me. I used to dream about what it would be like to dine with the world's most famous and fascinating people. In that respect, becoming prime minister was like acquiring magical powers. For example, if I want to dine with the world's most famous physicist, or with the Queen of England, I can arrange it. But of course, when it comes to the dead, I am only left to wonder what it might be like to share a meal with them. For example, I have always wanted to share a meal with Gavrilo Princip."

The name Gavrilo Princip was a rather esoteric reference these days, but Carver knew his history well. Up until the Kennedy assassination made Lee Harvey Oswald a household name, Princip had been the most notorious killer of the 20th century. His assassination of Archduke Franz Ferdinand of Austria sparked a series of events that caused World War I.

"When most scholars think of the First World War," Ito continued, "they think of the 38 million people that died as a result of Princip's treachery. I prefer to think of Gavrilo Princip and his employer, Emperor Taisho, as the great heroes of their time. World War I marked an era of great expansion for the Japanese empire."

"Everyone knows Japan exploited the war for its own gain. But it seems unlikely that Princip and Emperor Taisho were connected. The emperor was known to have a severe neurological disorder. He was unable to carry out even basic imperial duties, much less influence European affairs."

"Or so you were led to believe. History is written by the victors."

As much as Carver hated to admit it, he was riveted by Ito's story. "I'm listening."

Ito gestured to the waiter to bring more sake before continuing his tale. "From the time of Emperor Taisho's birth, the royal family received death threats on his life. And so over the years, they leaked a story that he had contracted lead poisoning as an infant due to the lead-based makeup worn by his wet nurse."

"You're suggesting Taisho's illness was all a ruse?"

"Just so. To create the illusion that he was no longer a threat. They went so far as to withdraw him from school, leading to more rumors that he was sickly and feeble-minded. The plan worked. Like Taisho, Japan was no longer seen as a threat to the world community. Meanwhile, he had in fact benefitted from the finest private education in Asia. He spoke several languages fluently. He was a brilliant tactician. And when his spies in Europe told him of the secret anarchist group Princip belonged to, the Black Hand, he immediately foresaw how Japan might profit from a great war in Europe."

"Let me guess. Taisho secretly funded the Black Hand, and in doing so, helped start the First World War."

"Very good, Agent Carver. Taisho convinced Princip that Ferdinand's assassination would be the spark that would collapse the ruling elite and unite the Slavic territories into an independent nation. And so Princip hired six conspirators. Together, they changed history."

"And while European and American troops were slaughtered by the millions in trench warfare, Japan captured Germany's islands in the Far East unopposed. All the while, the country grew into an economic superpower by filling wartime orders placed by its European allies."

Ito paused to sip his soup. "Your knowledge of history is impressive, Agent Carver."

"It's the present that I'm not so clear on." Carver unbuttoned the top button of his shirt. He was burning up. "I still don't understand what this has to do with me."

Ito downed the rest of his sake. "The wheels of history turn by blood alone, and now, you and I must play our final roles."

Carver felt dizzy. "I don't like the sound of that."

"Unfortunately, I have found that it is surprisingly difficult to start a war. I have brought down embassies and sunk ships and killed spies and cost both countries billions in economic damage. And yet, China and the United States refuse to fight."

"I wouldn't be so quick to assume that you can repeat the success of your forbearers. World War I was fought in Europe. The war you're trying to start will be waged right on your doorstep."

"As you and your companion have already discovered, the Kuromaku have quietly formed the most lethal army of cyber soldiers on Earth. Our enemies' fighting machines are dependent on connectivity with external systems, and that is what makes them vulnerable. The ease with which we took control of China's fighter jets to sink the American destroyer is proof enough of that. All that is needed now is one final shocking provocation. And that's where you come in."

Carver understood. He didn't have to *escape* to get to the Hotel New Otani. Ito was going to make sure he ended up there. Which got him to thinking about the target. Until now, he had assumed it would be President Hudson. But he now realized that notion had been wrong. If Kang was killed by an American – or at least appeared to be – then the public pressure to retaliate would be enormous. If that happened, there would be no turning back.

"You're forgetting one thing," Carver said, but his words failed him. His mouth seemed to be filled with cotton.

*The sake. There was something in it.*

Ito smiled as he watched his counterpart struggle. "The daydream of pacifism prevents the Japanese people from seeing the world as it is. But they will wake up soon enough. And as the U.S. and China cripple one another, the Empire of Japan will once again rise up, with me as its ruler."

The room spun. The American steadied himself with both hands on the table. He tried to stand, but was unable.

He watched helplessly as Ito rose from the table. "I will treasure the memory of this dinner. Because tomorrow, a new name will join the ranks of the world's great assassins. Gavrilo Princip, John Wilkes Booth, Lee Harvey Oswald…and Blake Carver."

# Air Force One
# Somewhere over the Pacific

Since their departure from Joint Base Andrews, the president had ensconced herself in the Oval Office aboard Air Force One, writing and rewriting her talking points, emerging only occasionally to confer with Speers and her National Security Advisor on the finer points of her speech. The United States military and intelligence forces would be actively engaged in operations during the press conference, making the task particularly tricky. She had to be both transparent *and* coy at the same time. Unless something changed in the next few hours, this would go down as the most important speech of her presidency.

Although Speers had agreed to get on board with the president's agenda, he had also not abandoned his own. Barricading himself in one of just three tiny private workspaces on the aircraft, he quietly worked the phones, personally reaching out to field agents in Japan. All were stunned to find themselves speaking to the Director of National Intelligence. The G8 was a powder keg waiting to happen, he told them. They were to close ranks around the city. They were to deploy in and around Akasaka Palace and be an extension of the president's secret service.

Speers was also mindful that Eri Sato was gathering moss at the U.S. Embassy in Tokyo. If her claims about Ito's government were true, then it wouldn't be long before they came for her. Still, in light of the president's visceral reaction to her claims, Speers had not yet passed her request for political asylum to the Department of State. To do so would be to create another political firestorm from which there would be no coming back.

Perhaps, he hoped, he could find another way to get her out of the country before the entire region was engulfed in war.

The phone on his desk rang. Odd. The caller ID read SUPERMODEL. That was *his* codename. And it wasn't even his phone. He answered.

"Hector?"

"Not quite," the caller said. Speers would have recognized Nico Gold's whiny voice anywhere. "Did you enjoy the audio files I sent?"

Speers put his foot against the door so that he wouldn't be interrupted. "I won't even ask how you managed to reach me here."

"Did you enjoy the audio files I sent?" Nico pressed.

Speers reckoned he was asking about the secret recordings from Zhongnanhai. "It was like Christmas. But some people in the White House no longer believe in Santa Claus."

Nico sighed. "I find Eva's lack of faith disturbing. But nevertheless, this *is* a business relationship. Carver and I have arrived at a compensation agreement for my services, which I am still executing in good faith. But he has unfortunately gone dark."

Speers had no idea what compensation Nico was talking about. The very thought of it made his bowels jitter. He saw no advantage to telling lies regarding Carver's whereabouts. If anything, perhaps Nico could help. "To be honest, we think Carver has been compromised. His last report looked like disinformation."

"What kind of disinformation?"

Speers told him everything. It was a Hail Mary. But he had nothing to lose.

Nico was quiet for a moment. Then he said, "I'm working on something that could turn even a scrooge like Eva into a believer."

# Hotel New Otani
# Tokyo

9:44 a.m. Carver woke sitting upright. His wrists were bound behind the wooden chair he sat in. His head ached, and his eyes clamped shut in painful protest to the blazing sunlight.

He smelled carpet cleaner. Heard the steady hum of central air conditioning. He rolled his head slowly up, left and right, stretching the tightness out of his neck and shoulders. From somewhere in the distance, another form of white noise crept into his consciousness.

The rumble of traffic. And crowds. *I'm in a city.*

He tried to swallow. He tasted leather and, unable to see his own face, ran his tongue along the soft edge of it. After a moment, its shape registered. A leather ball gag.

*Don't panic. Breathe through your nose. Slow your heart rate. Everything in its right place.*

He tried to move his feet. His ankles were bound to the chair as well. Ever so slowly, he forced his eyes open. What he saw startled him. A wall of glass overlooking central Tokyo.

He was in a hotel. On a high floor. Overlooking the city.

He broke out in an instant sweat, blood pressure skyrocketing. As his eyes adjusted to the view, he saw a labyrinthine concrete jungle that was Tokyo. And in the center of it, about 350 yards from where he was now, a large green pine grove and immaculate gardens. Akasaka Palace. The site of the G8.

Beneath sunny skies, Carver could see that the palace grounds were already crawling with security, no doubt anticipating the arrival of the leaders of the world's most economically influential countries. The surrounding streets were lined with crowds. And protestors.

The G8 was happening after all. That meant Julian failed. Nico failed. Eri failed.

He heard a click. It was behind him. The door. Someone was coming.

A seemingly random image came to him – the possum he had seen in the road at the Two Elk Ranch. To avoid harm, it had simply played dead.

Carver had played many roles during his intelligence career, but this would be the first time he had ever played possum. He closed his eyes and let his head fall forward, chin resting against his chest. He let his body go slack until he was dead weight. He let his tongue fall limp against the entrance to his mouth. And he slowed his breathing as he listened to two sets of footsteps crossing the carpet.

The smell of cigarettes and heavy aftershave was overpowering. One of them poked him hard in the shoulder. He allowed his body to jerk forward, but stopped short of falling out of the chair. Carver figured they might try again.

This time the impact hit him hard behind the left shoulder. Again, Carver's body jerked forward. This time, though, the wooden chair he was strapped to breached its tipping point. He surrendered to the sensation of falling.

*Focus. Stay in character. Don't break your fall.*

Carver's knees hit the mercifully thick carpet first, followed by his face. It hurt more than he had imagined it might, and he heard the frame of the wooden chair – which he now wore like an ungainly backpack – crack behind him.

Still, he did not move so much as a muscle. Did not emit so much as a grunt. He embodied the possum. He *was* the possum.

He felt fingers on his wrist now. Someone was checking his pulse.

"Is he okay?" the Eel said.

A second man answered affirmatively. "The drugs really knocked him out."

"Get his fingerprints."

The man lifted Carver's right hand and opened it so that his palm faced the ceiling. He felt the unmistakable comfort of a trigger guard. It had the feel of a heavy bolt-action rifle. His index finger was pressed hard against the trigger itself, and his middle finger, third finger and thumb were pressed against the surrounding metal.

Ito's words surged to the forefront of his mind. *Because tomorrow, a new name will join the ranks of the world's great assassins. Gavrilo Princip, John Wilkes Booth, Lee Harvey Oswald...and Blake Carver.*

He had to admire the audacity of the plan. Exiled or not, he was still technically a federal agent. If they succeeded in framing him for the assassination of President Kang, conspiracy theorists and rational people alike would naturally assume it was a government-sanctioned hit.

Unless he could stop it.

# Akasaka Palace
# Tokyo

The red carpet stretched more than the length of a football field, bisecting the perfectly symmetrical rows of Japanese soldiers in white dress uniforms, snaking up the palace steps, terminating where Prime Minister Ito stood in a black suit and white silk tie. To Ito's right was a space marked by a square of black carpet, memorializing the spot where the late emperor would have stood.

In future ceremonies, Ito mused, I will occupy both offices.

The flags of the G8 nations flew from the palace steps. The state-commissioned theme song for the G8 blared out of stacks of elevated speakers set around the property. Unlike in recent decades, when the theme song for state events was performed by J-Pop groups, Ito had hand picked a pair of brothers who were virtuosos in the shamisen, a traditional Japanese stringed instrument that looked like a guitar save for its square-shaped body. The accompanying music video played on massive screens, featuring the landscapes of the eight countries represented in the summit,

Everything was perfect, just as Ito had hoped. As the host, he had been the first to walk the red carpet. The Italian PM was up now, marching along to the strains of Italy's national anthem. Next up would be the British PM and the German Chancellor, each of which would enter as their respective national anthems played in their entirety.

A voice in his ear told him that the Canadian PM's helicopter would be landing at the far end of the property at any moment. Leaders from the two superpowers – the U.S. and China – would arrive by car.

Ito beamed as he stole a glance at the neighboring Hotel New Otani. The Eel had warned him repeatedly not to look at the shimmering building. *There can be no evidence of your involvement.* But Ito could not help himself. This was not simply the opening ceremony for the G8. It was the first volley in a battle of civilizations.

# Hotel New Otani

As quickly as the Kuromaku had come into the room, Carver heard the two men leave. But something was different. When they had come in, the heavy hotel room door had thudded shut behind them. This time, the sound of the door clasping was slight and tinny.

They had gone into the adjoining suite. He suspected that the real shooter – Sho Kimura – was there as well.

Over the noise of crowds and traffic, he now heard the German national anthem. *Deutschland, Deutschland über alles. Über alles in der Welt.*

Carver reckoned the German Chancellor must be walking the red carpet. The time for playing possum was over. He opened his eyes, twisted his body left, and with it, the fractured wooden chair he had collapsed in.

The first order of business was getting free. It was going to be a bit noisy, but hopefully the G8 hoopla would mask the minor racket he was about to make. He flexed his forearms, pulling the chair frame into his back. He heard another crack. Probably one of the chair legs. He jerked harder. He heard the crack spread, but not enough to splinter. He thrashed, left, then right, whipping the chair back and forth behind him like a bronco trying to shed its rider. At last he felt the wood pop and give. He rolled left one final time, and the chair back broke off into pieces.

Finally unsaddled, his hands and feet now free, Carver pulled the gag out of his mouth. He rewarded himself with some deep mouth-breathing. He hadn't had access to a toothbrush in three days, and the smell of his own breath repulsed him. But man, all that unobstructed oxygen felt *good*.

His eyes searched the room, finding only a king-sized bed, night tables at either side. A seating area.

Mounted over the bed was a blowfish. Taking into account the one-inch spines all around its body, it was the size of a cantaloupe.

He eyed the door to the adjoining room. One way or another, he was going in. But how?

# Near Akasaka Palace
# Tokyo

The motorcade carrying President Hudson and Julian Speers wound through block after block of anonymous-looking gray office buildings. As they came within sight of the palace walls, tens of thousands of protesters lined the streets. Police in riot gear formed a line on either side of the street, keeping the crowds at bay.

As the president studied the 70-page G8 economic brief she had been handed this morning, Speers checked his phone for at least the 200th time since landing on Japanese soil. Where was that supposedly world-changing report Nico Gold had promised him? He had promised that it would be like Christmas, Halloween and Easter rolled into one. Speers needed it now. Before the Pentagon could begin executing the secret operation that would take them to a place from which there would be no coming back.

And for that matter, where was Carver? Was he even alive? Speers noisily crushed what was left of a grape lollipop with his rear molars.

The president looked up. "Your dentist must love you."

"She loves my money."

At last, Speers' phone buzzed. He looked down and saw what he had been waiting for – an email from Nico Gold. The subject line: *Prime Minister Ito is a very Naughty Boy (Video)*

Holding the phone close to his chest, he donned his headset and watched excitedly as a video begin to load.

# Hotel New Otani

Now Carver heard a new anthem over the steady hum of the Hotel New Otani air conditioner - *O Canada, we stand on guard for thee. God keep our land glorious and free!*

He reckoned the Canadian PM had either just arrived or was walking the red carpet.

The American entourage couldn't be far behind. Nor would the Chinese.

The roar of the crowds 18 floors below him was growing louder.

There was no time for rest. The Eel's muscle would be back any moment now.

He scanned the room for a weapon.

Had they left the patsy rifle here?

No such luck, it seemed.

His eyes returned to the cantaloupe-sized blowfish mounted over the bed.

Some people might look at it and see just a fish. Or even a porcupine with gills.

Carver saw a homemade medieval chain mace.

He removed his paracord shoelaces and got to work.

# Akasaka Palace

The president held a compact, checking her hair as the car pulled through the palace gates. Satisfied, she snapped it shut and turned to Speers. "Any food in my teeth?" she said, smiling broadly so that he could inspect her veneers.

Speers instead offered his phone, which was cued up to play the video Nico Gold had just sent him. "Madam President, wait. You need to see this."

"Now?"

The car came to a gentle halt before the red carpet. Rows of self-defense forces flanked either side. The palace steps – along with Ito and the leaders of five other countries – loomed at the other end.

Rios tapped the roof twice and opened the president's door. "Showtime, Madam President!"

"Please," Speers said. "Eva. I'm begging you. This proves what I was saying before."

Disappointment darkened the president's face. "I gave you a chance to get on board. And this is how you repay me? By deliberately shaking my confidence as I'm due to step out in front of the cameras?"

"Of course not. I didn't plan this. It just – "

"Don't bother submitting your resignation. You're fired."

The Star Spangled Banner blasted from gigantic speakers on either side of the palace.

On cue, Eva lifted her heels and swiveled her legs to the side. She adopted a perfectly practiced smile as she emerged from the car.

# U.S. Embassy

In the two days since Eri's meeting with the CIA station chief, the television had been her lone contact with the outside world. She had been sequestered in protective guest housing within the embassy compound. Julian Speers had never responded to her warning about the G8, nor had the State Department answered her request for asylum.

The previous evening, she had come to terms with the fact that Carver had been killed or captured at Kyoto Station. She did not know whether she was capable of mourning another loss. Fujimoto. Taka. Carver. At some point, she knew, the emotional heft would all come crashing down on her. But for now, all she could do was keep breathing. She was the last living person outside the Kuromaku itself that knew the truth about Ito. As long as she was alive, and free, there was still a chance to expose him.

Now a guard arrived to escort her back to the conference room where she had had her only meeting with the station chief.

"He'll be with you shortly," the guard said. He shut the door and stood just outside.

Eri switched on the TV that was mounted high on the wall. The live broadcast of the G8 opening ceremony was on. The American national anthem played as President Hudson walked the red carpet. Prime Minister Ito, along with the heads of state from Italy, Britain, Germany and Canada, awaited her on the palace steps.

The crowds on the street erupted in a spasm of cheers and jeers. To many of the millions viewing at home, Eri knew, the slickly produced TV special was proof of Japan's relevancy among the world's wealthiest nations. She found the broadcasters' patronizing banter nauseating.

*"Ito looks every bit the statesman as he stands on the steps of Akasaka Palace, doesn't he?"*

At last, the conference room door opened. The CIA Station Chief entered. His hair stood on end in places, as if he had been pulling at it.

"Miss Sato," he said, holding a manila folder. "Please sit down."

"I have been sitting for two days." She gestured toward the TV broadcast. Her voice was full of emotion. "Look at that! The President came despite my warning! Did you tell them about the threat to the G8?"

"I sent your message," the station chief said. "It was read. That much I can tell you. But that's actually not what I came to talk to you about. I'm afraid we have a wrinkle in your request for asylum. It seems that the Public Security Intelligence Agency knows you are here."

A wave of panic migrated down Eri's neck and chest. She could scarcely breathe, much less speak. Her words came out as a whisper. "How?"

"I frankly don't know. But in the meantime..." He laid the folder on the table, turned it to face her, and opened it. Listed on the page were a number of infractions. "They are apparently bringing charges against you. There are 26 in all, including treason."

"Don't you understand? They are trying to silence me!"

The station chief stood and reached for the doorknob. "I'm sorry. I really am. My standing orders are to continue to forge a relationship of mutual cooperation between our two countries. They are due to pick you up in about 30 minutes. Unless I hear from Washington before they arrive, I'll have no choice but to hand you over."

# Hotel New Otani

Sho Kimura sat cross-legged before the heavy rifle, the brunt of its weight resting on the tripod. His eyes watered as a cool autumn wind blew through the 20 x 20 cm sniper hole he had so expertly carved out of the hotel window glass. The Eel stood behind him, chatting into his phone, quietly orchestrating a broad array of operatives in the hotel and on the palace grounds.

The patsy rifle with Blake Carver's fingerprints sat on the floor beside him. It was identical in size and make. He had been instructed not to touch it.

The identify of his target, President Kang, had been disclosed to him just three hours earlier, upon his entering the hotel. His previous targets had been ordinary people. A judge. An election official. Kang was anything but ordinary.

Although the practice conditions the Eel had simulated in Fukushima had been surprisingly accurate, he wished he had known about Kang earlier. He would not have backed out, as the Eel had feared. He would have studied Kang's gait, his build, and his mannerisms.

He leaned back and wiped his eyes. He regarded the patsy rifle. Out in the irradiated zone, he had realized that not getting credit for killing Kang actually bothered him. How sick was that?

It still bothered him. No one would ever know that *he* had pulled the trigger. No one would ever know that *he* had changed history.

Sure, he'd had his 15 minutes of fame as an Olympian. But he had finished 27th that year in an obscure sport that was mostly popular in Scandinavia. His name would appear in no records books. For all his years of training, he would never be anything more than a footnote in history. Less than that, in fact.

But this one deed – killing Kang – would actually *mean* something.

He thought of his mother. And his sister. And his little brother, who even now was at the restaurant, preparing that evening's courses. All he needed to do was take the Chinese leader's life, and his entire family would live. The inevitable decline of the superpowers would be set in motion and, at least according to the Eel, Japan would emerge a stronger nation.

The fingers of his left hand grazed the muzzle delicately as he watched the ceremony unfolding at Akasaka Palace through his riflescope. The SUV carrying the Chinese president finally came to a stop. Tiny red flags on its hood fluttered in the wind. The passenger side door opened to a magnificently long red carpet that stretched across the grounds and, like a snake, up the steps of Akasaka Palace. Japanese soldiers stood on either side, stiff as boards, saluting, staring at an imaginary place in the distance.

As the Eel had foreseen, Sho had an unobstructed view of the Chinese leader. There was a 10-meter gap of carpet between the limo and the first rows of Japanese defense forces, giving him perhaps three or four seconds to find a clean shot. An eternity.

"It's time," the Eel said. He turned and saw his handler stub the cigarette out into an expensive-looking ashtray. The two thugs in the corner stood. "Go untie the American. Don't bring him in until you hear the shot."

# Hotel New Otani

The deadbolt turned. Carver crouched behind the door with his improvised chain mace and waited.

Three steps into the room, the two invaders stopped in their tracks, tensing as they caught sight of the broken chair where Carver had been tied.

Even from behind the door, Carver recognized the muscle-bound pair as the two who had come to collect him at the sports bar in Kyoto. The one he had taken for a retired sumo wrestler actually looked big and athletic enough to play offensive line for most any Division I college football team. The other was the Rhino - spiky hair, massive head and barrel-shaped gut.

Carver rose up behind them with his weapon – the paracord shoelaces attached to the stuffed blowfish – as convincingly as if it was a real medieval chain mace.

The Rhino turned to look behind him. Carver swung, striking him in the temple. As he had hoped, the spines were sharp and sturdy enough to cut. The painful blow sent the bleeding Rhino wobbling left.

His more athletic accomplice rushed Carver head on. But the American was faster, sidestepping, swinging the mace in a windmill motion so that the fugu spines struck him at the base of the neck.

It was hardly a knockout blow, but his victim was stunned. Carver maneuvered behind the thug, driving the toe of his wingtip up into his ball sack.

Then he leapt sideways again, planted his right foot on the carpet, and drove the heel of his left shoe into the man's knee. The round, moon-shaped joint bent unnaturally inward with a sickening snap as both meniscus tendons tore away from the kneecap. The thug howled in pain and collapsed to the floor.

As he caught his breath, Carver heard the halting strains of the Chinese national anthem played on the street below. This was it. He was almost out of time.

The Rhino struggled to his feet. Carver wrapped the paracord around his neck – or at least where the neck should have been. As Carver tugged harder, he could see only the man's beefy shoulders. He even wedged a foot on the Rhino's back for leverage as he attempted to crush his windpipe.

The move might have finished a smaller opponent, but the dazed hulk seized the paracord with his right hand and yanked, pulling Carver onto his back with ease.

Now Carver felt a sensation he hadn't experienced since childhood. He was heaved up above the Rhino's shoulders. The Rhino's arms were fully outstretched overhead, as if he were performing an overhead press at the local gym.

Carver realized he was going to be tossed just before it happened. He curled up like a cannonball, hoping the walls were still as thin as he remembered.

# Hotel New Otani

President Kang emerged from the SUV and stepped onto the red carpet. Sho's finger grazed the trigger. "There!" came the Eel's voice from behind him. So close Sho could feel his breath on his neck. *"Take him now!"*

But the Chinese leader's movements were nothing like he had imagined. There was no pause, no wave. Now fully unfolded from the vehicle, Kang was taller than expected. He took enormous strides, as if he were gliding along a rail. Sho elevated the rifle slightly and nudged the sights to the right, leading the target.

Suddenly, white dust enveloped his vision. Something crashed into the tripod, jamming the riflescope against Sho's right eye. Blood pooled around his eye socket.

To his right, a gaping hole in the wall through which the Rhino had thrown Blake Carver. Now Carver and the Eel were struggling for control of the patsy rifle. Carver kneed the older man in the groin and jammed the rifle butt in his jaw, sending Ito's longtime partner hard into the window overlooking the palace.

He collapsed against the glass, pushing against it in an effort to get to his feet. Spiderwebs spiraled outward from the sniper hole in the center. A triangular wedge as large as a slice of pizza broke away. His hand punched through. He turned, trying to regain his balance as the integrity of the entire window collapsed.

Sho reached out, his hand grazing that of his handler as he fell back. He was too late. The man he had known as the Eel was gone.

# Akasaka Palace

Ito's public face was one of calm composure. Inside, he was a torrent of anxiety.

The Chinese president was already three-quarters of the way across the red carpet.

How was this possible?

His plan had been perfect. He had done everything right.

What was taking so long? Had the shooter been unable to get a clean shot?

Kobayashi had specifically told him not to look up.

And yet he *did* look. Up and to his left, at the Hotel New Otani. The shooter would be on one of the high floors.

And then he saw it. A man falling to Earth, his suit jacket billowing up behind him like a set of hopelessly broken wings.

*Kobayashi.* He couldn't possibly tell from that distance. But somehow, he knew. *Kobayashi.*

Surely the shooter was still at his post. And surely he would pull the trigger at any moment.

And yet President Kang ascended the steps before him. Hand extended. Oblivious to the unfolding disaster in the adjacent building.

Ito did not take Kang's hand. He did not bow. Instead, he stepped back, hoping against all odds that the shooter would take the shot.

# Hotel New Otani

A storm of broken glass fell. Holding the Sato patsy rifle in one hand, Carver watched the Eel clear the window and plummet to the concrete below. He fought a sudden twinge of vertigo, shifting his focus to Akasaka Palace, where a video of the Chinese flag flapped in the wind on giant video screens. The country's national anthem played its final bars.

Meanwhile, Sho had gotten to his feet. Despite his blood-rimmed right eye and the several thousand tiny glass beads bedazzling his hair and clothing, he pressed the butt of the real sniper rifle firmly against his shoulder.

"The Eel *lied* to you," Carver shouted. "Take that shot, and you'll start a war that will destroy all of us."

"Stay back!" came Sho's reply, swinging the rifle up to find Kang on the palace steps. His right finger tightened over the trigger.

At that moment, Carver realized just what he was holding. The very thing he had been longing for ever since he had arrived in Japan. A firearm.

There was just one wrinkle. He didn't know if the patsy rifle was loaded.

Now the Rhino was coming for him, charging from his position across the room. Carver lifted the patsy rifle to his beltline – there was simply no time to aim properly – and pulled the trigger.

Such a powerful weapon wasn't meant to be fired from waist level. Despite the rifle's muzzle brake, the recoil sent Carver off balance, propelling him backward.

The glass beads under his feet might as well have been marbles. He slid backwards as if on ice, feeling the cool wind at his back.

*Oh God. I'm going to –*

# Akasaka Palace

Ito watched as Kang walked to the end of the row of world leaders, taking his place beside the Canadian PM, who had volunteered to be the buffer between the Chinese and American presidents. The G8 theme song cranked up again. The eight heads of state smiled as they posed for photographers.

Suddenly, the music stopped. The giant screens went black, then flickered back to life.

The image quality was poor, but the screen was just bright enough so that Ito's face could be recognized. He was pictured in an office, addressing a small group of his closest aides.

The video paused for a moment as a message written in Japanese and English appeared on screen.

*PRIME MINISTER ITO HAS BEEN A NAUGHTY BOY.*

*...THE ATTACK ON THE CHINESE EMBASSY*
*...THE ATTACK ON THE AMERICAN DESTROYER*
*...THE MURDER OF THE EMPEROR*

*ITO IS GUILTY ON ALL COUNTS!*

The crowd gasped. The video restarted. A recording of voice was audible.

A new screen appeared:

*THIS WAS RECORDED IN ITO'S PRIVATE RESIDENCE THIS MORNING AS HE ADDRESSED HIS IMMEDIATE STAFF:*

*"Today at the G8, our hard work will at last pay dividends. The Chinese snake will be beheaded, and more than 1 billion Chinese people will*

*demand payback. Do not worry about reprisals. Should either the Americans or the Chinese turn its sights on Japan, their mutual dependence on a connected military force will be their undoing. The ease with which we controlled the American drone and the Chinese fighter planes is proof of that. As the U.S. and China fall from their lofty perches, the Empire of Japan will once again rise in the east. I will reign over this new era from the imperial palace as the rightful heir to the throne. My lineage is direct and pure. Power will at last be restored as it has been for millennia. "*

The screen went black. The crowd maintained a sense of shocked silence, seemingly unsure of what they had seen, or what it meant.

The video resumed, playing clips from Ito's campaign speeches.

*"Every Japanese woman should do her patriotic duty to give Japan at least three children."*

*"We must stop the flow of immigration and therefore the pollution of Japanese blood by foreigners."*

*"Japan must once again rise as Asia's lone superpower."*

*"One day, the Americans will look to us for protection — not the other way around."*

As the video played on repeat, Ito stepped back from the row of bewildered world leaders. Then he turned and walked purposefully toward the palace. Three guards converged before him, blocking his path.

# Hotel New Otani

Carver's feet dangled beneath him. A bed of concrete awaited him 18 floors below. So did the Eel's broken body.

His right forearm held fast to the window ledge. His left hand held onto the metallic window frame above it. The glass cut ever deeper into his flesh as gravity pulled him lower. Blood ran down his wrists and forearms.

Despite the pain, he was actually smiling. He couldn't see the video playing at the palace, but he understood by the crowd's reaction that something had happened at the G8. Now someone was telling the crowd to remain calm. The crowds were chanting for Ito's ouster. Maybe Eri had come through after all. Or Speers. Or Nico. They had done it.

*Now it's your turn. Let's do this. On three. One, two…*

With one final effort, Carver heaved himself up and into the suite like some fish flopping out of a raging river onto a bank of hot stones. His reward was a bed of broken window glass. Nevertheless, he crawled as quickly as he could away from the edge.

Only as he reached the couch did he see Sho, lying face up on the carpet. And the Rhino, face down, three feet behind him. The .338 caliber round Carver had fired at point blank range had gone through one man and into the other.

He collapsed onto the couch in the suite's generous sitting room.

He decided to close his eyes, if only for a moment. That felt *good*. It felt *right*. They had won.

# Air Force One

The president's Boeing VC-25 – the plane that had brought her to Tokyo as Air Force One – departed Japan as a decoy with a full complement of secret service personnel. The president was not onboard.

Hours later, a Gulfstream courier carrying President Hudson and her immediate staff left Tokyo's Yokosuka Air Force Base under strict radio silence. The tiny jet was now Air Force One. On her orders, Blake Carver, whose savaged hands and wrists had been treated with a gold-based solder at a local Tokyo hospital, was whisked aboard at the last moment. He now sat in the rear of the plane as the president's personal physician set up an IV that dripped fluids into his right arm.

Hector Rios sat in the opposite facing seat. He eyed Carver's left ear, which had taken on a greenish hue.

"I don't know what's nastier. Your ear, or those kids that get the ear gauges, then take them out and have all that loose skin flapping around like noodles."

The doctor looked up from her work. "Oh, that's easy. Carver's ear is *definitely* nastier." She turned back to Carver. "It's badly infected. Did you really think this would heal all by itself?"

Carver grinned. "On behalf of hopeless optimists everywhere, yes. But you know what I am sure of? I'll never use the expression *I would crawl on my hands and knees through broken glass* again. Because that's exactly what I did today, and it hurts like hell."

The president rose from her seat and made her way to the back of the plane. "Gentlemen, I need a word alone with Agent Carver."

Rios moved forward. The doctor also rose reluctantly. "And for God's sake," she told Carver, "Stop scratching it."

The president took Hector's seat, crossed her legs, and lowered her voice to a level that could not be heard by others over the hum of the white noise of flight.

"I just got off the phone with President Kang," she said. "I told him about what you did up there in the hotel."

"You're welcome," Carver said. "But between us, Sho Kimura was a B-grade assassin. Even without me there, who knows? Maybe he misses, and Kang just gets a haircut."

"You'll get the National Intelligence Medal for Valor for this."

"With all due respect, Madam President – "

"Please, Blake. Can we bury the hatchet and go back to a first-name basis? At least in private?"

"With all due respect, Eva, I appreciate the gesture, but I already have one. But I do have a wish. Or three."

"I'm a politician, not a genie."

"Right now, a Japanese government employee named Eri Sato is hiding out in the American Embassy in Tokyo. She's requesting –"

"Political asylum. I know all about it. Julian has already seen to that. Rest assured, Eri is safe."

Carver grimaced as pain shot down his right arm, and then subsided. "That's a relief. Moving on, the task force..."

"Disbanded. As for Ellis, we're offering her a position with the U.S. Small Business Administration in Anchorage, Alaska. I hope she'll take it."

"Then I wish her well. And the intelligence committee?"

The president reached for a crystal decanter filled with brown liquid on the bar next to her seat. "Committees are like fleas. Just when you've gotten rid of one, another pops up. How about a drink instead?"

"Yes please."

The president poured two tumblers full of bourbon. She handed Carver a tumbler, then clinked her glass against his. "To your health."

"I always drink to world peace."

"Anything else? Last wish."

"Yeah. This one is pretty important. It might even require a call to your counterpart on Downing Street. I hear you two are pretty close these days."

"That's none of your business. But if you want me to ask the British Prime Minister for a favor, it better be good."

"It is. Ever hear of the Lycurgus Cup?"

# EPILOGUE

## THREE DAYS LATER

# Las Vegas

From Nico Gold's suite high above the Vegas strip, Carver watched as his host began dismantling the wooden crate emblazoned with the stamp TRUSTEES OF THE BRITISH MUSEUM. Nico, dressed in a white tunic, took up a hammer and began eagerly removing nails from his new delivery.

Madge reclined on the couch with a glass of port and a Mona Lisa smile. Was she simply amused by Nico's enthusiasm, or had she already figured out how Carver had rigged the game? She had but a fraction of Nico's raw talent, but in many ways, Carver had decided that she was the adult in their strange relationship.

"Where's your sister?" Carver asked.

"You'll see."

Carver was careful not to stand too close to the window as he waited for his host to unwrap his presents. Another bout of vertigo was the last thing he needed. He focused on the orange sun plunging behind the jagged purple mountains in the distance. It reminded him of Tripoli. And the Butcher of Bahrain. And how badly he wanted to finish the mission that had been stolen right out from under him.

"Wait!" Nico said. "I want this moment to be perfect." He cued up Strauss' bombastic *Also sprach Zarathustra* in anticipation of the grand unveiling. Then he lowered the suite's power window shutters. A single floodlight illuminated an alcove where the cup would be showcased.

Carver cleared his throat. "If you don't mind, the British Museum kindly requested that you wear latex gloves before handling the cup."

"Request respectfully ignored."

Nico pulled the last nail from the crate. Then he reached into it, removed multiple layers of high-tech packing foam, and finally emerged with the ancient cup in hand. He held the vessel to the light and turned slowly. As promised, the cup was indeed a chameleon. It appeared jade green when lit from the front, but turned blood-red when lit from behind.

"Right," Nico said. He looked at Madge. "Time for authentication."

Carver took umbrage. "What do you mean, authentication? After all we've been through, you *still* don't trust me?"

"Please. In God we trust. In all others, we verify."

Madge got to her feet, put her phone on speaker and dialed. Octavia answered in Etruscan. It sounded as if she was in a cavernous room.

"Hello darling," Nico said. "I'm here with Madge and Agent Carver. Would you like to tell us where you are? And let's stay in English as a courtesy to our guests."

"I'm at the British Museum in London," Octavia answered. "It's half-past midnight here, the museum has been closed for several hours, and I'm with the assistant curator. Here he is!"

The live image of the half-lit museum streamed on Madge's phone. A balding man who looked positively petrified waved tentatively. Then the camera shifted focus to an empty glass enclosure. "The assistant curator has kindly turned the motion detectors off, and that empty enclosure in front of me is where the Lycurgus Cup should be. I'll get closer so you can read the sign they put up."

Nico mirrored the screen onto a large monitor on the far wall of the room. Carver watched as the image got close enough to the empty enclosure that the printed sign was legible. It read THIS ARTIFACT IS TEMPORARILY ON LOAN.

"Nicely done," Nico said. "And the vault?"

"Already checked. The space where the cup is held when not normally in rotation is empty!"

"Astonishing!" Nico cried. He lifted the suite's shutters and turned his gaze down the Vegas strip. "Eat it, Caesar's Palace! This Roman artifact is bloody well authentic!"

Madge clapped and hopped up and down. "Toast, toast, toast!"

"Yes, quickly, let me get the wine!"

He tore open the second shipping crate in search of the bottle of Château Lafite Bordeaux he had been promised.

"Careful," Carver warned, but Nico was not especially careful. He clawed through layers of protective material before locating the 15-inch long blast-proof container at the crate's core.

"It's locked!" Nico shrieked.

"Easy there, Titus. I'll have to give you the combination."

Nico keyed in the 24-character alphanumeric combination as quickly as Carver could relay it to him. Seconds later, he held the bottle of hand-blown dark green glass, sealed with black wax. There was no label, but hand-etched into the glass was the year 1787, the word "Lafitte," and the letters "Th.J."

"An authentic Thomas Jefferson bottle!" Nico said. He looked up at Carver. "You did it!"

"Yes, but as you know, the authenticity of all the Jefferson bottles is controversial. They were discovered behind a bricked up wall in Paris, and the consensus from some researchers is that – "

"Don't spoil the romantic mood with your cynicism! So long as this is one of the *alleged* Jefferson bottles, we are good!"

"It is," Carver confirmed. And it *was* indeed one of the Jefferson bottles. It did not, however, contain the alleged Jefferson wine.

While President Hudson was able to arrange a temporary loan of the Lycurgus Cup to Nico in the name of global security, she was not willing to allocate the $300,000 Carver estimated he needed to purchase an unopened bottle of Jefferson wine from a private collector. He went to Speers, who pledged $62,000 in off-the-books cash that had been confiscated from an Armenian arms smuggler. As much as he appreciated the moral support, how was Carver going to purchase a $300,000 bottle of wine at 80% off? His solution came in the form of a wine connoisseur in California who had purchased a bottle at auction some years ago – not as an investment, but actually to drink. He had kept the empty Jefferson bottle as a keepsake after finishing it. But due to an imminent bankruptcy filing, when Carver called, he was willing to part with it for $60,000 in cash.

Now Nico held the bottle up to the light for inspection. Carver prayed his host had not taken further authentication measures. If he had sent Octavia to London, would he then carbon-date the age of the wax that had resealed the wine cork just yesterday? Or obtain a gamma ray detector to test for the presence of radioactive isotope cesium 137 – an unnaturally occurring isotope that was the telltale sign of wines produced after 1945?

His host's nose wrinkled in scrutiny. He held the bottle closer to the light, peering not just at it, but also through it.

"Toast, toast, toast!" Madge insisted.

At last, Nico used his thumb to break the wax seal, and then retrieved an ordinary corkscrew from the bar.

"Careful with the cork," Carver said with manufactured trepidation. "It could be brittle." But of course, he knew that the cork was not brittle, for it had been custom-made and hand-painted just yesterday. And in the low-light atmosphere Nico had created with which to admire the ancient cup, he did not even notice.

Nico stuck his nose into the neck. "Moldy!" he said with enthusiasm. "Obviously old!" He sniffed much more aggressively. "Ah, I can smell burnt sugar and old undergrowth!"

He was mistaken. It was not moldy. There was no aroma of the autumn of 1787. It was simply a 30-year-old Paso Robles blend that Carver had purchased for less than the price of a plane ticket.

But as Nico drank, he was convinced. And watching the celebration live from London, Octavia was convinced. The fact that they believed was all that mattered.

Carver extended his hand and shook Nico's. "I think my work here is done."

"You're leaving?" Nico said. "For Jupiter's sake, no! The party's just getting started! We are going to invite some friends over, read Stoic philosophy, drink entire casks of wine and turn the second bathroom into a vomitorium!"

"Sounds like fun. But someone's expecting me."

"Ah. Eri. Right. Then Godspeed, old friend."

Madge showed him out. In the foyer, she kissed his cheek. "Thank you."

"Me? Nico earned this."

"I'm not talking about the cup. Or whatever wine is really in that bottle. Thank you for giving Nico something to do. He needs this. So don't be a stranger, okay?"

Down in the hotel lobby, Carver found Eri at the bar where he had left her. Upon arriving in Vegas, she had dyed her hair platinum as a security precaution, but it was the chunky non-prescription eyeglasses that really altered her appearance. It was a nerdy look to be sure, but Carver found that he liked it.

She rose and took his arm. Carver gave his ticket to the valet. They would be driving down to the Two Elk Ranch tonight, where his parents were no doubt scrambling to get the house ready for guests. They were no doubt more excited to see Eri than him.

He resolved to enjoy tonight, because tomorrow would be hard. He would finally confess that he wasn't a federal procurement consultant. Given the threat the Eel had made on his father's life, Speers had agreed that it was time to tell his immediate family what he really did for a living. Exactly how to do that was another matter. He had fantasized about this moment for years, and yet he still hadn't figured out how to tell them. *Mom, Dad, I have something to tell you. I'm a spy. But hey, don't worry. I'm still the same person you think I am.* Whatever he said would likely be met with laughter at first. Then it would morph into anger. He just hoped they would agree to keep it from his sister and her family for a bit longer. She had a big mouth.

He and Eri planned to stay in Arizona for as long as it took to secure the ranch to his satisfaction. Despite the fact that Ito was in jail, the Eel was dead and dozens more had been arrested on treason charges, the Kuromaku hadn't survived for two thousand years without solid plans for succession and mission continuity. That was why Carver had a security team scheduled to come out and set up a virtual perimeter. Cameras in trees, motion detectors programmed to detect human gait, and more. They would build a panic room in the basement with a failsafe communications system, and the entire ranch house would be outfitted with emergency blast-proof shutters. Carver also had a line on some anti-drone technology that was going to scare the bejeezus out of the turkey vultures.

Just as the valet brought the car, his phone rang. It was Speers. "The Butcher of Bahrain is in London."

Carver's breath left him. "How…"

"This, my friend, is why you debrief *relentlessly*. One of those little details Kyra mentioned in passing led to one thing, which led to another, and so forth. Good Christ, this is *big*."

Carver tipped the valet and held the passenger door open for Eri. He walked around to the other side of the car, but didn't get in. Speers was still on the line. "Look, Blake, I called you first as a courtesy. But after all you've been through, feel free to say no."

He didn't dare look at Eri. But she was watching him now. He could feel it. They had a chance for a new life together. What they had wasn't good yet, but it could be. He *wanted* it to be. On the other hand, he *had* to go to London. And he would have to leave right away. This time was different, he told himself. Eri would understand. This time, she would wait for him.

# Characters

THE FEDS

Blake Carver, intelligence operative.
Chad Fordham, FBI Director.
Haley Ellis, intelligence analyst.
Eva Hudson, President of the United States.
Dexter Jackson, Secretary of Defense
Kyra Javan, spy
Nico Gold, reformed hacker.
Arunus Roth, intelligence analyst.
Julian Speers, Director of National Intelligence.

THE JAPANESE

The Emperor, imperial ruler
Shoichi Kimura, informant/assassin
Eri Sato, intelligence analyst
Taka, bar owner

THE KUROMAKU

Akira Ito, Prime Minister of Japan
Maru Kobayashi/The Eel, Head of Security
Pizza Face, pilot

THE REST

Aldo, smuggler
Butcher of Bahrain, North African Allied Jihad Commander
Jack Brenner, engineer
Jessica Wu, spy
Mohy Osman, Allied Jihad security

## The Blake Carver Series

*Line of Succession*

*The Fellowship*

*Rogue Empire*

**Visit William online**

 ★WILLIAMTYREEBOOKS.COM★

Rogue Empire

Made in the USA
Middletown, DE
09 May 2022

65560368R00215